"...West brings to life native men and women who know the value of simple things like solitude, family, good whiskey, love...."
—*The Detroit Sunday News*

"...even as a simple story against a magnificent, magical island setting, West's new novel in his strong, musical prose will delight many readers thirsting for good fiction in a veritable desert. *Summer of the Red Wolf* is a love story, an adventure story, or it is something more."
—*Worcester Telegram*

"West is a storyteller of ingenuity and this book is an able testimonial to his craftsmanship."
—*Los Angeles Times*

"On the surface, this is a rattling good adventure yarn with a strong love interest.... However, probing deeper, the old West feeling for an epic theme is very much present, for the story represents modern man's debilitating weariness with the complexities of civilization...." —*Book Guide*

"...he gives you plenty of gunrunning, poaching, wenching and manly challenges of all kinds. It's fun, and quite forgiveable—and the ending is great, not only in the heroic sense, but in almost any sense you can name...." —*Milwaukee Journal*

"...both men and women will like the meaty plot, and there's so much more, with the wild beauty of the islands and the sea. It is a tale of conflict between two kinds of men, but there is a nobleness about them both; they don't wallow, they stride through life. The book leaves a good clean taste."
—*Charlotte Observer*

Summer of the Red Wolf
was originally published
by William Morrow & Company, Inc.

MORRIS L. WEST

Summer of the Red Wolf

A NOVEL

PUBLISHED BY POCKET BOOKS NEW YORK

SUMMER OF THE RED WOLF

William Morrow edition published September, 1971

POCKET BOOK edition published October, 1972

This POCKET BOOK edition includes every word
contained in the original, higher-priced edition. It is printed
from brand-new plates made from completely reset, clear, easy-to-read
type. POCKET BOOK editions are published by POCKET BOOKS, a division
of Simon & Schuster, Inc., 630 Fifth Avenue, New York, N.Y. 10020.
Trademarks registered in the United States and other countries.

L

For
JOY
with whom I have lived a long time
in the love country

A wolf must die in his own skin.
[George Herbert: *Jacula Prudentum*]

PRELUDE

SUDDENLY I WAS SICK OF THE SAVAGERY OF THE WORLD.
I was sick of the wars and the killing, the rise of new
tyrannies, the refinement of old ones, the lies and the pol-
itics, the drug culture and the arid pornography, the
midden stink of cities, the horror that hung over every
tomorrow. I was engulfed in a black despair. I was afraid
and ashamed and sad to be a man. I cried for a new
birth or at least a baptism into a new brotherhood. I could
not have the one or the other. The world would not stop
for me. I could only jump off it into a dubious eternity.

I began to suffer from a recurrent nightmare. I dreamed
of monsters, reptilian giants in a landscape of ferns and
lycopods and swamps leprous with strange flowers. The
skies were black with flapping terrors. The sea deeps
writhed with saw-toothed predators. I was there too,
wrenched out of time, set back in that vast slaughterhouse
which was the reality behind man's dream of the Garden
of Eden. I was alone, shouting my terror among the mind-
less megamorphs. I cowered from the spectacle of their
bloody battles. I ran, witless, through a primeval jungle,
deafened by nightmare discords. I would wake, sweating
in my tangled sheets, trembling under the impact of so
vast an obscenity.

I became, in the end, a stranger to myself. Even my
own hearth seemed a hostile place, as if all the talismans
which defined my identity had changed to hostile fetishes.
I felt myself cracking into scraps and shards. I knew that
if I could not sit down, collect the pieces and put them
together again, I might well go mad, or surrender all hope
of selfhood by an act of absolute negation.

1

Then happened a kind of magical accident, which even today I contemplate with wonder and awe.

It was a morning in early August. The black mood was on me and I was strolling, aimless, along the Old Appian Way, where the tumbled stones and the marble fragments and the spoliated tombs celebrate the futility of human endeavour. It had rained during the night, and I was poking around the damp earth of the verge, hoping to turn up one of those coins or amulets which sometimes come to the surface of the leached, friable soil. Then a voice called my name and gave me a greeting, in English, with a soft Scots burr to it.

I looked up, startled and resentful at this intrusion on my childish pastime. The speaker was a tall, muscular fellow, six feet and a half in his walking boots, with a shock of snow-white hair, a ruddy, freckled face and a grin that gave him the look of a satiated goat-god. I stared at him, gape-mouthed as recognition dawned.

"My God! Alastair Morrison! I thought you were still doctoring the heathen in Thailand."

"I gave it up a year ago—being confused as to who were the heathen and who weren't. What are you doing in Rome?"

"The same question to you—and a lot of others besides."

I was quoting him out of a time remembered. He laughed and so did I. Strange and sad to think I had not laughed in a long time. I took him home with me then and fed him wine and pasta, and we talked of a time when he had been a medical missionary in Chiengmai and I a writer, footloose and feckless in southern Asia. He told me he had retired to his family lodge and bought himself feu-rights and fishing water in the clan lands of the Lews. I told him what I had done and of the strange sickness that had crept upon me in the latter months. He listened, puffing on an old pipe, interjecting a laconic comment or a barbed question. When I had talked myself out, he poured himself another glass of wine and delivered himself of a diagnosis.

"Sometimes a man falls sick of the sunlight itself. He sees everything so clearly that he becomes blind and sees nothing at all. Sometimes he falls sick of reason because the juices which feed his dreaming dry up. It's time to

2

go then. Time to stick a shell in his hat, pick up the pilgrim staff and take the road."

"What road?"

"To the place of unknowing."

"And where the devil is that?"

"A place where you are strange and a stranger and lonely, and because of that, perhaps afraid."

"At this moment I'm afraid even to walk into the city, and I know it like the palm of my hand. I'm afraid to look into a mirror because I will see the fear in my eyes."

"You've got it bad, laddie."

"Yes, I've got it bad."

He fell silent a while, watching me from behind a cloud of smoke. I remembered, irrelevantly, that even the mosquitoes of Chiengmai were daunted by that foul briar of his. Then he made me the offer.

"Come to me if you like. Long time or short, it doesn't matter. The place is empty as a barn and you'll pay your lodging and your liquor, though you'll have the fishing for free, and a lot more besides."

"That's very generous of you."

"Och, we're a generous people. Most of the time, that is."

"Do you mind if I think about it?"

"Don't think too long, else the sickness will be at you again, and you'll do nothing. Besides, the air is soft now and the salmon will be starting to run and, if you remember the right prayer, the sea might set calm for your crossing."

"How will I let you know?"

"You needn't. I'll give you the address, and then you'll either come or you won't. But even if you take another road you'd better start walking, laddie, else you'll be like one of those old statues they have here: no ears, no nose, no parts to make love to a woman, no eyes to see the starlight or the sun on the hilltops."

It took me ten days to gather my wits and my courage; then I turned my face to the north and set out to find the road to the Isles.

I left in a state of panic, a man without a skin, all nerve ends and raw tissue. Fiumicino Airport was a horror of harassed tourists and polyglot confusion. London

3

was another; and I drank myself into anesthesia while I waited for the flight to Inverness. We were packed like sardines into a lumbering Viscount, we climbed into a low overhang of rain cloud and I slept, uneasily, until the touchdown.

Then a new terror took hold of me. I was born in the sun. I had lived all my life in the bright lands of the Pacific and cities of the Mediterranean littoral. Here was a black runway, shining from the last rain shower, a verge of brown stubble with green pasture beyond, a hillock of black pines whose topmost branches were veiled in ragged cloud. Here was a low sky and a cold unwelcoming light and myself a foolish pilgrim in vain flight from himself.

I had ordered a car to meet me so that I could move at will—and flee the faster if I needed to; but the car was not there, and I waited half an hour while the tiny airport emptied itself and the old melancholy grew and grew inside me.

The car came at last. An apple-cheeked girl gave me an apology, a contract, a set of keys and a road map of the Highlands, then left me. I remember that I sat behind the wheel a long time, pretending to study the map, which made as little sense to me as the writing on a rune stone. I was immobilized like a cataleptic, looking and not seeing, knowing and yet unable to direct myself to a single movement. Then the syncope passed. I started the engine, drove out of the gates and took the road to Inverness and the west.

If I linger over the retrospect of that journey, it is because I understand now that every stage of it was a preparation for what happened to me when I came to the Outer Isles. There were no accidents. Everything was predestined. I was an actor being groomed, all-unknowing, for a drama the text of which he had never read, the dimension of which he could never have dreamed in a lifetime. I, the man of reason, had forgotten how to dream; I, the once believer, had lost belief in destiny, benign or malignant; so I was very ignorant, very open and very, very vulnerable.

A mile or so from the airport there was a turnoff and a sign: National Monument, Culloden. I was tempted to drive past it. I had no mind to add an ancient sadness to my own very present ones. Then I told myself that this

4

was a folly. I was a pilgrim man and a pilgrim must offer a piety at the shrines along his way, else their saints might turn their faces from him and their demons dog his footsteps. I went, therefore, where I did not want to go and embraced a memory which was no part of my inheritance.

Or was it? Not all a man's heritage comes to him by will and devising. Once, in Rome, I had lived in the palace where died Henry Stuart, Cardinal Duke of York, brother of Bonnie Prince Charlie, last of the royal line. The Romans, a remembering if not a pious people, had set up a plaque in his honour; and I read it, perforce, at my comings in and my goings out.

Now I was standing on the field where the Young Pretender had fought the last, tragic battle for the Crown of England. I saw the grave mounds, where, they say, no heather has grown or ever will grow: the grave of the English, the graves of the clans, Camerons, Mackintoshes, Frasers and the rest, the grave of the Campbells of Argyll, who fought against the Highlanders for the German king. I laid a sprig of heather on their mound because, although there is no Scot in me, I am related to the Campbells by a marriage. I rested by the Keppoch stone where Alasdair, sixteenth of the name, died leading the charge of his clansmen. I remembered—how did I remember and why?—the lament that was made for him by his bard:

> . . . Worthy son of Coll, him of the battleaxes,
> Whom even the Southmen honoured,
> The hawk, bravest of the flight . . .

I saw the memorial to the Jacobite Irish, the Wild Geese, the sons of Mileadh, who fell in the rearguard action before Cumberland began his butchery of the Highlanders and their wild, sad hopes. Then I drove away through the avenue of pines, recalling what I had long forgotten: that I, too, was descended from the Wild Geese, who had taken wing in the bad times and flown to the far corners of the world, Australia and Canada and America and all the seaports of China.

Of Inverness I remember little except the courtesy of the folk who directed me, the English tourists and their prattle in the bar, the cry of gulls, constant over the grey rooftops, the first, unfamiliar lilt of the Gaelic. For the rest, it was a town, busy with people, and I was in flight from busyness and argument and congress and commerce. I was headed westwards to the Islands and the dark ocean. Only nightfall or the weariness of the road would hold me.

The weariness overtook me at Fort Augustus, the bleak little township on Loch Ness from which Cumberland launched his harrying of the glens. There was a cold wind blowing from the east, and rain in the wind, and the waters of the loch were dark and hostile. The hotel was jammed with the English; but there was an attic room if I could bear the cramp of it, and dinner if I could be ready in twenty minutes, and the night porter would serve me a dram any time I felt the need.

I accepted the cramp and the dinner, stodgy but generous; the dram I could not drink because the lounge was full of the English, little knots and enclaves, some talking softly and some loudly, because they were strangers in a land which their fathers had made desolate, and habit had made them too certain or too uncertain of themselves. I was uncertain too—God, how rickety a man I remember from that night!—so I walked out into the wind and the blown rain, looking for a place to drink and be cheerful with it. I found it two minutes away: a tiny stone tavern with a single bar, and that crowded to bursting, a peat fire, two barmaids, twins of the Earth Mother herself, and an old piper, blowing himself up like a bullfrog with reels and pibrochs.

I wedged myself into a far corner, ordered a double dose of malt whisky, brown as bog water, and tried to forget who and what I was. Soon I found myself singing —not the words, because they were in the Gaelic and I did not know them; but the melodies I knew, many of them, though I could not for the life of me remember where I had heard them first. Because I sang, my neighbours talked to me; and one tall fellow threw his arm around my shoulder and ordered me to drink with him, "to wet the pipes," he said, "because even a thrush canna warble without a dewdrop in his throat."

There was a wild and primitive merriment about the place that lifted the spirit. The pipes skirled. The talk rose high, salty and bawdy, Scots burr and Gaelic lilt intertwining, bubbling out of the same thirsty gullet. The girls, buxom as clover-fed heifers, shouted with the rest and poured brown ale into the mouths of their boys. The barmaids bustled and sweated. An elderly crofter did a flailing reel in the middle of the floor while his audience roared and stamped approval. The air was a blue fug of tobacco smoke and peat smoke and damp tweeds and human exhalations. But it was alive. It was a place of union, of warmth and brotherhood for those who farmed their tiny crofts on the uplands, grazed their sheep on sparse mountain croppings and wondered if the cash and the baled hay would feed them and their cattle through the winter.

For me, it was something else: a posthouse on the road to a place of unknowing. I could stay here a twelve-month and I would be no closer to them than I was now. I had no roots in their clan life. What to them was a poignant folk memory, a familial yesterday, to me was a chapter of history, closed, done, forgotten. They would never close their doors to me, or refuse me bed and board if I needed it; but themselves they would hold private behind the hedge of the old language and the old separatist faith, and their fear of the outsiders who, once and again, had robbed them of their lands to run sheep, and deer for gentlemen to kill in sport.

By ten o'clock I was awash with whisky and sentiment. The piper, drunk as a bard should be, played me out of the bar with the rest of them. But they went home, while I walked back in the rain, climbed three flights of stairs to my attic room and tumbled myself into bed, drunker than the piper himself. That night there were no monsters in my dreams; but with the head I had on me in the morning, I forgot to be grateful for so singular a mercy.

In spite of the hangover I was determined to be early on the road. A sleepy night porter fed me tea and toast and set the course for me.

"You'll go now by Glengarry and that will carry you into Glen Shiel. If there's mist on the mountains—and what with the early hour there might well be—then you'll drive slow and steady, because the road is high and narrow and there's many a poor body has tumbled off it into the lochs. When you pass the Five Sisters—they'll be the hills beyond Kintail—then you'll come to the Shiel

Bridge and then to the Croe Bridge, which is at the head of Loch Duich. After that, the loch is on the left of you always, and there's no place to go on the right, so you must come to Eilean Donan, which used to be the stronghold of the MacRaes. If you have half a crown in your pocket, then they'll let you see two rooms of the place, which isn't worth it, because with that much you can buy a dram at the hotel which is only a spit and a jump away down the loch. After that you come to Ardelve, where there's nothing worth a look. And after Ardelve there's Kyle of Lochalsh, and there, if the tourists haven't swamped it and the Board of Trade hasn't lifted its license, you can put yourself and the car on the ferry for Skye. After that it's MacLeod country, and may Saint Donan stand between you and harm!"

Whereupon, as the old chroniclers used to say, I paid the score and pointed myself in the direction of Glengarry. There was little traffic on the road, so I trundled along at a steady forty miles an hour, because I wanted to blow the whisky fumes out of my brain and rest my bloodshot eyes on the greenery, tall pines and feathery birches, and the heather climbing the rock banks, and bracken, knee high in the dells.

I was five minutes past Glengarry, still in the woodland, when I heard a long trumpeting behind me. I looked in the rear-vision mirror and there was a red sports car, coming up fast, with a woman at the wheel. There was a sharp curve in front, so I braked to let her pass. The shock wave slammed into my flank as she went by. She would have to corner tight if she was going to make the curve. She didn't make it. Thirty yards before the elbow a truck, loaded with pine logs, rounded the turn. She was forced to swing wide. Her wheels hit the gravelled verge and she plunged straight on down the slope and out of my sight. I heard the crashing as she plunged through the birch grove and then a grinding of metal as she brought up hard against the pine boles. The truck was already gone and I was left to deal with whatever I might find in the hollow.

There was less than I had feared. The birch grove had saved her from rolling and cushioned her impact against the pines. The left side of the car was stove in, but the driver was climbing out, apparently unharmed. She stood

8

for a moment, straddle-legged, surveying the wreck, then she sat down abruptly on the damp turf, her head hanging down between her knees. I scrambled down to her.

"Are you all right?"

"I think so. Leave me be for a moment, please." There was a touch of Scots in the voice but more of the English. I could not see her face, but her hair was raven black and her legs were good and she was wearing a skirt of the McNeil tartan. I let her be. I walked down to the car, switched off the engine, unlocked the trunk and took out the luggage, a valise, an attaché case and a small vanity pack. I carried them up the slope and stowed them in my own car.

When I came back she was sitting upright, smoothing back her hair from a pale, oval face. She announced, rather redundantly, "I'm a bloody fool."

"I agree. So now what?"

"You don't happen to have a brandy on you?"

"No. But I'll get you one at Glengarry. We can phone a doctor from there."

"I don't need a doctor. I am one. There's nothing broken and there's no blood. But I'll probably get the shakes very soon. Help me up, please."

I hoisted her up the slope, bundled her into the car and drove her back to Glengarry, where they fed her brandy and strong tea and telephoned the Auto Club to take care of the wreck. She did get the shakes and she was very terse and professional until they were past. Then she asked:

"Where were you heading?"

"Kyle of Lochalsh, for a start."

"Could you give me a lift?"

"Of course. I'll be glad of the company."

"And you're a safer driver than I am. Let's go."

We went; but before we went, we had—God help us!—one of those breathless formal introductions. She was Kathleen McNeil, Doctor of Medicine, Edinburgh and London; and, in a nice ladylike way, she was putting bedamned to any thoughts I might be having about wayside encounters and madcap drivers in distress. Come to that, bedamned to her too. Open your mouth, say "Ah," breathe deeply, now cough, once again, please, and don't think I'm not a good medico because I have good legs and a good figure

9

and I'm not a day older than thirty-two—or is it thirty-five? Well, dear madam, it's manners not to refuse until you've been asked; besides which, if it were the Queen of Sheba herself, I couldn't be interested at this moment. And, what's more, you may have the best cure in the world for gallstones and goiter, but you're a bloody menace behind the wheel of a car!

The mist was still down in Glen Shiel, so we climbed slowly along the flank of the hill, praying no crazy Highlander would come roaring out of the murk, sure that the God of the Free Kirk was holding his hand on the wheel. We were wrapped in an eerie stillness, broken only by the sound of cascading water or the bleat of a sheep, startling as the cry of a lost child.

Then, abruptly, we broke out into a brightness, a morning glory that I had never seen before, or hoped to see. The sky was a pale blue, clear of cloud. The hills climbed into it, royal with purple heather and the diamond-flash of springs and runnels, the shine of grey granite. Below, the land fell away, through peat beds and bogs white with swamp asphodel, to the shining water of Loch Cluanie. I pulled the car into a lay-by. We got out and stood together, the only humans in a primal solitude. The sheep were there, black-faced and shaggy, ambling over the peat mounds. High in the blue, a peregrine falcon planed in a lazy circle. For the rest, there was only the sky and the water and the harsh, alien beauty of the hills.

I remember that I was near to tears at that moment. I understood, very clearly, the impulse of the anchorites to flee the confusion of the ancient cities, their injustices and corruptions and cruelties. I understood the lure of the deserts and the high places, where a man could begin to *be* again. I found myself wondering how my private terror would end: in an explosive madness of frustration, or a passive imbecility in which I would simply survive, without hope, trapped in a desolation of my own devising?

"That's a grim thought you're having," said Dr. Kathleen McNeil.

"It is."

"Then you should leave it here and forget it."

"I'll take your advice, Doctor."

She laughed then; her face was suddenly young and

beautiful, and I was glad to have her there. At least we could talk and be easy for the rest of the journey.

"Where are you heading?" I asked her.

"To Harris. That's in the Outer Islands. I'm doing a locum for an old friend of my father's. It's the only kind of holiday I can afford just now."

"I'm for Lewis. I'm staying the night on Skye. Then, if there's a place, I'll take the first ferry from Uig in the morning. If you want to save a long bus ride and linger through the landscape, you're welcome to ride along."

"Thank you. I'd like that."

Looking back now, I marvel at the simplicity of that moment and the violence of the drama to which it committed us both in the end. We were strangers, met by chance in a Highland glen. We were private from one another. Each for a separate reason was determined to remain private. We shared only the casual intimacies of fellow-travellers—the hands' touch, the moments of common wonder and enthusiasm. We restrained our curiosities about each other. We offered no opinions that might touch the core of ourselves. We talked only of what was outside us, immediately visible, immediately experienced. Yesterday was a closed book because tomorrow would be another day and we would be strangers again. As well that neither of us guessed what Muirgen, the sea-born enchantress of the Celts, was weaving into the cloth of our mutual destinies.

The pattern she wove for us that day was simple and beautiful. If there were spells in it at all, they were all healing ones for me. There was a music of strange names: Morvich and Auchtertyre, Balmacara and Luib, Sligachan and Kensaleyre. There was the black boat beached on a pebble strand, and no man or woman or child within five miles of it; there was the old, old man, knee deep in a trout burn, casting with a ritual grace, as if he were performing a sacred rite; there were the Cuillins, high and magical, spent volcanoes from the age of the cataclysms; there was the golden bladder wrack spread like a carpet on the black rocks below the tide line, and the wheeling of white gulls over the white cottage by the seashore. There was the woman turning the scythed grass and piling it into stooks; there was the shepherd

11

with his kelpie, herding his black-faced flock, while we halted to give him the rights of the road, which were his due. And everywhere there was the heather and the green moss, and sometimes a pine stand planted by the Development people and sometimes a vast tumble of stones from an ancient glacier.

When we came to Uig, in the long, slow fall of the evening, there was the warm wind from the Gulf Stream with the smell of the ocean in it, and the promise of fair weather for the morning.

At the little hotel there was dinner for the two of us, but only one room with two beds in it, which we could have shared if we were married or looked like it; but we weren't and we didn't. So I found myself a room in a crofter's house where they promised me bacon and eggs for breakfast—with porridge if I wanted it—and guaranteed to wake me in time for the ferry. As for Dr. Kathleen McNeil, Edinburgh and London, I wished her good night, hoped she slept well, and truly cared not a tinker's damn whether she did or she didn't. I would call for her at eight in the morning, drive her down to the dock and, after that, good luck and good-bye.

That night I lay awake a long time, listening to the faint wash of the tide and watching the moon climb over Beinn Edra. I had never been so solitary in twenty years, and never, never so glad of the solitude. I had a sudden comical vision of Atlas, bone-weary from carrying the world on his shoulders, deciding one day to shrug it off and let it bounce away on its own crazy course. Now he was flexing his cramped muscles and wondering why the hell he had carried the thankless burden so long. What he might do with his liberty was another matter, for another day.

At eight-fifteen we were parked in the first line of cars, waiting for the ferry to Tarbert, the southern port for the Isles of Harris and Lewis. The boat would be late this morning, they told us, because of trouble with the hoists; so we had an hour to kill. Dr. Kathleen McNeil was in need of another cup of coffee because she had hurried her breakfast. She wandered off to find it in the little clapboard café on the far side of the jetty. I strolled down to the beach to look at the sailboat anchored in the inner pool. She was a beautiful thing, fifty-odd feet, built sturdy and beamy for the Northern seas, but still with a hull line that promised a close work and good turn of speed with it. The nameplate on her counter said, *"The Mactire, Stornoway."* There was a dory hitched to her stern and, as I watched, a fellow, with his arm in a sling, came out of the cabin hatch and began hauling the dory alongside. He scrambled into it awkwardly, picked up an oar and began sculling himself towards the beach with the oar over the stern.

He was a big fellow, half a head taller than I, with a shock of bright red hair and a red Viking beard and a chest on him broad as a herring barrel. I offered him a hand to haul the dory onto the shingle, but he refused with a grin.

"I still have one good hand. But you wouldn't happen to have a car, would you? I slipped on the deck this morning—fool thing to do—and I think I've cracked my wrist. I'd better find a doctor to splint it for me."

I told him I had both the car and a tame doctor, and he threw back his head and laughed.

"There's a providence if you like. Now all I have to do is find a sail hand to run *The Mactire* back to Stornoway with me."

It was then that I walked myself straight into the mesh that the sea-goddess had been weaving for me. On a wild impulse I told him, "I just might know one at that."

"A local lad?"

"No, myself."

"And what can you do?"

"I can set a sail and hold a compass course."

"And where have you sailed?"

"Sydney and the waters south. The Tyrrhenian and the Greek Islands."

"What about your wife?"

"She's not my wife. But if I can get her to drive the car onto the ferry and drive it off at Tarbert, you've got yourself a sail hand."

He gave me a long look, measuring me. His eyes were blue and cold as the sea. I read him for a man who could do murder if you crossed him on the wrong day, and yet tear down mountains for a promise made. Then he grinned and held out his good hand. "You're signed on then. And thanks. Now let's go talk with this doctor-woman of yours."

So it was done, easily and casually, in the manner of the Islands. So, though we could not know it, the magical square was completed—Alastair Morrison of the Morrison, Dr. Kathleen McNeil of Edinburgh and London, the big redbeard whose given name was Ruarri Matheson and myself, the stranger in the land of the Gael.

I wonder still why I was chosen to bring us all together. I have not yet determined how far I am responsible for the moon madness and the epic terror that overtook us all in the end.

I

"WE'LL RUN UP A PENNANT FIRST," SAID RUARRI Matheson, "just to show 'em who we are, then we'll make sail and take her out."

He was standing by the wheel, casting a critical eye on my handiwork as I hauled the dory inboard and lashed it to the hatch cover. The pennant was an odd one, a snarling wolf's muzzle, red on a white ground. I asked him the meaning of it. He laughed.

"You might call it my own house flag. It's the name of the boat, you see. Mactire is an old Gaelic word for wolf. It's also the name they've dubbed me with on the island: Red Ruarri the Mactire. I'm not sure it's a compliment, but they've laid it on me anyway."

"I thought you were an island man yourself."

"I am. Though I was away for ten years and only home the last three."

"What were you doing?"

"A little of everything."

"What do you do now?"

"I farm. I have a stake in the sea fishing. I sail this lady when I can."

I winched up the main, set jib and mizzen, cleated down so she would fall gently away, then scrambled forwards to get the anchor up. By the time I was back in the cockpit, Ruarri had her sailing past the jetty and out into the channel. We had to work from there because the wind was from the west and we had to push her into it to stay clear of the skerries at the mouth of the loch, and pull ourselves off the lee shore before we began the long reach northward through the Minch.

15

When I had tightened sheets, Red Ruarri gave me a grin and a laconic word of approval.

"Nice work, seannachie!"

"What the hell's a seannachie?"

"Och, the ignorance of the Sassenach! A seannachie's a storyteller, like you—though not quite like, because he keeps everything in his head: the histories of the clans that go way back, and the fairy tales of the time before the clans, and the histories that hang about the place-names. Sometimes he's a bard, too, and can sing you the old songs or make you a new poem for a wedding or a funeral. There are still a few of them around the Islands, and maybe when you go to a ceilidh you'll hear one, though you'll need the Gaelic to understand him."

"If I'm staying long, I'll have to learn it."

"And will you be staying long?"

"I don't know."

"Where will you be lodging?"

"With Alastair Morrison over by Laxay. D'you know him?"

"I know him. I like him. Though I'm not sure he approves of me always—or of what I do. Take the wheel now, and I'll make us a grog to keep the chill out. Hold her tight into the wind, else we'll start falling away to Vaternish Point."

He was paying me a compliment and, small as it was, I was absurdly proud of it. There is no purer or more healing pleasure for a man than to stand helm watch in a fair wind and feel the buck of the sea and watch the white, tight belly of a well-set canvas. After so long an imprisonment in myself and in a society in which I could no longer believe, I felt suddenly liberated, uplifted, free-ranging as the kittiwake that glided with hardly a tremor of wings just above the masthead.

Let me be honest and say at once I am no master mariner. I lack the muscle and the nerve and the nose for wind and weather, and the extrasensory mathematics that make a great navigator. I love the sea, but I fear it too. I fear its solitude and its mystery, the madness of its upheavals, the sinister threat of its calms. And yet I know, in my blood and guts and bones, that if the tyrants came again, with their spies and pursuivants and bureaucrats and manipulators, I would rather hoist sail, slip anchor and commit myself to wind and wild water and improbable landfall than risk the invasion of myself by a hireling man.

Then I found myself singing: an old song remembered out of a lost childhood.

Ruarri came on deck with two pannikins clasped in his fist: black coffee, heavily laced with malt whisky. He handed one to me, checked our heading, then fixed me with a bright and quizzical eye. "So you do have the Gaelic, seannachie!"

"No. Why?"

"The song. That's the tune they call 'Morag of Dunvegan,' and you were singing it in the Gaelic."

"And I don't understand a word of it. I learned it by rote, like a lot of other things. I was taught by an old Irish monk who was a harpist, and who claimed to know every tune of the Irish and the Scots and who wanted to turn us all into missionaries or junior Fenians."

He seemed relieved, as if he had suspected me of a lie and was constrained to make amends. "You're a good helmsman."

"I had a boat of my own. I used to race her, but I was never a real contender. I don't have the killer instinct."

"That's an odd word to use."

"Just a phrase."

He was a wary one this, soft-footed, edgy as a forest animal, every sense alert all the time. He was young to have seen war service, but he had that watchful, sidelong attitude of the commando, the leery eye and the quick reaction and the ready smile to hide the tension inside. There was a chameleon quality even in his speech. Most of the time he had the soft, singing burr of the Isles; he would turn the phrases as a Celt does. But there were moments when the accent slipped and there were hints of alien tonalities. He would never settle down to a subject the way a mountain man does, talking round and about it, under and over and through and back again, weaving the talk like a piece of cloth. His conversation was a series of sallies, now at one subject, now at another, so that you never knew quite what he was driving at.

"Tell me, seannachie, what's between you and this doctor-woman?"

"Nothing. She broke her car with damn-fool driving. I offered to bring her to Uig."

"Not interested?"

"Not in that one particularly."

"She's damty good-looking."

"There are lots of good-looking women."

"She might be willing as well."

"I didn't ask her."

"I might ask her myself one bright day."

"It's a free country."

"The hell it is, laddie!" He emptied his liquor at a gulp and set down the cup with a clatter. "I've been back three years and I'll tell you we're castrated with regulations, bloated as eunuchs with this bugger-you-jack disease they call British socialism. Even out here, round the Long Island, where the seas are jumping with fish and crawling with lobsters that would bring a fortune in Europe, what's happening? It's still hand labour on the crofts, and the weaving subsidized by the government, and the herring fleets dwindling because you can't get hands to run the boats even for a share of the catch. It's a tourist country, they tell us! Best salmon fishing in the world, but you can't get a bedroom with a bath from Berneray to the Butt o' Lewis. The money goes into the hotels all right—weavers' money and crofters' money and the money the Highlands Development Board pours in. But it all goes back to the mainland—across the bars and into the brewers' pockets. So the women still work like dray horses, and the men drink like fiddler's bitches on a Saturday and they all troop off to the Free Kirk for sulphur and molasses on a Sunday! Except on Eriskay and Barra, that is, because they're Romans there and Jacobites and a mite more tolerant of the lusts of the flesh—though it's hard to find much to lust after, because the girls go into service on the mainland and down to London, where they can use the new abortion laws!"

"So why do you stay?"

"That, seannachie, is a big question. One of these nights, if you can get me drunk enough, I'll try to answer it. Meantime, that's Score Bay to starboard, and the headland is Rubha Hunish. We'll hold on this course till an hour after we lose it, then we'll reach up towards the Shiants, where I hope to make rendezvous with a client of mine from Trondheim in Norway."

I didn't ask him who his client was or what kind of business needed to be transacted in the middle of the Minch. I was happy to sail the boat and watch the cliffs blur slowly into the summer haze.

But Red Ruarri had a mind to talk and talk he would. "Yourself, now. What brings you to the Isles?"

"I've been sick. I've had a bellyful of cities and arguments. Morrison suggested I come. Simple as that."

"But you're not a simple fellow, seannachie. You've done a lot of living, as any man can read in that face of yours. And you don't believe in the Isles of the Blest and all that medieval mist and moonshine."

"Maybe they had something we've lost. Maybe what they had is still left."

"In the Islands?" He threw back his head and laughed. Then he stopped laughing and frowned over a new thought. "Well, you could be right at that. When I was— no matter where I was, but it was wild and woolly and the risks were high, but the money was a golden shower while it lasted—I used to dream about the old Norsemen. They were a bold and bloody bunch of hell raisers. But, you know, they were dreamers too. Look at a map and see where they took their longships: to the Faeroes and the Orkneys and Shetland and Iceland and Greenland and the coast of America, and down the rivers to Kiev. There are runic words on the floor of Santa Sofia in Istanbul—did you know that, now?—and they ruled the Hebrides till the middle of the thirteenth century, and half our beaches have Norse names, Tolsta and Seilebost and Taransay and Grjomaval. We've still got towheads and redbeards from their sirings and a memory that's too mixed up with the Gael for our own good. You asked why I came back. There's one reason. I was sick of the sun and the sweat that leaches all the salt out of a man's blood. I wanted the dark water and the gale wind, and the deer in the high corries and the land that had to be made again, but could be made if a man put muscle and brains to work on it."

"So now you've got what you want."

"Not all of it, seannachie. But it's coming. Meantime, I

19

rove a little—and raid a little—and, if you want to stand well with the godly folk of the Lews, you'd best not spend too much time in my company."

"I'll make up my own mind about that. What time do you expect to make Stornoway?"

"If the wind holds, we'll make it in eight hours under sail. Which means we'll be home before the bars close. I'll buy you a drink, find you a bed and introduce you to a little blond pigeon who'll warm it for you any time you have a mind. And in the morning I'll run you down to Tarbert to pick up your car. Meantime, you'll do me a favour if you don't mention this little meeting we'll be having off the Shiants."

"That's your business. I'd have no reason to discuss it."

He relaxed then. He perched himself on the coaming of the cockpit and began to read me, in companionable fashion, the lore of the northern seas. For all his quirky temper, there was a vein of poetry in him and a hypnotic lilt to his storytelling that matched the rhythm of the swell and the warm lift of the western wind.

There were tales of the old whalers, and the fishing feuds and the seal hunters and wrecks in the great Atlantic gales. There were the legends of the giant Cochull Glas and the little dark pygmy men of Ness and the old, forgotten ones who raised the standing stones. There was the knowing of the sea birds, gannet and gull and fulmar, black guillemot and razorbill and Arctic tern. There were fisherman's yarns, too, of the killer whale that could coast at thirty knots and the basking shark that could drag a boat for miles and him with a harpoon stuck in his dorsal muscles, of the grey seal with his Roman nose and his shy, segregate ways, and the mackerel shoals that made a whipcrack music when they ran through a flat summer sea.

It was all rare and strange and wonderful, an ancient tapestry drawn between me and the world I had left behind. After a while I was drowsy with the wonder of it; so, when we had made our leg to the west and were reaching northward up the Minch, Red Ruarri took the wheel and sent me below to make a meal for us both.

The cabin was clean and bright as a new penny. There were two bunks, each covered with waterproof vinyl, each with a head lamp and a bookshelf within arm's reach of a resting man. There was a chart table, with a ship-to-shore radio above it. There was a big galley with a sink and a gimballed stove and a stool in gimbals for a rough-weather cook. Every movable article was bracketed, hooked, socketed so that it would not move even in the hardest blow. There was no bachelor clutter here, no shoddy carpentry. Every screw was tight, every lock oiled and secure. The pots were scoured, the cutlery was clean, even the dishcloths were rinsed white, and the head smelled fresh with disinfectant. Raw and randy and a rover he might be, but Red Ruarri the Mactire was a very systematic man. He ate well, too, and his liquor cupboard was stocked against the cold night watches.

While the meal was heating, I stole a look at his books. Another surprise. Here was none of the dog-eared trash one found so often on a sailor's bookrack. These were the books of a serious reader and a specialist at that. There was the Laing translation of *The Olaf Sagas* and *The Sagas of the Norse Kings,* Dasent's version of *The Tale of Burnt Njal,* and an early edition of *The Saga of the Men of Laxdale.* There was Frank O'Connor on Irish Literature, and a volume of the MacDonald Diaries on the folklore of the Lews, and a copy of Brøgger's *Ancient Emigrants.* There were two grammars, one Norwegian, one Danish. Whatever he felt himself to be—homecoming Gael or throwback to the Norsemen—Ruarri Matheson was reading himself back to his origins; or was he reading them into himself to fill the vacuum of ten years' exile? It was an interesting speculation, but I had no time to pursue it because the stew was coming to the boil and a hungry sailor was yelling down for his dinner and a mug of beer.

I took the wheel while Ruarri fed himself, one-handed, cursing the while at his awkwardness. Then I ate my own meal and went below to tidy the galley. I was halfway through my chores when Ruarri yelled again. The Shiants were coming up ahead and his client was running down to meet us: an old-fashioned trawler, timber built and belching brown smoke from very dirty diesels. I had to scramble then. Ruarri wanted the sails down and the fenders out. Then he took the wheel, while I handled the throttle and laid *The Mactire* alongside the trawlerman. I held her there with her engine idling while Ruarri

21

went aboard the trawler. He was greeted by a burly fellow whom I took to be the skipper. Then they both disappeared below-decks. Ten minutes later Ruarri was back with a small leather satchel under his arm and a bottle of schnapps clasped in his fist. Then we were off again. When I had made sail and we were back on our northward heading, he poured me a shot of the schnapps and vouchsafed his only comment on the transaction.

"Good fellow, Bollison. Twice as honest as most. Hard worker too. Trawls in the summer, hunts seal in the winter. That old tub doesn't look much. She's twenty years old, but he runs her up round the Arctic as if she were an icebreaker. I bought a half-share of her eighteen months ago and I'm in profit already."

"Where's he off to now?"

"West of the Isles. There are good herring grounds between Barra Head and Ireland. There's cod, and white-fish, too, if he's lucky."

We were back to fish stories again and I wanted to bait him. "So now you're a shipping magnate."

He gave me a hostile look and then that facile smile. "You're joking, seannachie, but you miss the point. In today's world a man has to have one foot on the land, the other in the sea. The land's for eating and for the capital gain and the national identity and all that, and for a place to retire when your sap dries out. But the sea's the free place still, where the legislators can't touch you, and the tax boys can't read your private log, and your ship's a kingdom, where no man has a right to set foot until the captain asks him. So long as you keep your nose clean in port, you get the best of every law and the worst of none. It's the sea that feeds the oil refineries and the steel mills and the cotton spinners, and it's the sea that'll be feeding a hungry world when half the land is turned into a bloody desert."

"So what are you trying to make yourself, Ruarri? The Onassis of the Hebrides? Or an old-style Lord of the Isles?"

He rose to that one, swift as a trout after a fly. "Maybe a little of each, maybe safer than both. Do you think I'm crazy?"

"No. I just wonder where you see yourself at the end,

when the sickness strikes, or the sap dries out as you said."

"And that's the point you miss, seannachie! That's what everyone misses. It's the doing that matters to me, not the being. It's the making that matters and not the thing made. Have you ever seen an Atlantic gale?"

"Never."

"Then I'll tell you how it comes—as it might come to-day—although it won't because the glass will hold high for a while. But there's the front first, cold sky, cirrocumulus, building and piling, until the wind hits and the sea rises and the spray starts freezing on your topsides. And there's the boat and the crew and the sea, and yourself only to master them all. If you don't master them, you're dead. But if you do, there's money in the bank—for another acre of sweet land, or the deposit on another boat—which gives you two chances next time—or a cargo that you can buy in Stockholm and sell at a profit some other place. That's what the old Norsemen did. They were butchers in battle, but they were traders too. And they took England from the Saxons and Dublin from the Irish, and the Danes are still trading teak from Thailand, and you're eating my haddock in Rome. Does that make sense or doesn't it?"

I had to admit it did. I had to admit that the doing of Red Ruarri the Mactire was infinitely more uplifting to the spirit than the bleak, meditative ennui into which I had lapsed for too long. But there was still another question I had to ask him.

"It seems to me, Ruarri, you're walking in another man's shoes. Leverhulme tried to do exactly what you're trying to do, and he owned the island! He was going to organize the fishing and the whaling and the spinning and the crofting, and he had a ready-made market for all the products, but he couldn't bring it off, for all his millions."

It was obviously no new argument to Ruarri, because he had his answer pat and ready. "And do you know why? Because he owned the island but he didn't belong. And he tried to do it in an old-fashioned way, the rich laird bending to confer favours on his fiefs. They wouldn't have that and I don't blame them. My way's different. I'm one of them. I'm the son of Anne Matheson, over by Gisla, but I don't know who my father is and I've given up caring. I'm the wild one, sure, and the boys who work with me are wild ones, too, but we belong. And though we attract envy, and the ministers and the missionaries don't like us, we mean hope, too, because we're staying and we're making good and we've got lots of brass in the bank. One fine day, when you're sick of fishing with Alastair Morrison, I'll drive you out and show you what we're doing with the peat land that's been sour for centuries. Come with me on a trawl and I'll show you what we're doing there. Give me a couple more years and I'll have myself a fleet like the Russians, with a mother ship to tend the small boats and process the catch. Lord of the Isles? Maybe that's what I'd like to be—but in the old way. Brother to all and better than all. And when I marry, if I marry, it won't be as Ruarri Matheson, the son of Anne Matheson. I'll be Ruarri Mactire, with the name changed by deed poll, and my sons will be the sons of the Red Wolf. So how do you read me now, seannachie?"

It was a bad moment and I was to blame for it. I had teased him into saying more than he intended and more than I wanted to hear. So I tried to put him off with a compliment.

"I read you as a driving man, Ruarri, and I think you'll probably get what you want—most of it, anyway."

"But you wonder what the drive is, don't you? You wonder whether there isn't a touch of madness in it somewhere?"

"A touch of the visionary, perhaps. But that's no bad thing, is it?"

"It's a haunting thing, sometimes."

"That's true."

"It's a lonely thing too. It's the loneliness of memories that other men don't have, of dreams that other men would hoot at if you told them. And it drives you to be more like them than they are themselves, to drink more, and chase more women, and take bigger risks, just so they'll believe the dreaming in the end. Or have you lost me already?"

"No. I just wonder how long you can live in other men's skins as well as your own."

"As long as I need to, seannachie! As long as it takes

to make 'em believers and followers and builders, instead of chattels with a social security number in place of a name."

"If you think you can bring it off, good luck to you. But don't expect flowers for every homecoming and a loving cup every dinnertime."

He took time to digest that one. I could see the anger in him and I understood why they had given him his name. Then the bright, easy smile was back again. "You're too clever by half, seannachie. I'm glad we're friends, otherwise we'd be giving each other a hard time. That's Kebock Head coming up to starboard. Call me when you have it abeam and I'll lay the homeward course for you."

He went below then and I was grateful to be alone for a while. He was too combative for comfort, and I had come away to be private from other men's quarrels. Yet there was something enormously attractive about him, a heroic dimension that set him apart from the grey townsmen and the shrill intellectuals who strutted so confidently in the twilight of a discredited civilization. There was a challenge in him too: a challenge to go adventuring, to break out of the closed frontiers and the crippling conformities, to measure oneself as a man against the primal elements and the tyrannies of a time out of joint.

I found myself wondering what kind of woman he would wed to breed the wolf-sons he wanted, how Dr. Kathleen McNeil would react if ever he set his roving sights on her. I wondered how he would handle a rival in business, or in love, and how far his ambition had or would set him outside the law. He had hinted at violence in his past, and the wolf pennant said that he took some pride in it. Then the wind began to freshen, coming in gusts and squalls out of the western fjords of Lewis. After that it was sail work and helm work and gunwales under, until we came to Stornoway.

It was near seven in the evening when we picked up our mooring in the inner pool. There was still light: a clear, cold light, alien and unwelcoming to the Mediterranean man. The water was grey as old pewter, the cliffs were black, the hills green and gold and purple, yet strangely melancholy in the waning day. The little town with its black roofs and its stuccoed walls, white and brown and

25

yellow, seemed to huddle for protection under the battlements of a very Victorian castle. The whole place was wrapped in a suppertime quiet, broken only by the plaintive crying of the late gulls. The high ferry dock was deserted, and the sea-scarred trawlers moored around the basin were empty of men. The few folk on the streets had a closed, uninterested air, as if they had turned their backs on the sea and wanted no more of it for a while.

"You're thinking it's a sad place," said Ruarri the Mactire.

"Something like that."

"Well, it is. You look at the sea and you remember the lives it has taken and the lives it has left. Over there's the lifeboat, which is a reminder that other lives will be taken tomorrow. Look at the hills and they're lonely for people, for the lost ones and the gone-away ones as well."

"The Happy Isles?"

"Aye, in spite of it all. Now we'll have the sails off, if you don't mind. We'll fold 'em and bag 'em, so they can be dried ashore. Then I'll show you where some of the happiness is to be found."

I was bone-weary and beginning to be cold, but at least the work was a respite from my brooding. As I hurried through the last tasks, I heard Ruarri curse explosively. I looked up and saw a Customs cutter putting out from the dock and heading towards us. I asked him what was the matter. He did not answer, but stood braced against the rigging, angry and hostile until the cutter came alongside. I went on folding the sails, ears cocked to catch the dialogue.

"I'd like to come aboard, Ruarri."

"Why?"

"Routine inspection."

"The hell it's routine, Duggie! It's harassment and discrimination and you bloody well know it. I've been in home waters since I left here yesterday."

"I'd still like to come aboard. Don't be difficult now, Ruarri."

"I'd still like to know why."

"Routine inspection. And you don't come ashore till I've made it. What happened to your arm?"

"I broke it."

"Who's that on board with you?"

"Fellow I picked up at Uig. A tourist. He sailed me back here."

"I'd like to talk to him too."

I judged it was time to intervene, so I stowed the last sails in the bag and stepped down into the cockpit. The Customs man, a dark, narrow-faced fellow with a knowing eye, gave me a professional smile and a sloppy salute.

"Sorry to bother you, sir. May I see your papers?"

"They're in my bag, in the cabin. I'll get them for you."

As I went below, the argument began again, low-toned now, but still vehement.

I am a wandering man and I have learned to travel light. I carry only a single suitcase which is never locked, because I lose keys and cigarette lighters and fountain pens with equal facility. I lifted the suitcase onto the bunk and snapped it open. The satchel which Ruarri had brought back from the trawler was lying on top of my folded clothes. I was startled and then angry. I unzipped the satchel and found it full of bank notes, English sterling and American dollars. Immediate dilemma: should I toss it onto the bunk and let Ruarri make his own explanations, or should I claim ownership and commit myself to a lie if the Customs man demanded to inspect my luggage?

I decided on a bluff, which might save face for both of us. I took the wallet containing my documents, shoved it into the satchel and clambered up on deck. I made a small play of fumbling inside the satchel and presented the documents to the Customs man: passport, air ticket, contract for the hire of my car, a receipted bill from the hotel in Fort Augustus. For good measure I gave him the name of my host at Laxay. He allowed himself a grin at the completeness of the dossier, then handed the papers back to me.

"Everything in order, sir. Hope you have a pleasant stay in the Isles." To Ruarri he offered only a curt command. "Now, laddie, let's get this over with."

He climbed aboard and immediately went below, Ruarri grumbling and cursing at his heels, while I sat in the cockpit, shivering and ill-tempered, with the satchel clasped on my knees. He must have done a very thorough job of inspection because it was all of twenty minutes before he came on deck again, announced, without rancour, that we were free to go ashore and left us.

Ruarri, cocky as bedamned, offered no excuse, only a grin and an offhand word of thanks. "I read you right, seannachie. That was quick thinking."

"To hell with you, Matheson! You're a bastard in any man's language."

"I don't like that name."

"I don't give a damn whether you like it or not."

"I could break your neck!"

"Not with one hand, Ruarri. So let's get the dory overside and I'll row you ashore."

"You wouldn't hear an explanation?"

"No."

"A drink then, to end the good day?"

"No, thanks."

We rowed ashore in silence. We parted without a handshake on the deserted dock. I trudged the town for half an hour before I found an indifferent room and a stodgy meal. I tumbled into bed, wishing the back of my hand to Ruarri the Mactire and thinking I should probably go stark raving mad in the Happy Isles.

I woke to a late, bright morning. Rested and bathed and fed, I strolled out to take another, less jaundiced look at this place of my unknowing.

The wind had blown itself out during the night and the sea was mirror calm. The first trawlers were heading out through the harbour mouth, a rusty freighter was discharging coal and there was life in the streets and round the docks: early housewives with their shopping baskets, a gaggle of gossips outside the harbour master's office, truckers loading baled wool for the spinners and the cottage weavers, a flurry round the inner pool as another group of fishing boats made ready for the sea. A small boy fished from an idle dory. A seal poked an inquisitive snout out of the water. An old man sat on a bollard mending a net. A pair of husky fellows were polishing the brightwork on the lifeboat.

Slowly I began to see a pattern to it all, a cool, austere, unraucous pattern that demanded respect, even if it did not provoke the swift rush of affection that comes in

28

sunnier places. The buildings were foursquare and drab, but they were solid against the gales and the spindrift. The people were drab, too, at first glance, tweedy and homespun in dress, the women apple-cheeked and sturdy, the men sea-scored and slow of speech. But when I asked a direction they smiled and spent time and ceremony to help me. They were very private and surprisingly incurious about the affairs of a stranger. And yet perhaps it was not surprising, for the men of the Lews had emigrated everywhere, and most had served time as merchant seamen, and the little port itself had given wartime haven to sailors from all over the world.

But the fear of the sea was here, too, nourished by the memory of old disaster and new risks. Five hundred yards from the harbour lurked the Beasts of Holm, where two hundred home-coming soldiers and sailors had drowned within sight of shore. Once the herring fleet had numbered a thousand vessels; now it was down to fifty, and never a season passed without a score of calls to man the lifeboat, for a coaster in trouble off the Flannans or a drifter blown helpless towards Cape Wroth. Small wonder that the joys of these folk were sober joys and their humour wry; small wonder that they had a healthy disrespect for those who lived their lives by the rule and rote of city men.

In the crowded lands, in the ant-heap cities of our time, men are made and unmade by men. They are ground and frayed and polished and shaped, or misshaped, by contact with each other, like stones in a turbulent river. The past does not dominate them because they are whirled along in the torrent of now. The land does not dominate them because it is buried under asphalt and concrete and their feet never touch it. The sea does not rule them because they neither smell nor hear it, as they tread their corridors of bricks and mortar like mice in a maze.

But in primitive places, in islands and uplands, man must adapt himself to the elements, to earth and water and changing air, else he will surely die. His past is always present to him, because the sap of knowledge and endurance must be drawn from it every day. His community life is less abrasive because it is more distended. It is more fraternal, more tribal, because it is closer to the mother earth; unified, too, by the sense of common risk.

Even the place-names tell the same story. They celebrate no ancient tyrants, no fustian politicians, no irrelevant idols; they celebrate the earth and the sea and the fruits thereof: Sheep Isles and Salmon Run and Seal Beach and Holding of the Herds.

As the pattern became clear to me, I saw Ruarri the Mactire as part of it, a man at risk with the rest of them. His small, insolent knavery took on another meaning: the rover cocking a snoot at the stay-at-homes, the privateer signalling up-you-Jack to the shore-bound merchants. I was sorry I had refused his explanation and his offer of a drink to end a good day. It was a small moment missed. There were too many such in too transient a lifetime.

It was midmorning now. Time to find a taxi to drive me south for my car; time to telephone Alastair Morrison and tell him to expect me at Laxay. When I walked back to the hotel to pay my bill and collect my bag, I found Ruarri waiting for me. He handed me a set of keys and a small package.

"I've had your car brought up from Tarbert. It's parked behind the pub. I've paid the hotel bill because you were supposed to be my guest. And the package is a kind of apology. I hope you'll accept it."

What could you do with a man like that? One minute he was at your throat, the next he was courteous as a prince. My own words sounded grudging and restrained.

"There was no need for this. I mislaid my own sense of humour last night."

"So we'll have that drink sometime, eh?"

"I'd like that."

"And maybe you'll come to a ceilidh at my house when you're settled down."

"Any time you like."

"Enjoy yourself now."

We shook hands and I stood watching him as he strode away, jaunty and swaggering as if he owned the town and all the fish in the sea. I sat in the car and unwrapped his gift. It was a chessman, four inches high, carved from walrus ivory in the semblance of a Viking warrior. There was a note with it, written in a bold but literate hand:

"This I found on my own land. They tell me it's nearly a thousand years old. If you feel we can be friends, keep

30

it. If not, send it back. Old things, like bastards, need a gentling in the house. Ruarri."

I have him still. He stands on my table as I write these words, an old, yellowing midget man, relic of a heroic age, reminder to me of a brief violence, a wild loving and a long regret.

II

THE LODGE OF ALASTAIR MORRISON OF THE MORRISON stands on a finger of land jutting into the waters of Loch Erisort, which is itself a long fjord opening into the North Minch.

To get there you take the road south from Stornoway —a single track of weathered bitumen, winding through peat lands and rare small crofts. On this road you keep your wits about you because there is no passing room, so that if you meet another car, or one of those big travelling shops of the Islands Co-operative, then one of you must pull into a lay-by to let the other go. Since the road is like a switchback, you must count on a slow progress. If the mist is down, then you don't drive it at all, unless it's a Saturday night, when God cocks a kindly eye on the men of the Outer Isles and keeps them safe for a tongue-lashing in kirk on the Sunday. When you come to Laxay, which is the Islet of Salmon, you turn east along a roughish track with dark water on one side and low heather hills on the other. It's the sheep that will hold you on this road—shaggy, spindly flocks with painted horns and rumps dyed red or green or yellow, so that each crofter may know his own after the gathering in. Finally you will see a small hump with two chimneys poking above it, as though there were a house buried under the ground. On the other side of the hump, face to the sunrise, you will find the lodge.

It is a lonely place at first look, built of grey stone, with sharp gables and narrow dormer windows, and a rock wall raised high against the sea winds. In front there is a beach of dark pebbles, spread with sea wrack, and beyond the beach there is grey water and the treeless headlands of the southern shore. But, once inside the wall, everything changes. There is a garden such as you might find in Kent or Surrey, with rhododendrons and azaleas and Dutch tulips and dahlias and a vegetable plot for the kitchen. Hannah welcomes you at the door, small, spry and ageless, with a wintry smile and a summery twinkle in her black gypsy eyes. A dumpling maid takes your bag and leads you to an upstairs bedroom, warm as new toast, smelling of wax and fresh flowers. There is a Bible on the desk and a shelf of other books for the secular man. When the dust of the road is off you, then you are taken down to a big room panelled in oak, lined with books and old prints, to be received by the kilted laird of the domain. He gives you the greeting of the Isles: "Ceud Mile Failte," the hundred thousand welcomes. He puts a glass of malt whisky in your hand, sits you down by the peat fire and then reads you what he calls "the hierarchy of the house."

"First, there's me. I collect the money, every Friday of every week. I listen to complaints, though I never do anything about them. I'm a mine of local history, mostly inaccurate. If I'm not fishing or sleeping or writing my memoirs, which no one will ever publish, I'm available for counsel, spiritual and temporal. If there's anyone you yearn to meet, I'll try to arrange it. If there's anyone you want to avoid, I'll do anything but lie for you, though I might interpret the truth slightly in favour of a paying guest. Then there's Hannah, who swears she's ten years younger than her birth certificate, which states she's sixty-nine. Hannah runs the lodge and the kitchen with two girls, who will be of no interest to you whatsoever. She serves breakfast at eight and luncheon at twelve-thirty and dinner at seven, and if you're not here, you don't eat—though I have known her leave a sandwich and a bottle of beer in the room of a favoured guest. Also she has the second sight, which she doesn't like to

32

talk about. But if she does talk about it, you'd be wise to listen. For the fishing, there's Fergus the gillie and his lads. He'll buy your gear and make your flies and give you more advice than you need for nothing. A bottle of whisky occasionally will halve the advice and double the catch. If you fall sick or break a leg, I treat you for nothing. So long as you're well, you treat me to a whisky every night before dinner. And if there's anything you're not happy about, tell me now, because tomorrow will be much too late."

"How long can I stay?"

"As long as you please."

"Can I entertain guests?"

"If I like 'em, you can. If I don't, you take 'em to Stornoway or Tarbert. Life's too short to be putting up with bores."

"I might be a bore myself."

"If you are I'll tell you. Which reminds me, there's a certain Dr. Kathleen McNeil coming to dinner tomorrow —a beauty like her mother, whom I once wanted to marry. You know her, I believe."

"We've met. Small world, isn't it?"

"Smaller than you know in the Lews, laddie. I also had an inquiry about you from one Duggie Donald of Her Majesty's Customs and Excise."

"The hell you did!"

"No need to worry. I gave you a character reference that belonged to a far better man, so you're quite safe— so long as you mind the company you keep."

"Meaning Ruarri Matheson?"

"Meaning you're a stranger with things to learn. Nothing more."

"Therefore. . . ?"

"Therefore you tread lightly and talk softly and say always a little less than you know."

"And what should I know about Red Ruarri?"

"Nothing that can't wait till the cheese and coffee. Come along now, else lunch will be cold and Hannah will be giving us the sharp edge of her tongue."

Luncheon was a lordly meal, served with fussing reverence by Hannah herself. There was barley broth and salmon from the loch, a rack of lamb with a good Burgundy to match it, a raspberry tart with cream, and a tray of cheese to take away the last hunger pangs. There was time, too, to enjoy it and to savour the talk of a man happy in himself and in his heritage.

". . . The lodge belonged to my father, who was a doctor like myself—except that he never travelled much, but spent all his life in the Lews. He served the hospital in Stornoway and he died there one morning on his rounds, which is a good way for any man to go. The land is poor, as you see—only good for sheep and the digging of peat—but the fishing is some of the best on the island. All the good land is to the west, where the sands have piled up over the centuries and the grass of the machair is sweet. You can run cattle there and grow hay and clover and vegetables. You take a buffeting in the winter, but in the good times the rain is soft and the air is warm off the Gulf Stream. . . . The people? Hard to know at first, because they hide behind the Gaelic and the clan life is tighter than you might imagine. You never have to lock a car or a house in the Isles, but you mind your manners on Sunday because they're all Sabbatarians and it's bad form to be seen fishing or driving while honest folk are walking to church in their best clothes. . . . Religious they are, and mystical with it, though a funeral will shock you because they're very matter-of-fact about dying; and, before the pill and sometimes after, a girl was apt to be pregnant at the wedding. The level of learning is high because there's respect for it and it's the only way to a job on the mainland, if you've a mind to go. Violence? None. It's a safe place to be young in, a good place to be old in. . . . Nonetheless, there's a sadness here because what we're seeing is the slow dying of a whole Celtic culture. The dying began at Culloden and went on through the Clearances, but now there are other executioners: television and radio and tourism, and the brutal economics of the twentieth century. The small language has to die eventually. The small people have to be absorbed or shrink back and back into a sterile enclave. It's no bad thing in the end, I suppose. Man has to adapt or lapse into extinction like the dinosaurs. But it's still a sadness because here's no one big enough to rally the Celts and give them an identity again, and the time is past, anyway."

Which brought us, by a round turn, back to Red Ruarri

and his fierce, private dreams. I told Morrison of my day's sailing with him, of its angry end, of the gift which he had given me this very morning. Morrison was a good listener, with a canny ear and shrewd, diagnostic eye. He let me talk myself out and then gave me his own version of the story.

"I told you it was a small world in the Lews, laddie. I'll show you just how small it is. Ruarri Matheson was born in this house, in the very room you have now. It was January, gale weather, and there was snow such as the Isles hadn't seen for ten years. Anne Matheson was in service here because my father had taken her when her parents threw her out from Gisla, after they found she was pregnant and no man around to marry her. She's dead now, poor woman, but in her day she was known as a local beauty. So there was malice enough to make things difficult for her, and for the boy later. Besides that, the kirk was a stern assembly in those days—as it is still, though it's softened somewhat—and a child without a father is a hard thing to live down in a small place."

"Who was the father?"

"She never told."

"Brave woman."

"Aye, there was iron in her, as there is in Ruarri. He grew up wild, as he had to be to survive his bastardy. When the old people died, the croft at Gisla came to his mother, and he worked it with her till she died. Then he sold it and he went away. About the next ten years nobody knows anything except what he's chosen to tell them, which isn't much, and he's a colourful liar when he wants to be. Three years ago he came back with money in the bank, lots of it. He bought up land over by Carloway in the west. He raised a loan for a trawler and paid it back within a year. And he's gathered a small crew of hard-drinking, hard-playing lads that they call Red Ruarri's buannas, which was the old name of the bodyguard of the Lord of the Isles. He works them hard and pays them well, and roisters around the island with them in between times."

"And why the interest of Her Majesty's Customs and Excise?"

"I don't know the answer to that, and Duggie Donald's

not a man to be telling. But Ruarri Matheson is no one to miss a quick profit, inside or outside the law."

"He's invited me to his house."

"I'd go. Have him here whenever you want. He's an entertaining fellow—just so you don't let him get you into mischief. If you feel like a wee stroll now, I'll introduce you to Fergus William McCue for the fishing."

So, for the moment, the subject was closed; yet I was left with the impression that Alastair Morrison was telling less than he knew and that, if I wanted to know more, I should have to find it out for myself.

It was ten minutes' brisk walk to the cottage of Fergus William McCue, gillie and factotum to the Morrison lodge. We heard him before we saw him: a high, nasal, old man's voice quavering through the tune which is called "Thoir a' Nall am Botul," the Song of the Bottle. In all the time I was in the Isles, I never heard him sing any other, and I am convinced it was the only song he knew. He was a true black Celt, small as a jockey, game and dancy as a fighting cock, with a set of false teeth that clattered every time he spoke. God only knows how old he was—or is, for only a thunderbolt could have killed him. He was sitting on a wooden bench outside the cottage, with a flat cap jammed on his head and his tweed collar turned up around his ears, making salmon flies.

When Alastair introduced me, he looked me up and down, summed me up and dismissed me with contempt. "Ach! The truaghan! The poor, poor fellow. Anyone can see he'll never do. He hasna the hands. He hasna the eye. So I'll be doing all the work for a poor fraction of the catch."

"But you'll try with him, Fergus?"

"Aye, God watch me, I'll try. But why do you bring 'em to me, Mr. Morrison, why?"

"Because you need the money, Fergus, and so do I."

"We do. Indeed we do." He fixed me with a rheumy, baleful eye and spread his flies on the bench. "Now let's see how much they teach you in Europe. Name the flies for me."

"I wouldn't know one from the other."

"Then how—may all the saints of God stand between

36

us and the storm!—how do you expect to fish? These three here are for the trout: Black and Peacock Spider, Golden Butcher and Heather Moth. This one we call a Hairy Mary, and that a Thunder and Lightning, both size ten for the salmon. These over here are all for the sea trout, Watson's Fancy, Black Pennell and Peter Ross. Have you got all that?"

"No."

"A slow learner, Mr. Morrison. A slow learner. Do you know how to cast?"

"No."

"What can you do then?"

"Nothing. That's why I'm looking to Fergus William McCue to teach me."

"And how much time do you think I've got? I'm an old man. I could be dead before you take your first half-pounder."

"If you die, I'll bury you—with a bottle of Glenlivet to keep the cold out."

"Make it two—one for the head and another for the feet—and I'll take you on."

"You have yourself a pupil. You name the times."

"Morning and evening, when the sun is off the water. You bring the vehicle. I bring the tackle. Is his credit good, Mr. Morrison?"

"For a week at least, Fergus."

"Does he drink?"

"I fear he does."

"God be thanked for small mercies. In the morning then, laddie. Nine o'clock. And be sure to bring a wee something to keep out the cold. Good day to you both."

Before we were ten paces away, he was busy again with his lures, singing the bottle song to the circling gulls.

"His wife died before he was thirty," Morrison told me. "He brought up two strapping sons single-handed. They're three times his size, but neither would dare raise his voice to the old fellow. He's well over seventy, but he still walks ten and twelve miles a day and his heart and his arteries are better than yours or mine. If you can put up with his rasping, which never stops, he'll teach you everything you need to know about fly-fishing, and a lot more besides. . . ."

I was sure he would; but I wondered how I would wear under the rasp in this sparse and quiet place, where every man's interest was particular to himself, where every small knowledge was refined, annotated and commented to the minutest detail. I was restless by nature. I had lived till this point in time a life of considerable diversity, in constant contact with men of every race, language and discipline. Now I was anchored in monotony, isolated in a culture so simple that it made me feel naked and afraid. I envied any man who could spend his days luring salmon onto a hook and his nights joyfully retelling his catch; I knew I could not always be content with such a divine simplicity.

We climbed back to the track and followed its winding round the high shoulders of the headlands, down into tiny dark bays and up again onto the peat land with its runnels of stained water and its dark, acid pools lined with sedge and swamp flowers. Striding along the high places, kilt flapping, white hair windblown, Alastair Morrison was the very image of the old clansman, a concordant element of the place and its history. Yet the concordance seemed too perfect, so that one wondered about the tenor of his inward life. I would not have read him for a monk, though he had obviously lived like one for a long time. I had known him first in a country where a man could indulge most sexual tastes without censure, yet all his reputation was for rectitude and sobriety. I was curious to know where he had spent all his passion and by what battles he had won his present contentment. I asked him:

"After the life you've lived, are you never lonely here?"

"Sometimes, laddie. Sometimes. But on balance I think it was wise to come back to the Isles."

"What decided you?"

"Nothing dramatic. I understood, I think, that there's a moment when it's too late for any man to go home."

"You never married?"

"No. I was in love once, a long time ago. I made a mess of that. Then, somehow, I had no heart for another loving. I liked the work I was doing. The service was a compensation, though it never filled the whole need. Still, by and large I've had a happy life, especially in the latter years."

"Do you ever miss the East?"

"I do. More than I expected. I dream of it often: of the wats with the sunlight on their towers and the demons with their breastplates of glass and porcelain, shining after the rain showers; of the fruit boats on the klongs and the spirit lamps floating down the river on the Feast of Lights; of the lotus in the jungle pools and the poppies red on the highland slopes. I wake sometimes thinking I hear the temple drums and the chanting of the monks and the small, beautiful women chattering like birds in the market."

"It's a far cry from the Lews."

"Not so far as you might think, laddie." His face lit up with that faunlike grin that made him look twenty years younger. "There's few people care to be reminded of it, but this island was bought in 1844 from the Mac-Kenzies for a hundred and ninety thousand sterling pounds—opium money, all of it, made by Sir James Matheson on the China Coast. It was the same Matheson who built Stornoway Castle—on the yellow mud of Asia. So what does that tell you?"

"That time makes saints out of villains. And never to believe the blather of the Tourist Board—or of those who rent lodgings either!"

"You make your point, laddie. And I'm the first to concede it. Sure, there's the other side of life in the Isles. We're a closed and slightly incestuous group. There are feuds that have gone on for twenty years. There's superstition and drunkenness and domestic tyranny and some very curious lecheries."

"And you've got a new Matheson on the way up."

"Ruarri?"

"The same. Where do you think he'll end?"

"Wealthy or in jail. And the odds are about even either way. You like him, don't you?"

"I do. Though I could see myself coming to holds with him if we were together too long."

"Then maybe you could do him a service. You're a travelled man. You've done things he respects. He's made a gesture that says he wants your friendship."

"What kind of service do you have in mind?"

"Persuade him back inside the law. He's been outside it too long, and the taste of outlawry is sweet and dangerous to him."

"That's a lot to ask of an outsider."

"I'd ask it of old Nick himself if I thought it would do any good."

"I couldn't take it on, Alastair. I'd risk too much, and I know too little even to judge the right words."

"Then I'll tell you the rest of it, laddie. And I'll claim your secrecy as a promise between friends."

"I'd rather you didn't tell me. I came here to be free. I can't wear new burdens."

"Then I'll beg you, laddie. I'll beg you in the name of whatever God you believe in, whatever charity you need for yourself. Ruarri Matheson is my son—and there's no one in the world knows that except you and me."

At that moment, I truly believe, I hated Alastair Morrison. He had seduced me two thousand miles on a promise of rest and healing for myself. Now he was dragging me into a domestic tragedy of which I wanted no part at all. I had trusted so much in him, in his Olympian calm and his pawky good humour, that this sudden humbling of himself seemed a craven betrayal. My anger was the greater because I was ashamed of myself and of the weakness that had forced me to depend on him. I was ashamed of my perilous facility in social intercourse, which passes for politeness, but is sometimes an indulgence of personal or professional curiosity. I am a willing listener, which makes me too often a wailing wall for the desperate or the eccentric. Now, of all times, I wanted no tears from man or woman. I was sick of the woes of the world and of my own. I wanted to learn to laugh again and be in love, and shout to hell with yesterday and tomorrow. And yet I could find no words to say it all. I could ask only a single resentful question:

"For Christ's sake, man! Why now, why me?"

He would not, or could not, face me. He stood, face averted, a ravaged giant on a high clifftop, staring out over the loch. "I don't know why now, laddie. Why does a dam burst suddenly when it's held for a century? Why does a tree topple or a bird drop out of the sky? Why you? That's easier. Because you took Ruarri's gift, and that said you were prepared for a friendship. Because you answered to something you found in him, as I could never answer because of all the silent years that had passed. It seemed a chance; I took it. If it was a mistake, I'm sorry."

"It was a mistake. And I'd be lying if I said it wasn't. I'll make you no promises except to hold the secret. I'll not make myself a missionary, but if a chance comes to speak a right word, I'll try to say it. I can't do even that if you spring surprises on me. Remember, I'm a stranger. I'm new to this sidelong Celtic way of things."

"If you want no surprises, then you'd better hear the rest of it. After that we'll close the question for good."

"Tell me then."

As we struck homewards across the peat lands, with only the painted sheep and the hooded crows for company, he told me. It was a poignant, strangely dated little tale of the first years of the thirties, when the shadow of the great depression hung over the land, when the gap between the classes was a chasm that only the bravest or the most foolish could leap over. The clachan folk, the people of village and croft, made one world. The folk of lodge and manse and castle made another. Alastair Morrison was a medical student, home on holiday from Edinburgh, looking later to London and a traditional career. He ranged the island, as any young blade might, for the fishing and the deer-stalking and the drinking and dancing afterwards. Outside his own world, Anne Matheson was his playmate. He was back in Edinburgh a month when she wrote to tell him she was pregnant. Marriage was out of the question. Abortion was a crime not to be dreamed of in the Lews. So the matter was arranged in the fashion of the time. Money passed, settlements were provided and secrecy enjoined. Alastair Morrison was left free to pursue his career and wrestle with his guilts as best he might. Silence, once imposed, became a way of life, and the cost of breaking silence might prove too heavy for all concerned.

". . . But you can't drive a stake through the heart of a truth, laddie. It lies there, buried but waiting for a day of particular judgment, and mine I think has come on me now. Ruarri is lost to me. I would like to think he might be saved to himself. I've burdened you, I know, but I feel a little better for the telling. I hope you'll forgive me."

I was humbled then, because there was more service done in his life than in mine, and more amends made for fewer delinquencies. By the time we reached the lodge we were friends again, though I knew in my heart I would never again be so free as on the day I drove through Glen Shiel and saw for the first time the wonder of mountains without men.

Even the lodge was changed for me. From the moment I reentered the garden, the walls seemed to fold around me like the arms of an unwanted lover demanding surrender and possession. Old Hannah herself seemed to look on me with different eyes. She clucked over me like a mother hen. The cushions must be plumped before I sat on them. The fire must be brightened lest I take a chill. The scones were fresh baked, and the cream new whipped, only for me, and she prayed the tea was drawn to my special taste. She could not leave us without a pat to my shoulder and a word to Morrison in the Gaelic. When I asked him what it meant, he hesitated, then gave me a wry, shrugging answer:

"An old woman's fancy. It's a local proverb. 'Na'm b'e an diugh an dé . . . Would that today were yesterday, and there were sons in the house!' "

Next day I went fishing. Let no one think this is a statement to be taken lightly. On the contrary, it is as pregnant and awesome as anything in Genesis: *"Fiat lux,"* or "On the seventh day God rested." Indeed, there is a whole sect of men in the Isles who claim themselves Christians only because there is a fish-image in the old traditions, but who would as readily bow the knee to Dagon, the fish-god of the Babylonians, or to Orpheus because he was a fisherman as well as a music-maker.

They are all fanatics, though in a quiet, monomanic fashion that makes them agreeable enough to live with. Some of them have attained a high degree of mysticism so that they can endure for days and weeks without women and with very little food or drink. They worship always in solitary places: by dark pools and mountain streams and hidden arms of the sea. They are jealous of these private shrines and apt to be hostile to intruders. They measure salvation by the pound, and the merit of a man by his skill with a fighting fish. You will recognize them by their ruddy, patient faces and their faraway eyes and the coloured flies stuck on their hats. They have a discipline of silence and of secrecy and they train their neophytes with constant admonition and frequent humiliation. They would submit to martyrdom rather than use a gill net, and some of them mourn the old days when a poacher could be legally killed with a spring gun or exiled to the Colonies for taking a trout from another man's water.

Fergus William McCue was a member of this sect and an initiate of its highest degree. He was a genius with the rod and a tyrant with his novices, of whom I was, as he told me many times, the most doltish and the least deserving. If I took one wee bitty brownie in a season, it would be a miracle for which I should fall on my knees and thank the good God.

He made me drive him five miles into the country, then tramped me another mile over the peat land to a private lochan where there would be no one to witness the follies I was about to commit. He took a long guzzle of whisky to wet his pipes against the ordeal and then read me a half-hour lecture on the rod and reel and their respective parts. He talked of lines, dressed and undressed, level and forward-tapered and double-tapered. He orated on wet flies and dry flies, on casting and shooting, and "fishing to the rise" and "searching the water." Then, when he judged me sufficiently confused, he put a rod into my hands and ordered me to make my first cast.

Immediate disaster! The line floated free as a gossamer and tangled itself in the sedge. Fergus William McCue shook his head mournfully, took another dose of whisky to steady himself and then abused me mightily. I had a wrist, hadn't I? I wasna one of them damty robots, all jerk and jiggle with the clockwork inside? Would I try again now and try to have a little respect for the fish, which was an intelligent creature and respected an intelligent angler? I tried again and again and again, with Fergus groaning and keening at my back, until I could manage a halfway respectable cast; but never a fish rose and the level of the whisky went down and down. Finally the master himself took the rod and within fifteen minutes had grassed a pair of brown beauties, neither far short of a pound. Thus humbled, I was ready for another lecture.

"It's a patient art, laddie, as you've now seen. It's like the painting of a picture or the carving of an angel out of a chunk of marble. It's the art of the hands, but it's also of the mind because you must know what a fish will be doing with himself while you're bending your wits to catch him. And even when you've hooked him, you have to know how far he'll run and when you can begin reeling him in. Four pounds' breaking strain is all you have in the line, and that's not much against a big fellow with a hook in his mouth and him racing away down the loch. No time then for philosophizing or writing poems in your head, or daydreaming about the girls you've never kissed. Would you like to try again now, before the sun is all over the water?"

I would and I did, and the first small miracle happened. I made a strike and I was so excited I forgot to throw the clutch on the reel, so that the line snapped on his first run and I lost fish, fly and leader all at once. Fergus William McCue abandoned himself to a Biblical despair. If Island tweed could be torn, he would have rent his garments. Had we had a fire, he would have poured ashes on his head and on mine. Nothing would calm him but a large tot of liquor and a grudging dram for me, to steady the hand and clear the mist from an addled Sassenach brain. Whether it was the whisky or a recklessness born of despair I cannot say, but the next time I was lucky. I hooked and played and finally landed a modest half-pounder. He looked small and insignificant beside Fergus' catch, but I was as proud of him as if he were the original white whale. Even Fergus' grudging compliment was a music in my ears:

"Nae so bad—for a beginner, that is. Had he been bigger, though, you'd never have held him. You have a hand like a plowman. No delicacy in it at all. But, given time from you and patience from me, there's a wee small hope."

"You're a hard man, Fergus."

"Aye. Indeed I am. How else would I put up with all the idiots that come to me in a season? You're bad enough, but God save me from the worst of them. Last year—would you believe it?—I had a woman handed to

44

me by Morrison himself. She was a great horsy creature with cruppers on her like a Clydesdale and a laugh to frighten even the hoody crows. She yearned to catch a salmon, she said; but it was a man she was after, and Alastair Morrison if she could have him. After a week I handed her back to Morrison and told him he could marry or murder her, but she'd never in her life make an angler. He, poor fellow, lost a guest, but he'd have lost a gillie if she'd stayed. So you'll understand the trials I have."

He was becoming garrulous with the whisky, but I was happy to let him run on. I was so stuffed with argument, so sick of controversy and clattering opinion, that his simplicity and his innocent malice were a refreshment. I was relearning, too, one of the primal arts of survival and I felt dignified by the experience. It was good to be a pupil again, good to be ignorant, good to be eager for the smallest accomplishment. It was like drinking spring water after a surfeit of wine, like tasting an apple fresh from the tree. I felt a sudden, poignant regret for all the innocence I had lost in a lifetime. Yet I had not lost the itch of curiosity or the habit of devious inquiry; so, as I searched the water for another fish, I searched old Fergus, too, for hints and keys to the secret life of the island.

"The Morrisons now, Fergus. They're an old name in these parts?"

"Aye, laddie. Old and respected—though not always respectable as they are now. For a long time the Morrisons were brieves of Lewis. And if you don't know what a brieve is, then I'll tell you. He was a judge of life and death in his own territory. Son succeeded to father and each one swore that his justice would be as even as the bones of the herring on either side of the spine. Not that they always kept the oath. For there was Hucheon Morrison, who sired a child on the wife of the MacLeod of Lewis, and the brothers Allan and Neil, whose heads were taken in a sack to Edinburgh. There was John the Tacksman, who was a bard, and Roderick, who was a harper, and one bastard son who was called the fire-raiser because of his habit of burning other folks' hayricks. There was a whole line of ministers in the clan, and some very good doctors, too, like Hugh, who was the father of this one. But the way it looks now, the doctoring's going to die out—unless Alastair makes a very late start, which I doubt he will."

"I'd have thought he'd have lots of women running after him."

"Aye. He's had 'em. And he's got a good eye for a filly himself. At least he used to have before he got religion and went away to serve the heathen. But he hasna been caught yet. And the way you're holding that rod, you're not about to catch anything either! Try another cast, right on the edge of the shadow. . . . Yourself, now, are you married?"

"Not now. I used to be."

"Are you looking again?"

"Not this trip, Fergus."

"But you wouldn't be averse if a good-looking lass happened along?"

"Do you have anyone in mind?"

"Not for you, laddie. I've got two sons of my own to settle and they're frisking a mite too freely around the local pastures. But old Hannah's the one if you want a list of the possibles. She knows 'em all, whether they're good breeders, how they can cook and keep house, and how much money's likely to be settled on 'em. Have a wee chat with her before you start walking out."

"They tell me she has the second sight. Does she use that for matchmaking as well?"

"She has. Indeed she has. She knew my own wife's death a year before it happened. She told the homecoming of Alastair Morrison before he knew it himself. As for the matchmaking, she'd read you a warning if she liked you, and if she didn't, she'd . . ."

I did not hear the rest of it because at the moment I got a strike and I hooked him. Fergus was on his feet immediately, dancing about me, yelling directions in Scots and Gaelic. If I missed this one, he would never forgive me. I would never forgive myself. To hell with second sight and all the Celtic humbug. I had a fish and I could feel the fight in him and damn me if I was going to lose him. Twice I nearly did because I reeled in too eagerly and misjudged his run, but both times the tackle held, and at last I had him netted and grassed, a pound and a half of saving grace that any man might be proud of. I shouted and laughed and did a crazy jig on the verge of

46

the lochan. Fergus, wise teacher, decided we had earned a drink. We had one and then another. We drank a toast to our noble catch. We had one more for the road, and then we set off across the peat land, singing in discordant duet "Thoir a' Nall am Botul."

When I got back to the lodge I was as elated as a schoolboy. Alastair Morrison was locked in his study, so I went straight to the kitchen to display my catch to Hannah, who, floured to the elbows, was rolling a vast pastry for the evening meal. She enthused over it as though I had taken the King of the Fishes himself. Then she admonished me with that winter smile of hers:

"If it's half a bottle every time you go out with that rascal McCue, you'll be in a sorry state when you come to leave. You need a dash of cold water now and a walk in the garden, else you'll be falling asleep over lunch."

"Hannah, you mustn't scold me. I'm a happy man today. I'm a fisherman, which I didn't know I was."

"You're two steps short of sober and you ought to be ashamed of yourself."

"Look into my eyes, Hannah, and tell me if you don't see a happy man."

"I've looked already. Get along with you."

"But you haven't told me what you've seen."

It was idle banter, and I was silly enough to persist with it. Suddenly she was no longer smiling. Her dark eyes clouded as if a membrane had been drawn over the iris. Her body stiffened and she stretched out a hand to touch the breast of my jacket. When she spoke her voice had a dull, monotone quality, as if she were reciting a rhyme learned painfully by rote.

"There is light at the coming and darkness for the going. There is life wanted and life refused. There is sleeping and dying and a waking afterwards."

Then, abruptly as it had begun, the catalepsy was ended. Her hand dropped to her side, she shook her head like a sleeper waking suddenly to full consciousness. She gave me a puzzled look and then a curt dismissal:

"Out of my kitchen now. It's half an hour to lunch, and I've no time to gossip."

The strange thing was that I was not perturbed. I accepted the brief phenomenon as though it were the most normal thing in the world. Why? I truly do not know. I had drink taken, as the Celts say, but I was by no means drunk. I knew about the second sight from my own forebears. I knew the old counsel that those who had it should never marry, lest they pass on the gift and the sadness of it too. But to witness the telling and to be unmoved, to be neither believer nor unbeliever, or even curious—that I cannot understand even now.

Only one thing I can say with certainty: from that precise moment, reality slid out of focus for me, and I began to live precariously but passionately in a dimension of dreaming. I might have done so anyway, but the moment was critical, catalytic. I was a man in flight: from the past, from a threatening future, from a self which I had found, suddenly and disastrously, incomplete and out of balance. I was seeking an impossible newness. If I could not find it, I would turn mythmaker and create it for myself. I would open myself to every impression, every experience. I would borrow every symbol that came my way and fit it into a cosmogony of private illusions. I did not understand how sick I was, how vulnerable in my imagined convalescence, how dangerous still to all those who had contact with me. I feel a guilt for this now, the greater because, at my coming to this small, strange place, I surrendered myself immediately to the delusion of innocence. I had changed my skies; I believed I had changed myself. At the end of Alastair Morrison's dinner party, the delusion was complete.

III

By MIDAFTERNOON THE WEATHER HAD CHANGED AND IT
had begun to rain, a soft, steady drizzle blown in from
the western ocean. The clouds rolled low over the hills,
making a cheerless murk, through which the painted
sheep moved lost and plaintive while the gulls settled to
roost along the furrows of the stripped peat beds. The
smoke drifted heavily around the chimney stacks, and the
only sounds were the slow wash of the sea, the drip of the
rain from the eaves and an occasional bleating from the
scattered flocks.

Morrison was anxious about Kathleen McNeil, who
was living in the doctor's house at the southern end of
Harris. She would have to drive forty miles of mountain
roads and then return late at night. So it was arranged
that I would drive down to get her. She would sleep the
night at the lodge and I would take her back in the
morning. The exchange would pass all her calls to the
district nurse, who would telephone the lodge in case of
emergency. I must leave at four to be back by seven because the roads were crooked and full of surprises:
humps and hollows and shaly verges and narrow cause-
ways and ambling sheep and mist in the defiles of the
mountainy country.

I recall the journey as vividly as if it were yesterday:
the monotone of the fine rain, the dark hills and the
darker water, the sweep of the wipers over the misted
windscreen, the sluice of the wheels through puddles and
potholes, the rags and tatters of cloud hanging from the
hilltops, the rare, yellow lights in the cottages. I remember that I sang to drive away melancholy and tried to
make rhymes from the place-names: Aglmachan, Ard-

hasig and Borvemore and Obbe. I remember the sense of relief and minor triumph when I saw the old Church of Saint Clement at Rodel and came, a few minutes later, to the dwelling of Kathleen McNeil.

I was early, she told me. She had been held late with a difficult case. She was still in her working clothes. Would I take a drink while she bathed and changed? It was not the warmest of welcomes and, foolishly, I was piqued by it. Then I saw that she had been weeping. When she poured the drinks her hand trembled, so that the decanter rattled against the glass and some of the liquor spilled on the silver tray. I asked her what was the matter.

She stiffened and tried to shut me out with a curt, professional summary. "I lost a child today. Breech birth, the cord tangled around the neck. I couldn't revive it."

"I'm sorry."

"It happens. But this was the first birth in the family and I'm the outsider."

"You can't blame yourself."

"No. They will. And the blame will be hard to live down."

"They'll make another child and forget this one."

"Perhaps. But there's so much promise in a baby here. So much hope against the sea and the loneliness of the hills."

I took the glass from her and set it on the table. I laid hands on her shoulders and held her while she steadied herself. "The hills will be here and children will be here when you're long gone. If you want to cry, be done with it now. Then go upstairs and change and make yourself up like a girl going out to dinner."

"I don't want sympathy."

"Then you won't get it. But it's a long drive to the lodge and I'd like some cheerful company. Agreed?"

"Agreed."

She gave me an uncertain smile, then left me. I sat by the peat fire and sipped my drink and thought about the sadness of life in the Happy Isles. Here everything was immediate, naked and potent. Here were no crowds to cushion the impact of events, no raree-show to distract the suffering or the fearful spirit. Birth, sickness and death came all in the same bed. Food was brought from garden plot to table. Man and beast were buffeted by the same storm, rejoined by the same thin sunshine. Mourner and merrymaker tramped the same rough road to the common meeting place between the mountains and the sea.

Withal there was a joy to be recognized. Here the primitive mystery of brotherhood and dependence was reenacted every day. No one lay hungry without some hand to feed him. No one was too old to be remembered. No child lacked a family to cherish him. No man died without one tear shed for his passing. The winter peat was cut by common labour, stacked by friendly hands for the aged and the infirm. The lifeboat was at the call of every sailorman, and there was no cottage so poor that a stranger would not be offered a strupach: food and drink and a gentle word for the road.

In the world from which I had fled, violence was preached as a surgery for the sickness of society. Children killed themselves with heroin. Juvenile lovers infected each other with gonorrhea. Diplomats peddled arms deals. Revolutionaries made hostages of the innocent. Citizens sent armed police against students. Students burned libraries like the tyrants of the Inquisition. Black man fought white man. Massacres were plotted on computers, and ant-heap cities devoured the sweet countryside. For all the loneliness of this place, for all the threat of the land and the elements, I was glad to be here. I felt that I might be glad to stay. When Kathleen McNeil walked down the stairs I was certain of it.

Even now, a century older, with all my follies for remembrance, I have no shame in the confession. I was in love with her from that moment. I wanted her in every way that a man can want a woman, passionately, urgently, with body and spirit. Laugh at it if you want. It was so wild a thing I would not blame you. Call it whatever name you will—the *coup de foudre,* midsummer madness—it happened. It was. I can no more reason it now than I could then. Unfashionable? Out of character? Juvenile? Clownish? All of that. But I see her now, dark hair upswept, cheeks glowing, lace at her throat and wrists. I see myself watching her, knowing with absolute conviction that this was my woman, this was the one for whom I would overturn mountains and hold for my own against all contenders.

Yet first I had to win her and I knew, even then, the game would not be easy. This was no foolish virgin, no light matron either. She knew the game, too, and she played it deftly and with charm. She would be outraged by a clumsy or incompetent suitor. Come the moment of avowal she would be ready—to accept or reject it out of hand. To time the moment, however, was my affair, and I, who had known more than one woman in a lifetime, was suddenly doubtful of my skill. I had a vision of myself, the comic fisherman, tangling his line in the rushes while all the trout in the loch thumbed their snouts at him.

"Something funny?" asked Kathleen McNeil.

"Yes. I haul you out of a wreck in Glengarry. We're as distant as moon from earth all through the Isle of Skye. And here we are going out to dinner together."

"You don't like the idea?"

"On the contrary. I'm trying to guess what you'll say when I ask you to come out with me again."

"Why not ask and find out?"

"Madam, would you one sunny, smiling day, when all your patients are recovering, please come driving with me through these Isles of the Blest?"

"Thank you, sir. I would be delighted."

"You have made me a happy man. Now let's get the hell out of here or we'll be late for dinner."

It was still raining and the twilight was mournful as we drove round the narrow track between the mountains and sea cliffs of the eastern coast. One skid, one incautious turn on an elbow would send us tumbling down two hundred feet into black water. It was a lonely road, haunted by the memories of clan feuds and old piracies and the bitter days of the Clearances. Both of us felt the haunting and the danger of the high crags, and Kathleen NcNeil drew close to me so that I breathed her perfume and felt the warmth of her body thrown against me at every tight turn. There was one bad moment when a wandering ewe bounded across the track in front of us. I hit the brakes too hard so that we lurched dangerously toward the drop. For an instant I thought we were gone, but a jutting boulder bounced us back onto the track and we were safe again. My heart was pounding and my palms were wet.

Kathleen McNeil sat rigid, staring out through the

streaming windscreen. When she spoke, it was as if she were talking to herself. "It always looks like that."

"What?"

"The moment of light when you're a second away from blackness."

"For God's sake! That's a happy thought!"

"In a strange way it is. There's no fear, no regret. Just a kind of wonder."

"If it makes no difference to you, Kathleen McNeil, I was scared witless. And there's ten more miles of this bloody goat track!"

She laughed then and laid a cool hand against my cheek. "So why don't you pull into the next lay-by and wait till your pulse rate settles down?"

"On the other hand, it might go a lot higher. And then we might never go driving again."

"Is that a warning?"

"Call it a confession if you like."

"Please," said Kathleen McNeil softly, "please, not yet—not for a long time yet."

"Just so you know."

"I know, but I can't play children's games any more."

"Nor I. So let's be friends, Kathleen oge, and see where that leads us, eh?"

When we came to the lodge, the other guests were already arrived. There were the Macphails, husband and wife, he a new minister of the Free Kirk, she a doe-eyed bride, eager to please and full of small embarrassments. There was Andrew Ferguson, from the coast-guard service, a sturdy barrel of a man with a grey spade beard and beetling eyebrows and Navy written all over him. With him had come Barbara Stewart, schoolmistress from Dumfries, a pert redhead, salty of tongue, with a slightly scandalous humour.

Alastair Morrison presented us with a flourish as "a bard and a bonesetter, unwed, unpromised, each a free spirit, the one a Scot, the other a Sassenach, but agreeable enough for a' that." Then he shoved whisky into our hands and stirred us about like a cook making a raisin pudding. For the first few minutes I found myself anchored with Minister Macphail. He was tall, ruddy and confident, yet so young that I had to ask what had drawn him to the Wee Frees, that last offshoot of dissent in Scotland.

They were a tiny group in Christendom. Their theology was primitive, their ritual austere, their morals rigid. They had no hymns but the psalms. No organ music was allowed in their assemblies. No food might be cooked on Sundays, or alcohol consumed. Blinds were drawn against visitors, and there were those who frowned on copulation—of man or farmyard beast—as a breach of the Sabbath rest. Yet their hold in the Isles was strong and unyielding. Macphail explained it to me with evangelical fervour:

". . . We're believers, my friend, not doubters. We're concerned to live the Gospel, not debate it. We stand, simple before God, free brothers in a free assembly. We keep the Sabbath holy because that's the Scriptural command. Our lot is harsh, our lives plain. We need a plain faith to sustain us."

"Boom! Boom! Boom!" Barbara Stewart cut in with a mockery. "That's only half the story, Jamie Macphail, and you know it. You're a bunch of old-line fundamentalists. Tyrants, too, when you get a chance to be."

"That's not fair, Barbara. Strict we may be, but not tyrants."

"No? If I want to drive my car on a Sunday, you scowl me off the road. If I want a drink—which I do— I'm the scarlet woman. Scriptural commands? You pick and choose the ones that suit you. Suppose I wanted to be like King David and dance naked before the Ark. Would you let me?"

"If you'd lose some weight, they might." This with a laugh from Andrew Ferguson. "Even so, the climate's hardly right for it."

"You're a fine one to talk about weight, Andy! Look at you. You're pickled in Navy rum and malt whisky and you sitting on your backside in a watchtower eight hours a day."

"I'm the guardian spirit of sailors, Babs! I brood night and day over the troubled seas, waiting to snatch men from disaster. I've got a newspaper cutting to prove it. Written by a woman too."

"And what did you pay her for that piece of prose?"

"Attention. Which is more than I get from you, my girl."

Minister Macphail turned to me with a grin. "You see why they need the kirk in these parts, tyranny and all. Without it they'd devour each other in a week. One of my professors used to say that Gaeldom was God's private madhouse, so he had to give a special love to the inmates."

"Love among the Gael!" The Stewart was not to be put down. "Now there's a theme for our bard! Scene One. The boy's drinking himself impotent in the pub on a Saturday night, while his girl stays home to finish the Sunday baking. Scene Two. At eleven he's knocking on her door, drunk as Chloe, with a bottle of whisky in his pocket. They drive off into the night to dance in a barn. Scene Three. Six in the morning. They're each in their own beds snoring off a hangover to be ready for church at eleven. Scene Four. The girl gets pregnant in the back of a car. They marry and live happily ever after in a little stone house in the middle of nowhere. Amen!"

She was a natural mime and she made such a comedy of it that even the doe-eyed bride dissolved into laughter. Alastair Morrison embraced her and swore he prized her above all other women in the world.

"More than that, she's the sweetest singer of Gaelic songs this side of Inverness. And that's a precious kind of madness in itself. Be gentle with her if you want her to make music after dinner. Will you come along now all of you, else I'll get a flea in my ear from Hannah!"

I have to tell you now that it was on this night I first learned the meaning of the word ceilidh. Look it up in a Gaelic dictionary—which is a hard book to come by in this complicated world—and you will find it means a visiting or a sojourning. It is the sojourning which carries the true colour. You come, a traveller out of a bleak land where there is no harbouring for man or beast. You are received with honour because in a place where men are few every human is precious. In the old days in the Isles, Bishop Knox had to promulgate a law against "sorners": shiftless fellows who moved from house to house battening on the hospitality of the poor. You are settled immediately into a security of lamplight and fire warmth and cooking fragrances and respect for the person you are presumed to be. This is the gift of the house to you. But you are expected to offer your own gift as well, however small it be. If you have news, you must tell it. If you have music or story or a special knowledge, then you must dispense it. If you have nothing but opinions, then you must toss them into the argument because one who sojourns in silence is a blight upon the tree of mankind. If you are lovers and have need of privacy, a ceilidh is no place to find it because your wooing and your bedding will be subject to comment and advice and even the prescription of herbs and spells if you need them. If the sadness is on you, it must be left at the door. If you are drunk, you must be happy and not quarrelsome. If another is drunk, he must be walked to safety lest he freeze on a lonely road. Scandal may be talked, but it may catch you up in another house. If there is a piper or a fiddler, you may dance, indeed you should because dancing is another kind of gift that gladdens the eye and sweetens the blood.

The ceilidh of Alastair Morrison was exactly thus. His guests made at first sight an odd assembly; yet by the end of the soup we were wrangling happily over a hodgepodge of subjects: morals and medicine, the Russian presence in the Atlantic, the missile base on Barra, Gaelic orthography, the follies of the Tourist Board, the troubles in Ulster and the latest tale of the island dispersion—a fellow from Harris who was trying to recruit mercenaries for the war in Cambodia.

Alastair Morrison stage-managed the affair with opulent good humour. He was the leading man and he played the role with elegance and relish. He was generous with the wine and with himself. He paid extravagant court to the women and to the men an ironic respect. Jack might be as good as his master in London or New York; but here in the Isles blood still counted, and Morrison the Brieve with power of life and death was only a page or two back in history. His performance brought out the best in the company. I had not heard in a long time so much vivid tale-telling, so much breezy, commonsensical debate. In Ireland they could be eloquent about nothing at all. In England they could be inarticulate about the end of the world. At the table of the Morrison each guest must say his mind to prove he had one.

For all the dazzle and the bravura, I could not keep my eyes off Kathleen McNeil. I was head over heels and gone for her, yet I realized, with a pang of jealousy, that I knew next to nothing about her. She was a Scot; she was a doctor; she was a madcap driver; she could weep for a dead child; she had fey moments when the fringe of life touched the hem of death. That was all. Had she been married? I guessed not, but only guessed. Had she a lover, now or then? She had not told me. To what did her heart respond, her body quicken? I did not know. So I watched her, hung on her every word and gesture, plied her with questions, displayed myself like a peacock to attract her interest. All her responses charmed me. She was an intelligent talker and a good listener. She laughed readily and her judgments were tolerant and compassionate. There were hints of a secret woman, too: a surprise politely veiled, a sadness quickly suppressed, an impatience covered with a laugh. I plotted, in fantasy, the private moment when she would drop all defense and say, "I am tired now. With you I won't pretend any more. This is who and what I am. Understand me and be tender."

We came near to the moment after dinner when Alastair Morrison unwrapped a beautiful violin, lustrous with age, and played accompaniment to the songs of Barbara Stewart. For all her sharp tongue she had a voice, high and pure and effortless, like the flight of a bird. The songs she sang I had not heard since childhood: "Kishmul's Gallery," the "Lovelilt of Eriskay" and that of Mingulay, which is sweeter still, the "Lament of Flora Macdonald" and the chants of the milk-maids in the summer shielings. They lifted us out of ourselves into the dreamtime of yesterday, so that we were like children listening to the same fairy tale, touched by old griefs, glad with the small joys of a life long past. For this while we were not ashamed of our emotions, but acknowledged them to each other with nods and smiles and hands beating out a familiar rhythm. The music was a golden thread binding us all, a small tribe in a lonely place, with the rain outside and the sea cutting us off from the commerce of a rowdy world. Then we sang together, each one calling a tune, until we were flushed and breathless and it was time for one glass against the homeward road.

When the last good-byes had been said, the three of us sat by the fire and relaxed in the afterglow of the ceilidh.

Kathleen McNeil put my own thought into words. "We've forgotten how to enjoy ourselves like that. It's all so simple. But we've forgotten. I wonder why."

"Perhaps," said Alastair Morrison, "perhaps because there's just so damned much to remember, like taxes and earnings and ownings and wars and revolutions and every salesman on the planet squawking at us every hour of the day. The world is shackled to us like a ball and chain. We never get rid of it long enough to lift up our heads or our hearts."

"But we can't go on like that. Half the patients who come to my office are sick because they're sick of the world and all its demands on their frailty."

"And what do you prescribe for them, Kathleen oge?" I used the endearment unconsciously, and Morrison gave me a swift, quizzical look.

Kathleen McNeil gave no sign that she had noticed it. She answered with a shrug and only the half of a smile. "Some loving, to take the weight off. Of course, you can't buy that in a pharmacy, and there's not enough to go round, anyway; so we use sedatives and tranquillizers instead."

"Yet there was loving here tonight. People gave something of themselves."

"There's a difference," said Alastair Morrison. "In the Isles we are forced to depend on each other. In the cities we are forced to compete. The quality of life is changed. The quality of people too. But that's all yesterday for me. I'm here and I'm happy and I'm ready for bed. So I'll bid you both good night. Sleep well, both of you."

We were not ready for sleep. So we sat, unwary, in the fading firelight and talked.

Kathleen McNeil seemed puzzled by our host. "Can he really retire like that? Can he close the door on yesterday and forget it?"

"Forget it? No. I think he's come to terms with it."

"But who laid down the terms for him?"

"Quite a question, young Kathleen. Who mediates between the man I'd like to be and the man I know I am?"

"Can you answer it?"

"No. You're the healer, young Kathleen. Can you?"

"I wish I could, mo gradh. . . ." Her use of the Gaelic word was so unexpected and my ear so untuned that I almost missed it. Mo gradh . . . my dear, my darling—my lover, too, if the heart were so disposed. My own heart missed a beat, but I dared not risk too much on a transient endearment. So I let her talk on because every small knowing of her was precious to me. ". . . Time was when I despised all religion as a tyranny over the ignorant. A man like Minister Macphail with his serene certainties I would have rejected out of hand. People need certainties. Even the certainty of dying is a help to many. The sickness of the mind is a sickness of unknowing and uncertainty."

"And the cure?"

"I think someone has to love you enough, to let you love yourself a little. I'm not saying it very well. But look . . ." Suddenly she was eager as a schoolgirl. "Two patients with the same constitution, the same sickness. One lives, one dies. Why? In the one the urge to live, the love of living, is strong; in the other it is weak. It's as if —as if life were a gift to the loving. And if you laugh at that, I'll spit in your eye."

"I'm not laughing. I've been down in the dark valley myself. I managed to climb out of it and get myself here—with a prod or two from Alastair Morrison."

"That makes two of us."

"What happened to you?"

"I fell in love and out of love—and lost my way in between."

"Do you want to talk about it?"

"Not tonight."

"There'll be other times."

"I know. I'm glad there will be."

We kissed then, new friends, still careful of the risks of friendship.

"Good night, Kathleen McNeil. Golden dreams."

"Good night, mo gradh. And a word for your pillow."

"Tell me the word."

She told me. It was an old proverb in the Gaelic and the words were a music to end a gentle day: "Is maith am buachaill an oidche . . . Night is a good shepherd. He brings home every man and beast."

My night, however, proved restless. I slept fitfully, plagued by erotic nightmares, and woke a dozen times in the darkness itching with desire for the woman who slept only a few paces away and yet was as far away as the galaxies. For too long now I had slept alone. It was a symptom of my malaise that I had felt unready and unwilling to enter into any new commitment. I had nothing to spend but seed—no caring, no concern, no self that would stand a sharing, no curiosity even for a casual encounter. Then, in one day, everything was changed. I was a lover, balked of possession, impatient to be possessed. I was stiff with lust, burning up with the need of the small sweet dying. Had I not been in the house of Alastair Morrison, I might have thrown caution out the window and gone to Kathleen McNeil in her own bed. Would she have taken me? There was one wild moment when I believed she would have. Then sanity came back and I switched on the light and read until the sun came up. When I heard the servants moving about the house I crawled out of bed, shaved the stubble from my grey, pinched cheeks, bathed and went downstairs to cadge a cup of coffee in the kitchen.

Old Hannah made me the coffee, then stood, hands on hips, mocking me while I drank it. "So you've got thistles in your bed, have you, and a wee bittie birdie perched on your pillow, whistling love songs all night?"

"Does it show?"

"Does it show? God save us from the wild winds! Last night you were all sheep's eyes and greensickness, and you ask does it show! It's the dark one, isn't it?"

"It's the dark one."

"Ach!"

"What do you mean *Ach?*"

"I mean that I'm paid to keep house for the Morrison. And what his guests do with their nights or their days is none of my business. Unless they do it in the house, that is, and scandalize my girls."

"Don't you like Dr. McNeil?"

"More coffee?"

"Yes, please. But you haven't answered my question."

"I think she's a good woman with the marks of the wrong man on her. I think you'll get her if you try hard enough."

"Hannah, I love you!"

"Aye, we all love the preacher with heaven in his hand and a word about the other place."

"I'll make you a promise, Hannah. You'll dance at my wedding."

"And I'll make you one. I'll not buy the shoes till I read the banns! Get about your business now. Go take a walk and put some colour in your cheeks before breakfast. You look like a drowned man dragged up from the beach."

I went out laughing at her and walked, whistling, into the bright morning. The rain was gone. The sun was on the water and the heather was gold and purple on the hills. All the omens were favourable. The scolding of an old, old woman was a kitchen comedy not to be taken to heart. Besides, there was strategy to be devised. The doctor must visit her patients at the hospital. I would offer to drive her to Stornoway and see a little of the country on the way. We would finish with lunch at the hotel in Tarbert. In the afternoon she would make her house calls, I would fish with Fergus. In the evening . . . Interesting point. If we were not lovers, or beginning to be, there was precious little to do in the evening but drink in a bar, or sit at home with a good book, or go quietly mad with Scottish television. As it turned out, I was a too anxious general. The strategy was overweighted and there was no battle to fight anyway. The district nurse had reported a quiet night and no emergencies. The doctor was happy to have my company on her rounds. She was happy to lunch with me. After that I could only pray that she had no better plans for herself than I had.

By nine-fifteen we were on the road to Stornoway Hospital. By ten-thirty the ward visits were all done and we were heading over the moorland to the western shore, where the rollers fetch clear across the Atlantic and break on white sands, with the dunes behind, covered by the sweet green grass of the machair. On a clear day, when the sea is flat—and if you have the gift of faith, which is rare in our time—they say you can look towards the sunset and see the legendary Hy Brasil, the blessed

61

stormless isle where all the men are good and all the women pure and God retreats for a recreation from the rest of us. I have to report, in all truth, that we did not see it because the sexual chemistry was beginning to work between us, slowly at first, but potently, through hands' touch and the closeness of bodies and the sharing of small wonders: a sculptured rock thrusting out of a sea of glass, an oyster catcher pecking for shellfish in the sand, the trill of a curlew questing through the kelp beds, a lapwing rising suddenly out of a meadow.

Of all the days of our loving, this I believe was the simplest, the most joyful. We were not children. Neither of us was innocent. Each of us had eaten the apples of knowledge and found them bitter. The moment would come—and we both knew it—when each must explore the other: the tastes of the body, the tangles of the secret spirit. The first declaration of need or love might open a Pandora's box of fears and guilts and bitter antipathies. On the other hand, it might unlock the gate of a lost Eden, full of bright fruits and singing birds. So by unspoken consent we deferred the risk and surrendered ourselves to the placid pleasures of the morning.

We walked a deserted beach. We visited the "black houses," ancient dwellings of the islanders built of rough stone, raftered with driftwood and thatched with grass. We scrambled up a hillside to stand in a ruined watchtower built by the painted men against the raids of the Roman colonizers. We took tea in a weaver's cottage and watched the making of the tweed. We leaned on a stone wall and watched a shepherd training a dog to the mustering of sheep. Then, as we drove out of Carloway on the road to Breasclete and Callanish, we came upon an activity rare in this isolated place.

There was a long peat slope, four, five acres of it, running down to a small brown lochan. A man on a bulldozer was stripping out the peat in wide, deep swathes and piling the spoil in mounds at each end of the slope. A tip truck was spilling beach sand into the excavations and three brawny fellows were spreading it with rakes and shovels. Two strips were already filled, and on these was spread a covering of dried sea wrack which smelled of salt and iodine. As the tractor came towards us, I saw that the driver was Red Ruarri the Mactire. He was stripped to the waist, his arm was still in plaster, and he drove the big machine one-handed. When he saw my wave, he accelerated and came lurching dangerously up the furrow, pushing a great load of matted rubbish in front of him. Then he cut the engine, leaped down and gave us a shout of welcome:

"God's good day! It's the seannachie—and the doctor-girl come to collect her bill! Stay where you are, else you'll be muck to the knees! I swore you'd come, sean-nachie. But the doctor's a bonus I didn't expect!"

He was bubbling with pleasure and with pride that we should see his work in the making. He pumped our hands and threw an arm about my shoulder and rattled away ninety to the dozen about what he was doing and how and why.

". . . This is where the money goes and the labour. The peat started to grow here about eight thousand years ago when the climate changed from warm and dry to cold and wet, and the moss ate up the forests of birch and hazel that once covered the land. It grows in a thick carpet, as you see, and the water lies underneath. There's little oxygen, so the microbes that cause decomposition can't work. The water washes out the lime, and the land becomes sour and useless. So we're writing history backwards. We're peeling off the moss and letting in the air. We're putting in sea sand and shingle, which is full of lime. We're laying in kelp for fertilizer, and in a couple of years we'll have sweet, good grassland . . . and subsoil building up every year. You can see the challenge of it, can't you? . . . But I'm talking your ears off. Drive me round the next bend and I'll show you where I live. . . ."

This was another surprise. He had taken one of the old black houses, long and low and ruinous, fit only for dwarfs to live in. He had rebuilt the walls, raising them another four feet. He had bought oak timber for the roof beams and ferried it from the mainland in his own trawler. He had laid withy hurdles over the beams and brought in thatchers from England to lay the roof and anchor it solid against the gale winds. He had built a stone enclosure and carted in loam and sand and made a vegetable garden to live from.

Inside, he had contrived, with more art than I had suspected in him, a modern adaptation of an ancient

Viking house. At one end were his sleeping quarters, at the other a kitchen, large enough to feed a troop of cavalry and modern enough to delight any housewife. In between was a broad chamber, dining hall and meeting place together, with a stone hearth in the center topped by a flue canopy of beaten copper. There were deerskin rugs on the floor; the chairs and the benches were up-holstered in Island tweed. There were bookshelves and a gun rack and a well-stocked bar and a refectory table to seat a dozen or more. The walls were hung with the spoils of a travelling man: Benin heads and a juju mask, a brace of claymores and a buckler, the fragment of a Norse rune stone clouted to the wall with forged nails, a Spanish guitar, a set of rusted spearheads, a length of carved wood which had once been the tiller bar of a longship, a shelf of glassware fragments and turquoise beads and a golden locket with the skeleton of a tiny snake in it.

". . . It's mine and it's me." Ruarri preened himself like a schoolboy who had just won a prize. "It lives comfortable too. The plumbing works and, though you can't see it, there's a heating plant that warms the tiles of the floor the way the Romans used to do it. I've slept a dozen bodies here after a late night's drinking, and no one complained of the cold."

"Where did you get this?" Kathleen McNeil held up the golden snake locket.

"I found it in an old chandler's shop in the Orkneys. I think it's a Viking piece. A fellow in Denmark told me the snake was a charm to protect the owner's virility." He gave her that cocky rogue's grin of his and added, "Since I've been home from the wars, I haven't had the need to wear it."

It was the old blade's trick: test a woman with a touch of bawdry and see how she likes the taste of it. If she does, you're up and away.

Kathleen McNeil did not smile; she looked at him with professional concern. "Does that worry you, Mr. Matheson—losing your virility?"

Ruarri—give the devil his due!—was bright enough to side-step the snub. "Not now. But in Africa it was the thing that scared me most. The local boys were very nasty to their prisoners."

"You were fighting in Africa?"

"I was a mercenary. In the Congo first, then for a while in Nigeria. We were a long way outside the Geneva convention."

"I've never understood what makes a man a mercenary."

"Money, ma'am. There's always a market for gun fodder. High risk. High profit. Ask the seannachie here. He'll tell you. There's a colony of Scots mercenaries been living in Italy for a couple of centuries, and there's a branch of the Leslies in Russia since the time of the Empress Catherine. Can I offer you both a drink now to set you on the road?"

I was glad that Kathleen McNeil accepted for both of us. She had humour enough to make her point and grace enough not to insist on a total victory. She gave Ruarri time to recover too. While he made the drinks she moved about the house, admiring his pieces, looking through the books on his shelves.

Ruarri gave me a conspirator's wink and whispered, "That's a filly with spirit, seannachie. Think you can handle her?"

"I think so."

"She'll give you a run for your money. Come to that, I might too."

"You play in your own backyard, Brother Wolf."

"Just a joke. Forget it." Aloud he said, "So you liked the chessman?"

"I did. I'd like to keep it."

"Good. And there's things we ought to do together while you're here. Some night fishing, maybe. And I've got my eye on a corrie where there's red deer that no one can claim. We might go after a buck one day, you and me and a couple of my boys. In the next week or so I'm taking a run up to Norway for business and trawling on the way home. You're welcome to come along if you like."

"Thanks. I'd like to try it all."

"I'll call you at the lodge and we'll fix it." Then, as Kathleen McNeil came back, he added, "And when we come back from Norway we'll have a ceilidh here. There'll be my boys and their girls and music to dance to. It'll be a late night, but you'll get the true taste of the Isles. You're invited, too, Doctor."

"I'll accept. If I can leave the doctor at home and be plain Kathleen McNeil."

"God love the woman! She's human after all." He grinned at us over his glass. "Slainte—and good luck to you both!"

Damn his smiling eyes! He had all the dash and style of a circus performer. He could do it all: the high-wire walk, the dizzy swing on the flying trapeze, the death-defying human cannonball. But he was not satisfied with skill; he had to play the mountebank as well: deliver the spiel, have the yokels gaping at the white rabbits and the ribbons, and the port wine pouring out of his elbow joint. The hell of it was he would still have you cheering at the end, while he walked off with the money in his pocket. Kathleen McNeil was no country schoolgirl, but before her glass was empty he had her hypnotized. I knew who and what he was, which was more than he knew himself. I had a commission to keep him out of jail if I could. I resented his quackery; still I had to laugh with him and make a reluctant salute to his talent.

I see it now, plainly, as I saw it then, obscurely: that morning in his house was the beginning of the battle between us. Let me confess it—I was jealous of him. Twice now he had put himself on record as a possible rival for Kathleen McNeil, but my own male vanity would not let me accept him in the role. There were deeper reasons. He was born without an identity. He had built himself one. I had mine handed to me on a plate, yet I was in imminent danger of losing it. I had worked as hard as he and travelled as widely and made more money and reputation; but the sheer impact of his physical presence, the magnitude and drive of his ambition made me feel inadequate, outclassed at every point, a painted clown beside the idol of the big ring.

". . . I like him," said Kathleen McNeil. "I'm not sure how far I'd trust him, but I like him. I think you're probably good for each other. He respects you and what you've done. He's anxious for you to respect him."

"I do, very much. He's a maker and a dreamer too. I admire that."

We had said good-bye to Ruarri and were driving down the winding road to Callanish to visit the place of the Standing Stones. The drink and the talk had relaxed

Kathleen McNeil. Ruarri's enthusiasm had communicated itself to her and she was freer and more outgiving than at any time in our acquaintance. I was uplifted, too, because I had to match her mood and prove myself no less a gallant than our rumbustious host. If he had baubles to display, I had them too. If he had tales to tell, I could cap them—and I did, shamelessly. But Ruarri, the Red Wolf, was hard to evade; he was there loping alongside us as we drove, a presence in her thoughts and in her conversation.

". . . There's a child in him as well as a man. A naughty child, but very engaging."

"Engaging, yes. But a child, never. He's a mimic. He'll make himself whatever it suits him to be at that moment."

"I thought you liked him."

"I do. There's no one I'd rather drink with, play with, sail with. But if I had something he wanted, he'd take it and walk away smiling."

"That's a hard judgment."

"I've proved it true, though I can't tell you how."

"Did he really kill for money?"

"He says he did. It's probably true. He made big profits somewhere, and it fits the pattern of his thinking—himself the Viking adventurer in the twentieth century."

"I'd rather not believe it."

"Does it matter whether you do or you don't?"

"Of course not."

She said it a shade too quickly and afterwards was silent a moment too long. It was then that I knew I could not do the simple thing and walk away with my woman on my arm and my pride intact. Muirgen the sea-goddess had woven the last strand in her net. I was snared now. I would not escape until I had done battle with the Red Wolf.

It was after noon when we came to the place of the Standing Stones, a high, grassy hump that falls away southwards towards Loch Roag with its tatter of islets and the black cliffs of Bernera heaving out of it. Even now it is a haunted spot, remote and silent always save for the crying of the gulls and the whisper of the wind through the rank grasses. There are no trees. The hill lies naked to the sky and the great megaliths rise out of it, twice and three times the height of man. There are four avenues of them, north and south and east and west, and, at the convergence of the avenues, a circular burial place and a stone, larger than the others, which faces the sunrise. Of the men who raised the stones little is known except that they were here before the Celts—three thousand years ago—and that this hill and the surrounding countryside was a place of congress where they worshipped the sun as the source of being and plotted their ritual life by its movements. They left no language, no history. Even their burial place was despoiled before history began to be written. But they are still there, frail, tenuous ghosts. We felt them, Kathleen McNeil and I, as we stood hand in hand under the stone of sacrifice and watched a golden eagle fly up and up until we lost him in the glare.

She shivered as if a goose had walked over her own grave. I drew her close to me and kissed her dark hair. Then, because the need was on me and the haunting was on us both, I told her:

"If it's too early or too late, I don't care. I'm not a boy any more and I'm too old to pretend. I love you, Kathleen McNeil. I'd like to marry you."

Do you remember the happy silliness of your own loving? If you do not, then finish here. Toss the rest of it out the window. Go ask the boys or girls to spell the story for you—four letters to a word, all words in monochrome, nothing else to it but what you can see in any barnyard between first light and first darkness. Any fool can draw two lines on a wall and call it love. Any drunk can weep and every half-sober clod can laugh at his tears. Only a poet can show you—and he no more than half—the sweet agony of a man and a woman, hung between heaven and hell, with nothing but the passion of the moment to hold them there. I am no poet, but a seannachie: a teller of tales, shabby and out-of-date as Blind Raftery with his harp or the grey-beard chalking his dreams upon a pavement stone for the rain to wash away at midnight. So I can tell you just the afterwards, when the ghosts had left us and we sat on a stone wall watching the placid sheep, while Kathleen McNeil pieced out her answer:

"Mo gradh . . . my dear, my very dear, I'm glad you

said it. I wanted you to say it. I know you, because what you say and what you do is what you are. But you don't know me. . . . No! Please listen to me! I like you, want you. Ask me to bed and I'll go—no questions before, no blame afterwards. But love? I don't know. I truly don't."

"Love's very simple, Kathleen oge."

"Is it? Was it for you? It wasn't for me. I'm not sure I want to risk it again."

"What happened?"

"What happened? God! It wasn't so long ago that I thought every man in the street could read it on me and every woman was ready to laugh in my face. The day after I graduated—seven, no eight years ago—I married. . . . You didn't know that? You were out of touch. He was the catch of the season. A knight, no less! Films and stage and a bloodline nicely documented in Debrett. We were happy. Even now I can't deny it. Happy as piglets in a clover patch. He needed a lot of mothering—what actor doesn't? I liked mothering him. I suppose that's why I became a doctor in the first place. I liked people depending on me. I didn't know I was depending on them twice as much. Then, four years ago, I became pregnant. Suddenly life was complete. There was nothing more I could ask for. When I told my husband he was horrified. The child, not even quickening yet, was a rival in the house. He could not tolerate the thought. He worked on me day and night, with tears and sulks and tantrums, until I agreed to get rid of it. I'm a doctor. It was easily arranged. When it was all over I hated him. I hated him for two long years until he gave me grounds for divorce. Ever since I've been hating myself. And that, mo gradh, is the woman you've asked to marry you. . . . What do you say now?"

"What do you want me to say, Kathleen oge?"

"I don't know."

"Suppose I tell you that I'm a jealous man, too, but not of a child—because a child is a love fruit for the cherishing of lovers."

"Then I'll feel safer, but still not sure."

"Why not?"

"Because I don't know who I am any more. I'm a lover and a hater. I'm a healer and a killer, both."

"And Red Ruarri's a killer too?"

"That's brutal."

"But true?"

"In one way, yes. In another, no, no, no!"

"Then we have a chance."

"Only if you say we have."

"We both have to say it. We both have to believe it. Look, my dear, dark girl, we all have murders on our hands, little or big, dreamed or done. Before anyone else can forgive us, we have to ask pardon of ourselves."

"Have you been able to do that?"

"Not quite. But you said it yourself. Someone has to love us enough, so we can love ourselves a little. Well, Kathleen?"

"Will you give me time?"

"Will you open your heart and let me in? It's cold outside the door."

"Please come in, seannachie. Please come in and tell me fairy stories again."

If this were a trite tale of faceless nobodies, I would tell you how we mated that night and what we did with these and those parts of each other, what wild pleasurings we had and what newness and what wonders. The truth is that we did none of it. We kissed and embraced like the lovers we nearly were; we parted at the milestone we had reached; she slept in her bed and I in mine and, wise or foolish, we waited for the day when the golden eagle would come plummeting down with the gift of the sun-god in his triumphant talons.

IV

THREE DAYS LATER—AND THEY WERE GOOD DAYS, WHEN
I caught my first sea salmon and earned my first down-
right praise from Fergus William McCue and hired a boat
and took Kathleen McNeil swimming off the beach at
Borvemore—Red Ruarri telephoned me at the lodge. He
had a mind to go night fishing; would I like to join him?
I could bring my girl, too, if she had a taste for that sort
of thing. We should take along a bottle of whisky and a
sandwich maybe, and wrap up warmly because it could
be cold on the loch at midnight. I told him we would be
happy to come and arranged to pick him up at his house
at ten the following night. When I told Alastair Morrison,
he didn't approve at all.

"If Ruarri's night fishing means what I think it does,
you're going on a poacher's picnic. Ruarri owns no fishing
rights that I know of. You can't use a rod and flies at
night. You have to use a net, and that's another offense
from the poaching. They're in touch with one another by
radio and with the police too. If you're caught with a
fish on you, or even the tackle, then it's a big fine and a
damage to your reputation and mine. And it wouldn't be
good for Dr. McNeil to be hauled up in a magistrate's
court, would it now?"

All of which put a new complexion on Master Ruarri's
invitation. If I went, I became a partner in the petty
outlawry of him and his buannas. If I didn't, I was a
mealy-mouthed moralist with no stomach for a foray
against the forces of privilege. There was no shame in
poaching, only in getting caught. Fishing and shooting
rights were an old sore in the Highlands, and whatever
the law said, no man had God-given rights over the fish

in the sea and the wild deer in the mountains. Also—I could see that crooked grin and those mocking blue eyes —a man who was scared of a gamekeeper could hardly hold his woman against the swagger of Ruarri the Mactire. On the other hand, I was a guest in Morrison's house. He had offered me friendship and support when I needed it most. If I was going to play games with the law, he had a right to be forewarned.

So I told him how it was with Kathleen McNeil and myself and with myself and Ruarri. He had trusted me with his own secret, I was entitled to trust him with mine.

He heard me out patiently, pacing the garden walk with me, and when I had finished he laughed. "You're in deep water, aren't you, laddie? When the tide comes full, you'll have to swim for it."

"Do you blame me?"

"No. It's probably the cure you need: one good fight for a woman or a cause—even if you lose. You could, you know. From all I hear, Ruarri's a dirty scrapper."

"I've thought of that too. This is just sparring and skirmishing."

"The last battle could be bloody."

"We may never come to it."

"I'll lay odds you will."

"So I go poaching, eh?"

"I'm an old man, laddie. I don't hear very well, and I suffer from night blindness too. I wouldn't know what you do with your spare time. But I'll give you a tip. Ruarri's tossed you a lure. He doesn't know you've seen the hook under the feathers. I wouldn't be in any hurry to tell him."

And there we left it. I called Kathleen McNeil and invited her to join our innocent expedition. Then I spent an instructive hour with Farran on the land laws of Scotland, where I found that salmon rights were called *regalia minora,* that they could be alienated, but that they were held inviolable by ruffians like myself under pain of fines and possible imprisonment. *Regalia minora* sounded like a good phrase to have handy when the gamekeepers were hounding us over the bogland.

However, in case it shouldn't meet all our needs, I shoved a small flask of whisky into my pocket and walked down to the cottage to share it with Fergus William Mc-Cue.

F. W. McCue on *regalia minora* was like the *Kama Sutra* on sex. He could give it to you upside down, inside out, left to right, back to front, with butter and honey, love and kisses and an anecdote to illustrate every mode of victory or violation. As a legalist he had his faults—some of his law had not been revised since the time of Morrison the Brieve—but as a tactician he had Farran licked to a frazzle. If he hadn't been a gillie, he would have been the noblest poacher in the land. In fact I'm not sure he hadn't been, and wouldn't have been still if he had kept his mind to it. He delayed his summary until the flask was almost empty, but the advice was worth the fee.

"If you had a mind to break the law—which I know you haven't, but I'm just supposing—then this would be the way of it. First, you stay off private land, because even if you're not had for poaching, you can still be caught for trespass. Besides, a man's allowed to keep a dog on his own property, and many do; and some of them are savage beasties that would take a bite out of your backside as soon as look at you. Also, a man's allowed to keep a shotgun; and I have to tell you no trout in the world is worth a charge of birdshot in the sensitive parts of the anatomy. So the trick is to poach in open water, because there's no danger from dogs or guns, and you can always claim you were outside one man's water and inside another's. If the wrong man swears out a summons, you're off free, with maybe a claim for damage to your unsullied reputation. Always providing, of course, that they don't find you with the fish or the tackle in your possession. Another thing about open water—if you're in a boat it's hard for a policeman or a gillie to identify you, and harder still to come at you. The shoreline's so long and the roads are so bad, the best he can do is sit and wait where he thinks you're going to land—and that's a long, cold watching when you're counting your catch a mile away. Of course if you've got a car and he finds it in a suspicious place, then he can ask embarrassing questions, but there's sweet nothing he can do unless he finds the fish. Have I made myself clear now?"

"Couldn't be clearer, Fergus."

"Then perhaps you wouldn't mind answering one question for me. Who are you going out with—and where?"

"That's two questions. And if I answered one or both, you'd never trust me again."

"Then I'll ask you another. Why risk a fine when you've all the Morrison water and me to guide your stumbling feet?"

"Because a fellow made me a challenge, and there's a woman in it, and you wouldn't want your pupil to shy away from a thing like that, would you, Fergus?"

"Never, laddie! And I'll drink a toast to your success. Next time bring a full bottle. These halves are just salesman's samples! . . ."

The night came down, cool and clear and full of stars: a gift to lovers, but no good at all for a poacher because by midnight the moon would be full on the water and any bailiff with half an eye would spot us a mile away. However, I was armed with Fergus' counsel, so I felt reasonably secure; also I was the innocent who was presumed to know only his prayers, so I made no comment. When we came to Ruarri's house we found him alone. I made no comment on that either, but I noted it as a nice piece of stage management which would display all his raider's skill and leave me, dumb and fumbling, in the background. He suggested we drive to the loch in his car. I balked at that. I wanted my own wheels under me and no crazy redbeard haring us round the country roads. He shrugged agreement, poured us a drink and then went out to stow the gear in the trunk. When he came back I asked him, ingenuously, what lures he would use for night trolling.

He laughed. "No lures, seannachie. Just an old-fashioned gill net and an otter trawl. We're fishing for the plate and for the pocket tonight, not for the sport of it. We'll set one net and trawl another, and whatever we get is profit—salmon, sea trout, or pollock."

"I thought gill nets were illegal," said Kathleen McNeil.

"Only if you're found using 'em ma'am."

"And you have your own fishing rights?" God love the dark woman! I had not prompted her and she was right on cue.

74

"Well, Kathleen, I'd have to distinguish. I claim I have a natural right to fish the waters of my own island. The law says I haven't. So the matter's in dispute. Tonight I'm giving myself the benefit of the doubt."

"So it's poaching we're at?" My question this time.

"Objections, seannachie?" He said it with a grin, but there was no smile in his eyes.

"None. Just so we all know the name of the game. Besides, we can't have the lady involved if we're caught."

"We won't be caught. If we were, my boys would never work for me again. Let's be on the road, shall we?"

We drove perhaps five miles down the main road and then cut off on a narrow, rutted track that led down to the loch. About two hundred yards from the shore we stopped. Ruarri unloaded a large duffel bag, hefted it onto his shoulders and led us on foot down to the beach. There was a boat hauled up on the shingle with a pair of oars in it.

Ruarri tossed the duffel bag aboard and, before we pushed off, uttered a cryptic warning. "Don't get your feet wet. You might just have to walk later. And keep your voices down. Sound carries far over the water."

Then we were afloat, and Ruarri was sculling round the rock fringes of the bay. He kept close inshore, I noticed, and his strokes were slow and careful so that there was no splash and no rattle of rowlocks. I noticed something else, too: a slight tightening of the tension within him, a new wariness in the eyes, a self-contemplative smile as if he were checking off his own skills and finding them still adequate for the task in hand. I had seen the same expression before: in the faces of men just before a night raid in New Guinea; on a desert tracker in the Jordan Valley, searching the sand and the shale for the tracks of Fedayeen raiders. It was the mark of the hunter, the professional, moving wary but confident in a hostile terrain.

Five minutes' rowing brought us to a spot where a long finger of water thrust deep into the land between two cliffs. On either side of the channel there was an iron stake, hammered into the rocks just below the high-water mark. Ruarri pointed them out with cheerful vanity. "I put those in last year. No one's tumbled to them yet. That's where we sling the gill net to catch the darlings as they run in and out with the tide. Lend a hand now, seannachie, and mind you don't topple overboard, or you'll spend a damn cold night."

A gill net is exactly what its name implies—a strong, coarse mesh into which a cruising fish will butt himself and tangle himself by the gills. To the honest angler it is anathema, but to a hungry fellow who wants food in the pan or silver in his pocket it is the invention of a genius. Ours was strung in a matter of minutes. We would leave it and come back for it on the way home. Then we were ready for the otter trawl: a large sock, winged open at the neck and trailed from a line astern. This one we had to use offshore where there were no reefs or snags but where we would be clearly visible when the moon came up.

When we had the trawl line cleated, I offered to take over the rowing to spare Ruarri's damaged wrist. He would have none of it. The plaster was firm; the muscles moved freely, and besides, he had more weight than I had. So I settled down with an arm about Kathleen Mc-Neil's shoulders and left him to pull his heart out if he wanted. Half a mile down the loch we hauled in the net. There were half a dozen pollock and one small salmon. We poured them into the duffel bag and tossed the trawl back into the water. I offered once again to relieve him at the oars. Once again he refused.

The moon was rising now, a globe of tarnished silver, with the hills black against its lower circumference. Its light was like the beam of a searchlight, refracted along the flat water. We were in the middle of it, with the trawl line cutting a silver furrow behind us. Another half mile and we were ready to haul in again. As I stood at the stern dragging on the line, I saw the lights: one, two, three, four of them, widely spaced, moving along the ridge of the northern hills. I pointed them out to Ruarri.

He nodded. "That's the gillies, without a doubt. And at least one of them has night glasses."

"So what now?"

"Let's get the net in and see what we've got."

This time there was a big salmon, eight pounds of him at least, and a few small whitefish. We emptied the net and left it inboard. Ruarri sat down again and sculled quietly to hold us against the run of the tide.

76

"Watch the lights, seannachie. Tell me how they're moving."

After five minutes or so the movement was clear. They were moving downhill in a half circle, gradually closing the circumference round the spot where we had left the car.

Ruarri swore softly. "Damn and blast them! They don't have to do any more. They find the car; they call the police for two roadblocks on the main road and they've got us trapped. Unless we want to walk ten miles across country, that is. Even then they can trace the driver of the car. Christ! I haven't seen them here for months. Why tonight of all the nights in the year?"

It was the moonlight that betrayed him: the one reflection thrown up by an oar stroke onto his bearded face. The bastard was smiling. His voice was mourning over us both, but inside he was laughing like a bloody leprechaun on a mushroom. We were supposed to register panic and concern. We would make a great act of faith in his skill and beg him to save us from mulct and mischance and the disgrace of a day in court. He would calm us with his courage and row us into a quiet cove to wait out the danger. But he couldn't save us all, only Kathleen McNeil and himself. The car was rented to me. I might dodge the gillies and the policemen tonight. Tomorrow they would be on my doorstep with soft, sweet talk and a list of questions I couldn't answer without a lie. And Ruarri would be laughing at my discomfiture. To hell with that for a joke in the Stornoway bars.

I was just opening my mouth to tell him the joke was stale when I remembered Alastair Morrison's warning. I wasn't supposed to see the hook under the feathers of the lure. Even if I did, I mustn't tell the fisherman. I shut my mouth and sat quietly, watching the lights draw closer and closer to the place where the car was parked. Then, as if at a signal, they all snapped out.

The moon was higher now and the shoreline was clear, a series of small, dark coves with headlands between. I marked the spot from which we had launched the boat. I turned to Ruarri and pointed to the next bay. "Row us in there, Ruarri."

"What the hell . . . ! The police are just round the corner."

77

"There's no problem. We'll be home free, with fish for breakfast. Take us in now."

"You're crazy, seannachie!"

"If I am, I'll pay the fines for all of us."

"At least tell me what you've got in mind."

"It's easy. Farran on land tenure and *regalia minora* appurtenant thereto: only possession of tackle or fish, or the means of transporting same, to wit a boat on prohibited waters, constitutes evidence of trespass or poaching. So you drop us ashore. We're lovers, in case you didn't know. We've been having a private interlude on the beach. This very night we've decided to become engaged —unofficially, of course. While we're explaining all that to the law, you'll row back and clear your gill net. We'll take your house key and drink your liquor and I'll be back to pick you up on the main road an hour after midnight."

He stared at me for a long moment, then dissolved into laughter, coughing and spluttering as he tried to stifle it. "You son of a gun! You slew-eyed Sassenach! Here's me sweating my soul out to save you from the hangmen, and you're six jumps ahead of me. Are you a good enough actor to bring it off?"

"If my leading lady's up to it?"

"How would you like it played, dear one?" The leading lady was enthusiastic. "Slightly drunk and singing? Or tender and brimming with happy tears?"

"Play as your heart tells you, Kathleen."

"Pass me the bottle," said Ruarri. "I need a big drink."

When we reached the shore, we had to walk the length of a stony cove and scramble over the rock and kelp of a headland to reach the car. The law was waiting for us: two genial constables and a sour-faced gillie with a big border collie on a leash. The constables were polite, if skeptical. Was this my car? It was. Would I mind telling them what it was doing at this particular place so late at night? I wouldn't mind at all; but was I in breach of any local law I didn't know about? Not at all. But it was a lonely spot and they were just doing a routine duty to the public. I told them: Dr. McNeil and I were friends, old and fond friends. We were out for a drive. We had stopped here to be private and watch the moon on the water. Lovers lose track of time so easily. We hadn't been fishing by any chance? Did we look as though we had? Had we seen anyone else fishing? We'd seen a boat on the loch. We had thought it rather beautiful in the moonlight. We wouldn't know who was in it by any chance? That was hardly possible. Both of us were newcomers. Dr. McNeil was doing a locum in Harris. I was a guest of the Morrison at Laxay. He would be quite happy to identify us if identification were needed. It wouldn't be. They were sorry to have troubled us. One last question: where were we heading now? Back through Carloway to the lodge. Anything else? Nothing at all. We were free to go. God rest you merry, gentlemen. I hope to God Ruarri's out of sight now; and I hope, more fervently, there's no patrol car on the road when I come back for him. . . .

Ten minutes later we were snug at Ruarri's fireside, drinking his liquor and laughing over the comedy.

"*Regalia minora,* for God's sake! How did you happen on that piece of jargon?"

"I didn't happen on it, my love. I dug it out this afternoon, just to be ready."

"You mean Ruarri planned what happened tonight."

"I'm sure he didn't. But he knew it could happen. He's a mischief and he likes to score off people. I wanted to be ready for him."

"Why didn't you warn me?"

"Because if nothing had happened I'd have looked a fool. And I'd rather not look a fool to you, Kathleen oge."

"But you think Ruarri would like it?"

"I know he would."

"I'm not flattered by that at all." She got up, walked over to the fire and stood with her back to me, warming her hands at the blaze.

"Are you angry with me?"

"Yes, I am."

"Why?"

She swung round to face me, cheeks flushed, eyes bright and hostile. "Because I'm not an object! I'm not a prize you quarrel over and then throw dice for. I'm me, Kathleen McNeil. I love whom I love. I give myself when and where I choose. I've been dirtied enough, thank you. Never again."

I was angry then, coldly and bitterly angry. I stood up,

took the car keys from my pocket and held them out to her.

"If you think you've been dirtied because I told you a simple truth, so be it! There are the keys, the car's yours. I'll pick Ruarri up in his own vehicle. But before you go, hear me out. I'm no great catch. I'm putting myself together after a crisis of my own, when I thought I couldn't believe or work or care or love again. I didn't ask you to mother me like your blasted actor. I didn't ask you to take me to bed to make me feel better. I asked you to marry me, because with whatever I am, I love you. I've lived rough, God knows! But I've never bought or sold or shared a woman in my life. I haven't talked secrets about any woman I've known either. Tonight? Ruarri's interested in you. You know it. I know it. I was warning him off the grass because it seemed there was a hope for us, and you were ready to cherish it too. If that's an insult, I'm sorry. If I'm the wrong man, tell me now, and let's be friends at least, respecting each other."

My vehemence shocked her. Indeed, it shocked me. My controls had worn thinner than I knew. She was very near to tears, but she was too proud to yield to them. For a long moment we stood confronting each other, the keys dangling between us, rattling in my unsteady hand.

Finally she said, "I hate quarrels."

"So do I."

"And I'd rather not drive home alone."

"You have a choice of drivers."

"I'd prefer the man who brought me."

Then we were together again, body to body, lip to lip; and for a while it was not Ruarri's house, but our own place with the world shut out and the fire shared and the hope a little stronger, if not yet wholly secure.

When the time came to pick up Ruarri, I left her drowsing over a book. I was glad to go alone and she, I think, was glad to be rid of me for a while. A quarrel is no bad thing when you can have it out and say all the bad words and then come to the moment when there are no words at all, only the you and the I becoming the we, and the we tumbling into sleep, knowing that tomorrow will be a better day altogether. But until that kind of sleeping comes, it is better to part a while and measure the need against the hurt and come back fresh to each other.

The moon was high now, unblemished by any shadow of earth. The hard land lay silver and gentle under its light. The lochans were bright. The houses were like the dwellings of sleeping dolls, white and peaceful in the hollows. Even the sheep were at rest, grey huddles beside the hayricks and the outcropping rocks. The wind had died. There was no voice of gull or curlew, only the faint susurrus of the sea, stirring around the black rocks and the yellow kelp. It was a place to be calm in, a time to be alone and yet not lonely.

I saw Ruarri first from a hundred yards away, a humped figure against the star line, a cigarette end glowing in the shadow. When I came up to him I saw that he was perched on a bag full of fish, with his nets piled in a heap beside him. He was weary and he showed it. He was a little drunk and he showed that, too, but he still had to make the last grandstand play.

"Fifty pounds of fish or I'm a Dutchman, seannachie! Six great salmon, three sea trout and pollock to feed a whole poorhouse. You're dead on time. That's a virtue I respect. Any trouble?"

"No trouble. Let's stow the stuff and be on our way."

"Where's Kathleen?"

"Sleeping in your living room."

"Ach, the poor, dark woman! Why not stay the night? The pair of you can have my room. I'll doss by the fire. It's forty miles back to Rodel and then you have to double the distance back to the lodge."

"It's a kind thought. Let's leave it up to her."

We drove in silence for the first mile, then he turned to me with a tipsy grin. "Seannachie?"

"Yes?"

"You're a bastard."

"So are you."

"But I like you."

"I'm a friendly fellow too."

"You called me tonight."

"You asked for it."

"So I did. So I will again, because that's the way I'm made. I'll call you on a card or a woman or a money deal. And if you don't raise me, I'll have no respect for you at all."

"Thanks for telling me. It'll help next time."

"Don't call me now, seannachie. Don't fight me. Just let me tell it and believe what I'm telling you is true, even if you never believe me again. I'm a bastard. That's legal, de facto, with a birth certificate to prove it. I'm a bastard by nature, and you don't need a document to prove that. So I'm a lone one, like the red wolf at my masthead. You know why I go poaching—and me a trawlerman with a hold full of herring every trip? I'll tell you. Because I was born poor and I lived poor, and I'm scared of being poor ever again. Tomorrow one of my boys will come and clean all the fish I caught tonight. The salmon we'll smoke and the rest we'll shove in a freezer against the winter. And I'll know I can always eat, without a call on the minister or the social service or the charity of friends."

"You make it too rough for yourself, Ruarri."

"Rough it was and rough it is. I still wear it. But you know one thing I miss? A brother. . . . A big brother to curse me out and slap me down and still put me to bed when I crawl home drunk with a busted jaw. That was you, seannachie. That was you driving *The Mactire* up the Minch, covering for me with Duggie Donald in Stornoway. That was why I sent you the chessman, hoping you'd understand."

"Jesus Christ!"

"He's dead, seannachie."

"I was damn near dead when I came to the Isles."

"But you're alive now, aren't you? The sap's running high. You've got a woman you care for. And you're spoiling for a fight—with me or the next man."

"We could have it, any time."

"I wouldn't mind."

"There'd be bad blood, Ruarri."

"Just so there's blood. I don't even know where I got mine. I don't know where it runs either. I've spilt seed in a hundred beds from the Piraeus to Port o' Spain and never cared. Now I'm caring—a little at least."

"So lay off my girl."

"I'll try, but I can't promise. I wish I could."

"So what are you asking?"

"Let's be brothers as long as we can."

"And when we can't?"

"Give me respect, seannachie. Just respect."

"You've got it. So take it easy now, eh?"

"Anything you say, brother. Anything you say." He lay back in the bucket seat, closed his eyes and slept the last winding miles to his house.

My grandfather, who was a much wiser man than I, used to say that if you wanted the truth about a man you'd find it in the last inch of the whisky bottle. There's a catch in the proposition, of course—there always is with the Celt, and the sooner you wake up to the fact the better! You'll get a truth out of the bottle, but you can't be sure whether it's the truth the drunk thinks he knows or the truth as it really is. And there's a world of difference between the two.

Ruarri the poor boy just wasn't true at all. Not bone-poor the way he told it, not charity-poor, not helping-hand-from-the-kirk-poor. The settlement from the Morrison was one guarantee against it, and his mother's croft was the second. Humble in circumstance, yes. Humbled by social stigma, yes again. And I didn't believe the fish-in-the-freezer story either, because I'd seen his kitchen and there just wasn't room for fifty pounds of anything with all the rest of his victuals. If my guess was right, he'd keep only the salmon and split the rest of the catch among his henchmen to make a big, bold fellow of himself. His need of a big brother? For *brother* read *father* and you'd have a more authentic text. The real truth was right down at the bottom of the bottle. Respect —that he had to have. The tragedy was he'd earn it ten times over and then toss it away with some silly roguery before he knew he had it. The remedy? In his furry, fuddled state, he thought I held it. Perhaps I did; but I had no license to use it, and it might poison him anyway.

We spent the rest of the night at Ruarri's house, because he insisted on it, and Kathleen McNeil was dead on her feet, and an eighty-mile drive at two in the morning made nonsense in any language. She slept in Ruarri's bed. Ruarri and I slept on bunks in the living room. I could not bear the thought of her curled in another man's sheets and him grinning at me across the darkness, so I was restless, falling in and out of troughs of sleep, like a boat hove to in a high sea.

An hour or two before dawn I found myself awake and trembling. The house was dark as a tomb but filled with a sound that chilled the blood: a high, unearthly wailing, like the cry of a man tortured to the limit of endurance. It went on and on, a long ululation of intolerable agony. I leaped out of bed, naked and shivering, and switched on the lights in the living room. Ruarri was tangled in his blankets, tossing and squirming and screaming like a man in delirium. His hair and beard were damp and matted. His lips were drawn back from his teeth in a rictus of terror. His hands clawed at the covers like the talons of a trapped bird.

I hurried to him and shook him, calling his name. On the instant he started up, eyes staring, his hands at my throat, throttling me. He was as strong as a baboon and I almost blacked out. At the last moment I drove my fist into his belly with all the strength I had behind it. His hands fell away. He doubled up, gasping and retching as he woke.

I stood well away from him while he recovered. For a while he stared at me, uncomprehending; then he shook his head to clear away the fog.

"What happened?"

"You were having a nightmare—screaming in your sleep. I tried to wake you. You damn near strangled me."

"I'm sorry." His chest was heaving. His face was running with sweat. "I'm sorry, seannachie. But never wake me like that. Stand at my head where I can't reach you, and press your fingers under my ears. I could have killed you. Get me a drink."

I poured neat whisky into a glass and handed it to him. He gagged on it first, then managed to get it down. He wiped the sweat off his face with the blanket and laughed unsteadily. "It's the old dream—the bad one. I'm pegged out in a clearing and the women are coming with knives to cut me up and then leave me to the ants. I wasn't joking about the snake charm. Oh brother, I wasn't joking! When we were camped at night I slept with a pistol under my pillow and a knife strapped to my shin, always an inch from waking."

"Will you sleep now?"

"Give me another drink and I'll settle down."

I gave it to him.

He sipped it slowly this time, holding it two-handed to his lips, watching me over the rim of the glass. "I'm not crazy, you know, seannachie."

"I know. I've had nightmares too."

"Maybe that's why you feel like a brother sometimes."

"Maybe."

"Did I wake the girl?"

"No."

"Thank Christ for that! Go back to bed. I'll be fine now."

I crawled back under the covers and watched him as he remade his tumbled bunk. He was as meticulous as a nurse, smoothing out the sheets, turning in the blanket corners as if for an inspection. Then he gave me an ironic salute, switched out the lights and bedded down again. Ten minutes later he was asleep and snoring.

I lay awake until a grey dawn crept over the ghost-ridden countryside. I understood now and was shocked by what had happened to me. Two men and a woman had shown me the secrets of their inmost lives, and I was the last person in the world fit for the burden.

V

As I drove Kathleen McNeil back to her house, I told her of my dialogue with Ruarri and his nightmares in the small hours. I did not want to discredit him. I did not try. I wanted her to know, and I believed I had a right to tell her, what manner of man he was and the explosive possibilities of any relationship with him. She was very professional about it—too professional for my taste, because I was frayed and edgy after a sleepless night.

". . . The nightmare is normal—a good sign. In sleep the controls are released, the safety valve opened. The violence we dream is the violence we never do any more. That's too simple, but you know what I mean. The terror behind it, that's the sad thing! I feel dreadfully sorry for him. He's too young for such a load of memory. The brother-need, that's a heart-cry too. You can't reject it, any more than I can ignore the call from a patient who has taken an overdose of sleeping pills. Even the warning that he will fight you is a plea for forgiveness for what he knows himself to be. He wants you to care. He's pushing himself up so high and so fast, he's scared that the props underneath him will be kicked away and he'll fall off his perch like Humpty-Dumpty."

"Why me for the brother?"

"Why anybody? Why did you come here when Alastair Morrison offered a refuge? A moment arrives and you have to lean to somebody, anybody, or go mad."

"Pick the wrong somebody and it's tragedy for both."

"That's the risk of living, isn't it?"

"I don't see what I can do for Ruarri."

"What he asks. Don't reject him. Be ready to forgive him."

"For anything?"

"The Bible figure was seventy times seven."

I remembered she hadn't been so damn casual about her own mistake. Or half so ready to forgive the fool she married. "You practice rough surgery, Doctor!"

"I think you're strong enough to survive it."

"Thanks for the compliment."

"Angry again?"

"No. I'm admiring your skill in diagnosis. I've got one more question for you."

"What's that?"

"What would it do to Ruarri if he found out who his father was?"

"How would one know? Is his father alive or dead? Would his father want him to know? Will he find out or be told? For what reason? Reconciliation? Inheritance? To help the father, or Ruarri, or both? I don't think anyone could answer all those questions."

"That's the problem. I know some of the answers."

"Oh my dear!" The words came out in a rush of penitent tenderness. "And I was being so damn bitchy to you. I thought you were making another jealous scene. God, what a mess!"

"You're the one bright light in the middle of it. How long are you going to stay in Harris?"

"Until the end of summer. Why?"

"So long as you're here, and so long as you're happy, I'll stay."

"But free, all the time. Please! No commitments yet."

"No commitments, young Kathleen. Just to enjoy."

The promise was easy to make. It was a new day. Summer was in full flush. The tents of the campers were like bright flowers on the dunes and the children were shouting already over the warm white sands. We shrugged off the memory of the night and drove, singing, along the fringe of a friendly ocean.

When I left Kathleen at her house, I took the cliff road to Tarbert. My time was my own, so I strolled down to the little port to watch the arrival of the mainland ferry with its load of tourists, timber, automobiles, baled wool for the weavers, newspapers, groceries, frozen meat, assorted hardware and homecoming islanders. It was a pleasant, bustling scene, though it lacked the gaiety and confusion of a Mediterranean docking—the shouts, the flailing gestures, the pounding of horns and the shrilling of police whistles just for the merry hell of it. The English took their pleasures soberly and the Scots wore a dour face for their sauciest jokes and the courtesies of a small, closed place must be jealously enforced. As I wandered through the crowd, keeping my eyes open for characters and my ear cocked for turns and lilts of speech—which is a writer's habit I have never lost—I came face to face with Duggie Donald, the Customs man from Stornoway.

We gave each other good morning and fell into talk: about the weather and the tourist trade and how I was enjoying my stay in the Isles and the trivial rest of it. As the crowd cleared I invited him to take a cup of coffee with me. He accepted and we walked up the hill to the hotel and sat on the verandah watching the morning exodus of anglers and harassed families making for the beaches in the west. He was a friendly fellow with a shrewd wit and a bright eye for the visiting talent. Also he liked springing surprises. He told me:

"I hear you were braced by the local constabulary last night—you and a lady."

"How the hell did you know?"

He chuckled happily. "Don't let it worry you. A man only has to sneeze and it's all over the island. There's little to do but gossip here."

"So I'm learning. Morrison said you'd called him about me."

"I did. Part of my job. He gave you a good character."

"Then you won't mind telling me what it was all about —the business with Ruarri Matheson."

"Well, now! How do I put it to you? I would mind in particular. I wouldn't mind in general. Our Ruarri's a wild boy, which is not to say anything libellous. He'll do mad things for excitement, and some things which he shouldn't do for profit. I'm keeping an eye on him, and I want him to know it."

"What sort of—things?"

"Why are you interested?"

"We've become friendly. He's asked me to take a trip with him on his next trawl."

"Has he now?"

"I'd like to go. I'm a writer. It's my trade to learn how men live. I'd like to know what I'm letting myself in for— if anything."

"Why don't you ask Ruarri?"

"Because he's done me a courtesy. It's courtesy for me to accept it at face value."

"Then it's safer for you to hear nothing, either from me or from Ruarri."

"Good advice. I'll take it."

"There's a rider to it, though. If you did, by chance, find yourself mixed up in an illegal activity, you could be required to disclose it in police inquiries and testify in court. If you refused, you could be charged as an accessory."

"That makes it very clear. I'm grateful."

"You're welcome. Thanks for the coffee. When you're next in Stornoway, drop into the office. I'll buy you a drink."

He left me then. I ordered more coffee and let it get

88

cold while I thought my own faraway thoughts. The English were the most practiced seducers in the world. They raped the girl first, taught her to love the child she didn't want, then sailed home to write a bible about it: bonds of Empire, Commonwealth unity, the long tradition of liberty under the law, sell arms to South Africa, boycott Rhodesia, liberate the Maltese, disprize the Americans, build white elephants with the French, bring in the Jamaicans, shut out the Pakistanis, fight the Spaniards for Gibraltar, woo the Portuguese because they're old colonials, subdue the Celts and turn them into nice competent public servants with a promise of pine forests all over the Highlands and new industry for Wales when the coal runs out and the last miner is dead with his lungs all black.

I didn't dislike Duggie Donald. He was a bright, agreeable man turning in a fair day's work for a public servant's wage. I was none too fond of Ruarri Matheson. He was a monumental liar, more than half a pirate, and I wouldn't trust him a jump and a spit with my checkbook or my sister. But in a grey world, with order in the streets, and a policeman on every corner, and a rubber stamp needed before you could take a pee or go to bed with a girl—God help me!—I was all for the man with a red wolf at his masthead and his pockets stuffed with free currency. The which being a seditious thought, it was time to go back to the lodge, before I talked it out in a bar and had myself gossiped up and down this very small island.

In the kitchen Hannah poured me a glass of beer and belaboured me with questions.

"You were away last night?"

"I was indeed."

"And you were poaching with Ruarri the Mactire?"

"Now who could have told you a tale like that, Hannah?"

"You'll swear you weren't?"

"I will not. The Bible says I shouldn't swear to anything—and it's the best of books!"

"Where did you sleep?"

"I didn't sleep, Hannah. My conscience kept me awake."

"As well it might. Did you sleep alone?"

"If I did or I didn't, you'd have no right to know. But the fact is, I did. And I didn't like it."

"Try it as long as I have and see how you like that! Did you catch any fish?"

"I'm told fish were caught, Hannah. But I never put line in water."

"A pity! I could have used a good salmon for lunch. Where's the doctor-woman?"

"Looking after the sick, which is a godly work of mercy."

"I wish she were here at this moment to take a look at the Morrison."

"He's not well?"

"Ach! He's as fit as a trout, he says. But I know better. Ever since yesterday he's been grey around the gills and blue around the lips. I've watched him going up the stairs. He can't make it halfway without a breather. He's got a little bottle of pills in his pocket which he sent Fergus to buy for him, and all morning, when he's been reading, he's had a glass of water and the brandy bottle beside him."

"Have you called his own doctor?"

"He'd have my head if I did. He's one himself, he says, and why should he pay a guinea for some other fool to take his pulse?"

"Where is he now?"

"Resting in his bedroom. But he won't thank you for disturbing him. You'll not tell him now that I've spoken to you?"

"I promise."

"You couldn't ask your lady friend to drop by, casual-like?"

"I could, but a doctor can't go scuttling round like a poacher."

"The master's worried about something, and that's bad for him."

"Do you know what it is?"

"I know it and I don't know it. You wouldn't under-stand that, not having the second sight. But the way it is, I can't find the words when I need them."

"Is it something I know too?"

For a moment she seemed to retreat into herself, then

she came back to me again. "Yes, it is. At least I think it is."

"Leave it then. I'll do what I can. I'm fond of him too."

"If you weren't, I wouldn't have you within a mile of him!"

She meant it too. When I looked into those old, dark eyes, I knew she would have a knife in my ribs and me buried in the cabbage patch before I brought a breath of harm to Alastair Morrison. She had handed me a problem, however, and I was at a loss how to deal with it. I was a guest in the house. I had no writ to prescribe for the health of my host. Even as his friend, I had no standing in his private argument with life and death. Yet I did have standing in the cause of himself and Ruarri. This I could abrogate on the grounds of disinterest or incapacity—or could I? Kathleen McNeil had given me an uncomfortable reminder of a thing I would rather have forgotten. All my life, albeit often wrongheadedly, I had battled to maintain the principle that all men were brothers, that an injustice to one was an invasion of all, that a sickness of one member was a disease of the whole organism. I had wearied myself to despair in the battle. I wanted to break it off now, cancel the blood pact, let the rest of the world go to hell in its own basket. This was the meaning of my flight to the Isles; but the battle was here, too, and I was involved again. Would there never be an end to it, a rest and a placid contemplation of follies I had managed to survive?

When Alastair Morrison came to lunch, he looked better than I had expected; a little peaky, perhaps, disinclined for food, a little less lively than usual. Still, he brightened when I told of our night's adventure, and he laughed uproariously over our encounter with the police. The rest of the story I did not tell him directly, but tried to come at it, crabwise, with the question Kathleen McNeil had put to me.

"I've been thinking about what you asked me to do for Ruarri. There's something I've wondered about. If it's not my business, tell me so. When you die, does Ruarri share in your estate?"

"He gets it all, through a trust. It devises down to his children, if he ever has any."

"So at that point he knows, doesn't he?"

"He guesses, maybe. The way the trust is framed, he doesn't know for certain. What's on your mind?"

"A waste, perhaps. A waste of what could be good years for you and him."

"They could be bad years too, laddie."

"I know that."

"Why raise the question then?"

I told him. I tried not to make a drama out of it, but simply to show him the need that Ruarri had expressed to me, and my own reservations about it, and the options that might be open between the two of them. He listened in silence. At one moment he took out a small comfit box, popped a pill in his mouth and washed it down with a mouthful of wine. When I had finished he sat a long time, with his elbows on the table, chin on his cupped hands, staring into space. Then, slowly and quietly, he began to talk, as if he were testing each phrase before he uttered it:

"I believe in Providence. I always have. The trouble is you never see how it works until the work is done. When you learn enough, you try to cooperate, but then the irony of creation shows itself. You never get the result you planned. Last night, when you were out, I had a warning. Not a bad one, just a knocking on the gate to tell me that the dark watchman was on his rounds and might be calling a little sooner than I expected. I thought of Ruarri then. I thought this was the time when a man would be grateful for a son to lean on when the stairs got too steep to climb alone. But you don't call in a son you've never acknowledged just to make a crutch of him. On the other hand, Ruarri has rights independent of mine. Those rights have been in breach too long. He's the victim of a conspiracy of concealment. I've perpetuated the concealment and called it protection. Now you come along and I bind you in a way I have no right to do. . . . Tally it up and it makes me a very selfish man. Small comfort with evening on me already, and the silent night inevitable afterwards. . . ."

My heart bled for him, but I could not help him. Once, years before, I had had a rude lesson and I had never forgotten it. A friend was stricken with an incurable disease. I went to see him. I was embarrassed for lack of words to comfort him. I offered a well-meant platitude. He cursed me in a cold fury: "Goddammit, man! The

92

death warrant's signed and delivered. Let me walk to the block with dignity." I dared not deny the same dignity now to Alastair Morrison. I waited, sipping a brandy, smoking a cigarette, until he went on.

"Of course, you can indulge yourself in guilt too. You want someone to tell you you're forgiven. But you're not —not without a reparation, or the injured one cancelling the debt you can't pay."

"He can't cancel it if he doesn't know the name of the debtor. Besides, you're talking in very limited terms, aren't you?"

"What do you mean?"

"All I've heard from you is debit and credit, fault and forgiveness. What about love?"

The word startled him. It was almost as if I had used an obscenity.

"Good God! Do you think that's possible now?"

"Yes. Your son's got size, Alastair—a ruffian streak, too—but size and spirit and a crying need that makes him reach for the stars. Why not have him here and judge for yourself? I owe him a meal. I'll invite him."

He did not answer immediately. He turned the suggestion over and over, as if searching for the flaw that would enable him to reject it. Then, with a shrug and a thin, grey smile, he surrendered. "So be it then. Invite him. Tell him to bring a woman friend if he wants. And you invite Kathleen McNeil. If you have a taste for irony, it should be an interesting evening."

"You could be pleasantly surprised."

"God give me good words that night, laddie! Now will you get yourself out of here, before I make a fool of myself?"

I shoved a rod and a pair of waders into the car and took myself off for Stornoway. I had shopping to do, and on the way home I would try a cast or two in one of the lochans over by Leurbost where I would have larks and blackbirds singing to me while I fished. I was glad to be alone, anyway. I was beginning to feel querulous again, frayed by too close contact with a small, enclosed group of intense and intelligent people. After the first exhilaration of space and newness, I was suffering the reverse swing of the island syndrome: a feeling of confinement, of scenic monotony, of exclusion and alienation. For a spirit in disorder there is no lasting Eden, only hints and snatches, elusive harmonies.

My first call was a book shop. I needed a Gaelic grammar and a dictionary. The freckled lass behind the counter gaped at me as if I had asked for a consignment of moon rocks. She spoke the Gaelic herself, of course she did, but she'd never seen a book of it. Maybe I should write to the Education people or take a wee stroll over to the Gaelic Society, whose office might just possibly be open. Gaelic music? That they would have in the television shop round the next corner. She herself wasn't much gone on it. They played it at the Highland games and sometimes at a concert, but not at the dances. There it was all the new stuff, the Beatles and the Stones and the soul music, that sort of thing, you know? I did indeed, and my knowing seemed to give her some small hope for my sanity.

I did not find the music either; but I spent an instructive half hour with an elderly antiquarian who sold me a gift for Kathleen McNeil—a Georgian locket on a fine chain of woven gold. Business wasn't bright, he told me. Most of the good stuff went to the mainland, to Edinburgh and London, and there wasn't the money or the taste in the Lews for fine old things. They were living on the tweed and the fishing; but half the money went back to the mainland in empty beer barrels, and television was making the young ones discontented with their life. Leverhulme had had the right idea, but he was half a century ahead of his time. There was this young fellow Ruarri Matheson who had great notions and talked high, but his past was against him, and though he spent money as if he had a hole in his pocket, he'd never make it. Lews folk were stiff-necked and stubborn—he was a Barra man himself, married into the island—and they resented anyone who was thought to be teaching his grandmother to suck eggs. If I wouldn't mind paying the little extra, he'd find me a nice box for the locket. Women were quick to notice the little extras, weren't they now? I paid him his money—none too little, for all the bad market in the Lews —walked out into the narrow street and turned down to the harbour.

There was some excitement here. An ambulance was

94

parked on the stone dock of the basin and a small crowd was gathered round it. A German freighter had reported a burst boiler pipe and two engineers badly scalded in the engine room. The lifeboat had been called to take off the injured men. It was a routine thing, they told me. Just a milk run. There were always accidents at sea. They remembered worse times in the war, when the U-boats were out and never a week passed without some poor devils picked up with their lungs full of oil or their limbs blown off or skin peeled off them from top to toe. The admission book at the hospital had the names of men from every nation under the sun, and some of them had died and were buried on the island, friend and enemy together, made brothers by the bitter sea.

There was a flurry of talk as the lifeboat drew into the dock, then a silence as the men were taken off, strapped to the stretchers, their faces and hands covered with white gauze. The doctor, a stocky fellow, incongruous in a tweed suit and yellow seaboots, climbed into the ambulance after them, and the day's drama was over. As the crowd dispersed I heard one woman say to her companion, "At last my Jamie has his scholarship. That's one the sea won't get."

It sounded almost like an invocation. The sea was a hell all women hated. They fought it as the missionaries fought the ancient demons, with prayers and exorcisms. Sometimes they won and then found the victory barren when their men turned sour with disappointed hopes and the workless days of winter. Sometimes they lost because the lure of it was too strong: the outcall to men penned too long in too barren a land, the promise of wealth and adventure, the seduction of exotic experience far from the eye of the elders and the kirk. But winners or losers, widowed or waiting, they were all sisters in their hate and their fear. Even the young and flighty ones would tell you they gave no welcome to visiting sailormen. They wanted their men home and safely bedded at nights—with or without benefit of clergy.

I heard a shout, "Hey, seannachie!" and there was Ruarri, his head stuck out of a wheelhouse, signalling to me. He was moored third in line, so I had to clamber across two other decks to reach him.

He thrust out an oil-stained fist to haul me inboard,

then handed me a wad of cotton waste to swab my palm. "I'm an engineer today. The main bearing was loose. But the boys are nearly finished now. This is the *Helen I*—so called because she's the first of a thousand ships—I hope! Iain, who's up to his balls in grease down below, skippers this one. I run the *Helen II*. That's the lady with the new paintwork over there! Where's Kathleen?"

"Working. I came up to do some shopping and fish on the way home."

"To hell with the fishing! Stay and have a drink with me and the boys."

"Fine! I've got an invitation for you too. I'd like you to have dinner with me at the lodge. You name the night. Bring a girl if you want. I'll have Kathleen."

"The lodge!" He gave a long whistle. "Och aye! The Mactire moves into society at last! You know I've never had a meal at the lodge in my life. Whose idea was this?"

"Mine. It's my party. I'm paying the score. Morrison will be my guest as well. When are you free?"

"Let's see now! We'll be out tomorrow at first light and away for two days. Let's say Friday."

"Friday it is. Seven-thirty for drinks. Dinner at eight. And you'll be bringing someone?"

"I will." He grinned a little self-consciously. "But who it'll be demands some careful thinking. I'll let you know. Come below now and I'll show you what a real trawler looks like. None of those clapped-out drifters for Ruarri the Mactire!"

It was no idle boast either. There was love and money lavished on his craft. The money was in the big diesels and the full panel of electricals: radar, sonar, direction finder, automatic pilot and the rest. The love was in the scrubbed decks and the clean bilges, and the bright paintwork and the fresh grease on the winches, and the fish-well free of stink and garbage, and every piece of gear stowed shipshape, as if it were an admiral's barge and not a stubby, workaday herring boat. There was power, too, in the skipper who could drive a tired crew to hose ship and chip rust and salt cake after days of hauling their tripes out in the Atlantic swell. Rogue and rapscallion he might be to the sober folk of the town, but in the tight brotherhood of the sea he was measured for what he was: a safe helmsman, a captain whose engines ran clean, whose crew would stand up and fight for him in any bar from Truro to Trondheim.

They didn't mind the swagger of him, the bawdy, jostling assurance. Age and the clouting of the sea would tone him down soon enough. With two trawlers and a yacht and his croft, he could buy and sell most of them; but he was still a working sailor, which kept him in the brotherhood. He was not one of them damty merchants or bankers who thought that money could buy you, body, soul and breeches, and who'd screw you into bankruptcy if things went wrong. Tough he was, and a bad man to cross; but he would never see a man without the price of a drink in his pocket or a family in distress because a fisherman was sick or injured.

I record these things because I heard some of them and sensed the rest as we clambered over other men's decks to visit the *Helen II*. I had, and I have now, small reason to love Ruarri the Mactire. I have still large reasons to hate him. But respect he had, and has, and I pay my tribute with the rest.

He had what too many lack in our monotone world, a sense of style and a talent for ritual. The style was a chameleon colour, shifting and changing with the company. The ritual was an instrument of power and he used it with knowing art. The "drink with the boys" was a case in point. When the hotels opened there was a general migration from the docks to the bars—no panic rush, but a steady, fated swarming, like that of jungle creatures to the water hole. Ruarri, contrariwise, held back. He would not submit himself to the indignity of the first crush at the bar, the first clamour for drinks. He held me in his cabin, yarning over a glass, until the confusion had subsided. Then he strolled me down the deserted dock to what he called "my own pub," a modest stone-built tavern under the sign of "The Admiral's Spyglass."

We walked into a fug you could cut with a knife and a crowd three deep around the counter; but the crowd parted to let him through, and ten strapping fellows at the far end shouted a welcome and pushed their girls along the benches to make a place for us and had drinks in our hands before we could sit down. Ruarri presented me to the group as "a friend of mine, a seannachie well known in other parts, and no bad sailorman either." Then,

97

as they pumped the hand off me, he added an order: "So we'll talk in English, because there are no secrets between us and he hasn't had time yet to learn the language." I was grateful for the courtesy. There is nothing quite so disconcerting as the Celtic habit—bad here, but worse in Wales—of shutting out the stranger just as the talk gets interesting.

There was a girl for Ruarri, I noticed: a busty blonde with a beehive hairdo and a kissable mouth and a very possessive look in her eyes. I wondered if this would be his guest at the lodge, though I had no doubt she had been his guest more than once at the croft. He sat with his arm around her and kissed her whenever he had the urge and drank from her glass when she offered it. The drinks went down with bewildering speed. Every man had to buy a round, and a glass too long empty brought a sharp reminder to the laggard. The talk was salted with bawdy words which nobody seemed to mind or even hear. This too was ritual—man's talk in a man's place and the women could like it or lump it. On the evidence none of them seemed to give a "fook in hell," though some were quite ready to give it in bed and told it plainly.

Ruarri handled himself like an actor, consummate in the role he had created for himself. He matched them drink for drink, joke for joke, and his audience adored him. The boys bellowed their heads off at every story he told, and there was not a girl in the group but would have had her clothes off at the snap of his fingers. Yet, in spite of the clamour, he managed to pass out work: stores to be ordered, papers to be collected from the harbour master's office, a telegram to be sent, a call to be made to an absent crewman. Ruarri had drilled them well. I noted that every man who received an order wrote it in a pocketbook and that all the books were identical. One hapless fellow who had forgotten his book was cursed out roundly and sent to fetch it. There was talk of the work done at the croft and of the next day's trawl. Then someone raised the question of the run to Norway. I pricked up my ears at that, but Ruarri quashed the subject with a frown and a swift sentence in Gaelic. However, at that moment the noise was high and one lad missed the warning cue. He gave a bellow of laughter and shouted:

"What say, Ruarri? That'll be one in the eye for the fooking Ulstermen. . . ."

What happened then I can tell you only in slow motion, with no true sense of the swiftness of it. Ruarri was out of his seat like a cat. He took the boy's nose in his fingers, twisting bone and cartilage so that he brought him out of his seat and down to his knees. At the same moment all the group came to their feet, shielding him from view. Then Ruarri slammed his boot into the lad's solar plexus, driving the wind out of him. Before he hit the floor, two of his friends had their arms under his shoulders, hoisting him up and carting him out of the bar as though he had fallen suddenly drunk. Then everyone sat down again and Ruarri was laughing and shouting to the barmaids:

"The rest of us are sober, lass! Another round and a double for our friend the seannachie! He's way behind the rest of us."

The drill was as perfect as any commando tactic. On-again-off-again-Finnegan; and though you saw it, you didn't believe it. The boys were laughing and the girls were twittering a second afterwards, and the drinkers at the bar had not batted an eyelid. Ruarri, I knew, was waiting for a comment or a reaction from me; but I was damned if I would give him the satisfaction. I took my drink and toasted the company, and then bought a round to return the courtesy and be free to go.

Ruarri came to the door with me and stood for a moment in the deserted street. "Dinner on Friday then, seannachie. Unless you've changed your mind?"

"I'll expect you, Ruarri."

"And I'll mind my manners."

"I never doubted it."

He smiled then, not cocky any more, but rueful and defensive. "It was yourself put the name on me—Lord of the Isles. Now you've seen what it might cost to wear it."

As I drove back to Laxay in the long, heather-scented twilight, I found myself wrestling with a very troubled conscience. The act of violence in the bar had revolted me. What revolted me even more was the sneaking approval I was prepared to give to it.

I hate all bullies. I was bullied myself as a child. I hate brutality. I saw enough of it in the war from comrades

99

and from enemies. Torture is abhorrent to me. I still have nightmares when I read of it, which is all too often in this savage time. I remember my nightly horror during the Pacific war: that I might be captured on patrol and treated like my friend, who had had his heart cut out, alive, by a Japanese surgeon to make him tell where the coast-watchers were hidden. If at the end of a none-too-noble life I shall have any claim to mercy, it will lie in this: that I have stood at risk against tyranny in all its forms, private and public; that I am on the record for the liberty of every man to say his credo in public and be held safe even by those who dissent from him; that I have never sold my pen to a liar, or my vote for personal advantage.

And yet, and yet. . . . Here I was, indulging myself in a secret and perverse admiration for a calculated act of cruelty. Why? Confused as I was at that time, I still knew that the question was radical for me. Did I lack the sheer animal courage to risk such an act? To that I had to answer yes. I have none of the qualities of a hero. I have had to lead men, but all my leadership was by manipulation, sometimes by superior knowledge, but never by the quality or even the posture of bravery. Was it the discipline implied? The instantaneous decision to protect the group, the family, against the aberrant member? To accept to lead is to accept a trust and to brook no breach of it by oneself or another. Yes, again; but still not enough. There had to be another reason; but I kept shying away from it, like a balky horse, scared of the water jump.

Finally I had to face it, because I had no confidants any more to whom I could gossip the story and let their judgments absolve me. Alastair Morrison was a sick man and I had charged myself to affect a reconciliation between himself and his son, in case death should come upon him unawares. I could not tell Kathleen McNeil lest I demean myself again by the jealousy with which she had charged me.

Jealousy—that was the root answer. Jealousy and the sum of all the personal insecurities that provoked it. I admired Ruarri and I hated him. What I was not, he was. Even his vices overtopped my puny virtues. To restore my dignity, to hold Kathleen McNeil against this clear attraction, I had to oppose him. To oppose him I had to use every tactic, however base. To use it I had to justify it, to prove it was good if only because it was necessary.

That moment of knowing, on the road from Stornoway to Laxay, was the moment of my self-betrayal. The proposition was as clear to me as to any casuist. By all that I believed it was false, base and immoral. Yet I committed myself to it. Once committed, I was calm: calm as a sniper sighting from a treetop, knowing that in the next instant he will kill the image of himself.

VI

THE RUARRI WHO CAME TO DINNER ON FRIDAY NIGHT was a man I had never seen before. He was dressed in full Highland rig and he wore it with the flair of the Lord of the Isles himself. From his buckled shoes to his Matheson kilt, to the jabot of fine lace held by a gold pin, he was as glossy and elegant a Scot as ever you saw on an advertisement for fine whisky. Even his manner was transformed and, if you had not known him, you would never have guessed the change. He was softspoken and respectful to Morrison, with Kathleen and myself, relaxed and urbane. One trifle more and you would have said it was overdone; but he hit exactly the right note: a compliment to the house in which he was making his first footing.

The woman with him was a surprise too. No country girl this, but an honest-to-God Irish beauty—red hair, green eyes, skin like peaches and cream, a soft Dublin accent and manners to match it. Her name, according to Ruarri's bill of consignment, was Maeve O'Donnell. She bred racehorses in Eire to win purses in England and France. What she was doing in the Lews and how the devil Ruarri had come to know her were matters left politely vague.

Alastair Morrison was impressed. I was myself. Kathleen McNeil was warm but wary, which I thought was no bad thing for my private interests. It always paid to have another pretty woman on the scene. Even old Hannah was startled into indiscretion.

As she bustled in with a tray of canapés she stopped dead in her tracks, stared the pair of them up and down and gave voice to a paean of praise. "God love us and protect us! It's Bonnie Charlie himself, back from over the water! Your taste's improved, Ruarri Matheson. I hope you have sense enough to hang onto this beauty!"

That took the weight off us all. We could laugh and begin to enjoy ourselves. I served the drinks so that Morrison could start the talk in his own way. He looked better tonight. He had rested during the afternoon; his colour was good; and, whatever the tension inside him, he managed a calm and courtly attention to his guests. I had not told Kathleen McNeil of his illness. I had explained the dinner simply as a return of courtesy to Ruarri Matheson after our night in his house. I did not doubt her discretion, but the occasion was critical enough without another undercurrent of unease.

Recording it now, I can hardly believe my own temerity in risking such a party: father and son, the one knowing, the other ignorant of the relationship; the son and myself, rivals for the same woman; she, uncommitted to either yet, and myself hugging a secret knowledge for a weapon to win her; Maeve O'Donnell, import from a territory of Ruarri's life which none of us knew about at all. The prime intention of it was good—I give myself that credit still—but the mixture was explosive, and the wonder was that it didn't blow up in our faces during the first ten minutes.

We fumbled the first passes of talk, but once we were settled with drinks in our hands and the fire warming us all, we managed to be easy together—at least as easy as folk could be who were acting out a fiction in the hope of a truth at the end. The memory of what was said is vague now, but the faces are still vivid and the attitudes and the tonalities. Morrison leaning back in his chair, his white hair fluffed about his ears, questioning Ruarri about his plans and projects; Ruarri, sober and deferent, explaining them with facts and figures and sturdy common sense; the two women fencing quietly with each other over fashions and travel and the inevitable surprise of having acquaintances in common; myself, withdrawn, only half listening, fingering the locket in my pocket and trying to find words with which to present it. Dinner would be a long meal. Hannah's food and Morrison's wine should shake us loose from the formalities. Maeve O'Donnell might help too. If I judged her right, she was too lively a one to sit through the evening in the shadow of another woman. She knew more than her prayers and read something more than the *Turf Register* and the Sunday supplements.

There was a small problem over the seating for dinner. I was the host, and Morrison argued that I should take the head of the table. I told him it was my privilege to decide the protocol and settled him in his own chair with the women on either side of him. I sat next to Maeve O'Donnell with Ruarri across the table from me. Morrison offered a grace, and I saw that the O'Donnell crossed herself, which gave me the word on her church but no firm clue to her virtue.

Ruarri, to my surprise, managed to turn a graceful compliment. "I like that. It's the first meal I've had blessed in a long time."

Morrison was pleased, and I was glad for him; but Hannah, standing by to offer the broth, made her own privileged comment. "More's the pity, young man!"

Morrison frowned, but Ruarri laughed. "Come and cook for me, Hannah, and I'll bless you three times a day."

She made no answer, but a gleam of approval showed in the dark, canny eyes.

Ruarri, however, added an unexpected comment. "It may sound strange, but there are times when I wouldn't mind having an anchor-hold in one kirk or another. Not the Frees, though, not ever. The Greeks maybe, or the Romans. They seem to have more experience of characters like me."

Was he making a ploy or a plea? He was so slippery a customer, I could not tell.

It was Maeve O'Donnell who took him up—and put him down. "You might do well in Ireland, Ruarri. You're

103

a good drinker and a slow marrier. Who knows, they might get you for a priest in the end."

"Then I'll hire you as my housekeeper!"

"The hell you will. I'd as soon peddle myself in Phoenix Park!"

"At least you'd be a better bargain than that nag you're trying to sell me."

"That nag, Ruarri Matheson, is going to win at the Curragh next June, and then you'll be crying your eyes out!"

We were in open country now, safe and laughing, and I began to relax. I reminded Morrison of that royal jockey club in Bangkok where every race was fixed and you could win yourself a fortune if you knew the right prince on the right day or the mistress of the Chinese merchant who was slated first on the roster. From Bangkok it was an easy stride to Chiengmai; and, when the salmon was served, Morrison was in a full flood of reminiscence about his years in the uplands. I wanted him to talk. I wanted Ruarri to know what manner of man he was and how much of gentleness and concern he had spent in his solitary penitential years.

My good intentions only laid another paving stone in the private hell of Alastair Morrison. Ruarri had been in Thailand too. He had spent six months ferrying opium into Laos with a loon of a French pilot. When his Thai patron was supplanted by a richer one, with a cheaper ferry service, he had to bribe his way out of trouble and head for Hong Kong.

He did not tell the story boastfully but with a kind of wry humour: one of the catalogue of follies of a footloose youth who had found the world was full of bigger bastards than himself. The irony was that Chiengmai had been a staging post for the opium runners and father and son must have been many times within half a mile of each other.

I did not dare to look at Morrison. I tried to lead the talk into safer channels by telling of my own troubles trying to write a book in Vietnam.

This time, at least, I was successful, thanks to Maeve O'Donnell, who demanded to know one good reason why I hadn't written a book about Ireland. I was ready for her on that. Every Irishman I've ever known has offered me twenty plots and a mission to tell the truth about the land of my fathers—although it was my mother and not my father who established the connection.

"I'll tell you why not, Maeve. Ireland's a lovely country. And if all the women were as beautiful as you, it would be next door to heaven. But ever since I was knee high to a tinker's donkey—which is a phrase my grandfather used till I was sick of it—I've had the place shoved down my neck: her saints, her scholars, her virgins and martyrs, Brian Boru, Oliver Cromwell, the Famine, the Fenians, Parnell, Daniel O'Connell, Clarence Mangan, Tommy Moore, Maud Gonne, the Easter Uprising, the Black and Tans and the IRA. Who needs me when you have all that, with Bernard Shaw and Jimmy Joyce thrown in for good measure?"

Maeve O'Donnell was not to be put off. My humour had fallen flat with her. There was a light of battle in her green eyes and a ring of steel in that douce Dublin voice. "That's all the past! It's now I'm talking about. We're back to civil war. Don't you read the papers?"

It was Ruarri who bailed me out and saved the face of the lady as well. "The truth is, Maeve, he can't read a line of print to save his soul. He's an old-fashioned sean-nachie. Does it all by dint of a prodigious memory and the services of pretty girls to write the stuff down for him. Seduces them all afterwards, I'm told."

This was the old Ruarri, and a glance at Alastair Morrison told me he liked him better than the bland fellow from the whisky advertisement.

Maeve O'Donnell showed her paces, too—with sickles on her chariot wheels! "Well! Well! I'd never have known it. He has such an educated look. You're not thinking of marrying him, are you, Kathleen?"

"He's asked me." She told it, bland and sweet as honey. "But I've told him I couldn't accept until he'd learned his letters and could write a check!"

We were saved by the roast and old Hannah waiting round with an ear cocked for scandal.

As he carved the mountain of beef, Alastair Morrison started a new line of talk. "You're an investor, Ruarri. You know there's loan money from the government to develop tourism. What would you do with a place like this if you had it?"

"With the land you've got? And the fishing rights tied to it?"

"Naturally."

"First I'd think about the season, which is short and chancy. So you have to make your money in three months, like they do in the Mediterranean. The rest of the year you close down, to cut the overheads. This house? I'd gut it. I'd put in a flat for the manager and the rest I'd turn into a central lodge—dining room, cocktail bar, television room and a quiet place for the old ones to read and write postcards. Then I'd go to the Swedes—no, better still, the East Germans or the Poles. I'd give them a design for cabins that would match the land and the climate. I'd have them prefabricated and erected around the shoreline. I'd buy boats from the same people, one boat to a cabin, each with an outboard motor. I'd charge high rents and top prices for drinks and food, and I'd have a three-year contract with a travel agency for ninety-percent occupancy. Anything over that would be gravy on the meat."

"If you'll forgive my asking, laddie—" Morrison paused with the carvers in midair—"did you give me all that off the cuff, or had you thought about it before?"

"I've thought about it every time I've passed the place."

"Would you like to buy it?"

"If I had the money, I'd give you a check now. But I haven't. I'm spread thin for the next twelve months at least. If you're serious, though, I'd like first offer."

"I'm serious, laddie. Not now, exactly, but possibly soon. I'd like to talk to you about it."

"I'll be here, whenever you name the time."

"I'd hate to see this lovely place spoilt." My Kathleen was very blunt. I was glad it was with Ruarri and not with me.

"Spoilt!" He rounded on her impatiently. "Come on, girl! If the building's good and it fits the landscape, where's the spoiling? The Isles are dying. They'll be stone cold dead in half a generation unless we get people back here. Tourism is the only thing that will bring 'em back—builders and gardeners and cooks and waiters and chambermaids and butchers and bakers and candlestick makers. I can't sell a lobster in London if it weighs over twenty-six ounces. I'm pulling 'em out of the pots three and four pounds apiece, and no one to eat 'em. Give me

106

a good chef and a good dining room and the guests will be shouting for lobster Newburg at New York prices!"

"That's a stale argument. There's a whole quality of life to be thought of first, and all the things you lose when you disrupt it without thought for the future. That's the ultimate horror of the puritan ethic. Work is sacred. Money is the key to a new earth and a new heaven!"

"It damn near is! Money's the variety and the lift and the drive that keeps you living. Money buys liberty. Money made you a doctor. Money changed deserts into farmland. Money put men on the moon. Money's what keeps us all from turning into little grey worms burrowing into the earth for safety."

"There are those who can never have it—and they're the majority on the planet." She was very terse with him. "There are those who want only enough for food and shelter and dignity. Where do they fit in?"

The implied reproof touched Ruarri on the raw. His answer was abrupt. "I wouldn't know. I wasn't born rich. I wasn't taught to be rich on nothing."

"Balls!" said Maeve O'Donnell. "You've never been hungry in your life, Ruarri Matheson, so what are you squalling about? You just love money. So do I. But you don't have to write a bloody gospel about it."

One instant I thought he would throttle her; the next he was bursting with laughter, as though she had made the greatest joke since Rabelais. "She's right! God help me—and my apologies to you, Mr. Morrison!—she knows me better than I know myself. Which is why I'd never marry her in a million years. You know what this woman does—this sweet, innocent piece of fashion plate? She breeds horses. She peddles 'em to princes and potentates. She touts for votes at election time. She foments civil disorder in between . . ."

"And if I were twenty years younger, I'd marry her myself," said Alastair Morrison.

"Try me now, Mr. Morrison," said Maeve O'Donnell. "I'm just in the mood."

There were some reckless things being said, and I thought I might as well add my own ten cents' worth and try my luck for the same money. So I called them to order and made them a little speech.

"Talking of marriage, ladies and gentlemen, Kathleen

McNeil has announced, without notice, that I have asked her to marry me. Ruarri Matheson has made it plain that I can't read or write. So I'm repeating the offer and putting down a small deposit for good faith and public witness."

With that I marched round the table and laid the locket in its open case before Kathleen. You know how you make omens for yourself? I made one then: if she wore the locket, I was home; if she put it back in the case, I was lost. She held it in her hands for a long moment, turning it over and over, feeling the worn surface of it, and the chain, pliable as plaited silk. I was standing behind her, so I could not see her face. Then she held the locket up to me. "May I wear it now, please?"

When I had clasped it round her neck, she drew me down and kissed me on the lips: a lover's kiss, with tenderness and time to enjoy it.

"Thank you, mo gradh—for the gift and for the loving."

Alastair Morrison beamed approval and raised his glass. "We should drink to that."

"It's a rare and beautiful moment." Maeve O'Donnell sighed like Deirdre of the Sorrows in rehearsal.

"I'll name the toast," said Ruarri the Mactire, and promptly did. "To the day when the seannachie signs the marriage register."

I laughed and said "Amen" and wished him roasting in hell.

Of course he wasn't and by all the symptoms he wouldn't be for a long time yet.

Still, we weren't doing too badly. The veneer was cracking off us all. There were sparks enough and smiles enough to keep the party alive, and Morrison enjoying himself.

Then—blast her green eyes!—Maeve O'Donnell dropped a match on the powder train. I was hardly back in my chair when she leaned across to Kathleen and announced, "The strangest thing! I've just noticed it."

"What's that?"

"Ruarri and Dr. Morrison. They're extraordinarily alike."

At that moment I thanked God I had told Kathleen nothing, because she reacted as normally as anyone who is asked to recognize a resemblance which has been missed at first glance. She looked from one to the other, then

108

said dubiously, "Well, I suppose there is a likeness. The eyes, perhaps, the facial bones. But I would never have noticed it."

"That's just the red hair and that great fungus of Ruarri's." Maeve turned the question to me. "You see it, don't you? Take away the beard now . . ."

By then I had had time to recover. I went through a pantomime of inspection, marvelling as I did so that Morrison could still sit, calm and smiling, on the edge of catastrophe. Then I made a joke of the whole idea. "You have to be in love with him, Maeve, or you need your eyes checked. That ugly mug of his belongs on a 'wanted' poster."

"I won't have our guests insulted." Morrison played up to the joke manfully. "It so happens I'm an expert on genealogies. Among the Morrison the women had the beauty and the men had the brains. With the Matheson it was the other way round—with some notable exceptions in both clans."

Whatever Ruarri's thoughts, they were hidden behind that facile smile. He would play whatever comedy was called. He turned to Kathleen and laid his head on her shoulder: the sad clown demanding to be comforted against the unkindness of the world. "Where would you say that leaves me, Kathleen oge?"

"Slap in the middle! Moderately brainy, moderately handsome, and much too opinionated for your own good."

"Kiss me, woman! You have the wisdom of Solomon himself and the beauty of Sheba—both wasted on that truaghan over there!"

I looked at Morrison. He gave me a faint smile of gratitude and poured himself another glass of wine. His hand was steady enough, but it was clear that he was tiring. His food was almost untouched and the grey look was creeping back. As the dessert was served, he begged to be excused for a few moments and left the room.

Hannah gave me a warning signal. I asked Kathleen, "Do you have your bag with you?"

"Yes. It's in the car. Why?"

"Morrison's not well. Hasn't been for days. He talked of a warning. I'm guessing it's his heart. Would you go upstairs and have a look at him? He won't like it, but I want you to insist."

"Don't worry. I'll insist."

As she hurried out of the room, Ruarri asked, "Would you like us to leave?"

"No. He wouldn't either. He's delighted to have you here."

"I'm glad. I'd like to know him better. He's a rare one in this dog's world."

"The liking's mutual. Why don't you come to see him as he asked?"

"I will."

Maeve O'Donnell laid a cool hand on mine, and the gesture said more than the words. "You relax now. We're all big enough to look after ourselves."

"He's a man with a conscience." Ruarri was at his old game again. "That's been the ruination of him. What about our day in the hills? Monday suit you?"

"I'm free, unless Morrison's in trouble."

"It's fixed then."

"A pity I'll be gone," said Maeve O'Donnell. "I'd have liked to spend a day with the pair of you."

It was on the tip of my tongue to ask what had brought her here in the first place, but I thought better of it. This lady was too bright by half and I had troubles enough.

We were alone for two minutes in the lounge while Ruarri went to the washroom and Hannah was still brewing the coffee. When I handed her the brandy, she gave me a big Irish smile and a nasty shock. "I'm in the racing business, so I never spread secrets. But I was right about Ruarri and Morrison, wasn't I?"

"I wouldn't know, lover girl."

"And you wouldn't say if you did. But here's a piece of advice from Sister Maeve. Take your girl to bed or to the altar or wherever and get the hell out of here. You'll never beat the local horse at a country meeting."

"A tip from the stable?"

"None better."

"When's the race?"

"They're at the barrier now."

"Who's the favourite?"

"The Mactire. The outsider's called Seannachie."

"I'd have a saver on him."

"I have. But the odds are against him. Hence the advice."

"You've got a personal interest?"

"Business and personal."

"Thanks for telling me."

"You're welcome. Good luck from me—but don't count on it."

Then Ruarri came back and a few minutes later Kathleen McNeil joined us for coffee. She was preoccupied and inclined to be terse.

"The ambulance will be here in a few minutes. If you don't mind, Ruarri, I'll pack the pair of you off as soon as you've finished your drinks."

Ruarri was on his feet in an instant. "Don't give it a thought. Get your coat, Maeve, we're on our way. How bad is it?"

"Not good, but he's safe for the night. We'll start the tests first thing in the morning."

"You'll let me know the results? And, seannachie, if there's the least thing I can do, call me. I'll come running. Good night to you both and our respects to Morrison."

"And thanks for the dinner," said Maeve O'Donnell.

Two minutes later they were gone and we were sitting by the fire with Hannah hovering over us, tearful but determined.

"You're giving me the truth now, young woman? You're not going to cut him up or anything like that, you promise me?"

"I promise you, Hannah. It's exactly as I've told you. His heart's damaged. It needs time and rest to heal, and doctors and nurses watching him until he's well again."

"How well? Tell me that honestly!"

"Never perfect. But with good years still."

"God bless you for that word, anyway. Can I go with him to the hospital?"

"No. He'll go in the ambulance. We'll follow in the car. When he's settled and comfortable, we'll come back here. Can you put me up for the night?"

"Can I put you up! The house is yours from cellar to ceiling. What do you want me to pack for the poor mannie?"

"Nothing, Hannah. I've done it all."

"But you'll call me before he goes."

"I will."

"I'll be clearing away then. Better than standing around just thinking."

She hurried out, nursing her private grief in the old dour way, the tears soon spent, the plaint going on and on inside like the cry of the gulls. I found myself grieving with her, for the presumptuous folly I had committed, for the needless, pointless hurt to the man who was lying upstairs, with the dark watchman just outside the door. I wanted to go to him, but Kathleen held me back.

"He's resting, my love. Leave him be. I need him quiet."

"Did he say anything?"

"To thank you for the dinner. And there's something in his desk he wants you to deal with."

"Nothing else?"

"That's all. I think I've guessed the rest of it."

"It wasn't hard. After that bloody comedy at dinner. Who the hell is Maeve O'Donnell, anyway?"

"I was going to ask you the same question."

"I know only what was said. And I don't give a damn for the rest. Christ! What a stinking mess!"

"Not all of it. I have my locket, remember?"

"I'm glad you wore it."

It was the conventional thing to say, the nice, polite, thoughtful, a-gentleman-never-gives-hurt-to-others kind of thing that I'd been saying all night. I'd been nursing Alastair Morrison, who'd had a good life, anyway. I'd been planning a prodigal's homecoming for Ruarri Matheson, who had whored his way around the world and sold himself for a killer at auction. I'd been playing a pretty, Edwardian love game with Kathleen, who'd had a child sucked out of her with a vacuum tube to please some half-grown actor and now wasn't quite sure whether she could or she couldn't be in love any more. . . . Well, to hell with it! To hell with them one and all! To hell with Kathleen, too, if the fruit was there on the tree and she couldn't make up her mind between apples and gooseberries. I was bone-tired, bitched and bewildered and bored to extinction by the antics of this inbred little group living on the edge of nowhere.

But when the ambulance came and they carried Alastair Morrison down, and he pressed my hand and murmured his private word of thanks, I was trapped again, seduced by the pity I would one day need myself, robbed

112

of the anger which was my only armour. But not all of it, not quite all.

We drove back from the hospital under a clear sky and a cold moon. When we reached the house, Hannah was still awake, with the fire built up and the tea made, waiting for our news. When she heard it, she murmured a prayer of thanks and, in a rare display of emotion, laid hands on our heads for a kind of blessing. She would sleep quiet now, knowing the Morrison was in good hands. She would pray for us both before she slept. We should lie late in bed and the girls would not disturb us.

We finished our tea and it was two in the morning. Kathleen carried the tray out to the kitchen. When she came back I took her in my arms and told her I wanted her—now, this night—and I would not wait for any tomorrow.

Her answer was swift and simple. "I want you too, mo gradh. I'm ready."

I have nothing to tell you of our loving, save that it was rich, and wild and wonderful, with a long, sweet calm afterwards. Once, in the early cold hours, I woke and heard her muttering and stirring in her sleep. There were names in the muttering and one of them was Ruarri. I felt a sudden, sharp pang of resentment, but when I drew her to me, she gave a small sigh of pleasure and woke slowly to be loved again. After that I was too triumphant to care. Sleep was the country of the dead and there was no threat to me in a jigsaw fantasy of dreaming.

VII

If you've been there, you know what it's like. If
you haven't, no poet in the world can teach you the
geography of the love country: the land always green, the
flowers spilling over it, the fruits ripe for picking every
day, the people all beautiful, private to themselves but
companionable, too, the sun warm and the dawn golden
and the nights secret and secure, and a soft, new language
easy to learn and apt for daytime or the hours of dark.
You can do the wildest things in it—stand on your head,
walk on your hands, shout, laugh, cry, roll in the flowers
without a stitch on your hide—and they all make wonderful sense. You can wear the country, too, like the
cloak of invisibility. You can carry it about, like a mirror
in your pocket, and see every colour of it at a single
glance. And others can see it on you, in you and around
you and wonder how you found the way to it.

In the morning Kathleen and I were there. Old Hannah,
who had a very knowing eye and the second sight as well,
needed no telling. She clucked over us at breakfast like a
mothering hen and made no secret of her approval.

"If that's the way it is, that's the way it was planned, I
always say. There's good in the bad and bad in the good,
and the pair of you seem to have grabbed the best of it.
How or when, it's not my business to know—and I wouldn't
ask. I'm a sound sleeper, thank God, even at the worst of
times; but this morning there were new roses in the garden
and that's always the making of a happy day. The Morrison will be glad too. Though maybe you won't want to
say anything until it's an engagement, legal-like. But he'll
need cheering and he's fond of you both. Tell him I wish
him well and want him back—but not a day before he's
ready. . . ."

Which reminded me that Morrison had left a message in his desk for me. Before we set off for the hospital, I went to see what it was. There was a sealed envelope addressed to Ruarri Matheson and a note for me, obviously written the previous afternoon. I read it, with Kathleen looking over my shoulder.

. . . I do not know how the dinner will go, but I am glad and grateful that you have given me the courage to attempt it. I have had so little courage of late, so little strength for unfamiliar situations. Even after I had invited you from Rome, I regretted it. I did not want a stranger in my house. Now you are not a stranger and I am happy you came.

After our talk that noontime, I made a decision. I want Ruarri to know who I am and who he is. He has been deprived too long of the fundamental birthright of identity. I beg you to believe that I am not afraid to tell him myself; but I want him to be free to reject the identity, and reject me, too, if he wishes, without the embarrassment of a personal confrontation. I am afraid of myself, you see. The condition from which I am suffering is such that any sudden emotion may bring on a heart attack, and I would not have that happen, lest he bend to me in pity and hate me for having to do it. If he comes, it must be because he wants to come. I have explained this in my letter, omitting all mention of my illness.

I want you to give the letter into his hands. I charge you with no other responsibility than this, which I know is already too much; but I have no one else to whom I can turn. I absolve you from all secrecy, so that you may answer any question Ruarri asks—if indeed he wants to ask any at all. I hope you will absolve me, in charity, from the guilt of this imposition. You came here for healing. I have done nothing but inflict a new wound. A sad comment on my own frailty. My thanks, anyway, and my regrets and my affection.

Alastair Morrison

It was a letter to weep over, but a noble one. Yesterday I would have read it differently, as an intolerable charge to lay on any man. Today I accepted it willingly, even, I

115

think, with joy. I was rich overnight. I was brim-full, pressed down, running over with happiness. I could be the greatest spendthrift in the world and still be rich tomorrow.

Which is one of the problems of living in the love country. You forget that it is a place of illusions and, once you step outside it, you are more vulnerable than before. You have forgotten the traps and the ambushes, the pits that open every mile under your unwary feet. The language you have learned is a meaningless babble. The cloak of invisibility doesn't make you invisible at all. You are just a silly fellow prancing along naked with all his parts a-dangle in the breeze. The mirror simply gives you back your own face, which is a clown's mask, smeared with custard pie. But how was I to know all that, with the glow still on me, and Kathleen leaning over me, with her hands inside my shirt, telling me I was the dearest, tenderest, wisest and most generous man in all the world?

So the decision was quickly made. This wise and tender and generous man would find a propitious time to visit Ruarri and deliver the letter and stand by him, in brotherly fashion, to help him bear the shock and adjust happily to the new and saving knowledge. After that we had a problem of our own to solve: another small matter of geography. Kathleen was a working medico, paid to keep the good folk of Harris healthy while the regular incumbent was on holiday. She had a few patients in Stornoway Hospital, but her practice was down at the other end of the island, forty, fifty miles away, depending on which road you took, and none of them were wonderful. She lived in the doctor's house with an elderly housekeeper for company. I did not dare spend a night there, else the scandal would be all over the village next morning. At the lodge we were safe so long as Morrison was in hospital, but there would be nights and days when we would be far apart or else coasting the bleak countryside and bundling in the back of a car. All this we discussed as we drove into Stornoway to see Morrison, and found no solution to it, only that we would meet whenever we could and take our comfort wherever we found it.

As it turned out, I did not see Morrison. They had him under sedation and did not want him disturbed. However, Kathleen's report was not too discouraging. If he survived the next few days, he would mend enough to resume a quiet life; but he would always be a man with a sword hung over his head. Which made it the more imperative that the weight of worry should be taken off him and the business of Ruarri favourably resolved. Kathleen drove me back to Laxay, then, after all too short a farewell, went on to Harris and her clutch of ailing islanders. I sought out Fergus William McCue for a couple of hours' fishing before lunch.

It was a mistake. Fergus William was in a maudlin humour. Morrison's illness had shaken him badly. I caught no fish, but I got two hours of theme and variations on the Grim Reaper and the grasses of the field. In that time—how long, dear Lord, how long—I was made cognizant of every creak in Fergus' bones, every flutter of his pulse, with drink taken and without, every wheeze and rhonchus in his pipes. I relived the last hours of his wife, "and her so patient, the poor bonny lass, but wasting away every minute and every hour with the horrible mess inside her." I heard the tragic tale of Malcolm Moray, a giant of a man, six feet three in his socks, with a chest on him like a barrel, who could toss a caber like none other in the Isles, and had begotten five sons and four daughters, and there he was, no more than forty, struck down in the middle of the night without warning. When they buried him it took eight men to carry the coffin, and although only two of them were drunk, they dropped it twice on the way to the graveside. Then, for the awesome irony of it, there was Alison Macaulay, still living at ninety, but she'd lost three daughters, all under thirty, one from the coughing sickness and the other was run down by a car, and the third—well, that was a sad story and not much talked about, though there was rumour of her dying in childbirth on the mainland, which could have been true, but there was never a record of the wedding. Before the litany of lamentations was ended, I was ready to move Job off his dunghill and sit there mourning my own imminent demise.

It was a soul-shaking experience, but at least it decided one issue for me. I might as well have all my griefs on the same day. So when I got back to the lodge I telephoned Ruarri's house, told him how Morrison was and asked if I could drop in to see him after lunch. He asked me to make it at six; otherwise he'd lose half a day's rent on the tractor. Besides, that way he could give me a drink and fix me a meal if I cared. That left me with an afternoon to kill. I spent it reading and dozing by the fire. Take it all in all, I had had a rather exhausting night, and I had no desire to be struck down with such promising days ahead of me.

By the time I got to Ruarri's house I had every gambit rehearsed. First move, the greetings and the pleasantries; then the first drink poured; then myself handing over the envelope and saying:

"Morrison asked me to give you this. I know part of what's in it. So pour me another drink and I'll wait outside while you read it. When you're ready, call me in or send me home. It's all the same to me."

Then I would take my drink and walk out into the warm, soft twilight and think of the brotherly words he would need afterwards. He would call me in; we would drink a little more to take the edge off the world; he would cook the meal; we would make a fraternal communion of it; he would be filled with the spirit of understanding and forgiveness and love; he would beg me to lead him to Morrison's bedside and leave him there, hushed and humble, to be gathered to his father's bosom.

In fact, the way of it was slightly different.

Shortly after six I walked into his house and found him, still grubby from work, sitting behind the bar with a glass of whisky in his hand. He gave a shout of welcome, then looked me up and down and sideways and laughed, "You smell of it, seannachie! The milk's all over your whiskers. And if you want to curl up by the fire and purr the night away, I won't blame you! Yes or no?"

"You stink yourself! Go take a shower. But pour me a drink first."

"Where's Kathleen?"

"Working. More's the pity."

"Morrison?"

"I called the hospital before I left the lodge. He's resting. They hope he'll make it. Where's Maeve?"

"In London by now, I should think. Then Paris."

"Did you buy the horse?"

"Not yet. What did you think of her?"

"Quite a girl. Are you interested?"

"Was. Not any more. She's too damned intelligent to live with. But we still do business together. Slainte!"

"Slainte."

"That was a good dinner party."

"Glad you enjoyed it. By the way, I've got a letter for you from Morrison."

"I'll read it in the bath. Help yourself to the drinks. Read a good book. Turn on the television if you're interested."

I wasn't. I poured myself another dram of malt whisky —fifteen years old, good enough to embalm an emperor —and walked out into the garden. The air was warm, but I was as cold as death. I plucked a green bean from the vine and nibbled on it the way the Italians do, but the taste was bitter and I spat it out. A homing shepherd called a greeting to me; I returned it mechanically and envied him the quiet incoming. Away in the distance a dog yelped and a child's voice went shouting after it. After that, silence. I paced the gravelled path up and down, up and down, like a monk telling an endless rosary of other men's dolours. Except that I wasn't a monk and Ruarri wasn't either and Morrison had been, but a trifle too late. After a long time I finished the whisky and went in to pour myself another.

Ruarri, bathed and dressed in fresh clothes, was waiting for me with the letter spread on the bar in front of him. His face was a wooden mask. I set down the glass. He filled it and pushed it back to me. He tapped the letter with his forefinger and said, "You had to know about this, seannachie."

"I did. But I didn't ask to know."

"I want to believe you."

I took from my pocket Morrison's letter to me and handed it across the bar.

He read it slowly, digesting every word. Then he folded it and gave it back. "I believe you now. Tell me the rest of it."

I told him the what and the how and the when. The why I could tell him only in the same fumbling way as the Morrison had told it to me: that a bird might fall or a tree might topple for no reason that could be put into words. He accepted that, too, reluctantly. Then the cross-examination began.

"But it was you who suggested the dinner party?"

"Yes."

"Therefore you made a judgment?"

"I was asked to make it."

"By Morrison only."

"That's true."

"You didn't consult me."

"I couldn't. I was bound by a secret."

"You were my friend. You kept the chessman."

"I couldn't be a true friend to one and a false friend to the other. Right or wrong, I was trying to do the best for both."

"Who else knows about this?"

"No one. Only Morrison and I."

"You'll swear that?"

"I swear it."

I was swearing a lie, too; but if I could not trust Kathleen, I might as well cut my throat.

"I hate you, seannachie."

"I'm sorry about that."

"But you don't know why?"

"No."

"Then I'll tell you. Because you knew when I didn't know. And you judged when I couldn't judge. And you can go on judging—right and wrong, black and white—when I'm still tumbling round in a confusion you'll never understand."

"You've no right to say that."

"I haven't, but I'm still saying it. Hating and loving come from the guts and the balls, not from the head. I'm telling you something true, seannachie. Believe it, for Christ's sake."

"So I believe it. Now what?"

"That's the big question, isn't it? Now what . . . ? Got any answers?"

"I'd like another drink."

"So would I."

He poured them, one and one, large enough for a horse, and pushed my glass back to me. We sat facing each other across the countertop, like a pair of heavies out of some old-fashioned movie. Finally I had to laugh, and Ruarri, ready as always, laughed too.

"Funny, funny, funny. Daddy has his son. Sonny has

his dad. They both live happily ever after. Sing, sing ye angel bands. Is that it, seannachie? Is that the way you'd write it?"

"I'm not writing it. I'm just the messenger boy."

"So you are. I forgot that. Let me write it then, and if you don't like the script, just remember I'm a poor, ignorant boy from the Lews with no learning in him at all. It starts like this. There's a father, Morrison, who in the gaudy days of his youth had a son whom his family for a hundred good reasons wouldn't let him acknowledge. Later in life—not too much later, mind you—he gets religion and goes off to look after the children of the heathen, leaving his own offspring still unacknowledged. Now he's old and tired and sick and feeling guilty and he'd like to cleanse his conscience and have his son back and love him tenderly and die at peace. Now is that a fair statement or isn't it?"

"It's true, but . . ."

"No! Forget the *but's!* Let's go back to the boy. He's not Morrison's son. He's Ruarri the Bastard, son of Anne Matheson of Gisla. That's the record. I've seen it written twenty times on a shithouse wall, carved into the top of a desk: Ruarri the Bastard. Not nice, mind you, but he wears it. Not easy, but he's growing tougher now. Soon he'll be having his first girl and getting his first beating in an alley and his first dose of clap. After that he grows up fast—still no daddy, but the need for him's fading now. After that . . . Well! You fill in the rest, seannachie—it's all the commonplaces you've ever read or written. And now Ruarri the Bastard's home again with money and ships and a croft and prospects bigger still. Does he need Daddy? The hell he does! Does he want Daddy—to fill the deep, dark holes in his spirit? The hell again! Daddy's a bloody albatross hung round his neck. Daddy's a gentleman, which Ruarri the Bastard isn't and doesn't want to be, because this is a rough, randy world, and he's seen it all and he knows it's going to get rougher still, and that's when the bastards will come into their own. You know what I think about Daddy? I think he's a good, sweet, stuffy Scots gentleman, and I'm sorry he's got a bad heart, but we all get something, and I hate his bloody guts from now to eternity. Amen."

"You'll tell him that, of course?"

"I don't have to tell him or not tell him. He'll know. Then he can sweat it out, just the way I did."

"I'll tell you something, Matheson. He'll do just that. He will sweat it out. And he'll never say another word about it, just because he is the stuffy Scots gentleman you think he is. And he'll do it with more goddam grace than you'll muster in a lifetime. Wrong he was. But it took a big man to write that letter—bigger than you are, boy. Much bigger."

I thought he might swing at me; and if he did he would get the liquor in his eyes and a broken bottle shoved in his face, because if I let him get close he could kill me. But he didn't move. He just stood there behind the bar, staring at me as though he didn't quite believe what he had heard. Then, damn me, he was grinning, then chuckling, then laughing, on and on as if he had heard the funniest joke in the world since Adam lost a rib and got a woman to make up for it.

"You're a rough one yourself, aren't you, seannachie? You don't look it. You've got all the literary talk, and the nice manners, yes sir, no sir, three bags full, sir, all present and correct, sir; but by Christ, you fight as dirty as I do! You had one hand on the glass and the other ready to reach for the bottle and smash it on the bar. You've been around, laddie. The only difference between us is that you know more words than I do, and you think like a snake, all sinuous and shifty. But you're stupid tonight. You're just hearing the words. You haven't one idea in all the world what they really mean."

"So you tell me, Ruarri. I'm a dumb Sassenach. You tell me!"

He told me. He told me quietly and bitterly, leaning across the bar, his red beard wagging at me, his eyes boring into me like live coals into a plank. "I'm bleeding, seannachie. I'm hurting as though someone has shoved a knife into my belly and is winding my guts round it like spaghetti. I'm crying, seannachie, but all the tears dried up twenty years ago and the grief can't get out any more. I'm hating, too, because the hate is the only thing I've had to keep me alive; and I lost the way of loving, with no one to teach it to me. You know what I'd like now? A woman! I'd like her to come and take me in her arms and let me cry on her breast and soothe me to sleep and

122

wake me when I'd forgotten all the shit of this lousy world. But if she came, I'd tumble her like a whore and pay her and send her home without a thank-you. So don't sit there, laddie, all toffee-nosed and secure in whatever little philosophy you have. Don't judge me for big or small, against Morrison or anyone else. You haven't the right. You haven't the knowing. Although I think you've got the caring, else I'd have been over the bar and at your throat a minute ago. And I could be still if I thought for half a second I was wrong in you."

I should have ended it there and then, because he had given me all the truth he knew about himself and I could not and would not tell him mine. He was waiting for it, I knew. He was waiting for the one good word that would crack the ice round his heart and let the spring flow and the tears run. I had all the words in the dictionary, but not that one. The best I could find to say was a banality. "I can't argue it with you, Ruarri. I haven't lived in your skin. I agree I have no right to judge you. I'm sorry for the hard words. Thanks for the drink. I'll be running along."

"I invited you to dinner, seannachie. I'm a good cook, though you mightn't believe it."

"I'll keep you honest then. Can I lend a hand?"

"Sure. You can peel vegetables and lay table. The cookery needs a lighter touch than you've got. Pour us another drink while I get started."

By the time the meal was ready, we were moving in a nice rosy glow, like the sunset after a big storm. We were eloquent, inconsequential, comical, anecdotic, bawdy and wiser than Socrates in all our conclusions. We were brothers-in-arms, gory and quarrelsome maybe, but, by God, brothers always. The meal was a masterpiece: trout and Black Angus steak and strawberries from the garden and a Burgundy of good vintage with not a penny of excise paid on it—which made it twice as good. Then, lest the glow should fade and we find ourselves back in the troubled outer darkness, there was a goblet of brandy and a coffee made from bean to cup, so that no whit of essence or aroma should be lost. All this time there was no word of Morrison or indeed of anything that touched the core of the matters between us.

We cleared off the table and stacked the dishes in the

123

washer, because we were both tidy fellows who could not be comfortable in a messy ship. We built up the fire and the brandy, stacked records on the player—En Saga and the Sibelius Fourth, which almost surprised me into sobriety—and settled down to be quiet.

This part of the evening was like our day on shipboard: free and easy, with the wind and the sea singing through the music, the talk spontaneous and the silences grateful. Ruarri was a great gabman when he wanted to be, but he had a gift of silence, too, when there was no one around whom he had to impress. Observing him now, drowsy in the fire glow, I saw that there was a rhythm in the silence and in the speaking. He would sink back, far into himself, in an almost animal passivity. Then something would stir in him, a half thought, a memory, and you could almost see it unfolding, growing, filling him up until it had to break out in a swift, tumbling torrent of words. When the words were spent, he was spent, too, and the cyclic renewal would begin again. But, even in the passive times, at the moment of deepest withdrawal, he was alert to every external stimulus, to every sound, every change of light, every tone of voice and attitude. He was never absent from things. Things were always close to him, always threatening, as though the energy locked inside them might explode at any moment if he were unprepared.

It was this sense of constant danger that made him dangerous to himself and to others. He felt himself so constantly besieged he could not afford the slightest risk. He had to compute every possible treachery, preempt every strike. If he were wrong, it was a pity, but at least he was still alive. Even the risks he took—and they were many and large—were preemptions against risks still greater which he either saw or imagined. I would not have you believe that I saw all this through the rosy glow of whisky and wine and brandy and Sibelius. I saw the phenomenon; I was blind to its meaning. When my eyes were opened at last, it was already too late for all of us.

It was late and I was thinking reluctantly of the drive home when Ruarri came out of one of his silences and said abruptly:

"We have to settle something, seannachie."

"What's that?"

"Morrison. You'll be visiting him, of course. What are you going to tell him?"

"Well, I can tell it three ways. I left the letter with you and I haven't heard from you yet. That's a lie, but I'm prepared to tell it for you. I gave you the letter, you were shaken and confused and you wanted time to sort yourself out. That's near enough to the truth to let us both off the hook. Or can I tell him that you understand why he sent it, that you respect his intentions but you'd rather not have any part of the relationship because it's too late in the day and too hard for both sides. Which is about the size of what was said before dinner. The last way's clean—if you're sure it's what you want. The others leave loose ends. They have to be tied off sooner or later. That's the best rendering I can give you, I'm afraid."

"Would Morrison leave it clean?"

"I know he would. I'd stake my life on it."

"Which is more than you would with me, eh?"

"I didn't say that. And don't spoil a good dinner."

"I'm sorry. I didn't mean it. Would Morrison leave it clean another way?"

"You've lost me now."

"You're drunk, seannachie. So I'll spell it for you. Morrison's old and he's sick and he's tried to do a decent thing. It's too late, but he's tried. I've got enough blood on my hands. I don't want any more. Are you hearing me?"

"I'm hearing you."

"So I give you another message for Morrison. I have his letter. I thank him for it. One day, when he's well and I'm less confused than I am now, I'll come and talk to him. I'll say hail and farewell just the same. But I'll say it like a gentleman because he's one and then we call it quits. Would he leave that one clean—no clinging, no tricks, no claim or judgment on what I do afterwards?"

"No claim, certainly. Judgment's a private matter always."

"You're a bloody Jesuit!"

"Just getting the message straight—in case you want to send it."

"Shut up then and let me think about it!"

He went to the bar and poured himself another brandy; then he went back into silence, long and deep this time,

125

while I closed my eyes and let the music roll over me like clean, deep water, free from all the offal of the world. The next thing I knew, Ruarri was shaking me awake. He was standing over me with a slip of notepaper in his hand and a rather tired grin on his face. "On your feet, seannachie! Time to go home."

"What's the message?"

"The way I gave it to you. I'll see Morrison when he's well. That's all. Except you can give him this to read. He might get a smile out of it."

He shoved the paper under my nose, and for a moment I thought I was still drunk because the words were unintelligible: ". . . ma's olc dhomh cha n-fhearr dhaibh."

"What the hell's that?"

"That, seannachie, is my summary of this whole goddam silly mess. When the great Conan went down to hell and his backside was frying on the hot plate, he looked around at all the rest of the damned and said those noble words: 'If it's bad for me, it's no better for them.' Now get the hell out of here, because there's a girl on her way over and I need no advice about what to do with her."

VIII

I DROVE HOME, SINGING, UNDER A SKY FULL OF MISTY stars. The songs were tuneless on my lips, but in my head, melodious and clear: "Ena Dilino," the song of the warring brothers, killing each other for an idea, dead and disproved already; "O Ilios," the sun that sees the stinking midden of man's earth and turns to ice; "Kaymos," the grief of every man feeling his sap dry out, his belly shrink, and half the wine of life still untasted.

The songs were sad. And yet I was not sad; at least I did not think I was. I had kept a friendship. I had re-

126

stored—or half restored—a bond between a man and his son. Today, this very new today, was the Sabbath, when no one under the dispensation of the Free Kirk could possibly fall sick and I could have the whole calm, beautiful, private day with Kathleen McNeil. Doxa to Theo . . . bless the Lord in all His works and days!

The Lord, for all the black marks against me, must have had a kindly eye on me that night, because I came safe to the lodge, with no bones broken and no scratch on the car. In my room I found a bottle of beer and a cheese sandwich and a scrawled note from Hannah: "The Morrison's better. The lady phoned. She'll be here after breakfast. If you're up by nine I'll feed you. If not there'll be coffee on the stove and you can fix for yourself." I drank the beer and wolfed the sandwich and blessed them one and all and went to bed.

The waking was sweeter than the sleeping: a kiss on the lips and Kathleen sitting on the bed and the house empty, because Hannah and her girls were off about their Sunday duties. It was a braw bright morning, but we drew the blinds to make a night for ourselves; and, when the night was over, I told the story of my meeting with Ruarri, and I was, all over again, the tenderest and wisest man in the world. Then we bathed together and dressed together and made ourselves a late breakfast and a picnic lunch and set off to tell the good news to Alastair Morrison.

He knew it already. In fact he had more news than I had. With his breakfast tray that morning he had received a note and a package from Ruarri. The package contained the snake locket which I had seen in his house. The note was dashed off in that bold scribe's hand, without erasure or alteration:

Dear Morrison,

Your courier arrived last night. We exchanged a lot of hard words; then we got drunk together. After that I went to bed with a girl, which made me feel better able to cope with a rather confused situation. I gave the courier a message to deliver to you. It included Conan's word on his sojourn in hell. It seemed rather apt last night, because hell's a place I'm very familiar with.

When I woke this morning, however, I felt that a Matheson should not be behindhand in courtesy to a Morrison. Hence this note. I find I'm glad I know who I am and who you are. I don't think we need to do anything about it at this moment. I'm not sure I want to do anything about it at all. You have to get well and I have work to do and neither of us needs a big drama.

Rights and wrongs I think we should forget. I've a list of wrongs as long as your arm and quite a lot are wrongs I've done myself. Forgiving? That's a Christian word I don't know much about. I'm not a Christian and the world I live in isn't either. There it's eye for eye and blood for blood. But I don't want your blood, since I share it with you.

For the rest, if and when we meet, we can meet with respect. If you want to sell me the lodge at some time, I'll buy if I can afford it, at a fair price; but I don't want wills and bequests or anything like that. What I own, I've earned; I am not beholden to any man. You gave me life. It's a gift with a sting in it, but I have it.

My gift is a Viking piece. It's supposed to protect the wearer against death or disaster to his sexual parts. You may find it appropriate on both counts. No more now. I want you to have this before your courier gets back to you. I like him very well, but I want to see him taken down a peg. He's a bastard, too, and you can tell him so from me.

Let things lie now. Get yourself well.

Ruarri Matheson

I folded the letter and handed it back to Morrison. His hand was steady, and whether it was the drugs they had given him or his true feeling, he seemed tranquil and satisfied.

"It's better than I dared to hope. Much better."

"And the locket says even more than the letter. It's precious to him. I'd do as he asks now. Let things lie a while."

"I will. I will. You must have had a bad time last night."

"A shouting match, soon over. A slight hangover. But

128

that's gone too. Kathleen and I are going off to the beach. She'll sleep at the lodge tonight."

"The place is yours. And I mean that. Enjoy it."

"We will."

He smiled and took my hand in his own. "Is that the way of it?"

"That's the way of it. Do you mind?"

"Laddie, I've just been looking over the wall. I'm not scared of the crossing any more. I've learnt something. The only thing that makes life bearable on this side is the loving you find along the way. If you and Kathleen have found it, good luck to you. If you can leave a little in my house, I'll be glad to have it."

"Thanks."

"Thanks to you."

"I won't see you tomorrow. I'll be out in the mountains with Ruarri."

"Good. I'm glad you're still friends. Look after your girl."

"She's waiting to see you now. Then we'll be on our way."

"God bless you, laddie."

I brought Kathleen in to him and left them to be private together. Ten minutes later we were a public scandal, driving out to the eastern beaches while the good people of the Lews were tramping to kirk in their best clothes. The scandal was soon over, however, because the crofts thinned out the farther we went from town and the tourists were all in the south and west, mercifully ignorant of the small corner of paradise to which we were heading: a narrow, sheltered cove with grassland running down to a white beach, and a great buttress of rock to shield us from the wind and hold the warmth of the sun.

The water was cold, but we plunged in, shouting, and swam a long way out, until the sandy bottom dropped away and we could feel the deep suck of the ocean current. Then we turned back to the beach and stripped off our wet clothes and towelled each other and stretched out naked on the warm, soft sand.

I wish I could celebrate for you—but more for myself —the quiet glory of that afternoon. I find I cannot. The coinage of love words has been so much debased that what was a sweetness to me might make for another a sadness or a laughter. We are such ridiculous animals in sum, but not all or always. When the mood is right and the hands are tender and the lips are hungry, the body is a shining miracle, a leaping ecstasy, a slow, sweet decline, repeated over and over again and always new. If you want a list of pleasures, go to a pimp. If you want an anatomy, go to a surgeon. Do not come to me. But for loving—yes, I know about that: the folly and the delight and the sometime terror of it.

That afternoon, when we were warm and placid and Kathleen was lying drowsy in the crook of my arm, I asked her:

"Do you think you could be pregnant now?"

"I know I'm not, darling. Why? Are you worried?"

"No. I thought it might be rather nice. We'd have to get married then."

"What's the hurry?"

"I'm greedy. I want you all to myself."

"You couldn't have any more of me, dear heart. There isn't any."

I was wondering about that, although I didn't dare to put it into words. The dictionary of love is very short. The words tend to repeat themselves. Once she had given herself to another man, as she was now given to me. I had given myself to another woman, no less generously in the beginning. For that first man she had done the ultimate: she had killed, she had violated her inmost self. I could never ask so brutal a proof, but I could and did ask myself the question: would her giving to me be as complete as her giving to him? My own surrender was absolute, unconditional. At least I believed it was. I did not see, being as blind as the little man in the fig tree, that the question itself implied a condition and a demand as brutal as dying.

She sat up, naked, beside me, scooped up a handful of sand and poured it slowly on my chest. She said:

"I don't want to get married yet."

"Scared?"

"No."

"Why, then?"

"Because . . . because we're here, and we're happy. . . ."

"Wouldn't we be just as happy afterwards?"

"Probably. But don't you see, we'd have to be happy then. We'd be forced into it, because a messy marriage is a hell and we both know it, and we'd have that over our heads all the time. As it is now, we're free, so we're giving freely. You could be off with another girl. I could be off with another man. But we're here, together. I like the feeling. It's a new experience. Do you understand?"

"I do, Kathleen oge. I do. . . ."

I did and I didn't. But I couldn't tell her that this wise man was a fool who couldn't take a flower as a flower and be glad of it, but had to pull it to pieces, petal by petal, to make sure it wasn't made of some clever synthetic. I couldn't tell her that this tender fellow had discovered in himself a child, jealous and possessive and insecure as any five-year-old; that this crusader for the rights of man was balking at the most fundamental right of all: to be private at the core of oneself, beyond the violation of words or questions. I couldn't tell her that her bold lover was so uncertain of himself that he needed a document to prove he had won a woman again; that he was so emptied of faith in his talent that he needed a hand to guide his reluctant pen back to work, and smooth his rumpled hair when he wrote balderdash.

So I surrendered to her, and she was happy and praised my patient understanding. She settled down beside me again and we lay close and comforted each other on the sand. The Eden apple was ours. We needn't rush the eating of it. I saw the tiny wormhole in the fruit, but I sealed it up and painted it over and told myself the worm would die very soon and the apple would still be sound for tomorrow.

In the fall of the evening we drove back to the lodge and found Hannah singing in the kitchen:

> Hear this, all people and give ear,
> All in the world that dwell,
> Both high and low, both rich and poor,
> My mouth shall wisdom tell.

It took a little exegesis to recognize it as the Forty-ninth Psalm in the version of the Scottish Psalmody; and it needed a more patient ear than mine to discern a melody in Hannah's high, nasal rendition.

But she was happy and there would be scones for tea and a fruitcake and shortbreads and honey and strawberry jam. It had been a grand service. Minister Macphail had preached a wonderful homily on the duties of spouses one to another, and when he came to the big ranty bit about the defilement of the marriage bed, there were one or two red faces and some sniffles from certain people she could name but wouldn't. The scones were from that young Mrs. Sinclair, who had made a better fist of them now she'd taken Hannah's advice about the sifting of the flour and letting the air into the mixture. The fruitcake came from Madame Jobson which was one of the few things she could cook and would be no better or no worse than it usually was. The shortbreads were out of a packet, but the Morrison liked to nibble them now and then. The poor mannie was better? God be praised. She would make time to see him tomorrow. One of Fergus' boys would drive her up. Oh, and there was a call for me from that Ruarri Matheson. I was to meet him at the croft not a minute after nine in the morning and be dressed for the mountains. And would the doctor be good enough to call the district nurse in Harris? Nothing urgent, just for some advice, she said. The number was on the pad in the Morrison's study.

When Kathleen went to the phone, Hannah gave me a conspirator's wink and beckoned me into the kitchen. There she took my hands and pressed them to her lips and still held them while she talked. She wasn't rasping or chiding now. She was just an old lady, clinging and caring.

"I prayed for you this morning, for the two of you, because you loved the Morrison when he needed it. The Lord spoke to me. He gave me words to say to you. You've had the light at the coming. If you go now, you can take it with you. If you stay, you'll lose it. And there's danger for you in the dark. That's the Lord's word, laddie, not mine. I don't even know what it means, but I'm too old for Him to lie to me."

"I'll go soon, Hannah. When Dr. McNeil is finished, we'll both go."

"I hope it's soon enough."

"It will be. Don't worry."

Then I kissed her on the cheek and the skin was old and dry, like parchment, with a whole life written on it.

For one brief moment she clung to me and then, always ashamed of tenderness, pushed me out of the kitchen and went back to her singing while the kettle boiled. Once again the odd experience was repeated. I heard the words, but did not understand them. I was an actor in the incident. The moment it was over, it was as if it had happened to another man. I walked back into the lounge, poured myself a whisky, picked up a book and read until Kathleen came down for tea. She could not stay the night, she told me. An elderly patient was showing signs of pneumonia. She had better see him and be on call during the night. It was a disappointment, but not a bad one. Our day had been almost perfect. Alone or together, we were ready for a quiet night.

When Kathleen had left, I hunted Morrison's shelves for books on *Cervus elaphus*—which, in case you're as ignorant as I was, is the red deer of the Highlands and Isles. I was a novice at the sport of stalking, and I didn't want to make a complete fool of myself. Besides, Ruarri, with his boys in tow, would be stalking me as well as the stag. Like the lads of the Mafia, he mightn't always get mad, but as sure as God made little apples, he had to get even, in joke or earnest. So I needed to be at least half ready for him.

Deer-stalking, I found, was a sport for gentlemen, with a very ungentlemanly history to it. In the old, old days, deer were the property of the king, the baron, or the laird, and any hungry lout who killed one was hunted and destroyed more savagely than the beast itself. They were hunted first with hounds that were slipped cold in packs to pull down any pasturing stag or hind. They were shot with arrows or crossbow bolts or, later, with leaden balls from a musket. Sometimes they were mustered into a valley by beaters, for a mass slaughter by hounds and men together.

In the more civilized days of Queen Victoria, the old nobility and the new gentry—brewers, shipbuilders, China-traders, coal-owners and iron-founders—built themselves castles, schlosses, châteaus, lodges, architectural follies of the wildest kind, in the wildest places, from which to stalk and kill poor *Cervus elaphus*. They ate his meat, coarse but exotic and therefore expensive; but, more importantly, they hung his antlered head upon their walls

133

for a warrant of their manly prowess—though many a man with a hundred heads upon his wall had a small pair of horns which he wore in private after the stalking season.

However, because they were civilized then, and used children only for hauling coal or cleaning chimney stacks, they gave up stag hounds and bred collies, handsome, intelligent creatures that would herd the deer but never pull them down, leaving that gentle task to their masters. The best kill was the beast with the biggest antlers—a curiously phallic thought since the size of the antlers, according to eminent authority, depended on the amount of male hormone in the stag. Rich gentlemen paid high prices for a good kill, so it was good business to drive the land clear of sheep and people to make room for the high priests of fashion and their sacrificial victims. It was good business to spread fodder for them in the winter so that they would kill better and bigger in the summer.

After Victoria died and Edward and George, and many millions of serfs, villeins, merchants, squires and nobles, minor and major, in a brace of wars, the killing of *Cervus elaphus* still continued, but with more refinement in the ritual. Now the killing season was more rigidly defined, and justified with clearer reasoning. The herds must be culled lest they devour too much land. The hunters must be controlled lest they destroy the best stock and leave only the worst to perpetuate themselves. The price of a gun must match the rise in taxes and the cost of labour. In the small islands of Great Britain—diminished but still great—the population of deer, like the population of humans, must be kept stable, and a little judicious murder was the best way to manage the operation.

Which brought me, close on midnight, to a consideration of my outing with Ruarri. It was, in essence, an exercise in tracking and killing a living creature. It was an exercise in which, once upon a time, I had been fairly expert. I had been trained to kill. I had been sent charging at a sack with a bayonet, leaping at a man with a naked knife, creeping to strangle a dozing sentry with a cheese wire. I had killed in fact and I had sworn I would never kill again, beast or man, though I still ate meat—which is a sad commentary on the value of human logic.

The stalking? Yes, I could accommodate that. Stalking was an exercise without penalties: human brain against animal sensors, reason against instinct and no violence threatened or done. There would even be a certain Godlike magnanimity in the victory: to know that one had won and yet exact no woe from the vanquished; to know that one could kill and yet not kill. A noble affirmation, surely? A small defiance of the dog-eat-dog world in which I wanted no further part?

Of course you could laugh at my sad and shallow argument. I could take a fish but not a stag. I could eat dead meat, provided another had killed it. I beg you, please do not laugh—not openly at least, and not contemptuously. I am trying to tell you as honestly as I can —but who is ever wholly honest?—my own part in this story of an island summer. I am not proud of it, though I am a proud man by nature. Why tell it, then? I suppose because every man must come sometime to his own Canossa with a halter around his neck, and ask forgiveness of the man he might have been. . . .

So I would stalk, but I would not kill. Or would I? Or should I? We would, with luck or skill, come upon the stag; Ruarri and I, half brothers, half enemies, with Ruarri's henchmen for witnesses. I would be the guest. Ruarri would, as courtesy dictated, offer me the first shot —and the last, too, because if I missed, the stag and the herd would be gone, devil take the hindmost. I could take the shot and fire high or wide; but he would know, even if the others did not, and he would be shamed and hate me more. I could tell him before we set out that I did not wish to kill, only to stalk and see. He would accept that; but he would laugh in his sleeve, as you are laughing now, and despise me, because neither the logic nor I would stand up in his eyes.

What did I decide? Nothing. I closed the books and put them neatly back in the shelves. I found myself a good, anesthetic thriller, full of blood and guts and sudden death, poured myself a large whisky and took them both to bed.

Which brings me to another point. If you find in this very personal narrative that there is much talk of drink-

135

ing, it is not by artifice or literary contrivance. I was drinking then, too much and too often. The days were long. My time with Kathleen McNeil was short and I had a deal of forgetting to do in between. Of course I wasn't a toper. I was on holiday in the Heather Isles, which were colonized by great, whoring warriors who drank their way to Valhalla. I had a long way to go to catch up with them, even with their twentieth-century descendants; but I was running. Praise the Lord, brothers and sisters, I was running . . . !

Next morning I was walking.

I was walking my feet raw and my shanks to numbness up fifteen hundred feet of peat slope and scree and slippery gneiss in the hills of Harris. That fifteen hundred feet was only the first slope. Beyond it was a saddle and then another peak which we must cross before we came to the corrie where the deer should be found. I hoped that the deer and Ruarri were in agreement on the location because, if they weren't, I might very well lie down and die and let the boys build a cairn over me for a monument.

Let me tell you about these hills of Harris. Did you know—but of course you wouldn't, such being the decay of knowledge—that Noah's Ark landed in these very hills, in the neck between Clisham and Uisgna Val More? Whether that was before or after it landed on Ararat, nobody knows for sure. But it landed here for certain. Everybody knows that. Noah sent out a magpie to scout around for him, and the magpie didn't like what he saw, which is why the magpie in these hills is a messenger of bad omen—especially if you see four of him together. Did you know also that these great, round stones on which I've been barking my shins all morning were once the castle of a giant who stole maidens and could only be bought off with sea pearls? Well, that's a fact too. And another is that to walk uphill on peat is purgatory, to walk on glacial scree is a fool's pastime and to scramble over tors and granite outcrops, greasy with moss and lichen, just to get a look at a deer eating his dinner is sheer hellish lunacy.

The pace Ruarri set was punishing. I thought I knew who was getting the punishment, especially when the two lads protested that he'd have us all with broken ankles if he didn't slow down. So he rested us at the first saddle, where to my other agonies was added a plague of midges. That, Ruarri explained with sardonic patience, was why we had to go high. The deer were wiser than we; when the weather was warm and humid they took to the high ground to be free of insects.

He further explained that in humid air scents carried farther and the animals were more acutely aware of them. So from this point we must stay downwind of the high valley for which we were headed. Up or down, it made small matter to me so long as I had wind left to make the climb, and enough control of my muscles not to make a fool of myself when the quarry was sighted and the stalk began in earnest.

We moved on, scrambling over the ridge that would lead us to the last summit, below which lay the deer forest, which was not a forest at all, but only a high basin in the hills covered with moss and grasses and not a tree breaking out of it. I was up with Ruarri now, striding more freely, breathing more easily, if only because I had to meet the challenge of him. We talked little and in low voices because the sound would carry across the peaks and startle the outrunners of the herd: the stags, cropping far from the hinds, and the matriarchs who would unsettle the whole group at one hint of danger. The rutting season was still a month away, so males and females grazed apart and the older hinds were still the group leaders. When we made our last halt, under the lee of a great tor, Ruarri explained the stalk itself:

"When we see the herd, they'll be grazing and quiet. The art is to get as close as possible without rousing them. We're downwind, and the breeze is steady, so they won't get the scent of us. But they have keen eyes and their ears prick up at any new sound, even the scrape of a shoe or the snap of a rifle bolt. So we pick out the leaders and watch them—all does, they'll be. If one of 'em gives a bark, you'll know we're spotted and you'll freeze. The herd will freeze too—forefeet planted together, heads up, waiting. If they start grazing again, don't move until every head is down, because the leaders will still be alert. You might get a bold one who'll come walking over towards you to get a better look or try to pick up a scent. . . . If we get close enough for a shot, I'll pick the buck we want. You can take him. Have you got all that now?"

"I think so. I hope I don't make a mistake."

"Stay close by me for signals. The boys can look after themselves."

"It's the army all over again."

He gave me a quick, suspicious look. "Does that worry you?"

"Hell, no!"

"How's your shooting?"

"I haven't handled a gun since I gave mine back to the government. So you might lose your stag."

"If you want him badly enough, you'll drop him. On your feet now and quiet from here."

If I wanted him badly enough. . . . Clever fellow, Ruarri! Clever, clever fellow, with every sense alive and every synapse in that brain of his ticking out the right answer every time! I wanted him, not for his meat or his hide or his head, but for Ruarri, to prove that I was as good a man as he was, as calm a marksman, as male a swordsman, and as ready as he to shed a little blood to get what I wanted and hold what I had. The oath I had sworn to myself? A wafer cake. I had forsworn myself already on the night I drove home from Stornoway to Laxay and accepted the proposition that it was right to kick any man in the belly, provided you got in first. Still, there was a chance that the final act might be avoided. The stalk had not yet begun. It would not begin until we had topped the last rise and seen whether the deer were even there.

They were there. They had to be. Their presence was written at birth on the palm of my hand, but I had not the eyes to read it. There were perhaps fifty hinds, some with calves at foot, staggies and does, grazing in four groups. The groups were spread around the basin, and aloof from them were two big stags, with antlers spread like trees above their heads. We stood watching them from a cleft in the rocks, bunched behind Ruarri as he scanned the valley through the field glasses. He pointed out the matriarchs, speaking in a whisper, using only the most restricted gestures. When we had them marked, he studied the stags and settled on the far one as the beast he would take. Then he had us worming our way out of the cleft, flat on our bellies, to mark the ground: where the shale

138

was and the rocks that would give cover, and where the peat moss began and would deaden a footfall.

The deer had all the advantage, it seemed. The wind was in our favour, to be sure, but we were on high ground and must come at them downhill, over rough and gravelly ground, until we hit the first humps of moss and heather. A hand's touch from Ruarri sent the two boys moving slowly round to the right of the valley. Then, slow and watchful, he handed me the rifle, pointing to the safety catch and telling me it was already cocked, with a bullet in the spout. I would be behind him, and I had to carry the gun, crawling on elbows and belly in the old commando way. He would make the cover. I must make the kill.

Once and again we almost lost them. The first time one of the boys scraped a metal boot stud against a rock. Instantly one of the matriarchs lifted her head and barked and the whole herd propped and stood poised like runners on the starting line. We lay prone, hardly daring to breathe, until a long time later we heard a second bark, and then a third. Then with agonizing slowness they settled down again and we made another twenty yards in the heather hummocks. The second time a sprig of grass caught in my nostril and the tiny sound I made as I dislodged it put the hinds on the alert again. By the time they were cropping once more, my muscles were knotted and the weight of the rifle was almost beyond bearing.

Finally we made our cover, a small rock crusted with lichen, jutting out from the bog. Ruarri held up a handful of fingers for me, his estimate of the range: five hundred yards, give or take a little. The hinds were quiet now and the big stag was cropping with lordly disdain on the farther slope. Inch by inch, I eased myself into a firing position and set the sights and slipped off the safety catch. Then I got him in the lens and held him, with the tiny etched cross just where his heart should be. When I fired he went down clean, buckling at the knees, with hardly more than a shudder afterwards.

It was a beautiful shot. Even Ruarri said he was proud of it. I remember only one other to match it: when I knocked a Japanese sentry off a rock at six hundred yards, just as he was lighting a cigarette. I had exactly the same reaction too. I wanted to be sick.

IX

I WAS A HERO FOR HALF AN HOUR, WHICH IS LONG ENOUGH for any sane man.

We inspected the kill. We admired the cleanness of it: no pain to the beast, little blood, only a tiny damage to the hide. He was a true royal, with a full spread of antlers, just right to die because next year he would be on the downgrade for breeding. All of which was a perfect absolution for the man who had knocked him off in his prime. The boys trussed his hooves together, slung the carcass on the rifle, carried him up the slope and dumped him far enough away so that he would not spoil our lunch: beef sandwiches large enough to choke a giant, washed down with neat whisky and a beer chaser. We were all great fellows, ten feet tall, with myself overtopping the rest by a couple of inches. Then, because a killing is like a mating and you shrink after it and are weary, we stretched out in the shadow of the rocks and swapped stories which had nothing at all to do with the poor dead buck lying fifty feet away, with my bullet in his heart and the flies buzzing around the hole in his side.

I was surprised at first by the tales that were told. They were all of faerie and of magic. But then I understood that killing is a magical act and that it demands a ritual: the chanting priest, the axman, all in black with his face covered, the processional afterwards, with the maidens dishevelled and the old women tearing their milkless breasts, the men solemn and swaying as if in drunken ecstasy.

One of the lads told the story of the two young men of Rodel who built a ship so beautiful that the sea grew envious and would not let it ever come back to the land.

140

He quoted the old saying: "The sea likes company, but it covets what it likes." Which led to another fable—or was it fable, being so deeply rooted in the folk memory? —that a sailor should always be buried on the beach, else the jealous sea would come back at night and swamp the land to have him back. Only those who were buried on the sacred isle of Iona would come dry to the judgment day, for in the last great flood Iona would float upon the waves so that God might recognize his saints.

Then there was lost Atlantis, so beautiful a legend from so rude a mouth. There were still old men living who had seen or been shown, not far from the shore, streets and temples and living men and cattle grazing among the grasses under the sea. And if there were no Atlantis, how come the woodcock tried to find it every year, flying as far west as they could and then returning, exhausted, to the Isles? How come the blue-eyed grass grew only in two places in the world: Bermuda and Ireland? The Atlantic was too wide for any bird to fly with a seed in his beak. Once upon a time there must have been a land in between.

I was the day's hero, so I weighed in with my bestiary of New Guinea: the sorcerer who could change himself into a cassowary and be in two places at once, a bird in one, a man in the other, the man talking like a bird, the bird like a man; the pig-god who demanded a sacrifice of the firstborn, so that the woman killed her babe and suckled a piglet instead.

After that Ruarri told his fairy tale and—God rot him for the poetry that contradicted the bloody rest of him— I could not tell how much of it was fact and how much fabulous nonsense. He talked of the place of the Stones, where Kathleen and I had first begun to know each other. Whatever the experts wrote, said Ruarri, the truth of it was far different. The great stones were not hewn in the Lews at all. They came from a far place, brought by priests in feathered robes, with black servants in attendance and wrens, a whole flock of them, flying around their heads. In the west country of England and in Wales, the wren was called the druid bird, and they used to kill it on St. Stephen's Day to celebrate the death of the old religion.

But the old religion wasn't dead yet. Not by a long

chalkmark. Ask the old folk in the Lews and they would tell you, in a whisper, that there were still families who "belonged to the Stones." Ask them again, gently and believingly, they would tell you that the Shining One still came on midsummer morning and stood by the great stone, and if you were there when the cuckoo called you would see him, plain as day. If you plighted troth among the Stones, the marriage would come to pass. If you had your first loving there, damp in the mist, the marriage would be happy and wholesome ever after. Had he seen the Shining One? Well, he thought he had, but he couldn't be sure. The way he told it, I couldn't be quite sure either, and I'm a storyteller, who knows the tricks of the trade. True or false, the magic worked, so that when we carried the stag away, two and two, resting each other every halfmile, it was just a carcass, ready to be hung and gutted and skinned and smoked for eating.

On the way back, when we were walking loose and unburdened, Ruarri asked me, "What did that do to you, seannachie?"

"What?"

"The killing."

"Nothing."

"You're a liar."

"So don't ask me damn fool questions."

"Did you get a thrill out of it?"

"Yes."

"And afterwards?"

"Oh, for God's sake!"

"I always want a woman. There and then. No waiting."

"I want to puke."

"I wonder what makes the difference."

"Who knows? Let's drop it."

We were both too tired for teasing so we dropped it, amicably enough. Nonetheless a damage was done. I was reminded of Kathleen McNeil and that strange moment when we hung, a foot from dying, on the cliff road. I remembered what she said: "There's no fear, no regret. Just a kind of wonder." Twist the words a little, give the phrase a male gender, and you had Ruarri's thought exactly. Twist the knife a little and you could have me jealous enough to kill Ruarri more happily than the stag —and take my woman afterwards.

142

True to form always, Ruarri leaned on the hilt and gave the blade just that little extra torque. He didn't do it immediately; he was much too shrewd for that. But later, at the croft, while the boys were in the outhouse dressing the meat and we were sitting over a drink, he began to quiz me.

"This trip we're taking, seannachie. We could be away ten days or more."

"Sounds interesting."

"You don't mind?"

"Hell no! Why should I?"

"I just wondered."

"About what?"

"You and Kathleen. Have you told her yet?"

"I've mentioned it."

"She doesn't mind?"

"She hasn't said so."

"Dangerous, laddie! Dangerous!"

"Why?"

"Well, let's face it, big brother. You and I are free to cut ourselves a slice of shortbread any time any place we want. In Trondheim, for instance, there's the sweetest little woman you ever saw, recently widowed, just crying to be comforted, and she has a house all of her own, clean, private, and never a tear afterwards. On the other hand—and this is brothers' talk, mind you—a woman just fallen in love, and getting what I know you have to give her, does have the right to complain if the comfort's snatched away. As it will be. Have you thought of that?"

I had, but my conclusions were none of his business. I had thought that a few days at sea would give me the purge I needed, a purge of liver and lights and brain box, so that I might enjoy the good things I had without this perpetual itch to analyze and this haunting of melancholy that came upon me unawares. I had thought that my absence might make Kathleen need me more and be more ready to trot off with me at the summer's end and get married. Also—and this, I thought, was a sign of healing —I wanted something new and simple to write about, to work my hand back into the trade. The answer I gave to Ruarri was a little different.

"Kathleen won't complain. She's working most days and

more than half the nights of the week. Besides, we'll be going off together after the summer."

"Getting married?"

"That's the general idea."

"Good for you, seannachie. Good for you. Have you given her the ring yet?"

"Not yet."

"Playing it loose, eh?"

"Not too loose. Just easy."

"How does she feel about that?"

"She likes it."

Then because he was getting too close to the bone, and I was beginning to feel some pain, I decided to do a little probing on my own account. So I told him of my meeting with Duggie Donald in Tarbert and gave him a carefully edited version of our talk. He frowned over it for a while, then got up to pour a new round of drinks. When he was settled again, he said:

"They're leaning on me, seannachie. I don't like that. This goddamned British bureaucracy is a pain in the arse."

"What do they have against you?"

"Nothing yet. Just rumour and loose talk."

"Like I heard in Stornoway the other night?"

He gave me a wary grin and nodded. "Things like that, yes."

"Any substance to them?"

"Some. But nothing they can build a case on."

"There's something I want to say, Ruarri."

"Say it."

"I don't want to know your business, but I'm making a run with you. If questions are asked of me, I want to have answers ready—true ones, if not whole ones. I don't want to be caught on the wrong foot, as I was the first day. I don't always think so quickly. Also, if there's trouble, I don't want it believed or hinted that it came from me. Clear?"

"Clear as a bell, brother. Let me think how I can put it to you."

He thought about it a long time and it gave me a secret pleasure to watch him. The more worries he had of his own, the less he was likely to push that red beard into my soup. Finally, with a great show of frankness, he spread his thoughts before me.

"I'm a fisherman, seannachie. The two *Helens* are registered as trawlers. They're not licensed or insured—and my crew aren't insured, either—for the carrying of freight or passengers. Board of Trade regulations and all that. Right?"

"Right."

"But you can't run a trawler profitably, any more than you can run a taxi, on dead miles. By dead miles I mean a run with no fish in the hold, nothing to sell when you tie up. That happens. It happens more and more, with the Russians and the Danes and the Norwegians and the Germans and the Portuguese, and the boys from Hull and Grimsby, all trying to haul a living out of the same sea. So one way or another we have to trade. Bollison, for example, whom we met in the Minch, he'll run into Stornoway to buy the fish he can't catch for himself, just because the market's undersupplied in the canneries he serves. We all do that and it's legal. Sometimes I'll get a radio call that there's a glut of whitefish in Orkney and none here. I'll make a run up and buy, just to pay wages on the profit. I'm getting rather good at this communications business. . . . But there are still dead miles. Too many. And in a bad season I could go broke, which I have no intention of doing just to keep the Board of Trade happy. So from time to time I do what a tramp skipper does, I carry freight: special freight for special customers, from ports where I'm known to ports where they're known, or the other way round."

"What sort of freight?"

"That varies and you don't have to know about it. The hold stinks of fish and you can't bear the smell, so you've never seen inside it. And you won't be round for loading or unloading because you'll be off in a bar drinking with a girl. You'll know where we've been, but why we were there will be the skipper's business, written in the log for all to see, including Duggie Donald. You don't have seaman's papers; you have a passport. You're a passenger—non-paying—come along for the ride, because you like the sea and you're writing a story about it. Simple? Complete?"

"Except for one thing. Do you carry drugs?"

"Good question, seannachie. And the answer is, never. Satisfied?"

"Satisfied."

"Of course, if you're not, or you're scared of involvement, you could call it off. I'd have no hard feelings about it."

"I'm not worried and I'm looking forward to it. When do we leave?"

"Any time this week. Half a day's notice. That suit you?"

"Fine. I hope I can be useful."

"You can split helm watch with me. There's not much to do on deck until the nets come in. You can lend a hand then if you feel like it."

And there we left it, with a lot of questions still unanswered, but none urgent enough to trouble us yet. I thanked him for the good day, took my leave and headed south to see Kathleen.

She was tired and inclined to be fretful. She had been called out twice during the night, and the day had brought a larger than normal crop of elderly bladders and rheumatoid joints and silted arteries. The house was closing in on her. The housekeeper was in a bad humour and the village folk were distant, but damned demanding the moment they got a bellyache or a cough. She needed some cherishing and she got it. Then she wanted to go out; but, as I was still in my climbing clothes and no fit company for the fashionable tourists of Tarbert, we decided to stroll down to Rodel, drink with the locals in the pub and dine there afterwards.

Rodel is a strange little place, almost uncanny in the stillness of a summer evening, with its ruinous dock, the old Church of St. Clement perched on the hilltop, the bay beyond, where, if the tide is right, you may see another circle of stones like those of Callanish, drowned in the deep water. Whether this is fact or fancy I do not know even now. However, with Kathleen on my arm and heads turning and faces pressed against windowpanes to watch the doctor and her gentleman friend, fact and fancy were the same thing: wholly pleasant and wholly believable.

There was an hour yet to sundown and the white cottages were bathed in a warm, soft light. There was still movement on the road: a group of little girls skipping and

146

telling a rhyme, over and over in the Gaelic; a small boy racing a dog along the verge; a crofter, home-coming, with his cap jaunty on his head and a mattock over his shoulder, his coat dangling from the haft like a banner; an old, bowed woman in a shawl, carrying a basket of groceries.

The peace of it was a blessing for bruised spirits. By the time we came to Rodel, we were back in the love country, hand in hand and singing with the joy of it.

The monks who founded the Church of St. Clement are all dead and gone centuries ago; the Free Kirk wants no part of its ancient imagery, so the Ministry of Works has taken it over as an ancient monument, and, if you want to look inside, you must get the key at the hotel. You can make a commentary on that if you have the heart for it. We did not, because the wonder was on us; and when we pushed open the creaking gate and stepped into the churchyard, grown high with nettles and grasses, we were outside of time. When we kissed, as we did, even the loveless ghosts were glad of us: the MacLeods of Mac-Leod; the MacCrimmons, who were pipers to the Mac-Leod; the MacVurrichs, who were their bards, son following son, and the Bearers of the Fairy Flag, whose bones lie, all together, forgotten in the churchyard.

But there are ghosts here older than the Macleod. High up in the tower, which sailors once used for a marker to guide them home, there are stones carved with strange symbols which came from the drowned circle in the bay; and sometimes at night the Little People visit the hill which used to be their place, before they were driven underground by the Saints of Iona. From this monastic house came the Great Clerk of Rodel, who journeyed to France and was befriended by Charlemagne and gave the Franks their first grammar school. Of course the French will quarrel with that. They quarrel with everything and everybody. But the best liquor always comes out of small bottles, and there was learning in the Isles long before the French ever heard of it. That may not be history, but if you stand under the square tower of St. Clement an hour before sunset, with your arms around a beautiful woman who wants the comfort, then you'll accept the truth of it.

With the comfort given and taken and the ghosts left quiet again, we walked down to the pub and found a place for ourselves among the gaggle of crofters and fishermen in the old-fashioned bar. We were strangers and they left us alone, until one recognized Kathleen for the new doctor and introduced her to the company. The Herries men were different from those of the Lews, less noisy, more shy and sidling, slower to strike up a talk. Even the musicman was a fellow so wispy a breeze could have blown him away; but he coaxed thin, sweet melodies out of an old sailor's accordion, and we could still hear him when we sat at dinner in a room hung with lace curtains and bobbled velvet drapes.

The food was simple, but the service was rendered with a smile and we were very content with our own company. Kathleen's megrims were chased away, and mine were locked out of sight in a distant closet of the brain. So our talk was light, drifting and changeable, like mist floating over dark, still water.

"You're good for me, mo gradh."

"And you for me, young Kathleen."

"I'm not really young, you know."

"Then I'm older than God."

"I think you've got younger since we met."

"Fresh air and exercise, malt whisky and the loving of Kathleen McNeil—a recipe for the elixir of youth."

"I missed you today. I wanted to play truant and come climbing with you."

"Thank your stars you didn't. I'm going to have knots in every muscle tomorrow."

"But you bagged your first royal."

"My last too."

"You're not proud of it?"

"The stag was beautiful and complete. The man was a less noble animal."

"You're hard on yourself, but I can understand."

"I'm glad you can."

"It's a problem, though. You respect life. You love it. But you can't cherish everything and everybody. Every ecology depends on death. The world's so small. So crowded."

"Not here, thank God."

"Even here, darling. When the land is cropped out, the people die. . . . How was Ruarri?"

"Fine. He's the best company in the world when the

148

good mood is on him. He ran me ragged at the beginning of the climb, just to see how I'd take it. After that, no problems. He's good at everything he does—even the telling of tall stories."

"Did you find out anything more about that Maeve O'Donnell?"

"Nothing much. Except they had some kind of a love affair that died a natural death. Ruarri says she's too intelligent for his taste. Which probably means she's one woman who wouldn't stand any nonsense from him."

"I'd say she's still in love with him."

"Probably."

"I wonder what a love affair with Ruarri would be like?"

"Stormy, I should think. Depending on what the woman wanted out of it."

"He's enormously attractive."

"To you?"

"To most women, I'd say."

"Could you take him on? And handle him?"

"I could be tempted. If I didn't have you."

"He talks about you every time we meet."

"And you?"

"I don't talk about you. There's a big, red 'no sale' sign that goes up every time your name is mentioned. But I think about you all the time. There's not a moment of the day or night when you're out of my mind."

"Will you think about me when you're away with Ruarri?"

"Too much, probably."

"I hate your going."

"Then I'll stay. It's no problem."

"No!" Her smile was grateful and her hand was gentle on mine. "You need to go. The days are long for you when I'm not free. I've been watching you, dear one, not just as a lover, but as a doctor too. You're overspent, scraping up resources to live just from day to day. You're better, but the restoration isn't complete. The physical things are what you need while the mind lies fallow a while. Come back to me laughing and new."

"When we're married, we'll take a boat and sail the Cyclades for our honeymoon."

"If the time comes, I have other ideas."

149

"If . . . ?"

"When."

"Kathleen oge, I think I've made a big mistake."

"What's that?"

"We shouldn't have had our first loving in bed. We should have had it in the place of the Stones. Then I'd be sure of you."

"Today I'm sure of you."

"Why today and not yesterday?"

"Try to guess."

"I haven't an idea. Tell me."

"No."

"Can I bribe you?"

"No. You have to guess. Now you can walk me home and tell me how much you love me."

"And then?"

"Then we'll have one drink and you'll be gone before old sour-face comes back from her ceilidh."

"No loving while we wait?"

"I have the curse on me, mo gradh. So it's just a kiss and a blessing tonight."

"That's loving too."

It was and it wasn't. I was too old and impatient for parlour games by lamplight, so I left early and took the long road home: round by the western beaches, where there were more ghosts, but no danger at all of driving over a cliff. Besides, this was the land of the story spinners, where even the frogs were known to be the sons of chiefs laid under a spell in the dreamtime of long ago; where the sands turned gold once in the year, and sometimes you could find the paw marks of the fairy dogs that walked by night when the tide was down.

I saw no fairy dogs. But I did hear the hoarse croaking of the frogs and I was sorry for the poor fellows. I wondered what charm was needed to break the spell and make them men again. It might be a kiss from a compassionate princess. It might be a single word: the answer to a riddle, set ten thousand years ago, never to be remembered, because even the enchantress had forgotten it.

Kathleen McNeil had set a riddle for me; but because I was dozy with fatigue and full of wine and kisses, I didn't try to answer it. Instead I played a game, trying to

150

turn the riddle into a rhyme in the Gaelic fashion. It took me twenty miles to set it, but I remember it still:

> The man I was, the man I am,
> She loves them both, but surer is
> Of am than was.
> I am who am, I am who was.
> I wish she'd tell the difference.

It was—as the minister said to the actress at breakfast —a pleasant conceit, but it did nothing for me. The riddle was fun. The answer, if in truth it was an answer, was no fun at all.

The only difference between me today and me yesterday was the fact that I had made a killing. Which set me at level pegging with Ruarri Matheson and Dr. Kathleen McNeil. If I wanted the lady, she was mine; just so I could be half an inch taller, half a pound heavier and one cut more ruthless than the Mactire.

A madness? Sure! But I have already told you of the day, a million years past, when I stepped out of reality into a dimension of dreams.

X

EARLY NEXT MORNING, WHILE I WAS STILL RUBBING THE sleep out of my eyes, Ruarri called me. Things had changed. He wanted to be off to Norway by one in the afternoon. Could I make it? I damned him to the last circle of hell; but, yes, I could make it. Clothes? He would lend me oilskins and seaboots. For the rest I should bring warm things to work in and something decent for the hours ashore. Money he could lend me, but I didn't need it. If I needed an hour with my girl—which I did, but couldn't enjoy—there was time for it; but he'd like me aboard, unpacked and ready for sea duty, a quarter before one. I damned him again and hung up.

I called Kathleen. She was only half awake and irritable, which made me glad to be gone. Then, in a swift somersault, she was tender and solicitous, which made me want to stay. I told her I would telephone her from the mainland. She told me not to bother. The lines were bad and she could be out on a call. I should forget about her and enjoy myself. When I came back—or did she say home?—we would enjoy together. Bless you, my love. Bless you, Kathleen oge. It's nice to have a woman to leave, because that's a woman waiting when you come home. I bathed and shaved and packed a bag and went down to breakfast.

Hannah was sure I had gone mad. Why any man with a warm bed and a comfortable house and a beautiful, loving girl should want to take off into the wild, wild ocean, she'd never understand. And with that rascal Ruarri? God save us all from sin and sorrow! Did I know what I was getting myself into? When that sea came up I could break an arm or a leg or my back even, and never be good for a woman again. Or I could be washed overboard, or be so seasick that I'd be crying kiss-me-mother before the night came down. Well. . . ! If I must go, I must, but I'd deserve every single horror that happened to me. Did I have warm clothes now? And shaving things? And money? And clean underclothes? No playing about, remember! No fornication in them foreign ports. Many's the poor laddie came home with what he didn't take away and was hard put to explain it to his wife or his sweetheart. I'd stop by to tell the Morrison? Good! There was decency left in me still. She'd seen him herself and he was looking brighter-like, but still not the same as he used to be. I should eat a good breakfast. The more in the belly, the easier it was to keep down, as her father used to say before the sea took him on a winter's night.

Morrison, on the other hand, loved the whole idea and lavished approval on it.

"You couldn't do a better thing in the world, laddie! If the weather holds good, you'll have a cruise that you couldn't buy. If it doesn't, you'll have an experience to shake the last cobwebs loose from that brain of yours.

I'm glad Ruarri still wants you with him. You were made to be comrades. I wish I were coming with you, but they've got me chained to this blasted bed, and a woman with snakes in her hair to watch over me. . . ."

So having discharged my pieties on the land, I bethought myself of those I owed to the sea. I needed a gift for Ruarri, to say my thanks for courtesies done and for the hospitality of the *Helen*. My antiquarian had just the thing: a sextant from the days of the windjammers, set in a teak box, bound in brass and engraved with the initials of some long-dead skipper. Since I looked like a constant customer, he offered me a modest discount and a paper bag to carry the prize. For the crew I decided on hard liquor and went to a pub in search of it. I had still an hour to kill, so I ordered a beer and sat myself in a booth by the window to drink it in comfort and watch the passage of people in the grey, narrow street.

I had been there perhaps five minutes when the bar began to fill with noonday drinkers. One of them was Duggie Donald, the Customs man. He ordered a pint and perched himself on a stool with his back to me. I had no desire to be drawn into talk with him or anyone else at that moment, so I slewed myself round in the booth and concentrated on the passersby. By the time I had finished my beer another man had joined Duggie, and they were talking in low, animated fashion. The newcomer was the crewman whom Ruarri had assaulted in The Admiral's Spyglass. Both of them, therefore, were ten minutes away from their normal haunts. I had nothing to fear from either, but I did feel an odd flutter of unease. I gathered up my parcels and walked out. I drove down to the dock, parked the car for a week in a nearby garage and carried my gear aboard the *Helen II*.

It was still early, and there was only one man on board: a tall, taciturn fellow who introduced himself reluctantly as Athol Cameron. I was to share the skipper's cabin, he told me. The port bunk was mine; I could go down now. I handed him the whisky and asked him to distribute it to the crew with my compliments. He cradled it lovingly in his arms and decided he would, after all, show me down to my quarters. By the time I had everything stowed shipshape and had scribbled a note to go with my gift, I could hear others of the crew scrambling aboard. I went topside to join them and wait for Ruarri.

I had a small dilemma on my hands. Should I, or should I not, tell him of the meeting which I had just witnessed? If it spelled trouble for him, I had some duty to warn him about it. If, on the other hand, the meeting was innocent of malice, the lad might find himself in needless bother with Ruarri. I was still mulling over the question when the fellow came on board, large as life, with a seabag slung over his shoulder. The greetings he gave and got seemed good-humoured enough, so I was inclined to forget the trivial affair. I knew nothing about the private relationships of Ruarri's buannas, and a brief flare of violence or rough discipline between shipmates was no rare thing. Certainly it was no cause to dub a man a Judas out of hand. The fact that he was still sharing whatever mission Ruarri had in hand was guarantee enough that the brotherhood was intact. So I decided to hold my tongue.

Then Ruarri came on board and called me to the wheelhouse to lay the course with him: a long northward leg, out of the Minch, past Orkney and Shetland, then northeast to Trondheim on the Norway current. The weather? Greasy in a couple of hours, with winds freshening from the east and rain in the blow. After that? Well, there was a cold front working its way down from Iceland. That could hit us just south of the Faeroes, but with luck we might miss it. Time for the journey? Forty-eight hours, more or less. Purpose of the journey? I didn't know, didn't ask, and cared not a curse. I was free as a soaring kittiwake and prepared to raise my voice and make ballads about it.

Our Ruarri was a punctual man. At one o'clock he had engines turning, lines cast off, and was easing out of the basin, past the ferry dock towards the harbour mouth. By one-thirty Chicken Head was falling away astern and we were heading north-by-northeast up the Minch, with the gulls screaming and wheeling above us and the overcast creeping in, blown by the stiffening easterly. There was no rain yet because the high hills of Sutherland had robbed the clouds already; but after Cape Wrath we would have the showers, and the wind much harder, funnelling through the Pentland Firth and across the roof of Scotland.

Ruarri handed over the wheel to the lad whom he had kicked in the belly—and who treated him as if he were Lord and Saviour—then took me below for a meal with the rest of the crew. The normal complement of the *Helen* was five men and the skipper. Ruarri demanded that every man should be able to do every job on the ship: keep the engines running sweetly, stand wheel watch, cook a meal in rough weather or good, handle nets and winches, scrape paint, clean and pack fish, splice cordage and hose decks. He himself could turn a hand to everything, so he would tolerate no scrimshankers on his boat. Every man might say his piece, but Ruarri was the master and there was no confusion about it.

I had met all his boys, boozed and shouting, in the bar. Here, in the ritual family of a small ship, they were different men altogether. They ate hungrily for the cold journey: a soup so thick you could stand a spoon in it, brown stew with a mountain of mash, canned peaches, and tea darker than peat water. They talked quietly, knowingly, of the weather ahead, of the grounds that had been fished out and others that seemed to be promising. The talk swung from Gaelic to English, and sometimes it was translated for me and sometimes it wasn't; but this I took for a compliment, since I was part of the family and a known friend who could down his drink and keep his mouth shut in an awkward moment.

They did not laugh so much now, I noticed. Their talk was less bawdy. Their jokes were the small, constant cryptic ones that ran from man to man, like the formal patterns in a weave. They were alert always to the rhythm of things, to the beat of the engines, to the sound of the wind, the lift and fall of the hull, the creak and grind and murmur within the body of the ship itself. Even at leisure they were still on watch against the treachery of the sea, an enemy always, however brightly it smiled, loving to be visited, but covetous always of new men to mate with the cold maidens of the deep.

Ruarri was watchful, too, but more of the men, it seemed, than of the ship itself. The men knew the sea as well as he did, better perhaps, because they had spent half their lives on it, while his wanderings had taken him off it and brought him back late. He was the master. But the master must sleep and rest, so there must be eyes to see for him and ears to hear and noses to smell the storm before it hit. Tonight and tomorrow we would be in wild waters, where the currents split and the sea broke every which way and the winds tore themselves into shreds around the island chains of the Orkneys and the Shetlands and the Faeroes.

I think I was the only one truly at ease at the table—because I stood in absolute dependence on them all. So I began to define them, one by one, as I had not been able to do in the fog and uproar of our first meeting. I began to hold their names and to establish their particularities of speech and attitude.

Athol Cameron, the dour and gangling one, was the mate. He looked like a jointed toy with hands and feet mismatched to the rest of him. His normal conversation was a series of grunts, among which, with a little practice, one could discern negatives and affirmatives. His orders were delivered in monosyllables and never repeated. When Ruarri spoke, he listened, sucking on the foulest corncob I have ever smelled. He assented with "Och aye." He demurred with "Hell, no!" delivered in a sharp explosion like a seal's bark.

Calum MacMillan, the cook, was a little black bantam, with a strawberry mark on one cheek and a nude woman tattooed on his chest. He was as hairy as a goat and as potent. He had served as greaser on a tramp line and served time as well for some sailor's delinquency in Port o' London. But to watch him handle saucepans and kettle and frying pan in a high sea, you would have thought him a professional juggler.

Jock Burns was the fellow for the diesels. He was a redhead like Ruarri, almost as large, with a mass of freckles from cheekbone to chin. But he had an ear like Toscanini for the tuning and a tongue like a whip for any damn fool who borrowed a tool and forgot to hang it on the right hook afterwards. Get him alone, though, with the sea quiet and the shaft turning sweetly, he would tell you tales of the China run that would hold you spellbound. He was the oldest of them all, forty-five or thereabouts, and he was Daddy Burns to everyone so long as they stayed in line. If they didn't, it was Mr. Burns and a bunch of knuckles, scarred and toughened from the spanners.

Then there was Donan McEachern, a big, muscular lad from Barra, who had tried for the Air Force but couldn't make it because of his eyes. He could lift a herring barrel as easily as you or I could a mug of tea. When he spoke English he stammered painfully, but the Gaelic of his home island flowed like a music from his mouth.

With the exception of Jock Burns and Ruarri, they were all under thirty years of age, and the boy on wheel watch, Lachie McMurtrie, was the youngest of them all—a stocky, talkative extrovert with twenty-three years, and more than that in women, notched to his belt—if you could believe him.

They would be a rude and dangerous bunch to meet in a brawl, and I made a mental note to stay away from any bars where they might be drinking in Trondheim. But here, yarning quietly in the cramped galley, they were all one breed, visitors to the jealous sea, loving it, hating it, cherishing one another against it, like the old adventurers in their longships.

Ruarri left us after lunch and went to his cabin. I stayed in the galley with Calum to help him clear the dishes: I had no thought of being an idle hand, with everyone tripping over my feet. Afterwards I put on an oilskin jacket and went out to take a turn on deck.

The wind was strong now, coming in gusts and sweeps out of the Highlands, with rain in it, and a lash of spray along the deck from the chopping whitecaps. Most of the gulls were gone, but there were still a few hardy ones clinging to the crosstree and the radar antenna, lifting off sometimes, then settling with wings folded against the buffet of the wind. I braced myself against the lee of the wheelhouse and watched the last outline of Lewis fade into the rain shower, and wondered what Kathleen McNeil was doing at that precise moment.

I was grateful then for the freedom which she had insisted to have for us both. I saw the reason of it, felt the need of it and was determined to enjoy every blessed moment and come back laughing to claim her. If the wind and the rain and the sea didn't wash the last black vapours away, I was beyond saving, anyway. Then Jock Burns tapped me on the shoulder and told me Ruarri would like

157

to see me in his cabin—and by the by, the boys were grateful for the liquor; it was a welcome gift, and thoughtful.

Ruarri's reaction to his gift was oddly poignant. He held it in his hands, unsmiling, and said:

"I've had presents from women, seannachie, for services rendered or wanted. This is the first gift I've ever had from a man. I'm touched. I read the thought behind it. It's like—like a birthday party, which no one ever gave me. I don't know what else to say."

"Don't say anything. Use it sometimes, if the calibration's accurate."

"Bound to be. It's a beautiful piece of brasswork." He closed the box and set it carefully on the shelf above his writing table. Then he turned back to me. "I want to talk to you about the trip, seannachie. Something's gone wrong, badly wrong. I don't know what it is, but I smell it. I was in town last night. I heard whispers I shouldn't hear. Hints I didn't like the sound of."

"What sort of hints?"

"Someone's been talking my business round the bars."

"Does that matter?"

"Christ! Does it matter! It only needs a telegram to Trondheim and we're all in trouble up to the neck—me, Bollison, Maeve O'Donnell, a lot of others you wouldn't know, even if I told you their names."

"What sort of trouble?"

"Police trouble, Interpol trouble, political backwash, everything in the book."

"In that case I'd better tell you something. It may have meaning, it may not. Just before I came aboard, I saw your Lachie McMurtrie chatting with Duggie Donald in the Crown and Anchor."

The change in him was startling. All the colour drained out of his face. Every muscle tightened. He was like an animal cornered and ready to attack. Then, very slowly, he relaxed, letting the air out of himself in a long exhalation, half whistle, half sigh. "You'd better tell it all, laddie."

"That's all. I saw them. They were talking. They didn't see me. I left."

"And it was in the Crown and Anchor. You're sure of the place?"

"Certain. I noticed the sign, which is one of the more colourful ones."

"And the time?"

"I went in at a quarter to twelve. I came out about five to. They were still there."

"Then our Lachie had better have a very good explanation. If he hasn't, I'll take the hide off him and feed him to the sharks."

"Not while I'm on board, Ruarri."

In an instant he was on his feet, savage and threatening. "You'll mind your own business, seannachie! This is my ship. These are my men! If you stick your nose in, you're apt to get it broken."

"Why don't you sit down and cool off?"

He swung at me then, and I didn't move fast enough, so that his fist caught me on the cheekbone and laid it open. The blow threw me back against the bulkhead. I pushed myself off it and came back to face him. His fists were down. He was gripping the edge of the table and shaking his head like a dog just out of a water hole. He wanted me to hit him; but, though I was blazing with anger, I could not throw the punch. I was full of bile and bitterness and I poured it out on him:

"Some other time, eh, Ruarri? Just you and me and no holds barred. It's your ship. Go run it, like a grown-up skipper! But if there are any accidents, you'll have a hostile witness at the court of inquiry. The Mactire, for Christ's sake! . . . The big bold wolf with—"

"Shut up, seannachie!" The words wrenched themselves out of him. "Please . . . shut up!"

He sat down heavily on the bunk and buried his face in his hands. I went in to the shower stall and sponged the blood off my face and found a strip of plaster to cover the slash. When I came back, Ruarri was calm again, and grinning, with an apology tripping off his tongue:

"I'm sorry, brother. I lost my head. And I'll give you the return match when you want it. Now you'd better hear what it's all about."

"I don't want to hear. I don't give a damn."

"You'd better listen just the same. Because you're in it now, like a noodle in the soup."

"I'm on the record, Ruarri. If I'm called, I'm a hostile witness."

"Amen. Now hear me out. I'm running guns, seanna-chie. Swedish army surplus, bought legally in Stockholm by Maeve O'Donnell and some other friends of mine, shipped overland to Norway, not quite so legally, and loaded by Bollison in a nice, quiet fjord where there's no Customs cutter. I pull into Trondheim for fuel and water and a final check on the arrangements. Then we meet Bollison, transship the crates and start for Ireland, which is where my market is at this moment because there's trouble in Ulster and the IRA is paying cash on the crate for clean goods still packed in the maker's grease. On the way home we fish, and the catch brings me back into Stornoway clean—provided our Lachie hasn't turned Judas and sold us all to the British. So how does that strike you?"

"It's blood business. I think it stinks. I think you stink too."

"You're entitled to your opinion. I have mine, and it wouldn't make any sense to a fine, moral fellow like yourself. But you see what happens if someone's blown the whistle on us?"

"I do."

"So I have to know for certain, don't I? And I have to get some signals out fast, don't I?"

"What you do is your own affair. I'll tell you what I'm going to do. If anything happens to Lachie McMurtrie while I'm aboard, or if I hear of anything afterwards, I'm going to blow the whistle myself. The first port we hit, I'm going to leave you and fly back to Stornoway. On what I've heard now, you're safe—and you know it. Otherwise you wouldn't be telling me. It's hearsay, therefore inadmissible, therefore useless in a case against you. But what I see, I'll testify, if I'm called—and if the boy's hurt, I'll file a charge. I gave you the warning because I owed it to you—and to the Morrison, for that matter. I just hope you're clear on what I'm saying now."

"Very clear. What I'd like to know is whether we're friends or enemies."

"Work it out for yourself."

"A drink, then, to take the taste away."

"No, thanks. I'll get some fresh air."

160

"Seannachie?"

"What?"

"You owe me a smack in the teeth."

"Leave it on the tab."

He was as bewildering as a diamond with lights flashing from every point, so that you couldn't really believe there was a flaw in him. He was so limpidly honest at times, so swiftly penitent, and yet so darkly and suddenly dangerous that you were always taken unawares. I did not doubt him for a killer. I did not doubt him either for a lost lad with a great, dark hole in the middle of his life. I understood even his need of me. I saw clearly that, the moment I bent to his need, he would be standing behind me with his boot up my backside.

Then, when I came on deck and the wind hit me and the scurry of sharp rain, I understood something else. I wasn't a free man any more. I was a prisoner on a bucking herring boat where the only writ that ran was the writ of Ruarri the Mactire.

Being a prisoner, I was impotent. I might as well relax and enjoy the experience. But there was small enjoyment to be found on a heaving deck, with the wind like a knife and the spray streaming down my damaged face. There was nothing to see any more but ragged cloud and squally wind patterns and the rearing white caps making a drunken dance. I was too proud to go below, but my pride was poor warmth with the cold creeping into my bones. I couldn't go into the wheelhouse and face the poor gabmouth, who didn't know what they were brewing for him in the galley. For that matter, I didn't either, but I knew that I wouldn't like to face those five husky fellows without an open street at my back.

Then Daddy Burns came on deck and beckoned me over. "Compliments from the Matheson. He thought as you'd be standing helm watch, you might like to get the feel of it with me."

"Good idea." And, better still, I'd be out of the cold, with something constructive to do.

So we went into the wheelhouse, took the heading from Lachie and sent him below. I must have given them a rough ten minutes while I got the hang of it, because the movement of a heavy trawler is vastly different from that of a sailing yacht with canvas above and a long fin below to slice her through the chop. Then I began to understand the rhythm: the slow roll, the steady hurdling of the bows, the stern drag, and the yaw that had to be corrected neither too soon nor too late. After a while I was able to relax and listen to Daddy Burns spinning a yarn about a typhoon in the Sea of Japan, and a rusty freighter with one engine out and the other turning over just enough to hold her nose into the swell. It wasn't until I checked my watch that I realized we had passed Cape Wrath and I was handling my first ship ever in the North Atlantic.

Then Ruarri came up and Daddy Burns left us, me still at the wheel and Ruarri, a message pad in front of him, fiddling with the transmitter.

He was grim, but he managed a flash of humour. "You can relax, seannachie. Friend Lachie is the original gutless wonder. There's no blood. He's less marked than you are. He'll jump ship in Eire, which is just what we want him to do, and he'll have enough inducement to keep him out of the Isles for a long, long time. Part of it's money. The rest is the certain knowledge that he'll end up in a peat bog if he shows up in under two years. For the rest, hold your heading and your whist and let me get these codes off."

"Ay, aye, sir!"

"Up your kilts, Mr. Christian!"

"And the same to you, Mr. Matheson!"

Suddenly and miraculously we were laughing as if the whole explosive mess were a schoolboy prank. Which it was, perhaps—except that men would be killed at the end of it.

Then Ruarri explained himself. "It's a foul-up. But not quite as bad as I feared. Lachie's a poor dumb truaghan who couldn't get his facts straight if you paid him—which Duggie Donald promised to do. So, with a little luck and good management, we're in the clear. We'll head for the Faeroes, where no one will dream of looking for us. Bollison can meet us there. He'll be away clear from Trondheim before the British and Norwegians sort out the dog's dinner they've got on their plates. A pity you're not staying with us."

"Better I don't."

"Will you say hullo to Maeve for me on the way back?"

"Where is she?"

"Just now, in Stockholm. Then she'll be waiting in Copenhagen for the news. Since she's put up the cash and guaranteed the delivery, she'll be having some nervous moments."

"Where the hell does she fit in?"

"That, seannachie, is a large question. She's an Irish patriot, she says. And it could be true, because her family was in the Movement way, way back. My version is that she's a wild girl who's never found a man to tame her, so she's now rearranged her priorities: money, horses, men and to hell with Ulster, in that order."

"I'd have thought you were made for each other."

"She still does."

"And you?"

"Women I love. Money I love. Horses I can take or leave, like oysters. And for the Irish and their squabbles, I don't give a hoot in hell. If they kill each other off tomorrow with the guns I'm bringing, I won't lose a wink of sleep."

"And up yours, Mr. Matheson."

"Yours, too, Mr. Christian. Now will you let me get my work done? And I hope you're making allowance for leeway, else we'll be halfway to Nova Scotia by morning!"

"I'm sailing the course you laid, for God's sake!"

"Do you want to finish the watch?"

"Unless you want to pull me off it."

"No. Whistle down for a grog for both of us."

"Aye, aye, sir!"

Say it, if you want, and I will not quarrel with you. We were brothers, two peas from one vine, rascals both, loving each other, hating each other, neither able to come to the final act of acceptance or rejection. And yet we had to come to it. I think each of us knew, each feared and both tried to postpone the moment as long as possible. It is the mystery of the brotherhood which eludes me still, the mystery which runs like an unbroken thread through the warp of history and of legend, too: Cain and Abel, the *Doppelgänger,* the man who lost his shadow, Absalom, hanging by the hair, run through by the spears of David's captains. We were very close that evening, plugging blindly through the half-gale towards a distant and dubious landfall, sipping the warm, sweet whisky, while the red eye of the transmitter stared unwinkingly at us both.

When he had finished his transmissions, Ruarri took a

radio fix on our position, gave me a new heading, wrote up his log and sat a while listening to a symphony program from Reykjavik, the reception clear and untroubled over the noise of the wind and the sea. He asked me:

"Have you ever been to Iceland, seannachie?"

"Never."

"We should go there together one day. Strange, fierce country, with a fire in its belly and steam and hot mud bubbling out of the ground. The sea's a monster there— shoals and mad currents, and rocks you've never dreamed of looming out of the mist, and the compass cockeyed, so you don't know whether you're coming or going. They talk the old Viking tongue, write literature in it still. They're a big and beautiful people, and you'll dream about the women twenty years after. That's where Parliament began, seannachie, with each man spouting his piece in the place of the Althing—and we've forgotten most of what they knew about democracy. Democracy. . . ! Oh brother! We're all slaves now, bound with paper chains and stapleclips! Are you free, seannachie? Do you feel free? . . ."

"Not often enough."

"Even sometimes?"

"Yes. Sometimes."

"Tell me when."

"Generally when I'm feeling most confined. As I am tonight. No offense, but that's the fact of it. I can't walk on the water. I can't go anywhere except where you choose to take me. You could toss me overboard with no one any the wiser. Something happens then. I know that I can always get away: into the past that someone else has created for me, or a present that I can conjure up from nothing, but keep, mind you, set down in words and keep and even pass on to you. . . . The real liberty is that no one can invade that private kingdom, no one can rob me of a passport to it. The only way you can destroy it is by destroying me. Even then you're not sure, because another man may have my manuscript or may have memorized the visions I recited. Dreams are dragon's teeth. Sometimes they spring up flowers. Sometimes armed men. . . . Does that make sense?"

"Too damn much!" His answer was abrupt and almost angry. "That's what I envy in you, seannachie. That's why

I want to throttle you sometimes. You've got something I need like life itself and can never lay my hands on. There's no private kingdom for me—never will be—because whichever way I turn there's some damned official with a piece of paper or a rubber stamp or a writ, or a bloody regulation that says I can't step farther until I've met his conditions. The only way I can get past him and his ilk is to shoot my way past. And how long can I go on shooting? . . . I dream, too, seannachie, wild and wonderful dreams. Why are my dreams a prison and yours liberty?"

"Perhaps because you want to make them all come true."

Truly I don't know why I said it. I didn't reason the answer. I wasn't trying to be clever or turn a phrase. I don't think Ruarri believed I was either. But he said it. He said it with a strange, haunted bitterness that was much more frightening than his rages:

"You're a clever son of a bitch, aren't you, seannachie? Too damn clever for comfort."

Then he left me and I was lonely in my tiny lighted box in the middle of the dark sea. I knew for certain then that the brotherhood could not endure. I wondered which of us would make the final rupture, and how and when it would come.

XI

By the time my watch was ended I was cold, hungry and aching in every bone. I needed a large drink and a quiet supper and a long, long sleep. I got my drink and my supper: hot cocoa and a dish of cheese sandwiches. I also got a surprise. Ruarri and Lachie McMurtrie and Daddy Burns and Athol Cameron and Calum the cook were playing a game of poker, noisy and as cheerful as though they had never had a cross word in their lives.

Now, if you have played poker, you will know it for gospel truth that you need only to watch a few hands before you know the name of the game and whether it is being played for fun, money or grudge stakes. I swear to you now—as I had once to swear it in affidavit—that this was a friendly game, for poor man's money, with lots of banter and random jokes and no tension at all. I sat in on it. I played a dozen hands and came out winning ten cents —and wondering if I had gone quietly mad in the wheel-house. Only the cut on my cheek told me I hadn't.

Yet there was Lachie, the Judas of the band, who had put everyone in jeopardy, shouting and laughing and scooping in his winnings, with never a twinge of fear or a word of resentment from his shipmates. Each man had a drink beside him, so tongues were loose enough. They weren't all actors. Ruarri, yes. But not the others—not Athol Cameron, or Daddy Burns, or Calum, who was a simple fellow, rowdy as a cock at sunrise. It made no sense at all, and after a while I was glad it didn't. So long as they landed me dry in the Faeroes, they could all go buccaneering for the rest of their lives—and whether they traded guns, women, shrimps, or salt herring, bless 'em all!

Just before ten-thirty, I tossed in my cards and went to bed. I tried to read for a while, but the effort to focus made me feel queasy; so I switched off the light and lay wakeful in the dark, listening to the buffet of the sea and the creak of the timbers and the muted gabble of voices from the galley. I thought of Kathleen McNeil, alone in her bed in Harris, and wished I were there with her; but there was small comfort in wishing and less in the fact that I would have to travel two thousand miles to get back to her.

Then I began to be obsessed by the bleak geography of the northern seas and all their legendary terrors of gales and fogs and drifting ice floes and black cliffs rearing out of millrace waters. I remembered the toll of ships and men exacted every year by the black widow-maker to pay for the harvest of fish. I saw the longships putting out from Norway and the coasts of Jutland, square sails bellying, shield bosses gleaming in the thin sunlight, serried oar blades striking the water to the rhythm of the helmsman's chant. I saw them scattered and labouring, rimed with ice from the driven spray, the sails shredded, the masts broken, the oarsmen furred like animals, blotched with frostbite, peering through the murk for a landfall in the dark. I saw them battling through the tide rips of the Faeroes, desperate for a beachhead where they could land their beasts and their women and begin to breed again to replace the lives taken by the sea. I saw Ruarri among them, always the survivor, the red wolf, run down to skin and bone, but snappish still and savage, howling defiance at the winds. Then, because I was deep in dreaming, I saw him changed: to the seal-boy with fur on his back, the love child of sailor and sea beast, who in the end must go back to the deeps. . . .

I woke in darkness, blear-eyed and unrested. The rhythm of my world had changed. The wind had dropped. The engines were running dead slow and we were slopping in a long, greasy swell. Then I heard the long, hoarse bleat of the fog siren repeated every half-minute. I groped for the light switch, and when I had rubbed the gravel out of my eyes, I saw it was six-twenty in the morning. Ruarri's bunk was empty and rumpled. I washed perfunctorily, climbed creakily into my sea clothes and went into the galley. There was no one there, but there was coffee still warm on the stove. I drank two cups and felt better. Then I climbed up on deck and stopped dead in my tracks.

The fog, so thick that I could not see the tips of my own fingers, stretched in front of me. It swirled and eddied like floating wool, stifling, blinding, solid enough to chew on. Even the sound of the hooter was muffled by it, and when I shouted it was as if I had fur in my throat and wadding pressed against my lips. Then I heard Daddy Burns's warning cry:

"Dinna wander aboot. Get up to the wheelhouse!"

I groped my way, inch by inch, to the companionway and climbed into the narrow lighted box where Ruarri stood, one hand on the wheel, the other on the button of the klaxon. He looked pale and strained and his eyes were bloodshot. He greeted me with a curt nod and announced:

"We've had this lot four hours and more. And we've lost Lachie."

"What do you mean, lost him?"

"Look outside. That's what I mean. I was on watch

from midnight. He was due to relieve me at four. He didn't show. I cut engines and went below to roust him out. His bunk was empty. He must have come on deck before his watch and walked overboard. It's happened before on other ships. We've had all hands on deck and we've been cruising in circles ever since, hoping to find him. I've called all ships and coast-guard stations."

"Can he swim?"

"I don't know. Even if he could, that water's bloody cold. He couldn't keep going for too long."

"Christ! Can I help?"

"Take the wheel. Make a slow turn, full circle to starboard. Watch the radar screen. Sound the hooter every thirty seconds. I want to make a round of the deck."

"Take care!"

"I will."

He left me then, and I could hear his calls and the answering voices receding into the fog:

"Athol?"

"Here."

"Calum?"

"Here!"

"Donan?"

"Here, Ruarri!"

Then there was silence except for the slow, ponderous beat of the engines and the hooter sounding out across the invisible sea. Mercifully the radar screen was clear; so, for the moment, we were out of hazard from collision with rocks or passing vessels. By the time I had completed one long, sluggish circle, Ruarri was back in the wheelhouse.

"Nothing. Not a sound. And you can't see a foot in front of you."

"What now?"

"Square search to port, two miles on each leg."

He left me at the wheel and bent over the chart, plotting the search areas with calipers and slide rule, making notations on each so that they could be read in concord with his log. Then he set to work on the log itself, writing slowly and meticulously the account that he must present to the Board of Inquiry. The log completed, he switched on the transmitter and called again, on the distress frequency, to all ships and coast-guard stations from Tórshavn to Stornoway. He gave his latest position and a curt account of the loss of Lachie McMurtrie and ended with the ominous words, "Search continues in visibility zero. If no success by 1000 hours will proceed to Tórshavn, Faeroes, for refuelling and filing of accident report. Please acknowledge. . . ."

Then he switched to receiver and jotted down the acknowledgements: from the Shetlands, from Tórshavn, from a Danish merchantman, from the coast guard at Streymoy, and finally from Stornoway itself. After that he sat a long time with the headset still clamped over his ears and his chin buried in his fists, staring out into the fog. At last he took off the headset and stood up. "I'm going to pass round a grog to the deck watch. Could you use one?"

"Thanks."

"Do you understand the routine?"

"What routine?"

"When we get to Tórshavn I file an accident report, accompanied by extracts from my log and my chart entries. The report is countersigned by Athol Cameron, with or without comment. The crew will be asked to make depositions. You may be too. When we get back to Stornoway there'll be a Board of Inquiry. It's not incumbent on me to show the log to any but the mate. As a matter of courtesy I'll show it to the other boys. You can see it if you want."

"Kind of you to offer, but there's no need."

"You'll still leave us at Tórshavn?"

"I think it's better, don't you?"

"Probably."

"Do you have any hope at all?"

"Precious little. But stranger things have happened. We might find him."

"I'll pass round the grog if you like."

"No. They need to see the skipper at a time like this. Steady as she goes, eh?"

Steady as she goes, two slow miles on one leg, then port again, and another two miles, checking the screen, sounding the hooter, blind searchers in a cloud world, listening for a cry from nowhere, hoping against hope that somewhere we might fish up a sodden bundle of flesh and clothes and find life in it still.

Was it Ruarri's hope too? I wanted to believe it was. I had seen him in many moods, bitter, mocking, mur-

169

derously angry; but I had never seen him so ravaged as in those ghostly hours. When, a long time later, he came back to the wheelhouse with a grog for each of us, his hands were unsteady and a nerve was twitching at the corner of his mouth, drawing his lips upward in a grin that had no humour in it at all. Even his voice had changed to a husky, tired monotone, as if his gullet were choked with fog.

"You know what this means, don't you, seannachie?"

"I can guess."

"They'll never believe it was an accident."

"Can they prove otherwise?"

"Never."

"So?"

"So like good Scotsmen they'll return an open finding: death by misadventure, circumstances unknown."

"Which leaves you in the clear."

"But never clean, seannachie. Never quite clean again."

"Do you care?"

"You're damn right I care. I'm owed as much respect as the next man."

"You'll have it, from those who know the truth."

"But who does know it? My boys? You? . . ."

"I know only what you've told me."

"And that leaves a lot of room for doubt, doesn't it?"

"Some."

"And you know I'm a good liar when I want to be?"

"For God's sake, man! Drop it!"

"You told me, seannachie, if anything happened to Lachie, you'd be a hostile witness. Now it's happened. Where do we stand?"

"I think my position is very clear. I was on watch from four in the afternoon till eight. When I came below Lachie was alive and happy. I played poker with him and his shipmates until ten-thirty. The game was friendly. I was in my bunk from ten-thirty till six-thirty this morning. End of testimony."

"And the rest of it?"

"The rest is words spoken between you and me without witnesses. As testimony it's useless. I would see no reason to present it."

"And your private opinion?"

170

"I have none. I accept what you've told me as the truth."

"Because you have to?"

"Because I want to."

"Well . . . !" The word came out on a long sigh of relief. "Thank Christ for that. Ever since it happened I've felt your hands on my neck choking me. I'm grateful."

"Forget it."

"Can you cook, seannachie?"

"Why?"

"You'd do me a favour if you could fry up a breakfast for the boys. They're damn near frozen out there. Call 'em down two by two. Send mine up here."

"Aye aye, Mr. Matheson."

"Thank you, Mr. Christian."

The joke was flatter than barley water, but it got me out of the wheelhouse and into the galley and took the sharp edge off a very uncomfortable stretch of dialogue. Now I had time and solitude to think through the events of the night.

At first blush, the story of a man walking off the deck of a trawler into the sea made incredible nonsense. Yet every sailorman had a sackful of such tales and many of them were true. There was the strange case of the Flannan lighthouse, found deserted in 1900 with the light trimmed, the boat intact, a meal on the table—and three men disappeared into thin air. In a fog like this one, on a stern trawler like the *Helen II,* where the deck fell away into a steel slide over the transom, a man, drunk, sleepwalking or unwary, could tumble overboard, and even if he cried out, his voice could be lost in the stern wash or the beat of the engines or the sound of the klaxon. On the other hand, he could as easily be taken by an assailant and toppled overside with no one to see or hear what was done.

Accident or assassination? There was no evidence either way. Except that a motive existed, and a strong one at that, for wanting Lachie McMurtrie dead. I knew it. Ruarri knew it. If my reading of the poker party was correct, no one else on board knew it. Which meant that Ruarri had lied to me about the confrontation with Lachie—or had he? He had suggested, intimated, created

171

an impression that a confrontation had taken place; but he had not said so, word by word.

Why didn't I ask him and settle the matter out of hand? Because it was safer and easier for me to take everything at face value and absolve myself from responsibility. After all, that was what Duggie Donald had recommended, and Duggie Donald was the representative of the Crown. If he couldn't make a case for Regina against Matheson, why should I do his dirty work for him? I couldn't prove Ruarri guilty. I could only suggest that he might be. Why make the suggestion when I knew that proof was impossible? Which was, of course, a highly correct point of view. A man is innocent until proven guilty, and the burden of proof rests squarely on the Crown. Somewhere out in the grey mist Lachie McMurtrie was floating dead and heedless, with his lungs full of water. I was safe and warm in the galley, cooking bacon and eggs and making myself a big fellow with his shipmates. Poor Lachie. Lucky me. All I needed was a bowl of water and a towel and I could be the most proper Pilate in the seven seas.

And Ruarri? Once again he would be off free, with profit in the bank, simply because he was as clever as a whore with that changeling talent of his. I could see the pattern of it now: the rage first, then the penitence, then the wheedling charm, each one a step towards the prize he wanted at that moment. He was like a child, but a child confirmed in selfishness, cold, cruel, infinitely seductive, with a perpetual promise of innocence, provided he got what he wanted. Well, today, tomorrow at the latest, I would be quit of him. Let Brother Wolf go range his own timberline; I would have him no more in my pastures.

Yet, when I carried his breakfast up to the wheelhouse and saw him grey and lonely on watch, my heart went out to him; and when he told me his thought, I was as haunted as he was.

". . . He'll never be buried, seannachie. The sea birds will peck out his eyes and sharks will eat the rest of him. He was a silly young truaghan, but he didn't deserve this. We'll hear him for a long time now, whenever the gulls cry, because his ghost will be restless. Do you believe in ghosts, seannachie?"

"No."

"Neither do I. But I'm scared of them, still. Over in the west where I live, they say a drowned man must be buried high enough on the beach so that he can shake the brine off himself at low tide. If he can't, he'll come flopping on someone's deck, just to be dry for a while. . . . I wish this bloody fog would lift."

"Why don't you go below and get some rest?"

"I can't. Not till we break off the search. After that, if the weather clears, we're going to trawl."

"No!"

"Why not, seannachie? Something to do to take our minds off Lachie. Besides, we're fishermen, and if we don't catch we don't eat. That's why the sea laughs at us. We always have to come back. . . . Thanks for the breakfast. Get the others fed, eh?"

Athol Cameron and Donan, the Barra boy, were the first to come below. They ate hungrily, in silence; and I ate with them, waiting for their reaction to the tragedy.

When it came, it was a terse epitaph from Athol Cameron:

"He's gone for sure. God sleep him quietly."

The Barra boy crossed himself and murmured something in Gaelic. I asked Cameron what it meant.

"It's a prayer they say: 'Saint Brendan, wish the fog away. God lift it for the sake of Holy Brendan.' "

"What do you think happened, Athol?"

"Man, I couldn't guess."

"Was he drunk?"

"Not when he went to bed. But he could have been tippling in his bunk, which he did sometimes, under the blanket."

"Could he have walked in his sleep?"

"Could have. Though I've never known him do it."

"If he were sober, could he still have fallen overboard?"

"In a fog like that, anything can happen."

"It's like a wall." Donan gave voice in a swift, stammering rush of words. "You think it's solid. When you lean on it, you fall through. . . . My uncle walked off a tanker near Hatteras years ago. My grannie had a vision of it the same night. She had the second sight and all. She said there was voices singing at him all the time, calling him to come . . ."

"Stow it, lad!" said Athol Cameron curtly. "Let's get

up on deck. There's others to be fed. Thanks for the breakfast."

From Daddy Burns and Calum MacMillan I got the same story in other words. At sea the improbable always happened. There were men blown sky-high out of tankers who lived to tell the tale. There were ships found adrift, with no living soul on board. Airmen flew upside down in cloud and never knew it. There were sailors who went into a kind of whirling madness when they lost their sense of direction. The yarns spun out interminably, with never a hint of malice or violence. There was pity always for the man lost, and some left over for the good-luck skipper whose fortune had turned sour overnight. Work? Of course they must work. The sea cared for its own dead. The living must make shift for themselves.

So, at ten in the morning, with the fog still down, Ruarri broke off the search and headed us northwards to Tórshavn. Then he handed over the wheel to Athol Cameron and went below to rest. An hour later we were free of the fog, in clear, bright air. With the trawl out and the first fringe of the cold front chopping up the sea again. By midafternoon we had taken half a ton of fish— cod, mostly, for which there was a good market in the Faeroes—and Ruarri was on deck, a new man, brusque, efficient, confident, watching the fish packed, ordering the decks hosed down, the nets stowed, so that we would come shipshape and worthy into Tórshavn. When the first is-lands came abeam, he read me a little discourse:

"This is the land of *kanska,* seannachie, and *kanska* means *maybe.* Maybe the sun will shine, maybe the sea will be calm, maybe the fish will run—but nobody knows for sure. This is the place where men fled from oppression into hardship and were glad just the same. They have their own currency and their own flag, and by courtesy they let the Danes handle their defense and their foreign affairs. They're dry, too, because a man can't buy liquor until he's paid his taxes. So when you go ashore you'd best take a bottle to keep the cold out. There's only one air-port, at Vágar, and you'll have a scary run by sea and land to get to it. There's one plane a day to Copenhagen— which reminds me I must give you a note to Maeve O'Donnell—and they grow rhubarb and potatoes and eat dried mutton, which tastes like tallow. Sometimes there's a killing of whales and the bays run red with blood, and after that they dance and drink all night, so there's a flush of births nine months afterwards. . . . There's a song they sing which goes back to Viking days: 'We are strong men, we love the killing of whales.'—And I wish you wouldn't leave, seannachie. I wish you'd finish the run with me."

"I can't."

"I know you can't. But what's the harm in wishing? I feel safer with you on board."

"You're not."

"I know that too. But listen."

"I'm listening."

"Don't shut me out, brother."

"I haven't."

"Not yet. But you want to, and you can't because I've still a foot stuck in the doorway. I need you, seannachie. With you I don't have to pretend."

"But you do."

"That's habit, and I'm not proud of it."

"Hear me, Ruarri. I'm older than you. I'm tired. I want a nice, quiet life, taxes paid, no sweat, no problems, the words meaning what they say, the bed warm and the waking happy. I've got ghosts of my own. I don't need yours."

"So, no ghosts. Just today. And tomorrow maybe a letter or two that says a greeting and that there's a place at table if I come."

"I wish I could trust you, Ruarri."

"I wish I could trust myself, for Christ's sake. But I can't. Don't you see that's the core of it?"

"Give me one straight answer."

"What's the question?"

"Did you kill Lachie?"

"I don't know, seannachie. I'd swear it to you if I had anything to swear by. I just don't know."

And there it was, tied with a pink ribbon and laid in my unsteady hands.

It was like a death or a wedding, when there's nothing to do but drink a toast to the dear departing and hope that everything turns out for the best—which it generally doesn't. I didn't have a drink, so I couldn't make a toast;

and, besides, I had no words to frame it. I braced myself against the bulkhead and gaped at him.

His mouth dragged upwards in that lopsided, humourless grin. "It's the truth, big brother."

"I believe you."

"So what should I do now?"

"You need help."

"That's what I'm asking—from you."

"I'm not a doctor."

"You don't have to be. I'm not sick, seannachie. I'm a man who's lived twenty lives, all of them violent. They run into one another, and I don't know which is which. What's the dream? What's the real thing? How can a doctor tell me that?"

"How can I?"

"You can. Because you're a seannachie. You live in two countries at once. You know how to keep them separate."

"Not always."

"But at least you understand the confusion when it comes."

"Mine I understand . . . not any other man's."

"But you write about other men and not yourself."

"What do you want from me, for God's sake?"

"Nothing. Just to know that you're there, that I can reach out and touch you and say, 'This at least is real, solid, a reference point that doesn't shift.' "

"It's too much."

"I still ask it."

"Tell me something."

"What?"

"If you knew now, for certain, that you had killed Lachie, what would you do?"

"Walk up forward with me."

We left the shelter of the wheelhouse and pushed our way up to the bows with the wind in our teeth and the spray beating against us with every pitch and yaw. Then, as the black cliffs of Sandoy thrust out ahead of us, he told me:

"If I knew, seannachie, if I knew truly, beyond all doubt, I'd finish whatever I was at. I'd write my log, cast up my accounts, pay my bills, leave everything tidy, call the police and the undertaker and blow my addled brains out."

"Why for this and not for all the other things?"

"You don't give any change, do you?"

"Not now."

"Then I'll tell you, and I hate you for making me say it, because I thought you were wise enough to know. When I came home—it was home, and it is, in spite of everything—I said to myself, 'This is a new day, a good place. The past is dead and buried. There's only to-morrow!' But it wasn't like that. Every man I met, and every woman, put a label on me from the first meeting. I put some on myself too! I'll say that, so you won't have to say it for me. But I did want the slate clean. . . ."

"So you run guns to Ulster! Come on now!"

"What's a few guns, for God's sake?"

"You put a bullet in the breech. You pull the trigger. The bullet comes out the other end and kills a man. Who's the murderer—the gun, the man who pulls the trigger, or the man who sold him the gun in the first place?"

"I didn't ask for a sermon. I want help."

"You don't. You want to be Ruarri the Mactire morning, noon and night, but you don't like the price you have to pay for it."

"Meaning I killed Lachie?"

"Meaning you could have and you would have if it suited your book. And whether you did or you didn't, I don't have enough blood left to bleed for you."

"So you'll sell me out?"

"There's nobody to sell. Nobody to help either, until you tell me who you are."

"I'm trying to tell you."

"You're lying, Brother Wolf."

"Then read behind the lie."

"Why tell it in the first place?"

"Because it's the only currency I know, seannachie. It's the coin I got for my birthday: Morrison's lie and all the others that were spawned out of it afterwards. After a while the lie becomes a truth, which is the way history gets written—and books like yours, seannachie. You'll give me that much, won't you?"

"Yes. I'll give you that much."

"So now I'll answer your question. The difference be-

177

tween Lachie and the others? Lachie was a friend, a fol-
lower. Maybe I pushed him too far and he turned traitor,
but he was still my man—mine! The others were just
shapes in a gunsight, shadows against the rising moon, not
men at all."

"So why do you doubt whether you killed him?"

"I'll tell you that, too, big brother. You're right, you
see. Sometimes I'm nobody. I'm the shadow. I'm the
shape in someone else's sights. When that happens, I
don't remember. How can I? Nobody is nobody is nobody. . . . That's why I do wild things and say wild
things, to get myself back again. Do you see that?"

"A little of it, yes."

"So what is it with us—good-bye or come again?"

"I'll be back to the Isles."

"And we'll have our ceilidh?"

"Let's wait and see. How long now to Tórshavn?"

"An hour. It won't be too rough. The Faeroese are
pleasant folk. And they understand the way of the sea."

They couldn't have been pleasanter. The Customs man
gave us a perfunctory inspection and the freedom of the
port. The fish broker offered a reasonable price for the
catch—just a shade under the odds, to keep the locals
happy. The harbour master found a bed for me in his
sister's house. The British Consul—no Britisher, but a
Faeroese—came on board and shared a bottle of whisky
in the galley while he took our depositions. He was sym-
pathetic, tactful and obviously impressed by Ruarri's careful logging of the incident. He engaged two airmail copies
of the documents to Stornoway, to inform Lachie's next
of kin, to do all else that law and decency required after
a death at sea. Then he went home to dinner.

Ruarri collected a check for his fish, paid out another
for fuel and announced that he was ready to put to sea
again. It was still only eight o'clock. He had the long, sub-
Arctic night to cruise in, and he wanted to be far away
from the islands before the cold front came down. Of his
rendezvous with Bollison he made no mention at all. He
gave me a note to deliver to Maeve O'Donnell at the
Hotel d'Angleterre in Copenhagen. We wished each other
luck. I stood on the dock and watched the *Helen II*
bouncing her way across the choppy harbour to the open

sea. I was glad to see the last of her. She had a ghost on board and I did not want to be there when his drowned body came flopping on the deck, shaking the brine off itself at midnight.

XII

I SPENT A RESTLESS NIGHT, TOSSING AND TURNING UNDER a feather quilt that kept falling off the bed while I wrestled with an exotic nightmare. I was searching vainly for Kathleen on a ghostly moorland while Ruarri harried me like a hunter and nameless monsters clutched at me from black bog pools. In the end I lost Kathleen and found Lachie McMurtrie, with fishes in his dripping hands and bubble weed where his eyes used to be, sitting in judgment on a black rock. Ruarri was behind me, his hands, gripping my shoulders, forcing me to kneel in penitence and confess myself for a murderer. Then Lachie was gone and Ruarri and Kathleen were lying naked on the rock, making love, while I fought my way through a tangle of sea wrack to reach them. Then they were gone and I was alone, with the gulls wheeling about my head, swooping to peck at me and crying all the time: "Lachie, Lachie, Lachie. . . ." I woke, sodden with sweat, to hear the rain beating on the windowpane and the cold wind whining round the eaves.

At breakfast my host told me there was a plane for Copenhagen that left Vágar every day at three o'clock—*kanska!* Maybe it would come. Maybe, with bad weather, it wouldn't. In any case, I should leave a couple of hours before midday, because Vágar was forty-five miles away and it would take me four hours at least to get there. In my fuddled state, I thought I had mistaken the mathematics. I discovered, painfully, that they were correct to the last particular.

First I took a taxi and was driven twenty-five miles across the island of Streymoy: a horrendous, switchback journey in driving rain, over mountain roads with never a guardrail between us and the cliff drops, and no moment at all to enjoy the tiny painted villages and the waterfalls, and the cloud patterns piled over the peaks. Then there was the ferry ride to Vágar, a bouncing, belly-churning passage across a tide rip; then another taxi ride to the airport, which was just a black runway, with a couple of hangars and a passenger office, perched on top of a rain-swept plateau. The aircraft was on its way. It would be half an hour late, but it would come. Not *kanska* this time; it had to get in because there was no other place for it to go except Iceland.

I sent a telegram to Kathleen to tell her of my change of plan and settled down with the small group of passengers to possess in patience what was left of my soul. There wasn't very much and I doubted whether it was worth saving, anyway. I had little to be proud of—much less than Ruarri, who at least had the courage to dare all the indecencies of life and battle, even to bloodletting, for his own foothold on the planet. I was still a running man, chary of small consequences, clinging desperately to a diminishing stock of certainties. I was a poor enemy, who would bluff, but never fight. I was a niggard friend, who doled himself out like alms to the needy. I was a purblind philosopher, who trampled on daisies in his blundering search for half-truths. I was a patchwork moralist with no charity in him at all, at all. The memory of the nightmare was still strong on me, and, though I am no reader of dreams, the message of this one was uncomfortably clear. Also I had a splitting headache and a foul taste in my mouth. I wished fervently that the aircraft would come and haul me out of this God-forgotten hole.

It came at last, forty-five minutes late: a Fokker Friendship settling down like a gannet on the strip, absurdly small in this waste of mountains and dark sea. When we took off it seemed smaller still and very fragile as it climbed precariously through the long gut between the cliffs, into the grey overhang. I looked back at the coastline with its hostile cliffs and its narrow, turbulent

180

bays, and I wondered where Ruarri was, and whether he had met Bollison and transshipped his guns and where he would land them, and what kind of homecoming he would have afterwards. I dozed most of the way to Copenhagen, and it was as well that I did because the shock of the arrival was greater than I had expected.

Kastrup Airport was crowded with tourists: Danes migrating to the sun, Germans and French and Dutch and English swarming in for the fleshpots of this happy-go-lucky town. Immediately I was panic-stricken. There was no space to move or breathe. The noise was an intolerable cacophony. I was sweating from every pore, choking with nausea. I was tempted to leave my baggage behind and run screaming into the open air. My panic increased when I realized that I had no hotel booking and no place to go. I stood, in a fever of impatience, waiting for my luggage; I stumbled blindly through Customs and found my way to the tourist office. The girl behind the counter smiled and was helpful, ignoring my boorish manners. I was in luck. Every hotel was full, but they had just telephoned a cancellation from the d'Angleterre. Would I take it? I snatched the slip from her hand and hurried away, jostling through the crowd to the taxi rank. I was halfway to the city before the panic subsided and I could breathe freely again.

Then a new fear beset me. I was not cured at all. I was still a man in fragments, pawing the air to retrieve the little bits of himself. How long could I go on like this? Must I always wander in solitary places, deserts and islands and tiny provinces, because I was unfit for the company of my fellows? If you have never felt this terror, then be glad and thank God, because it is a real madness, and if it goes on too long, there is no cure, not ever.

When we came to the Hotel d'Angleterre I found I had no Danish money to pay for the taxi; so I had to buy it from the cashier, which was a good thing because it planted me back, feetfirst, in simple sanity. I registered. A porter led me upstairs to a room the size of a shoe box, right next to the elevator. He apologized for it, took my tip and left me to unpack and bathe and make myself look like a man again. I did it all very slowly, testing each step as if I were walking near quicksands—as indeed I was. When finally I could look in the mirror without fear

181

or shame, I went down to the bar and sat a long time over a large drink, boosting my courage for the call to Maeve O'Donnell.

Her greeting was like a gust of clean air, blowing away the melancholy. "Seannachie! God love you! Where are you at?"

"Downstairs in the bar."

"Then come on up. I'm naked, but I'll be decent before you get here."

"I'll finish my drink and be there."

"To hell with your drink! There's better liquor here— and no charge for it. Come now."

I went. I rode up in the elevator, whistling "The Rakes of Mallow," which is a tune my grandfather taught me and which has a fine jaunty lilt to it. I knocked on the door; it opened before my fist was off the wood. Maeve dragged me inside and the next instant we were laughing and kissing as though we had known each other for a lifetime. Then she shoved me down on the couch and had a drink in my hands before I could wipe the lipstick off my mouth.

The suite was large enough for an army and the general's mistress as well; but Maeve curled herself on the couch beside me, wrapped her dressing gown round her legs and commanded:

"Now, tell me, seannachie! Tell me all."

"Read this first, while I get my breath."

I fished in my pocket and brought out Ruarri's note. She frowned over it a long time and then asked me, "Do you know what's in it?"

"No."

"Read it then."

I read it, and I was appalled.

Dear Maeve,

Your consignment will be delivered on time. I hope your payment will be as prompt, because there's a certain amount of trouble and I may need ready cash to bail myself out of it. One of my crewmen talked too loud, so the law is sniffing around my doorstep. He's dead now, which creates another problem; but I think I can handle it. Ask the seannachie for details. You can believe what he says, because he's a sad fellow with a passion for truth—God help us!

It's him I'm scared of, because, although I like him and I think he likes me, I doubt whether he's bright enough to get out of the rain—and the weather's likely to be uncertain for a little while. See if you can talk, or sleep, some sense into him. You're good at both.

Love,
Ruarri

I folded the letter and handed it back to her. "I think you ought to burn that."

"I'll do it now."

I gave her a lighter and she burned the note in an ashtray and ground the ashes into powder. Then she faced me and asked quietly, "Will you tell me, seannachie?"

"Anything you want to know."

"Why would you do that?"

"You did me a favour. I'd like to return it. And Ruarri's in a deeper hole than he knows."

"Are you his friend?"

"I don't know, Maeve."

"His enemy?"

"Not that. Something in between, perhaps. I'll tell you the facts. Then you'll judge for yourself."

"Before you tell me . . ."

"Yes?"

"I'm not going to talk, or sleep, you into anything."

"Forget that."

"I wish I could. Tell me now. . . ."

I told her as I have told it to you, hour by hour from the night of Morrison's dinner to the night of our parting on the dock at Tórshavn. I tried, as an honest reporter should, to separate fact from opinion, sentiment from the thing seen. I exposed my rancours and my doubts and my jealousies, my weaknesses, too, and the dilemmas they had created for me. It was a more honest confession than I had made to anyone—man or woman—in a long time. It was an indulgence and I admit it. But if Ruarri had need of indulgence and Morrison and Kathleen McNeil, so had I, and I admitted that, too, and felt a little better for it—if not more knightly or noble.

Maeve's comment was completely in character. "Ugh!

They're all mad in the twilight! I think you're a little mad, too, seannachie."

"I'm sure of it."

"Do you have any money?"

"More than I need. Why?"

"Because you're going to find me the best dinner in town. Then you're going to walk me round Tivoli Gardens and buy me anything I crave. After that we're going to drink with the sailor boys in Nyhavn, and if we're still on our feet, we'll go say good night to the Mermaid. What do you say, seannachie?"

"I'm your man, lover girl."

"Then pour yourself another drink while I throw some clothes on. . . . Holy Michael, what a mess of worms! And that Ruarri's the slimiest wriggler of them all!"

She was just what I needed that night, reckless and rollicking, with the wildest words bubbling out in that oh-so-douce Dublin accent. She was hurt and she was angry—and maybe at bottom she was scared—but she was damned and double-damned if she'd let it spoil her appetite for food, liquor and the soft summer air. So here beginneth the saga of a Jack and his Irish Jill, who didn't know each other worth a damn, but who had an awkward friend in common and wanted to forget him with a night on this ever-loving town.

We left the hotel arm in arm, because, as the lady said, we'd be coming back that way, so the help should get used to the spectacle. We turned in to Strøget, which is five streets of wonderful shops, where no traffic is allowed except a traffic of people, and they some of the most beautiful in all the world—and some of the weirdest too. Here you can buy everything from a stone axe to an ermine cape, and every purchase comes wrapped in a smile. We bought everything, but decided we wouldn't take it away, just leave it for other folks to enjoy—porcelain and goldware and silver jewelry and crazy clothes and fantasies in glass and teak furniture and tooled leather. Oh, we did take one thing, a book of poems from a barefoot genius with a Rasputin beard, who printed his books on a handpress and peddled them from a baby's perambulator. Maeve thought he deserved to succeed, and since we couldn't read Danish, we'd never be disappointed in the poetry.

We sat in the tiny square, at the center of things, with flowers blooming about us and watched the come and go of the burghers of Copenhagen and the invaders who were sweetly conquered the moment they arrived: leggy girls and blond, giant boys and peach-skinned matrons and children like beauties out of a fairy tale, a minor prophet in a caftan, preaching love, not war, a gypsy girl who needed a bath but who played sweet rebel songs on a guitar, a sad-eyed youth with beads around his neck and his wrists and his ankles and the smell of hash clinging to his hair, a trio of sailormen rolling arm in arm down the road and calling to the girls in Portuguese. Maeve said we were fools not to live here all our lives, because even the police were gentlemen and wore plain clothes so they wouldn't spoil the view. I told her I'd buy her a house that very night, but only after dinner, so we wouldn't be too anxious and choose the wrong one.

Dinner we ate at the sign of the Golden Cockerel, which is a deceptive place because it looks like a simple tavern; but there is a man who does miracles in the kitchen, and his dishes are delivered to you with a happy reverence and you are blessed when you eat them.

It was in the quiet of this shrine that Maeve first asked me about Kathleen. "How is it with the pair of you, seannachie?"

"Good, very good."

"You're lovers?"

"Yes."

"Good. Then you're in the home stretch."

"But not past the post. Is that what you mean?"

"That's what I mean. How much do you know about women, seannachie?"

"Less and less as I get older."

"Then you're growing wise. But listen, my love, there's a moment in every race when you have to make the running if you want to win. I think you're coming up to that moment now."

"Why?"

"Ruarri's letter. All you've told me. You have to understand him, seannachie. You have to be clear how his mind works. You're very alike—and that's a danger for you because you're very unlike as well. Comes a moment with that boyo when he drives off at a tangent, cuts clean across the track in front of you, and tumbles you on the turf. Your weakness is that you expect him to be running the same race as you are. He isn't. He's trying to run twenty others at the same time. The only way he can get at you—and he will, just because he's fond of you—is through Kathleen. He'll try it. Mark my words."

"She's a big girl. She knows her own mind."

"But she doesn't. Not with him, not with you either. She's been honest enough to tell you. So you'll have to make up her mind for her in the end."

"How?"

"That's for you to say. But Ruarri comes into it."

"Tell me something, Maeve."

"What?"

"Does he really believe I'm as big a fool as he says?"

"Of course. He believes it of everybody. He has to."

"He's a sick man then."

"How sick?"

"If you're asking me about Lachie, I don't know the answer."

"I think he did it, and I know him a lot better than you."

"Were you lovers?"

"Too long."

"But you still use him."

"For the mercenary he is. I pay him, and I like that."

"If he killed Lachie, you killed him, too, Maeve mine."

"So I did. But there's a difference."

"What?"

"There's two of me, my brave bard, and I know exactly who each one is. There's Sister Maeve that you're out with tonight. She breeds horses and she likes to wear expensive clothes and have fun and go out with good-looking men—which you are, seannachie, especially when you smile—and she'll move mountains for her friends and drink a deep damnation to her enemies. Then there's Maeve O'Donnell, daughter of Patrick O'Donnell, granddaughter of Michael, who was shot by the British after the Easter Rising. That one's a patriot, seannachie—which is an old-fashioned word but a good one—and she hates the British and will spend the last drop of her blood to get their filthy feet off her own land. That's the Maeve you shouldn't take out to dinner, and if ever she tried to seduce

186

you to the cause, you should spit in her eye and send her packing. . . . Now pour me a drink and tell me I'm beautiful."

"You're beautiful, Maeve O'Donnell."

"I'm also frightened as hell at this moment. The British —and the Irish government, too—are breaking their backs to stop the flow of arms into the country. This business of Ruarri's could wreck our whole organization."

"I hope it does."

"You could do it yourself now. With my name and Ruarri's and what you know of us both, you could put us out of business."

"You're a bitch, Maeve O'Donnell."

"And you, seannachie love, are just not enough of a bastard. Which is a pity for you and a blessing for us. Now let's drop it, eh?"

I should have been insulted, but I wasn't. She was being a sight more honest than others I could name; and she was giving a lot of herself and asking nothing more than bright company in a bright town and to forget the rest of the dog's world we lived in.

When we left the Golden Cockerel we were mellow as the old brandy we'd had with the coffee. We sauntered down to Tivoli Gardens and wandered, hand in hand, under the festooned lights, watching the people, listening to the band, buying silly trifles at the booths, smelling the flowers, laughing like children at the flea circus. We danced to old-fashioned waltzes, and fox-trots from the twenties, and beat music and soul music and God knows what else. We ate spun sugar. We pitched hoops round kewpie dolls. We shot at jumping rabbits in a gallery. We rode swings and roundabouts and had coffee and sweet pastry at midnight. And with all the people and all the noise and all the narrow places we were in, I was as happy as a colt in a meadow full of buttercups and dandelions. Even Maeve noticed the change; and, when we were sitting, languid but content, over our coffee, she said, "You're another man, seannachie. Where did you spring from?"

"I think I just got lost for a while."

"How?"

"It's a long story. I don't want to tell it."

"Not even a short version?"

"All right. Short and not very sweet. There are women

who want to castrate the man they love and coddle him ever after like a gelding in a paddock. I married one like that. I loved her, too, so it took me a long time to understand what she was at. I don't blame her now. I feel sorry for her. I escaped and then fell apart—confidence gone, talent dried up, or almost, spent and aimless after a wasted battle. Boh . . . *Finita la commedia!*"

"Thanks for telling me."

"You're welcome."

"Now take me up to Nyhavn."

"Why Nyhavn?"

"That's another story. And I'm a sentimental Irish slob."

"The hell you are, Maeve O'Donnell! On your feet now."

So, with midnight long gone, we came to Nyhavn, that long, black canal with the fishing boats moored along it, and the old houses lined along its bank, chandlers and tattoo shops, and Chinese chow houses, and sleazy bars where you can meet sailormen from all the world and lumpish country girls and the oldest whores in Denmark. There are always police there, walking two and two, ready to pick up the drunks as they roll out the doors or to wade in if the brawling gets too loud and too violent, which it does from time to time. And yet it's a cheerful place, rowdy, boisterous, and healthier than the sad clubs on the other side of town, where pretty girls and handsome boys copulate on a mattress for the paying guests, and lesbians make public love and handle the men afterwards, and you can even mate with a poodle if you have a mind to and be paid for it. Which is the other side of the ever-loving city, and not the better one either.

I let Maeve choose the bar she wanted: a blank housefront with the windows painted over and the panes bulging from the raucous music inside. It had no name, only a number hung over the door, with a yellow light to guide the customers in. Once they got out, they had to be sober enough to find their ship, or they would end up in the canal or the police wagon.

Inside there was a fog of tobacco smoke and a smell of stale bodies and spilled beer. We fought our way to a table in a corner, and I struggled back to the bar to buy our drinks over the rows of nodding heads. I tried to find an easier way back, across the dance floor, but was almost mown down by a prancing giant with a fat girl hoisted up to his bosom. When I got to Maeve I found her fending off the advances of a young Portuguese. He bowed himself out with an apology to me; and I was glad he wasn't a Norwegian, who might have eaten me for an early breakfast.

Maeve was flushed and exuberant. "I love it here, seannachie! I love the noise and the stink and the hefty maleness of it all."

"It's fun. But if someone throws a bottle, you upend the table and duck."

"Have you been here before?"

"Not here, but in other places like it."

"This is where I met Ruarri for the first time."

"Good God!"

"I was out on the town, just like I've been with you tonight. Except I was a little drunker and a little wilder. The man I was with doesn't matter—he didn't then either. I'd sold him some horses, which I found he liked better than women. I was kicking up my heels and making eyes at any man who was interested, and most were. Ruarri was sitting just over there with his boys and a few girls. He came and asked me to dance. I thought he was just a fine-looking fellow with a leery grin and an over-good conceit of himself. So I teased him. I waved everything I had at him like the banners of Brian Boru. Then, somewhere along the way, it wasn't a tease any more. We both went wild. He had me dancing on a table with my skirt spinning and my blouse down to my navel, and everyone shouting and clapping at the exhibition. I'd lost my escort by then. So, when it was all over, I went down to Ruarri's boat and slept there the night, and he's had my heart in his hands ever since."

"And then?"

"Then, seannachie, just like you, I discovered Ruarri the Mactire. It wasn't quick and it wasn't easy, because he is a wolf, soft and prowling one minute, then snarling and ravening, a loner this night, the next, loping up with the whole pack at his heels. And treacherous always, seannachie, playing good doggie with his feet up in the air until you reach out to scratch him—then he's bitten your hand off. I took it for a long time, because he's wonderful in bed, soft and knowing, then hard and driving like a piston—am I shocking you, seannachie?"

"No. Go on."

"He beat me sometimes. Not badly, but enough to scare me and make me want him gentle again. I didn't mind too much. I've got claws myself and I know how to use them. But came a moment when I couldn't take any more. I saw what he was doing—unbuilding me, brick by brick, to shore himself up. He's a coward, seannachie. He's scared like a little boy in the dark, but he won't let on. Try to pick him up and carry him to bed and he'll tear your eyes out. . . . So one day last year—it was just before the Curragh, I remember—I threw him out."

"You did?"

"Me, seannachie! Little Maeve O'Donnell! I told him what I thought of him, cold and quiet, in very simple words. Do you know what he did? He cried! He cried like a baby, torn from the tit. He loved me, he said—and he thought he did. I told him I loved him, but no loving was worth all the pain I'd paid for it. He asked could we be friends. I told him yes. And so we've been ever since, in just the way you've seen. When I hear the consignment's been delivered, I'll go back to him for a day or two and hold his hand. Then I'll go home again and cry for him in the night, praying he'll never hear me. . . ."

"Does he love you, Maeve?"

"He doesn't know how to love, seannachie. That's the pity of it. He wants to, but he doesn't know how. That's the way he is with you. He wants you for a brother, sure! But he doesn't know what a brother is. He's like a blind man hearing about colours, but never seeing them."

"Dear God! How sad!"

"Sure! But sad for you, too—and for me."

"What's the remedy?"

"I don't believe there is one. If there is, you're nearer to it than I am. I've slept with him, you see, I'm known, used up. He doesn't have to respect me, though, by Christ, he should! You he does respect, but he'll never admit it fully and honestly until you've rubbed his nose in the dirt and lifted him up again. It's the father he wants, seannachie. It's the father he never had. A woman can't be that. She can be mother, mistress, wife, whore, all in one

—but never a father. . . . Please, seannachie, it's the truth!"

"I know it is."

"I'm a bitch, but not here, not now."

"I know that too."

"So will you take me out now? Walk me home, slow and easy, and say sweet things to me on the way?"

"Come on, Sister Maeve."

"But, seannachie. . . ?"

"What?"

"Don't back down. Promise me you won't **back down** to Ruarri any more. If you do, you'll be a **killer like** the rest of us."

"I promise. Let's go now."

She wasn't drunk and she wasn't sober. She was full of tears, but she shed never a one. So I walked her all the way down the King's own street to the water and back again to the hotel. I said the sweet things that she wanted and I meant them all, although she was not my woman, nor ever would be, because of the past she carried and would carry all her life like a hoary giant on her back.

When I took her to her door, she said very softly, "Seannachie, don't leave me alone tonight."

"I won't. Wait for me."

There's no secret and no guilt about it. There was never need for any. I stayed with her that night and the two nights after, until Ruarri's message came. We were in a strange land and lonely, and no one cared who or what we were. It wasn't the love country, but we were happy in it for a little while. If, when I left her, I was whole, or nearly whole, it was because of the laying on of her hands. If she was calmer, and I think she was, it was because of the gentling she'd had from me.

XIII

I SENT TELEGRAMS TO KATHLEEN AND TO HANNAH AND to Morrison in the hospital, announcing my arrival. I flew from Copenhagen to Glasgow, spent one night in that dreary city and then took off the next morning for Stornoway. When we landed in a drizzle of rain, I found a reception committee: Duggie Donald, a local police constable, and a tall, grey-haired fellow who was introduced as Chief Inspector Rawlings of the Special Branch. Rawlings hated to bother me, but he was making certain inquiries and he hoped I might be willing to assist him. He was so polite about it that I had no thought of refusing. In fact, though I didn't tell him, I'd been preparing for him, or someone like him, all the way back. He thought perhaps the police station would be the most convenient place to talk, if I didn't mind—and of course I didn't. He would be happy to drive me down with Mr. Donald. The police constable would take care of my luggage. So, ten minutes later, I was seated in a rather bare room with Duggie and Rawlings and a young policewoman who sat in the background and wrote shorthand.

Rawlings, I found, was a very leisurely man with a taste for colourful detail. He was also very solicitous for my well-being. Would I like some coffee? I would. The coffee was brought. Had I had a pleasant trip? Well, the latter part of it. Copenhagen was a very pleasant city, was it not? Very. He travelled there himself occasionally. Where had I stayed? The Hotel d'Angleterre. Splendid place, though a little beyond the means of a working policeman. I had come back by way of Glasgow? Yes. How long had I stayed there? Only one night. He agreed it was more than enough. He was a Londoner himself, although his work often took him abroad, to the Continent, to Eire, the Six Counties, though rarely to the Hebrides. He supposed I was wondering what all this was about. I imagined it had something to do with the death of Lachie McMurtrie? That and certain related matters, yes. I presumed he received the deposition which I had made in Tórshavn? Oh yes. And it was very concise. He appreciated that. He hated to bore me, but perhaps a little amplification here and there? He was welcome to all the information I had, which I feared wasn't very much. Might he see my passport? Of course. He leafed through it carefully, then laid it open on the desk on top of his files. Then he began to question me in earnest.

"I see you're a novelist, sir?"

"Yes."

"This is your normal profession?"

"Yes."

"Your passport was issued in Rome. You are normally resident there?"

"Yes."

"May I have your address and telephone number, please?"

I gave them to him. He asked me to spell them out, for the benefit of the stenographer.

"Now, sir, may I ask what brought you to the Isles?"

"I came for a vacation, at the invitation of Alastair Morrison of Laxay. He's in hospital at present."

"We know that, sir. Thank you. This was your first visit?"

"Yes."

"You had no other friends in the Isles?"

"Not before I came. I have now."

"Among them Ruarri Matheson?"

"Yes."

"How did you come to meet him?"

I told him that in great detail.

He listened attentively, leaning back in his chair with his hands locked over his midriff. Then he said, "So this meeting on Skye and this first day's sailing were the only basis of your friendship."

"I'd say it was the beginning of the friendship rather than the basis of it. I liked Matheson from the first moment. He's a colourful character, well-read, well-trav-

193

elled, hospitable. He was my first contact in the Isles. I was only too happy to cultivate him. Our later contacts have proved friendly and interesting."

"For instance, you've been poaching together?"

"Correction, Inspector. We went fishing and deer-stalking, both legal recreations unless otherwise charged and proven."

"Forgive me. You have also visited Matheson's house?"

"Several times."

"Once or twice in the company of Dr. Kathleen McNeil, the locum from Harris?"

"Yes."

"And Matheson was your guest at dinner in Morrison's house?"

"Yes."

"So you have, in fact, established a fairly intimate relationship with him?"

"The word *intimate* is too coloured, Inspector. It sometimes bears unpleasant connotations, especially in court examinations. I would say a friendly relationship."

I wasn't trying to be clever, believe me. I wasn't trying to show what a bright bush lawyer I could be. I might, if he pressed me too hard, be forced to make some very fine verbal distinctions. So I wanted it fixed in his mind that I was a very academical fellow to whom all words had sharp edges. Also I had to be righteous, at least as long as I could. So I asked him a little testily:

"Would you mind if I made a comment, Inspector?"

"Not at all, sir."

"Then, Inspector, let's be frank with each other. I understand the meaning of words. I understand the import of questions. I want to help you in every way I can, in whatever inquiry you are making. I can best do that if you come straight to the point and stop rehearsing me in information which you already have. I have no intention of lying to you and no reason to, either. I hope I make myself plain."

"Admirably, sir. If I've offended you, I apologize. In our business we have to cultivate a method and a routine of investigation. Sometimes, I admit, we stick to them a little too rigidly, especially with a cooperative witness. Now, where were we? Ah yes! We've established your friendship with Ruarri Matheson. Now Mr. Donald here has told me of a talk you had together at the hotel in Harris. From that talk it appeared you knew that Ruarri Matheson was engaged in some illegal activity within the purview of Customs and Excise."

"Another correction, Inspector. It was Mr. Donald who suspected the illegal activity. I became aware of his suspicions because he came aboard Ruarri's yacht when we landed in Stornoway, and because he saw fit to telephone my host to check up on my identity and personal history. I questioned him about these matters. I also asked him whether he could give me any information that would keep me clear of illegal activity, if such were going on. Is that a fair summary, Duggie?"

"That's right, Inspector. And, if you'll remember, that's the way I told it to you."

"Of course. Of course. But, in spite of Mr. Donald's suspicions, you elected to make this trip on Mr. Matheson's trawler."

"Was that illegal, Inspector?"

"No."

"Then why do you use the words *in spite of?* Mr. Donald could not and did not suggest a contrary course of action. I would like the stenographer's record to show that I object strongly to such loaded questions."

"Does the young lady have that noted? Good. Then let me ask you a very direct question, sir. Did you at any time during your sea voyage see any sign of any illegal activity, of whatever kind?"

"No. I did not."

"You mentioned in your eulogy of Ruarri Matheson that he was well-travelled. What do you know about his travels?"

"Just things that came out in casual talk. He seems to have been in most places round the world."

"And done a lot of strange things?"

"Probably."

"Could you give me any examples?"

"I remember only two. He did say that he had run opium in Thailand and that he had been a mercenary in Africa. The rest, I'm afraid, was generalities."

"So we have a smuggler and a hired gunman."

"I don't know what we have, Inspector. I've seen only

195

a farmer and a fisherman. The rest is hearsay. I can offer no proof of it."

"You're an admirable witness, sir. I wish all my subjects were as clear as you. Tell me, do you know a lady called Maeve O'Donnell?"

"You know I do, Inspector. She was Matheson's escort at the dinner party which I gave. That was the first time I met her. The second was in Copenhagen a couple of days ago. She was staying at the same hotel as myself. I spent a very agreeable evening with her and we took a couple of outings in the country as well."

"So you have a friendship with her too?"

"Yes."

"In fact you went to Copenhagen to visit her?"

"No. I visited her in Copenhagen. I did not go specifically for that purpose."

"But you knew she was there?"

"Of course. Matheson told me. He asked me to look her up."

"Why did you go to Copenhagen then?"

"Because, Inspector, I left the trawler in the Faeroes, and the only way I could get back here was through Copenhagen. It's a pleasant city, as we agreed. I decided to stay there and enjoy it."

"Why did you get off in the Faeroes? Why didn't you finish the voyage as you apparently intended at the beginning?"

"Several reasons, Inspector. The trip proved rougher than I'd hoped. I found the quarters cramped, myself slightly on the outside of a tight-knit crew whose principal language is Gaelic, and finally and most importantly the death of Lachie McMurtrie cast a gloom over the whole voyage. It may sound cruel, but I came for a holiday after a bout of ill health. I felt no call to assist at a long requiem."

"You didn't feel a call to lend support or even assistance on board to your good friend Matheson?"

"I felt he would be better without me."

"Or yourself safer without him?"

"I don't think I understand that question, Inspector."

"Let me put it another way then. It could be argued, without discredit, that you found yourself in rather unsavoury company and wanted to get out of it as fast as you could."

"But that would contradict my previous statement."

"Which one, sir?"

"That I knew nothing of any illegal activity on board the trawler."

"So it would. So it would. But I'm still troubled by the nature of this relationship between you and Matheson. All our evidence is that you are good friends, close and cheerful friends, yet you walked away from him at a crucial moment. How do you explain that?"

"I could just be a very selfish man."

"That's not in evidence either, sir. Rather the contrary. You bought liquor for the crew, which with British taxes is very expensive. You also bought a rather costly gift for Matheson, to wit an antique sextant. These are not the gestures of a selfish man. Why did you leave the boat at Tórshavn?"

"For the reasons I've given you, and one which I haven't."

"Which is?"

"Just before the tragedy, relations between myself and Matheson had become a trifle strained—on my part more than his."

"Over what?"

"A private matter. I do not feel at liberty to discuss it."

"Then, sir, I must caution you in the strongest terms. We are investigating not merely a Customs matter, but a possible murder."

"Murder!"

I hoped my surprise sounded genuine. I had been rehearsing it long enough.

"Yes, sir. Murder. So if you attempt to withhold relevant information, you may find yourself in very serious trouble."

This wasn't playtime any more. I could not afford either to tell a lie or to conceal any truth that might become known. On the other hand, I could not let him think he had frightened me, else he would be snapping after me like a ferret. So I gave him a surprise to keep him quiet for a while.

"I understand the warning, Inspector. But I find myself in a very difficult position. Certain information, which has nothing to do with these events, was communicated to me in confidence. A certain, very personal service was asked of me. I performed it. As a result, an element of, shall we say, abrasion was introduced into my relations with Matheson. We were and still are good friends, but there has been embarrassment and, at that moment of crisis, I thought he would be happier without me."

"The information and the service, what were they? You must tell me, sir. You are neither a lawyer nor a doctor. You are not entitled to privilege in this matter."

"Then may I ask that a decency be observed and that this information be kept secret if it is found irrelevant to your inquiry?"

"You may ask, of course. The best I can say is that we will try to keep the decencies. We generally do, you know."

"You, Duggie?"

"If I can, sure."

"Inspector, you've made a great deal of my close friendship with Ruarri Matheson. I'm afraid the conclusions you're trying to draw from it are not valid, because you don't know the true nature of the relationship. My first and closest friend on the island is Alastair Morrison. We met, a number of years ago, in Thailand. He has been a sick man for some time. One day, under great emotional stress, he told me that he was Ruarri's natural father. When he was taken to hospital, he charged me to communicate that information to Ruarri and try to establish some kind of reasonable relationship between them. He also asked me to maintain my friendship with his son and tone him down a little. I did everything I was asked. It wasn't easy. Ruarri was shocked and he's still not adjusted to the idea or its consequences. So our relationship has been slightly unstable ever since. That's all, Inspector. Alastair Morrison will confirm it, but I'd rather you didn't ask him."

"The poor, poor mannie!" said Duggie Donald fervently. "Poor Ruarri, too. It's a hard thing to learn after all these years."

"Thanks for telling us," said Inspector Rawlings. "Naturally we'll do everything possible to spare Mr. Morrison pain or embarrassment."

"Thank you. Now would you like to spare me some, Inspector?"

"If I can, yes."

"Then since we're talking about a friend of mine, and the son of a friend, let's lay the charges or the suspicions on the line. Murder's one. What's the other?"

"Gunrunning to Ulster."

"Oh! . . ."

"It's quite big business. Dangerous, too. We don't want another civil war, do we? Are you Irish, by the way?"

"On my mother's side only, a generation back. But if you're wondering about my sympathies, I can tell you they're all the other way. I think we're stuffed with violence today. I crave, like most people, to see the end of it."

"Talking of violence, would you say Matheson is a violent man?"

"I would say the capacity is there, yes."

"Have you seen any evidence of it?"

"Yes—but in fairness I have to say that, on both occasions, I saw contrary evidence of enormous control."

"What were the occasions, sir?"

"Once when I delivered Morrison's letter informing him of his parentage. He was very shocked, very bitter. We nearly came to blows, but didn't. The other occasion was in The Admiral's Spyglass, when I saw him use a certain amount of violence on Lachie McMurtrie."

"Kicked him in the belly, I'm told," said Rawlings mildly.

"That's right. But again he was in control in a moment."

"Do you remember the reason for the attack?"

"I've never been clear on it, Inspector. There was a lot of talk, a lot of noise, a lot of Gaelic flying back and forth —if you go into the pub yourself tonight, you'll see what I mean. Apparently Lachie said something out of place and Ruarri took after him."

"Did you ever discuss the incident with him?"

"No."

"Why not?"

"It goes back to the curious nature of our relationship. Ruarri has always tried to impress me with his skill, his accomplishment, how he has overcome the handicaps of his birth. Physical prowess was always one of his boasts.

199

If he thought he saw me squeamish, he would have a chance to tease me. Also—and this is minor, but I think it makes sense—I've travelled a lot myself. I've been in rough places. I've learned to keep my mouth shut and mind my own business."

"So now we have a violent man. We have a calculating one, too—you mentioned his swift control. We have an attack on his crewman for an indiscreet word. We have the crewman lost overboard in mysterious circumstances. You see what's building up?"

"I see a lot of gaps, Inspector. Where do the guns come in?"

"Through Miss Maeve O'Donnell, who is a known agent of the Irish Republican Army with a long revolutionary history in the family."

"I thought she bred racehorses."

"She does. And good ones. I won a nice packet on one of 'em last year at Ascot. But she still does the other thing on the side."

"Do you know for certain that Matheson was running guns?"

"We do. With Lachie dead we can't prove it."

"I'm afraid I don't understand."

"Matheson chose and trained his men well. They're all seasoned seamen, closemouthed as oysters. Ruarri took them at least partly into his confidence. He had to, but Lachie was the weak link. He couldn't keep his mouth shut. And he resented bitterly being beaten in front of his comrades in The Admiral's Spyglass. He came to Mr. Donald here and told what he knew: that Matheson was going to Norway to pick up guns and deliver them to Ireland. We had everything set up to catch him in Trondheim. Then Lachie was murdered—or we believe he was —and Matheson went to the Faeroes instead."

"And after that?"

"He fished for three days between the Faeroes and the Flannans and came home."

"So he didn't pick up guns and didn't deliver any?"

"Not a one."

"How can you be sure—if you'll forgive my asking?"

"Because we were tracking him. We had a Navy Corvette and a spotter aircraft reporting his movements, and we know he never went near Ireland."

"You're very efficient, Inspector."

"So is Matheson. And that's our problem."

"I'd like to say something, Inspector."

"Yes?"

"I'm a friend of Ruarri's. I like him. I'll stay close to him until this thing is settled. But, if he is a murderer, I hold no brief for him, nor will, in spite of my relations with the Morrison. . . . But I was on board the *Helen II*. I talked with the crew after Lachie was lost. I'm a logical fellow—you have to be to construct the simplest story. I truly don't believe you can prove murder in a million years. If you could prove the gunrunning, you might be closer to it, but even then you have only a motive. There's no body, no witnesses, no scrap of evidence on which to build a case."

"Oh, we do have some evidence. I'd like to work through it with you now. Have you ever heard Matheson speak of a man named Bollison?"

"Bollison . . . Bollison? Yes, I have. When we were cruising up the Minch that first day, we met a Norwegian trawler. We stopped alongside. Ruarri went aboard for a few minutes. He told me he owned half a share of the boat and that the captain's name was Bollison."

"You never met the captain?"

"No. I saw him on the deck. That's all."

"You've never seen him since?"

"Never."

"Heard of him?"

"Yes. Matheson mentioned we would meet him in Trondheim. He talked of our having a drink with him."

"And in the Faeroes?"

"Not a sight or sound."

"Thank you, sir. Now let's come to your time on shipboard. I'm interested in the roster for the wheel watch."

"Yes? . . ."

"How long were the watches?"

"Four hours."

"When you left Stornoway, who was at the wheel?"

"Matheson. It's normal for a skipper to take his boat in and out of harbour. When we were clear of the island he handed over to Lachie McMurtrie."

"What time was that?"

"Two o'clock, or thereabouts. We had a late lunch."

"Normally, then, Lachie would have stayed at the wheel for four hours, say, until six?"

"Well, I don't know what's normal on a trawler. It's fairly informal. But I'd say the normal thing would be for Lachie to stay on till four, take a split watch, so that the hours would run four, eight, twelve and so on."

"What time was Lachie relieved?"

"About four."

"Who took the wheel then?"

"I did. I spent maybe an hour with Jock Burns beside me, showing me the handling of the boat."

"So that was the first abnormal thing?"

"In the circumstances I would say it was quite normal. Ruarri knows I love boats. He was paying me a compliment. I was delighted."

"You finished the watch at eight?"

"Yes."

"Who came on then?"

"Donan McEachern. He's the boy with the stammer."

"He was on till midnight?"

"I'm told he was. I went to bed at ten-thirty."

"After that?"

"Again by hearsay, Ruarri."

"And after him? . . ."

"Ruarri told me he was to be followed by Lachie Mc-Murtrie at four in the morning."

"Exactly. . . . Lachie McMurtrie, for the second time in twenty-four hours, and there were two other men—three, if you count the cook—who had not stood watch at all. How do you explain that?"

"I can't. It's curious, now that you mention it, but I couldn't tell you why it was done. It's a skipper's business, and I was not part of the crew. So I had no cause to ask."

"But you see my point! A man is rostered for a watch out of normal order. During that watch he disappears overboard. What does that say?"

"What does it say to you, Inspector?"

"Murder—by collusion!"

"No, I'm sorry. It's too elaborate. And quite unnecessary. Five husky fellows against one, in the middle of the North Atlantic. They could toss him overboard at will."

"So we cut the collusion and we have careful planning

by the skipper alone. . . . With you as the convenient odd man out who changes the roster."

"It makes better sense than the other. But unless you can fill that hole between midnight and Lachie's watch at four, you have no case."

"We're filling a few others round it. Matheson's log, for instance, did you ever read it?"

"No. He offered to let me see it. I declined."

"You heard him, I believe, sending a number of radio messages in code?"

"Did I?"

"You had to, sir. If the times you have given us for your wheel watch are correct. There was one to Bollison in Trondheim, one to Miss Maeve O'Donnell in Stockholm, and another to a man called Fermor in Oslo. We've traced those messages to their destinations. They were transmitted ship to shore before you cleared the Minch—in other words, while you were on watch."

"Yes, I remember now. Some messages were sent."

"And later, during the search for Lachie, other messages were sent?"

"Yes. I heard one of them."

"Now here's the curious thing. Those last messages were logged. The first ones weren't. What does that suggest to you?"

"Nothing, Inspector."

"Please."

"I'll spell it for you. Murder is alleged against person or persons unknown. I am obliged to give you all facts in my possession. Nothing would be more dangerous or unjust than for me to indulge in hypotheses or interpretations. I won't do it. And I mean won't."

"You're a very faithful friend."

"I am also a friend of the law, and you, Inspector, are its servant. Now, if there is nothing else, I would like to go."

"No, there's nothing else. The transcript should be typed tomorrow morning. Perhaps you'll drop by and sign it then. We have your address at the lodge. Thank you, sir."

"You can buy me that drink soon, Duggie!"

"Don't be too hard on the inspector here, laddie. He's had a rough passage."

"Haven't we all? Where's Ruarri now?"

"Over at his house, so far as I know."

"I might drop over and see him later. Objections, Inspector?"

"Not at all, my dear chap. A kindness, in fact. We put him through the wringer yesterday. Quite a lad! I like him."

"Good day, Inspector!"

In spite of my show of irritation, I was not too unhappy with the interview. I had told no lies. I had established a position as a meticulous, if somewhat tetchy, witness. I had made it clear that I was unwilling to be drawn on points of speculation or hearsay; that I was a friend of the suspect and would be until he was proven something more. Of course, Rawlings hadn't been too convinced by the comedy; he was too seasoned a fox for that. But so long as we relied on the record and due process, I wouldn't be too much annoyed.

Ruarri. . . .? He didn't need me. He didn't need anybody. The bastard was a genius in his own right. He could lie like a Münchausen and give every word the luster of truth. He could cheat his women and have them mourning over him for a lifetime. He could have the noose round his neck and the next instant conjure it round somebody else's. He would get away with murder, and in his old age —if he lived that long—they would canonize him as a captain of industry. Everybody had been out to get him, Customs and Excise, the Special Branch, Interpol, the Navy and the Air Force, and he was home, scot-free, cocking a snook at them all. Bollison had delivered his guns for him. Bollison had sent the final telegram to Maeve, and Bollison would be paid well enough to keep his mouth shut in the unlikely event that anything went wrong. Then I saw the irony: I was the one man in the world who could really bring him down if I set my mind to it. Why hadn't I done it five minutes ago? Why didn't I turn back and do it now? The truth, when I came to face it, was fascinating in its very ugliness. I wanted him exactly where I had him now, held in the hollow of my hand, impotent as I had once been, so that he could never again stand up and challenge me on level ground. I was the giant now, and he, the dwarf. I could take him anytime I wanted, just by closing my fist. Whether I could

204

live with myself afterwards was another question. I didn't have to answer it just yet.

I telephoned Kathleen. She was out; I left a message that I would call again as soon as I got back to the lodge. Then I drove to the hospital to see Alastair Morrison. I had decided to tell him most of what had happened, leaving out only the darker aspects of the whole affair. He would have heard most of it, anyway, in one version or another. The word of Lachie's death would be all over the island, and the police investigation would be raising rumours everywhere.

I didn't have to tell him anything. I didn't have to soothe, encourage, protect, or strengthen him any more. He was up and about. He was ten years younger. Very soon he would be fishing again. . . . Ruarri had been to see him! Had he indeed?

". . . I tell you, laddie, when he came through that door, it was like life itself striding in—although, God help me, this old heart of mine did a double somersault and I thought the fibrillations would start again. However, there he was, with an armful of books and a bottle of old brandy and a funny, boyish grin under that beard of his. We talked a long time, round and about—feeling for each other, you know? It was like blindman's buff—touch and run and grope again in the dark. Then suddenly he called a halt to it. He looked me square in the eye. He took my hands in those great paws of his and said, 'Morrison, let's get it over. You've got a son you didn't want. I've got a father I thought I didn't need. I need him now because a lot of things have caught up with me, and I'm sick of standing alone like a rock in the middle of a bog. But you have to know what you're getting, too—and I'm not a great bargain. I've got a bad conscience and a bad reputation and I've deserved a lot of it, but not all. Right now they're even whispering murder about me, because I lost a man at sea. . . .' I tell you, laddie, I wept to hear him; he was so blunt and honest about himself, so easy in his absolution of me. He'd like me to acknowledge him, he said. And that was the happiest word I'd heard in a lifetime. When I'm out of here I'm going to file adoption papers, which I find I can do, and he'll join the name of Morrison to his own, which is a happy thought and a notable symbol of something good in both our lives. So what do you think of that, laddie? What do you think of it, eh?"

I did not dare to tell him what I thought. It would have sounded like a blasphemy and I would have had him dead on my hands. I lied to him instead. I lied eloquently and emotionally, swearing that it was the most wonderful news, that I was happy beyond words for them both, that Ruarri was out of his gaudy past and marching towards a glorious future, that God was good and everything turned out for the best if you prayed long enough and were blind enough to believe it.

Underneath it all I was sour with rage and contempt for Ruarri's duplicity and his selfish manipulation of an old and ailing man. He didn't want a father. He wanted a protector. He wanted a decent name to take the stain of roguery and murder off his own. He wasn't content to be safe—if indeed he was; he wanted to be honoured as well, and borrow another man's respect.

The words I said were sawdust in my mouth, but at least they made Morrison happy. . . . Which, come to think of it, was just what Ruarri had done, though I was damned if I'd give him any credit for it.

XIV

MY HOMECOMING TO THE LODGE WAS STRANGE, BUT I find myself hard put to explain the strangeness.

Suddenly everything was small: the houses like toytown cottages, the fields like pocket handkerchiefs, the hills squat, the lochans muddy pools, the road a country track and the sheep like animals from a children's crib. I was not large, you understand. I was just a middling man, looking through glass into a lilliputian landscape, set by some shopkeeper for the summer trade. I did not feel superior—this you must understand—only separate, different, faintly resentful, like a child who could not fly out the window with Peter Pan.

Even old Hannah was changed. There was no mystery about her any more, no gypsy wander-thing, no mist of tomorrow or of yesterday. She was just a little old lady, wrinkled like a prune, who clung to me, possessive and loquacious, because I was a man come back to a house too long without one.

"You're home! God be praised in all his wonders! I saw you swallowed by the black sea. But it wasn't you, it was that poor Lachie—God save his silly soul! You'll come in now and take a bath—I'll draw it for you. And you'll throw out your soiled things for the laundry and spruce yourself up for the dear young woman that wants you to call her. Ach! There's a smell of sin on you! You'd better get rid of that before you go calling. Not that I'd ask who it was, but she might, and I hope you've got your lying well prepared. And what's this with the police, running all over the island, asking questions as though we're criminals? Don't tell me! I don't want to hear—not till you're clean and rested and we can have a strupach together. And then don't tell me what you don't want talked about, because I'm a garrulous old woman who'd drop her false teeth in the soup if she had a good story to tell. . . . Out of your pants now and into your bath. And if you're worrying what I might see, I've seen it all and enjoyed it long before you knew what it was. Tea'll be ready when you come down—and there's scones ready and smiling for the oven!"

It was good to be home. Except it wasn't home. It was a pleasant enough lodge on the Isle of Lewis, in Ross-shire, where I was resting my tired brain for a while. I lay in the hot bath, like a demigod on Olympus looking down on the provincial comedy and wondering how and why I had become involved in it all. I could be gone tomorrow and they would trot on their little rounds with never a thought of me. I could come back in ten years and it would still be the same: the heather blooming, the fish jumping, the peat smoke rising and a few more stones in the churchyard, to mark the cycles of the years. . . .

But when I went down to the lounge and found the tea-things laid out, and Hannah sitting with her hands folded

207

in her apron waiting for me, everything grew back to size and I grew down again.

She fixed me with her bright, black eyes and stated categorically, "You know about Morrison and the Matheson boy?"

"I know, Hannah."

"I've known for thirty years and more, and never a word has crossed my lips—for which I hope God will reward me one day."

"I saw the Morrison on the way home. He's very happy."

"I hope he stays that way."

"So do I, Hannah."

"That Ruarri! There's trouble in every wind that blows round him. Now it's murder they're talking about, and guns being smuggled, instead of whisky and silks like it was in the old days."

"How do you know that?"

"Everybody knows. Or they think they do. It's a shame such talk should touch the Morrison."

"He won't mind, Hannah. Now he has his son back."

"And is it his son? That's what I keep asking myself—as I did the very day he was borned. There's fairy children still, you know—and I know some of them! Changed in the cradle they were, by the Little People, and they're mischiefs always till the day they die."

"Hannah, if that kind of talk got back to the Morrison! . . ."

"And how could it, since I never say a word outside the house! So let's talk about you instead. You should have gone away when I warned you."

"I didn't. So that's the end of it."

"Not the end, young laddie."

"So what is the end, Hannah?"

"I wish I could tell you, but I can't. I know the sea's gone from it, because the sea's satisfied for a while. I know there's fire in it, but where, I don't know. And I know there's three in this house, and Matheson isn't one of them."

"How do you know it, Hannah? I'd like to know. I wouldn't tell."

"And how could you since I can't tell myself? It just comes. That's all. Sometimes when I'm lying in bed, some-

208

times when I'm saying my prayers, sometimes when I'm in the garden or in the kitchen."

"Does it frighten you?"

"Having the sight does, but seeing doesn't. It's like knowing a bit of what God knows. And He's not frightened now, is He?"

"He ought to be sometimes, Hannah."

"Well, if He is, He doesn't tell. And that's a lot more virtue than we've got."

"I'm not laughing at you, Hannah."

"I know you're not. You've little to laugh about, anyway."

"What's that supposed to mean?"

"Laddie, whatever I've seen, you're in it: in the sea and in the fire as well."

"Was there anyone with me at the end?"

"I wasn't shown that, laddie. That's the terrible tease. The good God gives you only half a gift and holds the rest till you've earned it. Which I haven't done yet. . . . Now tell me, will you be in or out tonight?"

"I'll be in, Hannah. We'll have the company of Dr. McNeil."

"I know. I've ordered the meal and I've set her room to rights—though there'll be little use made of it, I know."

"Hannah, you have an evil mind."

"Evil, is it? And look who's talking! With all the seven deadly sins writ large across your visage. Go telephone your woman and tell her you love her. I hope she's easier to convince than I am!"

I couldn't convince her, because I couldn't find her. Her housekeeper told me with relish that the doctor was uncommon busy, and it was hard to know when she might be home. Yes, she'd tell the doctor about the dinner, but she couldn't give any guarantees about it. I understood that, didn't I? I understood. God love you, madam, and send you comfort and a sweeter temper before you die! . . . It was still only three-thirty so I decided to cut across and see Ruarri at his croft. For all the lies he'd told, and the sweet little surprises he'd pulled out of his hat, he owed me an explanation, though I'd be a fool to believe it, if I got it.

When I reached the croft I found Ruarri and three of his boys hand-sowing the newly made land. I leaned on the stone fence and watched them at this simple, biblical task and wondered how they or I could possibly be caught up in all the other madness. Ruarri saw me and waved, but he continued his work until the bag on his shoulder was empty. Then he came over to me, walking heavily and awkwardly in the soft sand. I don't know why, but I had expected some kind of dramatic change in his appearance or his manners. There wasn't. He was the same old Ruarri, full of piss and vinegar, with that same old grin spread over his face and the same come-all-ye greeting.

"Welcome home, seannachie! You look ten years younger."

"That's clean living and clean girls. Also I've stopped worrying about you!"

"And when did you do that?"

"This morning in Stornoway. I had a long, long chat with Chief Inspector Rawlings."

"And what did you tell him?"

"Nothing he didn't know already."

"Like what?"

"Like that you're a friend of mine and so is Maeve, and I've heard of Bollison but never met him, and the order of watches on board, and that there was an incident between you and Lachie at The Admiral's Spyglass, and that messages were sent during my watch on the *Helen II*."

"And what didn't you tell him, seannachie?"

"What has passed between you and me on various private occasions."

"What point did he hammer the hardest with you?"

"Why I left the ship at Tórshavn. Why didn't I stay like a friend and support you in your hour of trial?"

"And what did you answer to that?"

"I told him you and I were rubbing each other the wrong way."

"About what?"

"About yourself being Morrison's son and my having to tell you, and you not liking me very much for it."

"That was clever, seannachie. What made you think of it?"

"Because I was determined not to tell a single lie. If he'd pressed me about our relationships and our talks, I'd have had to invent things—and you've been doing enough invention for both of us."

"Do you think he'll question you again?"

"Very probably. I have to sign my deposition tomorrow morning. I'm sure Rawlings will be there for another little chat."

"What do you think he believes, seannachie?"

"That you killed Lachie."

"He'll be hard put to prove that. . . . He hasn't got enough even to file a charge, let alone make it stick in court."

"But I have, Ruarri."

"And what's that supposed to mean?"

"Walk me down to the house, pour me a drink and I'll tell you."

We walked in silence down to the house and sat at the bar. While Ruarri was pouring the drinks I lit a cigarette and pulled a clean ashtray towards me, a large shallow bowl of African ceramic. When I dropped the dead match in it, I saw, lying in the bottom of the bowl, the locket and chain which I had bought for Kathleen. Ruarri had his back to me, replacing the bottle on the shelf. I picked up the locket and shoved it into the pocket of my coat.

Ruarri turned round, perched himself on the stool and toasted me. "Slainte!"

"And to you."

"Now what's on your mind, seannachie?"

"There's quite a lot, so let's take it slowly. On board the *Helen* you told me you weren't sure whether you had killed Lachie or not. You couldn't remember. Do you remember now?"

"Yes. I didn't kill him."

"What convinced you?"

"Lack of evidence. I'm in the same position as Rawlings, you see."

"Also on the *Helen* I told you I believed you were innocent."

"Now?"

"I still do. For a negative reason like yours. The moment I cease to believe it, the game is over. I can't compound murder. I have to tell everything I know."

"Which is. . . ?"

"That you uttered in my presence a threat to Lachie's life; that when I protested, you struck me and threatened me, too, with violence; that you told me a lie about a

211

confrontation with Lachie which did not take place. . . . And how do I know that? Because I sat in on a friendly poker party, and because you never had any intention of going to Ireland. Bollison was already on his way there and you were fishing innocently between the Faeroes and the Flannans. You see the way it shapes, don't you? As of now, Rawlings can't touch you because all he's got is motive and opportunity. The moment I speak, he has motive, expressed intention, a display of violence, the beginning of a plot to murder. I think he'd take you in on that. Even if he didn't win his case, he could hold you on remand for quite a while and leave you discredited for ever afterwards. . . ."

"I'm trembling, seannachie."

"I haven't finished yet. Maeve gave me the letter you wrote to her."

I didn't tell him she had burned it. I wanted to see how much he could take without flinching. To this point he was doing very well. He was cool, half smiling, weighing every word said, estimating the consequences, patient as a cat with a bird hopping in front of him. But the letter got him. The letter was a document. If I had it, the noose was really round his neck. But he still tried to bluff. He said lightly:

"I don't believe a word of it, seannachie."

"I quote, then: 'See if you can talk, or sleep, some sense into him. You're good at both.' She loved that. So did I. Big motion of confidence from Ruarri the Mactire to his friends."

"Where's the letter now?"

"Safe in Copenhagen."

"So it's blackmail, is it? How much, seannachie? And how often?"

"One installment, Ruarri. Don't hurt the Morrison."

Now he truly didn't believe me. He stared at me as if I were something odd, kicked up from under a stone. He shook his head. He blinked, and then he started to laugh, in a queer, stuttering chuckle. "You can't mean it . . . You just can't. . . ! How could you police a bargain like that?"

"You miss the point. I don't have to police it. Because I'm one man in the world who can prove you're shit—A to Z, right down the line. And you're going to break your back just to prove I'm wrong. That's the way you are, brother."

"I could also be tempted to kill you one dark night."

"You won't do that either. There's no need. Maeve burnt the letter after I read it."

"And you're fool enough to tell me?"

"I'm fool enough to believe your neck's worth saving and that you and Morrison might have some joy together."

"Then why the hell did you go all that way round to tell me?"

"You want respect. You cry to get it. You have to give some too. As of now the only one you respect is the man with the big stick. I just wanted you to know I'm holding it and that I could have used it this morning and didn't. So how does that grab you, Brother Wolf?"

"Right where it hurts, seannachie. But not for the reason you think. You're such a patronizing bastard, you're so chockful of wisdom and righteousness that there's no room for sap and blood. You wouldn't give me the smack in the teeth you owe me. No, brother! You come sliding in with a stiletto and shove it between my ribs. You won't give me one single credit, will you? Not for the boys working out there that wouldn't be working without me. Not for the land that's going to be a model for other lands like it all over the Islands. Not for the promise I made to see Morrison and kept, and the bending I did to make him feel I needed him and that he could really offer me something. No! . . . To you I'm all shit—A to Z. Amen! Amen! Amen! I think I'd like you better if you turned me in to Rawlings. Then at least I wouldn't owe you anything."

"That's just the point, Ruarri lad. You do owe me something. I want you to know it, remember it and pay it— not to me, but to Morrison."

"Oh, seannachie, seannachie! You'll have to do better than that!"

"Any suggestions?"

"Yes. . . . Ask Kathleen about the locket you just stuck in your pocket."

This time he did get the liquor full in his face. The wonder of it was he didn't make a move. He stood there, a long moment, solid as a rock with the liquid running down his cheeks and into his beard, blinking against the sting of the raw spirit. He picked up a paper napkin and dabbed at his eyes. Then, unsmiling, he said:

"I think we're even now, seannachie. And I hope you'll apologize to the girl when you get home. She came here for dinner because I asked her, and she went home at midnight without my asking or getting anything else but her company. Now have another drink and let's have a little brotherhood between us, eh?"

To save the shreds of my dignity I had to stay. I had to apologize and take one drink with him and give him the last word in his own house. He took time to say it, and I had to give him the time as well, though every minute there was a purgatory.

"Seannachie, we're very close, but it doesn't work. Why?"

"God knows."

"Don't put it on Him, seannachie. He's not around that much. I lie to you and you snarl at me. Why?"

"You tell me for a change."

"So I will and all. Here it is, straight from the horse's mouth—or the other end of him, if you like. You want to make a statement about yourself—an act of faith, a saying of love or hate, or a shout against injustice—you do it. You write it in nice clerkly periods. You print it, black and clear, and it's on the record. They can love you or hate you or daub you over with paint, but you're there! Me? . . . I can't do that. I've got two languages, seannachie, and I'm schooled in neither. I've got a bad name and a checkered history, so any man who wants to discredit me can do it with a wink or a nod before I'm heard. That's a bitter thing, seannachie, a cruel thing. There's no absolute judgment—though there ought to be. It's all relative to unrelated things. Result? I can't speak and be heard. I'm clamped down like a pressure cooker. So I spout steam from the cracks. I bubble and spit and sometimes blow my lid off. If I can get a lie believed easier than the truth, why not tell it? They're as like to hang me either way. And you, brother, you've been lynching me in your own mind these last few days, haven't you?"

"It's only half true, Ruarri. Because you never give yourself more than half a chance with an honest word. You have to wait a space until your credit's past impeachment. You won't wait. You want laurels hung round your neck every time you recite, 'It's a braw bricht moonlicht nicht . . .' "

"You're not overly patient yourself, brother—as we proved a minute ago."

"Agreed."

"So if, just for once, I asked you to sit something out with me, wait on me, not judge me till the end, would you do it?"

"What have you got in mind?"

"Come to my ceilidh, two nights from now. Bring Kathleen."

"For God's sake, man! You can't give a ceilidh now. It's an indecency."

"You've judged me already—wrongly!"

"I'm sorry."

"In the Isles, seannachie, we mourn the dying, but we drink for the burying. Lachie'll never be buried, but there's honour to be done to him, and something needed to be arranged for his family. So everyone who comes will bring a gift of money—you too. And for every coin that's brought I'll put in two. So there'll be a fund for Lachie's mother and her young ones. I'm inviting all my boys and their girls. Maeve's coming and Duggie Donald will be there, and even Inspector Rawlings, if he wants to come."

"Now you're right off the rails."

"No, I'm not. Because this is my statement, seannachie. Just as it would be if he were buried like a Christian in a churchyard. I'd be there, large as life and twice as ugly, to say I was clean and I had nothing to fear from God or man. Whatever anyone thinks after that I won't care. Now do you see what I'm at?"

"Yes."

"Will you come? Both of you?"

"We'll be there."

And because he could never resist the last turn of the thumbscrew, he added, "You'll be like God, seannachie, with a secret in your bosom that no one else in the world knows. A man can get drunk on a thing like that. . . ."

It was still early when I left him, and the rain had cleared and I could not bear to go back to the lodge and Hannah's scolding affection; so I drove to the place of the Standing Stones and sat, facing the east, with the Great Stone at my back and the empty burying place under the

215

soles of my feet. I saw no sacred wrens; I heard no cuckoo. I wish I could tell you that I saw the Shining One, but I didn't. I did have other visions, though: of Kathleen sitting in candlelight at dinner with Ruarri, of myself with Maeve in Nyhavn and her telling me, "He's treacherous always, seannachie, playing good doggie with his feet up in the air until you reach out to scratch him—then he's bitten your hand off!" None of us was a match for him in the devious arts of betrayal, because all of us loved him— yes, even Kathleen—and each of us was victim to one or other of his dazzling potencies. We had only one defense against him: pack and go; step outside the magic circle he had conjured around us; meet him, if we must, like a vagabond friend, on far and neutral ground, among a press of people. I wondered what spell he had laid upon Kathleen and how she would act and what she would say when I handed her back the locket. I was resolved on one thing: I would make no jealous scene. She had asked to be free. She had left me free. I had exercised my freedom. So had she; in what fashion I had no right to ask. But now, for me, the waiting time was over. It was forward for us, caps over the rainbow. If she wanted to come with me, fine! We would lock the gate on the past and throw away the key. If she wanted to stay, then I wouldn't be here—the Isles were too small to hold me and the Mactire together.

When I got back to the lodge Kathleen was waiting for me, and she was in my arms before I kicked the door shut behind me. Don't ask me what we said in those first ten minutes, because it was all in the babble of the love country, and it would make no sense at all in cold linear print. Later, when we were calmer, sitting by the fire, I told her everything that had happened on board the *Helen* and part of what had happened in Copenhagen and of my talk with Rawlings and my afternoon meeting with Ruarri. Then I put the locket round her neck again and sat on the rug at her feet while she told me the other side of the story:

". . . The news of Lachie's death was all over the island in a day. Even in Harris, where they don't worry much about the doings of Lewis folk, it was gossiped in every household. There was talk of a fight over a girl, a drunken brawl on board, a fight with the Russians or the Norwegians over fishing rights. . . . There were hard words about

Ruarri and his violent ways and even about you, darling, because they said you'd run away to avoid answering to the police. When I heard that one for the first time, I lost my temper—and a couple of patients at the same time. So, when I heard Ruarri was back, I called him. He was very guarded on the phone—they're not very private here, as you know—and asked me to have dinner with him, so that he could tell me the whole story. He asked would I mind going to his house, because he didn't want to raise talk by a public appearance with me. . . . I won't lie to you, mo gradh. There'd be no point. I was glad he made the suggestion. I wanted to be alone with him. I wanted to experience what he was like and I resented your being off in Copenhagen, and knowing that Maeve O'Donnell was there at the same time . . . Oh yes, he told me that, very brotherly and man of the world. So by the time I got there I was just light-headed and reckless enough to enjoy myself. And I did. He made cocktails and we cooked dinner together and flirted while we were doing it—and I enjoyed every minute, because I knew I was a big girl who could handle any situation. . . . Over dinner he told me everything, much as you've told it, darling. I was surprised at how much he said, but he told me he knew you and I were lovers and we had no secrets. Or did we? He asked when we were getting married. I told him the truth. I said we hadn't decided whether we would or wouldn't. Then he laughed and said the seannachie was a shrewd old fox who knew how to arrange himself coming and going. . . . He is like that, isn't he? Lots of little pinpricks, never enough to hurt, just enough to let you know you're alive and make you want to justify yourself to him. After dinner we danced, and I knew we were dancing on a trapdoor, but I didn't care. He had me on fire for him. . . . You lit me, darling, but you were away and he was there, blowing on the coals. Then he asked me to go to bed with him—and I'm ashamed to say it, but I was ready. . . . Then he laughed and held me close and said, 'What price the seannachie now, princess? Pity he's not here to watch the fun.' I went cold all over and I wanted to run away and be sick. I pulled free from him, and when he came after me I couldn't bear him to touch me. Then . . . then he walked over to the bar, poured a glass of brandy and held it up in a kind of toast, grinned at me, a cold, beastly kind of grin, and said, 'Your very good health, Dr. McNeil. I know you'll be very happy. You and the seannachie are made for each other. . . .' And that's all. After that I went home. I had to tell you, mo gradh, because I love you and I couldn't bear to think you would hear that story from Ruarri one day and hate me ever after. . . . Now, if you want me to go, tell me."

"What will you do if you go home?"

"Go to bed. Lie awake and stare at the ceiling—and despise myself the way I've been doing for a long time now. Sometime or other I'll get used to the notion and make terms with myself."

"Rather a waste, don't you think?"

"Any better suggestions?"

I stood up and pulled her to her feet and held her at arm's length from me. "Just one, Kathleen oge. The first and the last. Do you see where you're standing now?"

"Yes. . . ."

"When the Morrison comes out of hospital, we'll be standing here again, and Minister Macphail will be reading the marriage service, I'm going to take this woman for my lawful wedded wife, and she's going to take me . . . On one condition: that she tells me now, because there's banns to go up and licenses to get and some unfinished business I have to tidy before the wedding day. It's yes or no, Kathleen oge. And if it's no, you go home to that bed and the blank ceiling and a woman you'll never come to terms with until you die."

"And if it's yes?"

"It's love and honour and cherish and shut the door on memories until the sunset comes for both of us."

"Yes . . . yes, please, my love."

. . . And if you think it's all too simple to be true, let me tell you that's the way most important things happen in our lives. We go through reasoning, fantasies, fears, frustrations, vast, dreary do-nothing acres of time. Then, one fine day, the doctor comes and tells us we're dying, or the girl comes and says she's pregnant, or the bottom drops out of the market and we're poorer than church mice, or a plane falls out of the sky and we're dead and standing in judgment without our notebooks. We were engaged to be married. We had all dinnertime to talk about it, and all coffeetime, and all the time after the loving. And when all that was done most pleasantly, and Kathleen was asleep beside me, there was still time for me to think about Ruarri the Mactire.

I had to take him now. I had to rub his nose in his own dirt, lift him up again if I could; and, if I couldn't, to hell with him. But how? Unless I knew him guilty, I could not and would not turn police informer. I could not and I would not face him in private, because I would be caught once again in that shouting apocalypse of self-justification, and afterwards no one would know anything except the lies Ruarri told with so much conviction. How then? And where? And on what issue, so that he could not leap away like an acrobat and go bouncing up to the high wire, where I couldn't follow him?

I could see no other time or place than the ceilidh—his own house, his own occasion. Kathleen didn't want to go. She had said as much, but I had insisted, because we must walk in there and face him down and spit in his blue, smiling eyes and let him know that he hadn't harmed us at all. I could not plan what would happen. I knew only that he would be vain for the company and drunk and talkative—and that a moment must come when I could bore in and fight him openly.

XV

Now that I must tell it, I find I am hesitant and solicitous for the small truths.

You must not see this as an epic, all thunderclouds and clashing furies and portents scrawled everywhere like Chinese laundry tickets. The Isle of Harris and Lewis is a small place. Put all its people together and you would not make a decent football crowd. The habitations are sparse. The houses, even the largest, are modest. The roads are single tracks. So a ceilidh for thirty or forty people is by local measure a large affair. The only epic things are the eating and the drinking and the tales that are spread afterwards, wild and wonderful, with miracles and moralities on every page. Which, I suppose, is the way of history; the smallest peoples have the most potent gods and the largest cities have men so tiny that you can hardly tell one from another.

The ceilidh of Ruarri the Mactire was timed for eight o'clock in the evening, so that the girls could beautify themselves after work and the boys could oil themselves in the pub before the festivities began. Kathleen and I decided that we would arrive late, so that there would be less danger of embarrassment with Ruarri. Kathleen chose to wear Highland costume, which is a most becoming dress for a woman—the velvet corsage, the arisaid plaid, the gold Celtic brooch worn like an order of chivalry. My own wardrobe was sadly light, so I had to settle for a dark suit, of a cut rather too Italian for the climate and the local fashion. Still we were not unpleased with ourselves and, if Ruarri or anyone else wanted to tread on the tail of my coat, he was welcome to try it.

There were cars parked for twenty yards on either side of Ruarri's house and there was a piper at the gate to give a skirl or two for every guest. He was there for the dancing, he told us, and later there'd be a fiddler and a man with the squeegee box. It was them he was waiting for; but why waste the music, which was the best part of the hundred thousand welcomes!

Ruarri, kilted himself in the Matheson rig, met us at the door with a glad smile and a hearty handclasp, and never a blink or a blush to say we weren't the best friends in the world. Then he presented us, with a sweeping gesture, to everyone at once and carted us over to the bar, spieling away like a comedian.

"I was just about to send out search parties. For one bad moment I thought you'd never come at all. You know a lot of the people, seannachie. And those you don't you soon will. Take Kathleen around now and introduce her. We'll talk later when things settle down. Maeve's on her way, and—I told you, but you wouldn't believe it!—there's Rawlings in one corner and Duggie Donald with the dark girl in the other. Maeve just called from Stornoway. She'll be here shortly. Enjoy yourselves now!"

We perched ourselves on a pair of stools and took stock of the company. There were the boys from the two trawlers, the lads from the farm, a girl for every man, including this time the blond and kissing one from the pub in Stornoway. She too was in Highland dress—which made her as near to a lady as she'd ever get. There was Duggie Donald; there was Rawlings; there was Fergus William McCue and his two sons, and one of the constables who had questioned Kathleen and me on our poaching foray. There were three young couples whom I hadn't seen before, whom I took to be neighbours from the crofts around Carloway. Thirty people, thirty-five, enough to fill the broad chamber and make a steady clatter of talk and laughter.

The fire in the open hearth was banked high with peat sods. The kitchen bar was loaded with food. The table was pushed to one side so that the floor was open to the traffic of drinkers and for the dancing afterwards. I noticed that some of Ruarri's more precious things had been moved off the shelves, lest some high-riding laddie had a mind to play games with them at midnight.

I took Kathleen on a round of the people I knew: Athol Cameron and Jock Burns and the rest. Then we came by inevitable progression to give a salute to Chief Inspector Rawlings. He was in fine humour; and when he saw Kathleen in all her finery, he brightened even more.

"My God! I'm beginning to be glad I came. In spite of all the trouble I'm having."

"Are you having trouble, Inspector?" Kathleen was wide-eyed innocence itself.

"Let's say, Doctor, I've got my nose rammed against a brick wall so hard that it's hurting, and I'm thinking of going home. Now that I've seen you I might reconsider."

"I'm bespoken, Inspector. I'm engaged to one of your suspects."

"This fellow! Good Lord! Well, I'll just have to concentrate on Miss O'Donnell, though I'm not very popular in that quarter, I'm afraid."

"Why?" It was my question now. "Have you seen her?"

"Not only saw her, my dear chap. Damn near turned her back at the airport as an undesirable alien. Then I

221

thought better of it, because I'd never really had a chance to chat with her before, and I thought I might pick up a tip or two to beat the bookies. All I got was a flea in my ear and some language I never expected to hear from those ruby lips. I hope she's mellowed by the time she gets here. . . . This looks like a good party."

The fiddler and the piper and the squeegee man marched themselves in with a flourish, dumped their instruments in a corner and begged to be led to the drink because of the chill outside and the warmth that was needed to make decent music. Then Maeve O'Donnell walked in with the air of a virgin martyr, kissed Ruarri, waved to the rest of the company and presented the inspector with a sealed package.

"It's a present from Ireland, Inspector, and I dare you to open it without a bucket of water handy."

He was a game bird and he knew a gamy joke when he smelled it. He opened the package, fished through layers of sawdust and brought up a small bottle of clear liquid. He opened it, smelled it, tasted it and then shook his head.

"What is it?"

"Holy water, Inspector. We used it for the baptism of the heathen, the purification of mothers after childbirth and the exorcism of the evil one. I thought you might find a use for it."

That got her a laugh, and the inspector got himself a kiss for his decency in letting her into the country, which was a doubtful privilege but appreciated this time.

Then, with a piece of footwork that left me gasping, she prized me away from Kathleen, put the inspector in my place and backed me out of earshot of them both.

"Now tell me, seannachie. What the hell is all this? Has Ruarri gone out of his mind?"

"I'm beginning to think he has, lover girl."

"What's he trying to prove?"

"He calls it his statement. He's saying he has no guilt before God or man."

"In a pig's eye, he hasn't."

"Would I joke about it, Maeve my love? With the inspector and Duggie Donald and all this bunch? Who knows what'll be said when they've all got their drinks in?"

"And you, seannachie? What's with you now?"

"We're getting married as soon as Morrison's out of hospital."

"And what brought that on?"

"I'll tell you later. But if Ruarri gets a pie in his face tonight, you'll know who threw it."

"Are you really that mad? Are you really, seannachie?"

"I'm out for blood, Maeve O'Donnell."

"Whose blood?" asked Ruarri from behind us.

"Yours, Brother Wolf."

"I'll bottle some for you, seannachie." He shrugged it off with a grin. "Help yourself to the food."

Maeve watched him swaggering away and let out a long, soft whistle. "Holy Patrick! I think you both mean it this time. If it comes to a donnybrook, seannachie, watch him! He fights dirty. . . . Let's go and eat. I'm starving."

In the crush around the food we were separated, and by the time I had a plate in my hand I found myself once again shoulder to shoulder with Rawlings. Kathleen was in the far corner, deep in talk with Daddy Burns, who would keep her busy for a while.

Rawlings said, "Why don't we sit at the bar? I hate standing around trying to balance food. It makes me feel like a performing seal."

"Enjoying yourself, Inspector?"

"Better than I expected. I'm learning something too."

"What's that?"

"Everybody knows what I want. Nobody's going to give me a word to cheer me. I might as well pack up and go home."

"You're back to the tribes here, Inspector."

"Off the record, I like it."

"Also off the record, Inspector, how do you read our host?"

"I like him, very much. I imagine he'd be first-rate company."

"You answered the wrong question, Inspector."

"So I did. It's a bad habit. This job really does make one unfit for polite company. How do I read him? . . . He is a man who's chasing something he doesn't want. When he gets it, he'll break it."

"Why?"

223

"I don't know him well enough to answer that. But I know I'm right. This party tonight . . ."

"Ceilidh, Inspector. You're in Gaeldom now!"

"Whatever you call it, it's the same thing: an act of contempt. Matheson knows he's in the clear. I know it. So do you. There's no way in the world we can fill in the last blank hour on the *Helen II*. There's no way we can nail him for the guns, but he'll slip up on that one day. But the murder—I'm convinced it's murder, and I'm telling you because there's no one near enough to shout libel—he's waving that at us all like the flag of the revolution. Don't you agree?"

It was a tempting discussion and I knew he was tempting me to embark on it with him. Regretfully I had to refuse.

"Sorry, Inspector. No go. You build your own theories."

"I've got one that might interest you."

"Oh?"

"I think you're hiding something because it would throw more suspicion on Matheson, but still not convict him."

"And why would I do that?"

"Because you hate his guts—and yet you're too meticulous or too squeamish to get at him through the law."

"You're very astute, Inspector."

"Aren't I just? Problem is I always get my best ideas when I'm off duty. . . . Excuse me. I think I'll try some of that roast beef. . . ."

I had enough to digest, so I poured myself another drink and went over to rescue Kathleen from Daddy Burns. Before I could get to her, I was ambushed by Fergus William McCue, who fixed me with a rheumy but triumphant eye and told me of the twelve-pound salmon he had landed in my absence. Fergus sober is eloquent enough, but Fergus drunk—and I don't mean tipsy; I mean ripe, slopping-in-the-scuppers drunk—Fergus drunk would silence the last trumpet and shout the dead from their graves himself. Finally his boys rescued me by the simple expedient of hoisting Fergus under the elbows and carrying him out into the garden to cool off. By the time I reached Kathleen, she was staggering under another of Daddy Burns's typhoons, so we found ourselves a quieter spot near the door while the fiddler tuned his instrument and the piper and the squeegee man were hoisted on the table and enthroned above the multitude, as bards should be. Then Ruarri took the floor, clapped hands for silence, waved everyone to seating places and delivered himself of a speech in Gaelic.

The effect of it was curiously moving: the big red-beard in Highland costume, standing in the center of the floor with his own small tribe about him, the very image of a chieftain or a prophet at his first acceptance. He spoke, very quietly at first, with many gestures and a kind of lyric challenge to the emotions of the company. Then he brightened and made them smile first and then laugh. Whereupon he turned to me and to Rawlings and to Maeve at our different points in the room and made a slightly offhand translation:

"For those of you not fortunate enough to have the Gaelic this is what I've just said. This ceilidh is for the memory and the honour of Lachie McMurtrie, a shipmate of many here, a crewman of mine, lost at sea. We're here to raise money for his family, and there's a big glass bowl by the door that you'll drop it into before you go out, if you've got any left after the games and the forfeits, in which I hope you'll all join. Whatever money is given, I'll double it from my own pocket, since no man who sails with the Mactire will ever be afraid for his family. . . . Let's have the music now and a little dancing to limber up."

As the fiddler and the piper and the squeegee man launched themselves into a lively disharmony, Ruarri brought Maeve onto the floor and led the dance himself. I danced with Kathleen and Rawlings reached out for the other one in the plaid, which made six people on the floor, each with murder in the mind because, if ever a woman was jealous of Ruarri, the blonde was dying of it. . . . The others followed a little sheepishly at first; but it was lively in a moment, and risky, too, because some of the boys were rearing and kicking their heels like stallions in clover.

We danced in couples; we danced in squares; we danced, men and women in concentric circles, scrambling for partners each time the music stopped. And when Ruarri judged us exhausted, there was a pause for drinks, while the piper played a pibroch just to prove he had lordlier themes in his head than country dances. Then we played the forfeit game, which, in case you've forgotten your childhood in this quick-changing world, goes like this:

You put names in one hat and the tasks to be performed in another and the forfeit to be paid in a third. You draw out a name at random. You draw out a task at random: to sing a song or recite a verse, or tell a story, or stand on your head, or dance a jig. If you don't want to do it, or you can't, you pay the forfeit which is named on a card from the third hat. It's a game with infinite variations and one which can be very easily rigged if you put your mind to it and have a sense of malice or humour. Ruarri had both, and a considerable ingenuity as well; but, in the beginning at least, he played the game for laughter. The forfeits were all to be paid in cash to Lachie's family, and there was a comical penalty tacked on just for the fun of the thing.

Donan, the Barra boy, had to bob for an apple in a bowl of water with his hands behind his back, and transfer it without a hand's touch to the lips of his girl, who had a bosom like a pouter pigeon. Athol, the taciturn, had to sing two verses of "Scots wha hae" with his pipe stuck in his mouth, which almost gave him apoplexy and lost him his money. Calum had to talk for three minutes on any subject of his choosing without mention of a woman and without a swear word. He lost in the first forty seconds. Maeve had to dance a jig with Daddy Burns playing the fiddle; and they did it to vast applause because Daddy played with a rare sweet tone, better than the fiddler we had. . . . It was all good, simple fun with drinks to help it along, and Ruarri, the master of village ceremony, heading the laughter and clapping and totting up the fines like a happy banker.

It must have been towards midnight, when we were getting down to the last names in the hat, that Ruarri pulled his first little trick. It was staged for my benefit. It had to be because no one else in the gathering knew all the relationships involved. Ruarri walked across to the wall where the claymores were hung behind their buckler. He took down the two blades and laid them crosswise on the open dancing space. Then he held up his hands for silence and announced:

"This next one should earn some good money. Two girls will dance the reel and the swords against one another. The winner will be chosen by popular vote. Each girl has her own man to back her. The loser pays ten pounds into the fund for Lachie. I close my eyes now and dip into the hat and bring out the name of . . . Miss Flora Jamieson! Come up here now and let's see you. . . ."

It was the blonde from Stornoway, with I-love-you-Ruarri written all over her. And damned if he wasn't admitting it to one and all.

"This young lady is a special friend of mine, worth much more than the bet we're putting up. So dance for me, Flora love. Dance your feet off."

He dipped again into the hat.

"And the contender, ladies and gentlemen, is a beautiful visitor to these Blessed Isles, Dr. Kathleen McNeil. Of course, if she doesn't want to dance, we'll excuse her. You do? You're a gallant woman, Doctor. I presume you're backing this lady, seannachie? If you are, it's a fiver on the table and may the best girl win."

There was no time to say anything, but the touch of her hand was enough to tell me that she would go through with it. I led her out to the floor, placed her in front of her opponent and joined Ruarri at the table. There were ten years between them. The one was a thoroughbred, slim and lightly built; the other was a big country girl who would be wide as a barn at forty, but she had good legs and a good body, and if Ruarri had picked her, then he knew she could dance like a champion. As for Kathleen, I just didn't know, except that she was game, and I was backing her, and before the night was out I would settle with Ruarri for this very refined insult.

He was finishing his spiel now. "There'll be two sets solo for each girl, and the third will be in twosome. No break in the music, piper, and no applause until the dance is over. We'll toss a coin now. Loser begins. You call, Dr. McNeil."

She called tails and won, and I breathed a sigh of relief. The young one could warm up the piper and get him into rhythm. At a signal from Ruarri he puffed up his cheeks and began.

Now if you know the Highland dancing, there's nothing I can tell you. If you don't, there's little enough, because to recite the steps means nothing; but the feel of it, the lift of it, the wild, waking visions you get as the fiddle scrapes

227

and the piper skirls and they go, heel and toe, tripping round the sword blades—ah! that's something else. There's one piper playing, but there's a hundred others you can hear distant in the glens; and it's girls that are dancing, but it's men in kilt and bonnet with buckler and sword striding down the sheep tracks for the gathering of the clans and one last, losing fight for the lonely cause.

Flora Jamieson looked like a tart, and on the evidence she was; but she danced like an angel, with never a slip or a falter. Her big body seemed light as thistledown, her feet sprung like a ballerina's, her back straight as a rod under the arch of her arm. My heart lifted with her and then it sank for Kathleen, who must repeat the set after her and then join her in the final reel. When she had finished, there was a spontaneous burst of applause, and Kathleen moved in to pick up the beat of the pipes and fiddle.

The change in her startled me. I had known her in many moods, but never in this one. Suddenly she was proud and disdainful as Lucifer. Her head was high, her eyes full of fire and contempt. And she could dance. . . . Praise the Lord! She could dance on any Highland green from Inverness to Oban and you'd still be proud of her— and every twirl of the tartan was an up-you-brother for Master Ruarri, who couldn't take his eyes off her. When the two girls came together for the final set, they were at the top of their form, and no man in his right senses would have wanted to choose between them. We clapped them off the floor and shouted and stamped and declared in one voice that it was a drawn match.

Ruarri picked up the swords and clashed them over his head for silence. "So what do we do now? It's up to the men to decide the outcome. We're the backers and it's even money on the table. What do we do, seannachie? Dance for it? Spit for it? Toss double or quits? Maybe a hand of poker? Maybe you're a swordsman . . ."

He tossed one of the claymores to me, and I caught it, just as the boys caught the dirt in the joke and laughed.

"Hold it now!" Ruarri was laughing with them. "That wasn't what I meant at all. I know he's a writer and all, but for the rest of it, how would I tell? What about it, seannachie, are you a swordsman?"

He made a sham pass at me and I parried it and lunged instinctively.

He stepped back and stood grinning at me triumphantly. "Och aye! It's like that, is it? Are you game? They're not foils and they don't have buttons."

"I'm game, Brother Wolf. You name the stake."

"A hundred pounds for the fund. That suit you?"

"Fine. We need an umpire."

"That's me," said Inspector Rawlings out of the silence. "I'd hate to see either of you two fighting cocks get hurt. It's Olympic rules for saber and I know 'em, so you'll do as you're told. Right?"

"Right you are, Inspector," said Ruarri and then addressed himself to the assembly. "Let's clear some space, shall we? I'll stoke up the fire. Get yourselves a drink and settle down. . . ."

Then Maeve O'Donnell stepped in and gave everyone a chance to laugh. "I'm making book. For anyone that's interested. If someone'll give me pencil and paper, I'm offering two to one against the Mactire."

In the flurry that ensued, Inspector Rawlings asked me a bland question. "What is this, trial by combat?"

"For the record, Inspector, it's an exhibition match to raise money for charity."

"I hope you can fence."

"I hope Matheson can't, otherwise I'm in bother."

"If there's an accident, so am I," said Rawlings with a grin. "When I lose my job, you'd better stage a benefit for me. At least there's a doctor in the house."

The doctor was more worried than he was because she knew a little more than he did about sliced tendons and cracks on the skull and what happens when you drive a steel blade through a bunch of muscles. Womanlike, she was glad I had called Ruarri out, but she was angry at my stupidity. She would rather have me shamed and whole than carved up like a turkey and covered with blood and honour. She was right, of course, and while I waited beside her for the room to be cleared and Maeve to record all the bets that were being thrust at her, I knew I was more than stupid; I was stark-raving, motherless mad.

I can fence. I learned it when I was trying to be an actor, for which I found I had no talent at all. However, the fencing I liked and was good at, and I kept it up for a long time with a notable Hungarian of my acquaintance who had more slashes on his bosom, and more girls to lie on them, than you would ever have believed possible at his age. But let me tell you now, plainly, you can't fence with a claymore. The word itself means *great sword,* and in the old days that's what it was, a great, double-bladed, two-handled chunk of bad steel, more useful for chopping trees than men. By the time of Culloden it had been somewhat refined, to a blade with a single edge—though sometimes two—and a big basket hilt, which cut out all wristwork, if indeed your wrists were strong enough, because this was still a cut-and-slash weapon which handled more like a machete than a fencing saber. But, of course, if you got cut with it or pierced with it, or clouted on the shoulder bone, it could make an awful mess of your beauty.

So what was I going to do? It all depended on whether Ruarri could fence. If he could, then he would have the advantage. He was younger, lighter on his feet and in much better condition than I. Given an equal skill, he had to win. If he couldn't fence, then I could take him because, even with an awkward weapon, the man who knows the moves has the advantages—although he's always vulnerable to a lucky slash that incapacitates him. Also, as Maeve had said and I knew, Ruarri was a dirty fighter, and there are more than fencer's tricks for a man with a steel blade in his fist. Inspector Rawlings might umpire by Olympic rules, but Ruarri was going to fight by his own. . . .

He couldn't fence. He came awkwardly to the *en garde,* presenting the whole front of his body open to me. It looked ridiculous, but it made me scared. He didn't know the rules and didn't care. He was out for blood. What vein he tapped it from made no matter. I would have to attack because my defenses were all based on the high and low lines of the rule book. Ruarri wouldn't worry if he hit the jugular or the Achilles tendon, just so he brought me down. When Rawlings gave the signal to engage, I went in fast, striking upwards, in pronation, going for his right cheek, to scare him. He didn't parry. He swung away like a boxer does, then leaped away from the line of my lunge and came chopping at me from the left. For a moment it was more like quarter staves or kendo than swordplay, until I was able to pin him in line and attack again, always for the high line because there is nothing more disconcerting than a steel blade slicing near your naked face.

It was like trying to cut a bouncing ball. He was away again, spring-heel-Jack, leaping and turning, then coming in, slashing as if with a billhook. Then I got what he was trying to do. He was working me like a boxer, trying to tire me with his free-for-all tactics until I couldn't turn fast enough and he could catch me with one, final stroke. Like all orthodoxy, fencing is limited by its dogmas and its rituals. It is a beautiful art, but it isn't war, and Ruarri was making war, not love.

I needed more than the six guards and parries of the saber school to save my skin. I changed tactics. I began attacking the low line, belly to breastbone, tempting him to strike for my head. He wouldn't be tempted. He pulled back from my last lunge and left me short-reached; then as I straightened he did the old, knife-fighter's trick: dropped on his knee and drove for my ribs. He almost had me; but he missed by a fraction, and because he was immobilized just long enough, I went in on a risky flèche and opened an inch of his cheek with the cutting edge. Then Rawlings stepped between us and the match, if you can call it a match, was over.

We shook hands and made a conventional ceremony of compliment to each other, but the applause was scattered and uneasy. Rawlings took the swords from us and tossed them onto the table. Kathleen came to Ruarri and examined his sliced cheek and took him off to the bathroom to bathe and tape the cut until it could be stitched in the morning. Maeve came over to me and put a drink in my hand and said, "You look as though you need this," then walked away with no smile and no compliment. I warned you, didn't I? This was no epic encounter. It was two grown men playing silly-ass with lethal weapons, and drunk or sober, the Lewis men had sense enough to see it.

But the evening wasn't quite dead yet. Ruarri came back, with a slightly one-sided grin, waving a checkbook. The takings must be counted and his own contribution added and the whole sum consigned to Lachie's mother by the hands of Athol Cameron. Maeve must pay out on the bets. There was time for one more drink and a dash of lively music to send us home dancing. While the count-

ing was going on Kathleen drew me aside and told me
Ruarri wanted me to stay behind and talk to him after
everyone else had gone home. I could see no point in it.
He had put me through enough, and Kathleen too. I
wanted no drunken dialogues at two in the morning; I
wanted to be home in bed. The Mactire was out of my
system now. The sooner he was out of my life, the better.
I was surprised and irritated when Kathleen insisted:

"I want you to do it, darling. I want you to do it for
me, if not for Ruarri. He knows he made a bad exhibition
of himself. He feels deeply humiliated. He apologized for
what happened after my dinner with him. I think he wants
to apologize to you. You can afford to be magnanimous.
If you're worried about me, Maeve or the inspector can
drive me back to the lodge. I'll be waiting for you there."

I argued with her; but, of course, she convinced me. If
she hadn't, there would have been some other thing to
keep me, because that, too, was written on the skin of my
hand and a man, like a wolf, must live and die in his own
skin.

XVI

WE SAT, AS WE HAD SAT SO MANY TIMES BEFORE, TO-
gether at the bar, with the shambles of the ceilidh spread
around us. We had drinks between us, but they remained
untasted in the glasses because the time for drinking and
the time for playing was over, and now, or nearly, it was
time to walk away. Ruarri was calm and direct. The only
time he smiled was at the beginning.

"So you finally called me, seannachie."

"You asked for it."

"So I did. I've been asking for it ever since we met.
Tonight I want to tell you why."

"Look, it's late and—"

"Seannachie. Please do me this favour. It's the last, because you're going away and so am I. Don't say a word. Just hear me out, right to the end. Will you?"

"Whatever you want."

"Thanks."

Then he began to talk, haltingly at first, then in a steady flow of simple vivid words.

". . . We met on a strange day, seannachie. You were running away from whatever was in your past. I was cruising the Minch, single-handed, trying to make some sense out of what I was doing with my life. Oh, I know! I was always very sure with you. I could see all the rewards hung like baubles on a Christmas tree. All I had to do was reach up and snatch them off. But underneath, and for a long time and about a lot of things, I wasn't sure at all.

"Now, if you're living a life like mine, and all the other lives I'd lived before, you have to be sure. If you're not sure, you're dead or rotting in some lousy jail in a flea-bitten country where they don't have habeas corpus and the British Consul has a short memory and no funds to spend on roving rascals. You have to be sure because you've only half a second to pull a trigger or duck from a judo chop, or decide whether to tell a lie or risk the truth with a son of a bitch who won't believe it anyway.

"On that day, seannachie, I wasn't sure any more. I had money enough—and even in a legal way, I'd have more. I had comfort enough and friends enough—and though they're simple fellows, they are good friends, as you saw tonight. I had women enough, too, though from the day Maeve threw me over, there was always the doubt whether I had the brains or breeding to hold the kind of woman I liked. I had some things going, on the edge of the law, like the guns, and wholesale pharmaceuticals that you can buy cheap and sell in bulk for a good profit if you know the market. That didn't worry me too much. I liked the thrill and I liked the profit even better. But I was beginning to wonder how long I wanted to play games with the law—not for the morals of it, but the comfort really, and being able to sleep at night and walk into a bar without the Duggie Donalds of the world tapping me on the shoulder for a little chat.

233

"Then you came along. . . . Now I don't want you to take it amiss, seannachie, but I want to talk about you for a little while. You don't talk much about yourself, except in your books, and I've read a couple now, though I've never told you. But you've got some dangerous talents. For instance, you're always curious and questioning, so that people are flattered to talk to you. They think—and don't we all like to think it?—that you're interested in them. You are, some of the time. But for the rest you're interested in what they have to tell you, because it's grist to the writing mill and sometimes it's a clinical thing, like a chemist looking into a test tube. I'm not blaming you. I'm just saying what I've seen and felt. You've got good manners, seannachie, which are part gift and part practice. But when you're using the practice and not the heart, it shows and it hurts.

"Also, seannachie, you're well-read and you have a logical mind, chop-chop-chop like a lawyer's, but that's hard to take for ordinary folk who live half by their wits and half by what they feel with the tips of their fingers. You want to reason with everybody, and the only exception you'll make is with people you're very close to, and them you'll love and protect even if they're the biggest bastards in the world. So you're a hard man to live with, laddie, easy to be jealous of, and a bloody obstruction on the horizon of someone like me because you stand in your own light and won't let us get at ours. Another thing, you're alive and twitching all the time, so whatever you feel communicates itself: fears, doubts, angers, love and hates too. You won't—or you can't—let anyone ignore you. No one can float on the surface with you because you're not content there either. . . .

"So there's you and me on that morning in Uig, each with our separate histories catching up with us, very alike and yet very unlike, and we sail back together into Stornoway. I wonder if you've ever understood the real meaning of that day—my meaning? You were trespassing. No man should have all that you have and be able to sail a boat like that. No man should have a nice clear mind, and cheat the law like you were prepared to do for me.

"Then, when you came to the croft, I saw that in your own way you were jealous of me. You saw me riding the tractor and you were ashamed of your soft hands and the fact that you were a wanderer with no land under his own feet. I saw you when you looked at my house, how you felt the beams and knew how the stones were laid and the joinery done, though you'd never done any of it yourself —or maybe you had, but you'd stopped doing it a long time ago. You'd been a fighter, too—I've never forgotten that night when you were all set to take me with a broken bottle. But somewhere along the line you'd given that up. And I wondered why. I wondered about you and Kathleen, too, because when you brought her to my house, I didn't know what you wanted from her—although I knew you had balls, seannachie, and I thought you knew what they were for. . . .

"So I started to play a game with you. At least I told myself it was a game, but it wasn't. I was looking for myself and I thought I might find me through you. You spoiled the game, seannachie, when you brought me Morrison's news. I had to take you seriously then. You weren't outside my life any more. You were like a cow tick under my skin. I couldn't scratch you out or laugh you out. You were there, drinking my blood and itching me day and night.

"But I had to play out the game. I was the rogue, you were the nice, scholarly gentleman with a well-known name and good table manners and a lawyer's mind. You couldn't be as good as you looked just as I couldn't be as bad as I was painted. I took you poaching. You proved a cleverer rascal than I. We went after the deer, and you made a kill clean as the next man.

I made a play for Kathleen and you were in bed with her already. On board the *Helen,* you told me about Lachie, which meant you could think as well outside the law as inside it. The closer I looked, the more you seemed like me.

"That's why I called the play tonight. You couldn't see yourself, seannachie. You thought I was playing rough— but it was you who drew blood and you who had death in his eyes. I know we're the same, and I think you do too.

"And yet there's such a difference. In a funny way, I think I've cured you of what was ailing you. But you haven't cured me, seannachie. You've left me weaker and more puzzled than before. I'm not blaming you. Don't think that. I'm just stating a fact. The ceilidh was my public statement. This is my private one to you.

"You made me question everything I did, said, or believed. That's not a bad thing, except you have to prepare the subject for the experience—and you didn't do that. It's just as hard to see yourself plain as it must be to see God for the first time when you didn't believe He was there at all. You never understood that. You wouldn't let me have any secrets from myself; but you have to have them sometimes, otherwise you can't bear to live with yourself. I thought I was doing a good thing when I went to see Morrison. You saw it, and said it, as a total selfishness. Well, part of it was, but not the best part.

"You thought I was a shit because I told you a lie about my dinner with Kathleen. The lie was to protect her, because I could have taken her, seannachie, and I didn't. And the insult I laid on her was the only way I could send her home with her pride unbroken.

"When you told me about Lachie on board the *Helen,* I was blazing mad. I said wild things—but it was you who read murder into them, seannachie. I know that murder was in the back of my mind. But you pulled it out and showed it to me . . . made me look at it, made me weigh chances and consequences I'd never thought of, might not have thought of if you'd let me cool down.

"As it turned out, I did kill him. . . . I chopped him while he stood at the wheel just after he came on watch. I carried him out of the wheelhouse in the fog and tossed him overboard. . . .

"Don't look shocked, seannachie. You've had the knowledge buried in your own mind ever since it happened. And there's nothing you have to do about it because all the arrangements are made. . . . No, I'm not going to give myself up, because they'd have me mad and raving after a week in prison. I'm going away, as I told you. How, I'll tell you in a minute. I'd like you to understand the why, first of all. . . . Lachie's death was because of the guns. Now my boys were in that and Maeve O'Donnell too. The boys followed me. I have to protect them. And my deal with Maeve was that I would hold her and her organization safe. I want to honour both friendships.

"Then there's Morrison. He's my father—and you may think it strange, but I've started to think of him like that.

He's old and ailing, and I know he's told a lot of people about me and I won't have him shamed now. When I'm gone, you'll have to tell him, and I know you'll tell him the best, and only so much of the worst as he would guess anyway.

"I know what you're thinking, seannachie. You can't figure out why, if I'm the bastard you know, I don't stay and bluff it out, because I can. Even what I'm telling you now I can deny in the next breath.

"It gets back to you and me and the difference between us. I know what the difference is now. You're a reversible man. I'm not. You're open to change. You're open to believing, to disbelieving, to forgiving, to starting again. You're one of those who can be—what do they call it?—converted. You can believe in a better tomorrow, a better you even. I don't. I can't. And I'll tell you, seannachie, you and those like you had better beware, because there's a whole dark world full of people like me, and you haven't seen the half of it yet.

"I'm programmed, seannachie, like one of those great whirring machines that will soon be used to run the world when men give up trying. My little memory bank, seannachie, is loaded with everything I've ever done in my life. And I can't live with myself any more because I know one day someone else like you is going to come along all naïve and respectable and press the starter button and have me spew out another and bloodier answer on the tape.

"You remember I told you at dinner that I'd wished once I could join the Romans or the Greeks or some old and tolerant religion. You never heard why. It's because they still raise a hand over you and bless you clean in the name of God and let you crawl away into a desert or a monastery until you grow new and fit for human commerce again. Of course I missed the bus, because I was too proud and stupid to lift my hand and yell for it to stop. That's where you and I failed together too. We couldn't forgive each other's being what we are. It's a great shame, but there it is.

"Now let's talk about my exit, seannachie. It'll be clean. All the paperwork's done. The will's made. The legacies are as just as I can make them. There's no confession because that would have to implicate my friends. The law

237

will have to be content with what it gets—a closed case and no more. When you leave here I'm going to fire this place. And then I'm going to take the capsule I've carried round with me all these years—which will have me cleanly dead in four seconds maximum.

"Don't look shocked, seannachie. You've heard it, maybe written it, all before. This is how it looks when it happens. I'm exercising the last liberty of a man, seannachie, to pull out his own plug before the computer takes him over. The fire? That's always been in my mind, seannachie. It was the way the old Vikings did it, and it's clean and final. And no police surgeon will be poking round inside my guts to find what I died of—which is an obscenity I've always shrunk from. When you're on your way home, turn back, just once, and you'll see a light in the sky. That'll be me . . . on the way to Valhalla, wherever that is!

"Funny! I've never been much worried about the afterwards. I've seen so much torment and terror on this side of time that I never saw the need of hell on the other. Just being alive is punishment enough for whatever you do. I know the kind of heaven I'd like, though. Just to see it all plain, just once and calmly and wholly, and be able to say it was good. Because there is good in it, seannachie—except you need some kind of a gift to enjoy it. Maeve's got the gift, seannachie—for all she's a crazy loon dedicated to putting the clock back. Your Kathleen's getting it—which is maybe what loving does for people. I think you're getting it, too—or maybe you just lost it and are picking it up again.

"Me? . . . I missed the gift. Or maybe I threw it away in the days when I was young and bitter. There were moments with you when I thought I had it back, but that was just fairy gold, which goes away when you close your fist on it. . . . Your sextant was real, though. There was a care and a gentleness in that. And you're the last here, to say good night to me. You're not arguing with me either. Not that it would do any good, but it shows you understand.

"You should go now. I've things to do, and I have to be alone for the last of it. No tears, seannachie. That wouldn't be fair. I haven't any left to share with you.

238

Just one favour—when you go, don't shake my hand. Don't say anything. Just do what I've seen in the sunny places and laughed at first and then envied. Put your arms round me. Hold me a moment and lay your face against mine. Then get the hell out of here! It's a silly thing to ask, but I never had a father to kiss me good night."

When I left him he closed the door on me and turned the key. The sky was blown clean and the moon was riding high and cold among the faint and distant stars. The roadway was deserted. The hills were black, and Rawlings was dozing in the front seat of my car. He gave me that blank little smile of his and said:

"Thought you might like some company, on the way home. You've had a rough night."

"I'm not going home yet."

"Waiting for something?"

"No. There's a visit I want to make. You're welcome to come."

"I think you mean that."

"I do."

"Are you friends again?"

"As near as we'll ever be."

"Where are you taking me?"

"A little way and a long way, Inspector. . . . Trust me now."

I drove him up to the place of the Standing Stones and walked him over the damp turf and down the great colonnade to the burial place. I told him the history of it, and the legends of the Shining One with wrens flying round his head and the cuckoo that heralded his coming. I told him how good it was to make love and plight troth in this place, and how there were still families on the island who belonged to the Stones in a way that they would not explain. He was very patient with me and very polite, which is no small compliment to pay because I was very voluble and, I think, inclined to ramble. He let me talk myself to a standstill before he asked me:

"Why do you tell me this? And why here?"

"Because this is one place where we don't belong. It's a great monument on a tiny island. All its history begins around here, and all the people, whether they know it or not, are touched by the history. They can't escape it. They're still living the consequences of the Ice Age, when the peatbogs were made. . . . There are so few of them now, everything that happens to them is large and talked of and full of consequences. Every death is a diminishment greater than you or I can understand. Every despoilment is a tragedy, and every going away is one pair of hands lost and one heart less for the loving of the harsh place. . . . So you want to ask me a lot of questions because that's your job. Here in this place I've got all the answers. Tomorrow, because of the magic and the night air, I may have forgotten them all. I want to make a bargain with you, Inspector. . . . I want to make it not for myself, but to save more grief for those who have enough already and will have more tomorrow."

"I never make bargains, my dear chap. I'm not free to do that. Sometimes, though, I make decisions on my own responsibility, which is what I'm paid for. Also, I have a conscience, and you would pay me a compliment if you believed that."

So, because there comes a time when you have to believe or else go mad in unbelievable horrors, I turned him round, not to the east, from whence the Shining One would come, if he ever did, but to the west, where he could see over the rise of the hill the leaping flames of Ruarri's funeral pyre.

He stood there watching, a long time, in silence. Then he said, "Of course he was alive when you left?"

"Yes."

"He was well and in good spirits?"

"Yes. He was tired, though. He said he was ready for a long rest."

"I suppose the place was still in a mess, glasses, cigarette butts, all that sort of stuff?"

"It was a shambles. That was quite a wild party, one way and another."

"A generous gesture, though. And it did make quite a bit of money for a good cause. . . . He didn't give you any letters, depositions, anything like that?"

"No."

"Any messages to deliver?"

240

"None. Of course I'll have to break the news to his father . . . and I should talk to Maeve O'Donnell. She was very fond of him."

"She's at the lodge now with your Dr. McNeil. You might give her a message from me."

"Of course."

"Tell her I'll be busy tomorrow and I'd be happier if she took the first plane out—and left the United Kingdom the same day."

"You're a gentleman, Inspector."

"I'm a policeman. I have a closed case. . . . And as you say, there'll be enough grief tomorrow. Can you stay on this road for Stornoway?"

"We can. It's a long way round, that's all."

"I don't like fires. They scare me. There's a big one building up. I pray God I won't be round to see it."

I had never heard a policeman pray before. Which shows you how ignorant a man of letters can be and how little you can trust him in his ignorance.

It was four in the morning when I got back to the lodge and found Maeve and Kathleen still awake by the fire. They had to hear the story and I had to tell it all—because the weight of it and the guilts which Ruarri had laid on me was suddenly beyond bearing. There was a crushing horror in the vision of myself triggering a programmed man to acts of murder and self-destruction. And yet I could not gainsay the truth of what Ruarri had told me. Maeve could, would and did.

". . . To hell with *de mortuis* and all that crap! He was a man with a flaw in him. He knew it, hated it, but wouldn't do anything about it. He loved it. He had a ready-made excuse for everything he chose to do. I'm sorry, seannachie, you're tired and you've had a rugged night of it, but you've got to think straight. Ruarri's exit wasn't clean. The flaw was there still. You beat him at all his games. He had to trick you into believing he'd won the last one of all. He'd have the glory and you'd have the guilt, and you'd remember him always because of it—which isn't the kind of immortality any half-sized hero would be wanting. He's done something good, though. He's cured me. . . . I wish him luck wherever he's gone—and, by Christ, he'll need it! But he's out of my life at last. Thanks for the rest of it, seannachie. I'll be off in the morning. Good night, children. Be kind to each other."

It was a gallant effort and she had my salute for it; but it still wasn't the whole truth, and I knew it and so did Kathleen. For what was left of the night—and there wasn't much of it, because I had to face Morrison soon after daybreak—Kathleen was firm and tender and would have no argument at all.

". . . Ruarri loved you, like a brother. You loved him too. And the proof is what you're doing now, cleaning up the mess he's left. That's the good thing you'll remember in the end. The rest of it? You have to forgive yourself as you taught me to do, for something much worse. . . ."

"What do I do about Morrison?"

"Tell him the truth."

"Can he take it?"

"There's something I've learnt from you, mo gradh, and now I'm teaching it back to you. It's only the lies that kill us and only the truth that keeps us alive. Come on now, sweetheart, close your eyes and lie on my breast, and I'll wake you when it's time. . . ."

There was a time, and I have told you of it, when I condemned Morrison for weakness and was angry at the burden he had laid upon me. It is for this reason that now, before this chronicle is ended, I must show him to you in respect. He was still in bed when I went to him, and he did not need to be clairvoyant to read bad news on my face. He asked me to hand him his Bible, and while I talked he lay back, eyes closed, holding it in his hands. What strength he drew from it I do not know. All I know is that he did not weep and exclaim, but listened silently, until the long, sorry tale was done. So, I imagined, some noble patriot or martyr might have listened to his death warrant from a hireling messenger. When finally he spoke his first words were for me:

"I blame you for nothing, laddie. I thank you for the best of it. I'm alive and Ruarri's dead, and that's the irony of God we talked about, the kind of harsh dispensation you have to accept or lapse into despair. Perhaps it's the way I'm asked to pay for a kind judgment on Ruarri. I'll be out of here tomorrow, and there'll be a service for him in the kirk. But he should have a prayer now. I'd be pleased if you'd read it for me."

His hand was steady as he opened the book and his voice firm as he recited the psalm with me.

"Have mercy on me, O God, according to thy great mercy.
And according to the multitude of thy tender mercies, blot out my iniquity.
Wash me yet more from my iniquity, and cleanse me from my sin. . . .
Cast me not away from thy face: and take not the holy spirit from me.
Restore unto me the joy of thy salvation: and strengthen me with a perfect spirit.. . . ."

When I had finished he laid a hand on my head and said gently, "Go home to your woman now. You've earned some loving for yourself."
But she wasn't there; she was out ministering to the sick. So I drove as far as I could, to the loneliest beach in the west, and swam until I was exhausted. The water was very cold, but it was clean; and the sands, when I came back, were as empty as I was.

EPILOGUE

THE EMPTINESS WAS A KIND OF DYING. I WAS ABLE TO recognize it because, many years before, I had lain in hospital, desperately ill, waiting for the doctor to tell me the result of his last test. If the result was positive, I was a dead man. I had waited so long and so painfully that part of my dying was already done. I felt no sadness, only a relief that the time of waiting would soon be over. I felt no fear, only regret that I had been so inadequate a sharer in the experience of life. People I loved came to visit me. I was glad to see them, but not unhappy when they were gone because the effort to hold them was too great, and they must be about a business which was no longer mine. My perspective was different from theirs. Everything was in sharp focus, but receding to a point of infinity which was as clear to me as the glass of water on my table or the red tulips in my flower bowl. Even my own body was a detached object which I could contemplate in all its anatomy of bone and musculature and declining vitality. Try as I might, I could not get myself back into it, and finally I gave up trying. Even when the doctor came, smiling, to tell me that I would survive, I remained for a long time detached and disinterested because this meant only that I must go through the same experience another time, and by now I was familiar with it and would have preferred it completed.

For days after Ruarri's death, I endured in this state of syncope. I made the depositions required of me by the law. I brought Morrison home from hospital and bore him company whenever he felt the need for it. I filed applications for marriage licenses. I went fishing with Fergus William, and caught sometimes big and sometimes little fish, and listened to his prattle, laughed at it, too, sometimes, watching myself all the time and wondering why I was going through such a useless ritual. I went with Kathleen and with Morrison to the service which Minister Macphail held for the resting of Ruarri's soul; but it left me cold and unmoved as though it were some alien cult at which I was a spectator only and not at all a participant. Whenever she could, Kathleen came to spend a night at the lodge and I slept with her and made love desperately, hoping that the little death would be followed by a resurrection and I could begin to live again.

She was very patient with me, and she would not let me be ashamed or apologize for the strange body which she received so generously into her own. Over and over she repeated to me the same admonition:

"I've been where you are now. I know the feeling. And the life I lost was inside me, part of me. I was much more guilty than you are. You have to be patient, patient. . . . Every mending takes time. You are not robbing me. I'm rich and happy now. . . ."

But she could not be there all the time, and the days were long without her and the nights a bleak wasteland. Old Hannah was brusque with me always, but solicitous, too, constant with small cares and comforts for me and for the Morrison. He seemed much older now, more stooped and lined and slower of speech. On his good days he would walk in the garden, pacing up and down, hands clasped behind his back, like a monk in meditation.

Then one day I had a telephone call from a lawyer in Stornoway. He asked me to call upon him at my convenience; he had something to communicate to me "of a testamentary character." He was a fussy little man, dry as a stick, full of legal quiddities. He was charged, he said, to execute the provisions of the will of the late Mr. Matheson. I was a beneficiary. There would, of course, be the usual delay in probate, but the late Mr. Morrison had left his affairs in reasonably good order and there were liquid funds for the estate duty, so my legacy would probably pass to me unencumbered. He would read me the whole will if I wished, but if I would be content with the relevant clause? . . . I would be. He read it to me:

". . . To my friend . . . who is known as the seannachie, I leave my sailing boat, which is registered in Stornoway

245

as *The Mactire*, together with everything by way of sails and equipment which is aboard or belongs to her. I would ask him, though I would not charge him, because I have laid enough on him already, to keep the name of the boat so long as she remains in his possession; and perhaps, one day, he will scribble an epitaph for me. He has found it hard to think kindly of me; and I don't blame him, because I do not think very well of myself, but I would like to be remembered sometimes and gently . . ."

The lawyer was at pains to be precise. The request did not constitute a condition of the legacy. No undertaking was required on my part. The sentiments of testators were one thing, their intentions with respect to their property were another and so on and so on, until I wanted to shout at him and tell him to go jump in the harbour. Finally I was free of him and I walked out into the sunshine and down to the basin, where the trawlers were clustered along the wall and *The Mactire* was lying at anchor, placid on her moorings.

Suddenly the dying was over, and I was back in my own skin, looking out through my own eyes at simple, familiar things: the wheeling gulls, the gossips round the bollards, the grey houses, the busy housewives, the silly seal poking his snout above the water, the wool baled ready for the weavers, and the two men mending the nets, which were laid over their knees like shawls of brown lace. They were very old men and they must have seen many departures and many dyings and all the griefs of the sea over the years; but they were still here, working at the same simple tasks, glad of the sun while it lasted, and glad of the warm, foggy bar when it wasn't. For them, life was its own absolution, and time brought in its own healing, soon or late. I was no better than they, and certainly no wiser; so why should I ask more? It was time to be up and doing and to hell with yesterday. . . .

A week later, Kathleen and I were married in the parlour of Morrison's lodge. It was a very simple ceremony because its only use was to set a seal upon what was already consummated between us. Minister Macphail read the service, Hannah and Fergus William McCue were the witnesses, and Morrison passed the bride from his hand into mine. Which again meant very little, because

246

we had already accomplished a giving that signified more than possession.

Still, it gave Hannah a chance to have the last word. This was what she had seen, she told me: the three of us together, Morrison, Kathleen and myself—and Ruarri Matheson not one of us. You don't have to believe it. I'm not sure I believe it either. But she had seen the fire, and the love given and the love refused, and all the rest of the misty things that added up to a truth in the end. She had something else to tell me, she said, but that would have to wait until the last moment before we left for the airport.

By then she was tipsy with excitement and champagne and the joy of seeing Morrison more like his old self. She called me into the kitchen. She drew me down and kissed me, holding my face between her old, dry hands. Then she said:

"You're lucky, laddie! And if you're ever unkind to that sweet lassie of yours, I'll rise up from my grave and haunt your pillow. So I'm giving you something to remember and you'll repeat it after me: 'Cha robh bàs fir gun ghràs fir . . . Never a man died, but another was grateful.'"

It was a hard saying to hear on a wedding day, but later I understood it better and how many meanings it might have.

We live now, happily, in an old, old country where daisies grow out of the mouths of men long dead, and roses out of the loins of saintly virgins who never bore a child—and these are gentler epitaphs than the ones you read on gravestones. There will be no roses for Ruarri the Mactire, because he went away in the fire, and what was left of him after the dusty usage of the law was buried in the Morrison plot under a granite stone.

But there is an epitaph—this book—and there is love in the remembering and the writing. These are the last words of it:

I miss you, Brother Wolf. . . . God! How I miss you!

Daphne du Maurier

The best-selling author of Gothic novels

▼ **AT YOUR BOOKSTORE OR MAIL THE COUPON BELOW** ▼

Mail Service Department **POCKET BOOKS** Dept. P-34
A Division of Simon & Schuster, Inc., 1 West 39th St., New York N.Y. 10018
Please send me the following:

QUANTITY	NO.	TITLE	AMOUNT
....	78135	Mary Anne **1.25**	____
....	78122	The Breaking Point **1.25**	____
....	77011	The Dumauriers **95¢**	____
....	75656	I'll Never Be Young Again **75¢**	____

Mailing and handling   .25

Please enclose check or money order.
We are not responsible for orders containing cash.   **TOTAL** ____

(PLEASE PRINT CLEARLY)

NAME..

ADDRESS..

CITY...STATE.................ZIP.................